Étude

Melinda R. Morgan

Silverton House Publishing • Silverton, Idaho

This book is dedicated to Mom and Dad.
Their inspiring love story
has withstood the tests and trials of mortality
for three quarters of a century.

Étude
Book One of the Birthright Legacy

Copyright © 2012 by Melinda R. Morgan
ISBN 978-1-60065-010-9
Library of Congress Control Number: 2011919596

Front cover image by Pi.Kos.O Studio (www.pikoso.kz). Original musical manuscript by Frédéric François Chopin. Spine image by Liliboas (www.istockphoto.com/liliboas). Cover design by WindRiver Publishing, Inc.

The characters and events portrayed in this book are fictitious. Any similarity to real persons, living or dead, is coincidental and not intended by the author. Silverton House Publishing, the Silverton House mark, and the Silverton House logo are trademarks of WindRiver Publishing, Inc.

Printed in the United States of America
10 9 8 7 6 5 4 3 2 1

Silverton House Publishing
an imprint of WindRiver Publishing, Inc.
72 N WindRiver Rd • Silverton, ID • 83867-0446

http://www.SilvertonHousePublishing.com

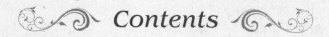

Contents

A vortex is a mass of energy that moves in a rotary or whirling motion, causing a depression or vacuum at the center. . . . These powerful eddies of pure Earth power manifest as spiral-like coagulations of energy that are either electric, magnetic, or electromagnetic qualities of life force.

Page Bryant, *Terravision: A Traveler's Guide to the Living Planet Earth*

Vortices are high energy spots on the Earth. . . . Yellowstone Park is a mixture of positive and negative energy, as are many such places. Yellowstone Park is a catastrophe in wait and it will affect people hundreds of miles away.

OfSpiritAndSoul.com

The locals of Andersen, Wyoming, believe the earth has a soul, and that those who are sensitive to its spirit will experience enhanced creativity and inner strength. They also boast that it's the eighth "vortex" of the world, and that Andersen is the place where the earth's energy is at its zenith—where mystical forces merge to unite humanity with the spirit of the planet.

Hattie Lee Arrington

Prologue

*H*attie Lee Arrington watched her daughter's reflection in the bedroom mirror as she pulled a wide-toothed comb through the child's long auburn hair. It was a big day for Elizabeth, or Beth Anne as her mother affectionately called her. Today was her fourth birthday and she had been waiting for it impatiently, drilling her parents daily about why it took so long for birthdays to arrive.

Beth started working on some drawings while her mother struggled with yet another difficult mass of tangles.

"Ow!" she hollered, "you're pulling again!"

Hattie chuckled but kept gently working the comb through the snarls.

"It's not funny, Mom!" Beth complained.

"Just a few more sections," Hattie promised, "then we get to the good part."

Beth hated having her hair combed, but she knew once the tangles were out her mother would exchange the dreaded comb for a brush. That was the part she loved.

Suddenly, she frowned. "Do I have to count again?" she asked.

Her turned-up nose made Hattie laugh. As soon as Beth had been able to count, Hattie had made her number the brush strokes aloud—all one-hundred of them.

"Well," her mother teased, "if you don't, you might forget the numbers."

"I won't . . . I promise. Cross my heart," Beth pleaded.

"All right. Since it's your birthday I'll give you the day off."

"Yea!"

"But—" her mother added quickly, "tomorrow you have to add twenty extra counts."

Beth let out an exaggerated sigh. "Okay. Deal."

Hattie grinned. "It's all about negotiation, Beth."

"Negoshy what?"

"Negotiation. It's a valuable life skill."

"Oh." Beth frowned. "One of *those.*"

Hattie glanced down to see how Beth's drawings were progressing. On one of them, four cartoon-like figures with over-sized heads stood in line next to what appeared to be a piano. The figure closest to the piano had extra large hands.

"Who's that?" Hattie asked, pointing to the picture.

Beth scowled with disapproval. "Mom!" she whined. "That's me."

"Oh, okay. I see the resemblance now," Hattie lied. "Why did you draw your hands so big?"

"'Cuz when I grow up I'm going to play the piano, and I'm going to play better than all these guys." Beth pointed to the other three figures.

"Who are they?" Hattie asked, curious.

"They're the mirror people," Beth replied innocently.

Hattie stopped mid-stroke and looked into the mirror.

"Who are the mirror people?" she asked—but she already knew the answer.

She watched Beth's eyes carefully as they flashed up to the mirror. All at once, Beth broke into a wide grin.

"Them!" she said as she pointed to the mirror.

Hattie swallowed hard. She had known this day would come eventually, but she'd hoped it wouldn't be so soon. She tried to smile and act casual, but her senses shifted to a state of heightened awareness as she continued brushing her daughter's hair.

"Mommy?"

Hattie shifted her focus to Beth's face in the mirror. "Yes?" She smiled in spite of her nervousness. She so cherished her little girl. How had four years passed so quickly?

"Can it be time yet?"

Hattie set the brush down and wrapped her arms around her daughter.

"Okay, let's go have a birthday party. What do you say?"

Beth giggled with excitement and struggled to get free from her mother's grasp.

Hattie glanced again at Beth's finished drawings—and froze. Her arms stiffened around her squirming daughter.

"Mommy, let go. Come on!"

Hattie released her grip, but continued to stare at the pictures sitting on the desk.

"Beth," she said quietly, pointing at the top picture. "Who is this one?"

Beth looked at the figure and broke into a broad smile. "That's Bailey. He's my friend."

Hattie stared at the dark shape standing next to Beth in the drawing. He was noticeably different from the others. The others looked somewhat human; they had distinguishable faces, hands, clothes, and hair. Bailey was nothing more than the shadowy image of a man. She could discern his features, but it was like looking at a black and white photographic negative—only the negative had bright yellow eyes.

She quickly flipped through the other drawings. "Bailey" was in all of them.

As Beth scurried from the bedroom and down the hall to find her father, Hattie picked up the drawings, folded them several times, and tucked them into her pocket. Before she left the room, she paused in front of the mirror and reached her hand slowly toward the glass. She stared fixedly into the mirror, but no matter how intensely she focused, she saw nothing but Beth's empty room in the reflection.

"Hattie?" her husband called, his rich baritone voice smooth and low. He smiled as he entered the room, his eyes tracing her figure from behind. The gesture was so automatic and her body so distracting that he had to remind himself why he'd come looking for her.

Hattie turned. He knew immediately by the look on her face that something was seriously wrong.

"What's happened?" he asked quietly.

"It's time, Jim," she said, resigned.

"Time for what?" He tilted his head slightly and searched his wife's wary eyes.

Hattie glanced over her shoulder at the mirror and shuddered. "Time for us to move."

Andersen

CHAPTER 1

*T*he rumbling vibration in the back pocket of my khaki Bermuda shorts alerted me that I had an incoming phone call. I didn't have to look to guess who was calling. I flipped open my phone and stared at the familiar picture in the caller ID box. It was the face of a very distinguished and very handsome, middle-aged man. I smiled and in true teenage fashion, rolled my eyes.

"Hey, Dad," I spoke into the phone.

"Hi, honey. How's the train ride so far?"

"It's good. Quiet." I shrugged, noticing the reverberating noise of the train's engine. I adjusted the worn, blue velour seat back a notch and checked my watch—8:40 a.m. It had been less than an hour since we'd said goodbye at the depot.

By train, the journey from San Diego, California, to Jackson Hole, Wyoming, takes a little over twenty-two hours—definitely not the preferred mode of travel under normal circumstances. But in my case, it was a pleasant alternative to flying. I looked forward to the time alone where no one could analyze what I was thinking or worry about whether or not I entertained suicidal thoughts. My father normally would have protested; he didn't think it wise for an eighteen-year-old girl to travel alone—especially on a train—but I had insisted. And this time he didn't argue.

"Are you sure you're okay?" There was desperation in his voice—it told me he had a guilty conscience.

"Dad, trust me, I'm fine." I was . . . for the most part. "When does your plane leave?" I asked, trying to mask the uneasy tightness in my voice.

"We're boarding now." There was a slight hesitation as he spoke. "I just wanted to hear your voice one more time before I left."

A stabbing ache pricked my throat. "I wish you didn't have to go."

"I know honey. I wish things were different."

"Tell them it's too soon," I pleaded. I knew it was a fruitless request. My dad, James Ethan Arrington, served with the Special Forces of the military. I understood very little about his job but I knew that he had to leave immediately whenever a "situation" arose, and it could be anywhere in the world.

"Beth, honey, you know I can't do that."

"I still don't see why they can't send someone else," I murmured under my breath, not sure he could hear me. He did.

"Because," he sighed, "this is something only I can do." The sadness in his voice made me feel guilty for questioning him—again. I hated to cause him pain. "I promise I'll join you before you know it, and we can put this whole past year behind us."

"I know. I understand, really." I glanced out the window and watched the waves break into thin white lines across the Torrey Pines shore where ant-sized sunbathers were already dotting the sand. The crystal water was calm today.

"Besides," he added, shifting moods, "your Uncle Connor's cool. Isn't that what you're always telling me?"

"Yeah," I couldn't help but chuckle.

Uncle Connor *was* cool in a quirky sort of "new age" way. He was my mother's twin; the two of them were like peas in a pod. I adored my uncle. I was pleased when he finally convinced my father to let me stay with him.

"Uh . . . I have to go honey," my father said, serious again. "I promise I'll contact you as soon as I receive clearance, okay?"

My throat throbbed as I struggled to force down the lump that had lodged there. "Okay," I managed to croak into the phone.

"Oh, and Beth, don't forget to—"

"Yeah, yeah, I know. Call grandma and let her know I made it. I will." We had been through this at least a thousand times.

"And let me know what you think of Connor's new wife."

"Yeah," I laughed to myself. Uncle Connor had been a widower for a long time. The thought of him married again would take some getting used to.

An indistinct noise on my father's end of the phone made my heart race with a sudden sense of finality.

"That's the final call, Beth. I have to board now."

"Dad . . . wait."

"I love you, honey." His voice broke before he could get the words out.

That was the last time I would hear from him for several weeks. I watched as the display on my phone faded from my father's face to the current time. I sighed, flipped the phone closed, and stuffed it neatly back into my pocket.

My dad and I had spent the last several weeks with my grandmother in San Diego, after he sold our home in Carlsbad and put in his request for early retirement. His plan was to purchase some land and build a new home in Wyoming so we could be closer to my mother's side of the family. He thought the change would be a healthy one for us both. Then he got the call. They needed him for one last assignment—an assignment that would take him to Eastern Europe for at least six months. Originally, he planned for me to enroll in high school in San Diego and remain with my grandmother until he returned; but in the end, he feared my mental state might be too upsetting for her.

In my opinion, *he's* the one everybody should worry about; my mother's sudden death over a year ago deeply devastated him. He does everything in his power to behave as though things are normal and he foolishly believes that in time, I'll be normal again too.

But what's *normal?* Normal would be coming home from school and telling my mom about my day. Normal would be sitting at the glossy, black, baby grand piano that once stood proudly as the focal point of our family room with my dad accompanying me on his guitar and my mother pretending to sing.

Normal would be *before* the accident that left me in a coma for seven months, only to awaken and discover that my left hand was permanently disfigured and useless, my future as a concert pianist was over, and my mom was dead! No matter how hard my dad tried, life for me was never going to be *normal* again.

My father and I never spoke about my mother's death; in fact, we didn't speak much at all during the first few weeks after my release from the psychiatric trauma center. He was too worried that he might say something to upset me. Instead, we danced around each other, politely avoiding any topic of conversation that went beyond the mundane tasks of the day. He approached each day robotically, void of emotion. That is until the morning I found him slumped over my piano, his hands clinched into fists and pressed angrily against the keys. His shoulders were shaking and I could tell by his labored breathing that he was crying.

My first instinct was to leave him alone and sneak quietly back up the stairs—I had never seen my father cry—but I could not bring myself to turn away. When I rested my hands on his shoulders, I expected him to straighten immediately and compose himself. Instead, he whirled around, wrapped his burly arms around my waist, and sobbed.

That's when I noticed the gold embossed paper lying on top of the piano—results of my piano competition held the winter of my junior year of high school. Playing the piano was the one talent I had developed beyond the level of mediocrity, the one area in which I was not merely average, and the one impressive achievement I could claim. I had placed first in the competition and received a full-ride music scholarship to the Berklee College of Music in Boston. Had things gone as planned, I'd be preparing to begin my first year of college at Berklee as a music major, but those plans died in the crash—along with my mom. My disabled left hand was a permanent reminder of losing both.

When I challenged the "official" version of what happened the night of the accident, my account was dismissed as that of a traumatized brain or an overactive imagination. They said that was to be expected from coma patients. But I knew the truth. I wasn't alone as I lay trapped beneath the tangled remains of my mother's green Chevy Malibu. Others were present, searching, moving frantically around our overturned vehicle. One of them pulled me away from the burning wreckage.

"No! Not this time! Not again." A tortured voice pleaded on my behalf. "Hold on, Beth."

The voice was calm, but commanding.

"Did you see them?" the one holding me asked.

"Sorry, I only caught a glimpse," another voice replied. "What are they after?"

"Her."

"Why?" A long pause followed.

"It's . . . complicated."

"I don't understand. Why take her mother?"

Another long pause.

"I don't know," he replied in hushed tones. He continued to hold me next to him and even though an ominous darkness encompassed me, the firm pressure of his hand on my forehead comforted me.

"Where's the ambulance?" he snapped impatiently.

"On its way," the other voice answered. "Be patient."

"Hold on," he whispered lightly in my ear.

His arms tightened, holding me securely so I could not move. I struggled to open my eyes, to see who they were. I wanted to ask them about my mom, but the murky darkness that surrounded me only grew denser until there was nothing—nothing but the sound of deafening silence.

"But someone else *was* there!" I had insisted. "There were at least two—"

"Beth, we've been through this," my father interrupted, exasperated. "The police investigated the scene of the accident. There were no footprints, no unexplained fingerprints, no physical evidence of any nature to suggest that anyone else was there."

He was right. We'd had this conversation several times since I had awakened from the coma. The fact that I couldn't let it go convinced my father that he had no choice but to admit me to a mental health facility. When the doctors brought in a hypnotist specializing in accident victims—specifically accidents that resulted in a fatality—they expected her to uncover where the "invented" memories had originated. I disappointed them all when my account of the accident remained adamantly unchanged.

I suspect that was the reason my dad decided to sell our home. In his opinion, the best way for both of us to reclaim any sense of normalcy was to begin with a fresh start somewhere else. He had made a healthy profit on the house; he could put a big down payment on a new home anywhere in Wyoming and still have enough to send me to college—a necessity now that my scholarship was no longer valid. I didn't plan to go to college after finishing high school, but to pacify my father I kept that little piece of information to myself.

Instinctively, I began to rub the palm of my wounded hand. Once graceful and gifted, the fingers in my left hand were now bent inward into the shape of a near fist. Although I retained some slight mobility and feeling in my thumb and index finger, the other three fingers rested involuntarily against the palm of my hand where, mercifully, they hid a grotesquely puckered and discolored scar— compliments of the hot, dripping oil that had destroyed the tendons and nerves through most of my hand. The only feeling that remained in that area was a phantom ache that the orthopedic surgeon assured me would fade with time. To him, my hand was a medical miracle; he had managed to save it from partial amputation. But no miracle could restore all that I had lost in that accident and no miracle could give me back the missing year of my life.

My dad clearly had his reasons for sending me to Andersen, but I had my own agenda, and it had nothing to do with normalcy or putting the past behind me. I didn't *want* to put the past behind me. I was determined to find out what really happened the night my mother died, and I was counting on her twin brother to help me.

As I watched the last sliver of ocean slip from view at Dana Point, I plugged the headphones of my iPod into my ears and settled into my seat, prepared for the complete collection of Hungarian Rhapsodies by Franz Liszt. By the time they concluded, I would be in Barstow—with another eighteen hours to go.

Uncle Connor met me at the train station in Jackson Hole and immediately enveloped me in a huge hug that lifted me off the ground. He held me tightly and patted my back, just as he'd done when I was a child. His freshly shaven face smelled of subtle spice and fresh mountain air—always a perfect blend.

"Ah, Beth, you look great," he said sincerely.

"Thanks for letting me come," I muttered breathlessly.

"Wouldn't have it any other way." He pulled back and examined me for a moment. "You look more like Hattie every time I see you."

I winced at the mention of my mother's name, yet I felt comforted knowing that he saw some of her in me. My mom and my uncle used to argue over which one of them I resembled the most. They were twins, so it always seemed like a silly argument to me. The truth was I didn't look like either of them; I looked more like my dad. I had his clear brown eyes—deer eyes he called them—and his cinnamon brown hair.

Uncle Connor noticed my reaction and was instantly contrite. "I'm sorry," he said regretfully. "You must miss her terribly."

"Yeah," I sighed.

He laid his hands gently on my shoulders and looked squarely into my eyes, giving my shoulders a gentle squeeze. "I'm really glad you're here."

A shield of moisture threatened the corners of my eyes, so I shook myself free and we walked in silence across the deserted train depot to retrieve my bags. I glanced sideways to watch him as we strolled through the long, narrow station. He hadn't changed. Nothing about Uncle Connor ever seemed to change. His features were identical to my mother's. He had the same bright hazel eyes and the same creamy shade of caramel brown hair and although he was well over forty, his face revealed no sign of wrinkling except when he smiled—just like my mother.

My uncle, a successful hay broker, had lived in Andersen for as long as I could remember. He maintained that Wyoming's Teton Mountain Range housed the oldest elements on the planet, and that the surrounding foothills carried mystical powers because they flanked the heart of one of the earth's vortexes. He believed that to fully experience our world, we must learn to tap into these powers. He also insisted that the earth has an aura which, of course, he claimed he could read. Naturally. That was another thing he had in common with my mother—they were both a bit whimsical. I liked to blame that on the fact that they were half Irish.

When she was alive, my mother enjoyed discussing metaphysical theories with Uncle Connor, particularly those related to the physical laws that limited humanity. Their conversations went over my head, but I remember watching the two of them lock horns in heated debates that would sometimes go on for hours. I blame that on the fact that the other half of them was German.

Had I known then that their eccentric theories were a precursor to her death I would have paid more attention to them.

Because they were twins, the bond between my mother and my uncle had been immensely powerful. Being an only child, I had no way of relating to the connection among siblings, let alone twins. Instead of playing with brothers and sisters as a young child, I resorted to playing with imaginary friends; they became my family.

"Beth?" Uncle Connor said, interrupting my thoughts. "You okay?"

"Yeah, sure," I shrugged. I studied the varying lines of the treetops as they passed lazily by my window. If I squinted just right, the tree line looked like giant green ocean waves.

"When does your father leave?"

"He's already gone. He left right after he took me to the train station."

"Oh." Uncle Connor paused, watching me carefully. A dull silence followed. Uncle Connor opened a water bottle and offered it to me. "You know," he said reassuringly, "he would have stayed if he'd had a choice."

I took an obligatory drink and nodded understandingly. Uncle Connor and I both knew that my father *did* have a choice. He could have stayed if he'd really wanted to.

The drive east from the train station in Jackson Hole to the small town of Andersen took about 30 minutes. The town was nestled on the relatively flat valley floor between the enormous Teton Mountain range to the West and the Gros Ventres to the east. Bisecting the picturesque valley was the meandering Snake River. If you traveled very far north of Jackson Hole, you'd wind up in Yellowstone National Park. A trip south would take you into the "Grand Canyon" of the Snake where a lot of white water rafting took place. At an elevation of 6200 feet, the mountain air was crisp and clean, something I felt pretty sure I would get used to in a hurry after San Diego's humidity.

The city of Andersen boasted several charming streets of rustic shops, a few food stores, some small government buildings, a library, an elementary school, and Andersen high school. Uncle Connor lived at the east edge of town in a two-story house that backed up against an uneven field of wild grass. The field was edged by several rows of pine trees and eventually merged into a series of long rolling foothills. Uncle Connor's kitchen, living room, and guest bedroom were on the main floor of the house. The second floor housed another two bedrooms (formerly belonging to his sons) and the master bedroom suite. There was also a full basement.

Decorated in earth tones, the main living areas of the house boasted a rich southwestern decor. Large picture windows cast a cheerful glow along the warmly painted walls, reflecting the vibrant colors found in Wyoming sunsets. Family pictures lining the wall parallel to the staircase chronicled the passing years. On the far side of the entryway hung a large oil-painted tapestry displaying the grandeur of the Tetons. I paused briefly to admire the beauty of the rugged mountain peaks, and I pondered the powerful forces that had combined to create such a majestic sight.

"I figured you'd be more comfortable in the guest room," Uncle Connor said as he directed me to the room that was to be my living quarters for the next six months.

Painted a cheerful shade of icy mint with accents of navy blue and white, the New England-style room was a definite contrast to the rustic western theme dominating the rest of the house. A queen-size bed, centered strategically along one wall, was covered with a thick white and navy blue-patterned comforter and a mix of throw pillows in mint, navy, and white. A white rocking chair upholstered in navy blue sat in the corner near a window that filled most of the back wall. White shutters had been pulled back to frame a stunning view of the rolling hills and forest that meandered aimlessly across the horizon. A set of free-flowing, sheer lace curtains hung delicately along each side of the shutters, giving the room a soft, graceful appeal. Between the bed and the window was a teak desk covered with an array of empty picture frames, a printer, and what appeared to be a brand new laptop computer. Uncle Connor told me that the computer was a gift from my dad.

"This room has a bigger closet than the upstairs bedrooms," Uncle Connor explained after giving me a minute to browse. "And it has its own bathroom, so you'll have more privacy."

"It's perfect," I whispered. I carefully ran my thumb and finger along the edge of the lace panels and then turned around to face him as he set the first of three large suitcases on the floor. "When did you do all this?" My obvious approval pleased him. His smiled brightened and I couldn't help noticing that his eyes were like clear, jade-colored crystals.

"As soon as your father agreed to let you come. I chose a Cape

Cod theme to remind you of the beach. It was your mom's favorite. I had Marci tackle the remodeling job after she informed me that it needed to be more feminine."

"Marci?"

"Er . . . yes. I guess the news of my marriage must have come as a surprise, eh?" he replied sheepishly, a slight blush coloring his cheeks.

"You could say that again. I didn't even know you were, uh, dating someone." The thought of Uncle Connor dating someone seemed totally weird to me.

"Well, your cousin Carl had a hand in that. He sort of introduced us," he chuckled. "I don't think he expected us to get married, especially not so fast." Uncle Connor looked positively youthful. "I'm sure you'll appreciate having another female around. After all, I don't know a thing about raising teenage girls."

That was true; having me here would be a major adjustment for him. It had been years since a female had lived in Uncle Connor's house. His late wife, my Aunt LeAnn, died shortly after the birth of their second child, Carl, leaving my uncle to raise their two sons on his own. Nick, the oldest, married immediately after high school a little over seven years ago. He and his wife Gina and their two boys were now living in South Dakota. Carl, the youngest—and my favorite—left home right after graduation.

"When do I get to meet her?"

"Well," he scratched his head and grinned, "we're still working out the logistics of the living arrangements. She owns a home in Jackson near the college where she teaches."

"She doesn't live with you? Isn't that kind of the purpose of being married?"

Uncle Connor laughed, "It's one of them, yes." His cheeks burned bright red, and the moment I realized why, mine flushed with embarrassment as well. "Things are a little complicated right now, but we're working it out. You'll meet her this weekend for sure."

I stretched on my toes to kiss Uncle Connor on the cheek and give him a hug. He was taller than I remembered. I lingered, absorbing the clean, mild musk scent of his skin. Something about his smell reminded me of my mom. He hesitated for a moment, then smiled and backed away.

"Well then," he nodded politely, "I'll leave you to get settled. You make yourself comfortable, all right?"

I returned a quick nod and smiled. "Thank you, Uncle Connor." Then I started the long process of unpacking and organizing, transforming the guest suite into a place that felt like home.

Because I missed the last quarter of my junior year (and my entire senior year for that matter), I was forced to enroll in a home study program for the remainder of the summer in order to earn credits toward graduation and prepare for university entrance exams. The program was tedious, but it helped me keep my mind off the inevitable. I would turn nineteen in October and therefore, I would be older than everyone else at Andersen High School. I could have taken a test and earned a certificate of high school completion, but the team of psychiatrists specializing in coma recovery recommended that I not miss the experience of a senior year. In their opinion, it was an important part of the healing process.

With no social life to distract me, I managed to complete the home study requirements in plenty of time to qualify as a senior for fall semester. Classes would not begin until the day after Labor Day, but it was necessary to register early in order to assure placement in the courses required for graduation. In addition, school policy required me to sit through an orientation program and hook up with one of the senior student body officers for a tour of the campus. I knew the drill well; I had done the same thing for new students at my former school.

When I arrived on the morning of registration, a platinum blonde woman with ashy-gray roots greeted me at the front desk of the attendance office and directed me across the main quad of the campus to the multi-purpose room. I rolled my eyes at the thought of sitting through an hour-long presentation intended to acclimate ninth graders to high school culture. I imagined little benefit would come from attending, but I dutifully obliged.

When I entered the oversized double doors of the spacious auditorium, a very enthusiastic girl with highlights in her bouncing blond hair welcomed me.

"Hello. I'm Darla Reeder," she announced vivaciously. She handed me a prepared packet for incoming students. "And . . . you are . . ." she eyed me respectfully from head to toe, "obviously *not* a freshman. What's your name?"

"Beth Arrington," I responded, though not as enthusiastically. "I'm a senior."

"Oh? Where are you from?"

"Southern California."

Immediately her eyebrows rose. "Really? Did you live near the ocean?"

That was always the next question when I told people I was from California.

"Depends on what you mean by *near.* Just about everywhere in Southern California is *near* the ocean." I probably sounded condescending, but she didn't seem to notice.

"Oh. I guess that would be true." She tilted her head to the side and smiled. "What brings you to Andersen?"

"I'm staying with my uncle for a few months, until my dad gets here."

She watched me quizzically and waited politely for me to explain.

"He's overseas right now, in the service. My mom passed away a year and a half ago." I had rehearsed the words so many times in my mind that they came out more abruptly than I intended.

"Oh, that sucks," she said. "That's gotta be hard."

I shrugged and looked away. This was not a conversation I wanted to have. "My uncle's cool," I replied, emotions in check.

"Hey," she said suddenly, flashing an abnormally perfect smile, "you already know this stuff. How 'bout I take you on a quick tour, and then you can help me with the incoming ninth graders?" She hesitated, dissecting my expression thoughtfully. "Unless you have other plans."

A sarcastic chuckle escaped as I thought about her comment. I definitely had no plans for the afternoon, so I decided to take her up on her offer.

Darla's enthusiasm never waned throughout the day, even through the myriad of repeated questions spewed at her by the incoming freshmen as she warmly welcomed each of them by name. Following a brief presentation, she gave me a tour of the campus which, I admit, was much larger than I expected. Afterwards, she walked me to the library so I could check out my textbooks, then we returned to the multi-purpose room for the rally with the freshmen.

When the program ended, Darla insisted that I meet a few of her friends, so we walked to the field where the varsity football team was finishing the second set of their two-a-day practices. I followed her to the stadium stands where we sat and waited for the coach to conclude his comments to the team. Darla held her hand up to shield her eyes from the sunlight while she glanced from side to side.

"Is something wrong?" I asked.

She shook her head quickly. "No. I was just hoping some of the girls would be here. Guess you'll have to meet them later."

More than once, a couple of the boys glanced in our direction. I couldn't blame them; Darla was exceptionally pretty. At a willowy 5 feet 8 inches, she was at least two inches taller than me with long, wavy blond hair that cascaded in soft curls to the middle of her back. She clipped the bangs away from her forehead revealing a lovely oval-shaped face with high, perfectly placed cheekbones. Her almond-shaped eyes were crystal blue. They turned up slightly at the corners, almost paralleling the corners of her mouth, which also slanted upward, suggesting the hint of a smile even when her lips were closed. When she smiled her entire face lit up, making her impossible to ignore.

Darla watched the boys, pointing each one out to me and giving me their background. One particular boy, the tallest of the group, made no attempt to hide the fact that he was staring at us. He was the best looking of them all, at least as far as I could tell from a distance.

"That's Eric." Darla gestured towards him. "His parents and mine are close friends, so we've known each other ever since we were little kids." She let out a forced laugh, but never took her eyes off him. "He's definitely popular with the girls, if you know what I mean."

"Oh." I nodded, but I sensed there was more behind her warning tone. "You guys don't get along?"

Darla frowned. "We used to. He was my best friend the whole time we were growing up. But then we were . . . a thing." She looked at me and shrugged. "We broke up over a year ago."

"What happened?" I flinched as soon as I asked. It was none of my business.

Darla smiled and shook her head. "He had too many options to explore." She scrunched her nose and nervously scratched the back of her neck.

I studied her reaction for a moment and then gasped. "He cheated on you?"

"Something like that." She chuckled darkly. "He has a . . . reputation."

I thought of Adam, my boyfriend of nearly two years and ex-boyfriend since just before junior prom. "Yeah, I know the type."

"Sucks, huh?" She threw me a knowing smirk.

"You could say that." So, Darla and I shared something in common.

I squinted, trying to get a better look at Eric who was still look-ing in our direction, then I looked back at Darla. "Are you guys still friends?"

"Well," she shrugged, "Andersen's a small town, so we sort of hang out by association. Besides, like I said, our families are really close. We had to get over it."

"Hmm," I nodded. "What about now? Are you with someone else?"

"Not yet," she replied, shaking her head. Then she grinned and shifted her eyes toward one of the other boys. "But I'm working on it."

I followed her gaze to the boy in the number five jersey. He still had his helmet on so I couldn't see his face clearly.

"That's Derrick," she informed me. "He just moved here this summer. I was hoping he and Eric wouldn't become friends, but it might be too late."

"Too late for what?"

"Isn't it obvious?"

I looked at her questioningly and shook my head.

"There's a 'code,' you know? Friends don't go out with their friends' exes."

I nodded understandingly. I was all too familiar with the "code."

Darla shifted her gaze away from the cluster of boys and looked me over from head to toe. My body straightened instantly under her scrutinizing gaze.

"Maybe having you here will work in my favor." She tilted her head to the side and giggled.

"Excuse me?"

She glanced quickly at Eric and then turned back to me. "When Eric gets a look at you, he'll be all over you."

"I don't think so," I snorted. The implication made me uneasy.

"I know Eric," she smiled. "He'll find you irresistible."

I couldn't think of an appropriate response to that, so I just stared at her in disbelief. I wasn't sure how to take her.

"Trust me, I don't mind," she grinned. "It might just give me a chance to work on Derrick."

"You are clearly crazy." I eyed her skeptically, but she laughed.

"So I've been told." She nudged me with the side of her arm; her smile was angelic. Then her expression altered. "Seriously, Beth, be careful of Eric. You always have to keep your guard up with him. He's really good at playing the game."

"He's really that bad?"

She shook her head and smiled pitifully as if I were missing something obvious. "I'm just saying . . ." she shrugged, "you're pretty, and you're new blood."

"Well, I'm only here for a few months. I don't plan on dating anyone." I frowned, pulling my forehead into tight creases. This conversation was way too weird. "Besides," I added, "the guys here are too young for me."

Darla turned up her nose and eyed me curiously. "What, you only like older men?" she said with a hint of judgmental sarcasm.

"No," I laughed, feeling suddenly foolish. "I just meant because I'll be nineteen in a couple of months."

Darla looked confused. "Were you held back or something?"

"No, nothing like that." I didn't see the need to explain further.

Darla waited for a moment and then said matter-of-factly, "Well, you're not *that* much older than the rest of us."

"Whatever." I shrugged my shoulders. That was the same argument the psychiatrist used when convincing me to enroll in high school instead of a junior college.

Darla ignored my comment. She leaned closer to me as if she were afraid someone might overhear us. "One more word of advice about Eric. If you're easy, his interest won't last for more than a few weeks."

"Gee, thanks," I replied, offended by the assumption behind her words. As embarrassing as it may sound, a tiny part of me felt challenged to prove her wrong. I had to shake the thought from my mind.

"No, no," she said quickly, her eyes wide with regret, "I don't mean to imply anything negative about *you*. It's just that I know Eric so well. He's shallow."

I couldn't decide if she was nuts or just brutally honest, but at that moment, something inside me decided that I liked her.

Just then the huddle dispersed and Eric and three other boys walked toward us. Darla waited patiently for them to approach, and then one-by-one she introduced them to me.

"Hey, guys, this is Beth," she began. "Beth, this is Eric Daniels, Tom Stewart, Derrick Miles, and Evan Bradley."

I suddenly felt self-conscious and very small in the presence of the four gigantic football players who towered over me. It was easy to see why Eric was so popular; his captivating smile and larger-than-life presence were almost unnerving. After the "Hellos," we went through the usual questions: "Where are you from?" "What brings you to Andersen?" "How long are you staying?" Then the conversation shifted to finalizing plans for an upcoming boat trip. I was given a courtesy invite, which I politely declined.

Of the four boys, Evan Bradley was the one I found most intriguing. His unusual combination of dark hair and green eyes were a definite contrast to Eric's blond hair and golden brown eyes. More reserved than his teammates, Evan seemed content to allow the others the spotlight, yet he seemed equally confident and at ease. What caught my attention was that he never took his blazing green eyes off Darla. He carefully scrutinized her every move, and when she spoke directly to him, he glowed.

Derrick, the one Darla flirted shamelessly with, showed no interest in her whatsoever, which was surprising given that she was so undeniably pretty. In spite of all her attempts to charm him, he remained unresponsive. He made eye contact with me once, and the only thing I saw in his expression was annoyance. Darla had her work cut out for her.

The politics of the school were pretty complex, something I didn't expect in such a small town. The seniors were divided into three main social groups: the jocks, the losers, and the nerds. The jocks consisted of the athletes, the cheerleaders, most of the student body officers, and those accepted into the elite group by association. The losers were those who showed no interest in any part of the school culture: no clubs, no sports, and no activities. In class, they were the perpetual underachievers. The nerds were the stereotypical brainiacs with little or no social skills or physical appeal. If a high achiever was good looking enough and "cool," he was included into the circle of jocks. Eric and Evan had the best of both worlds; they were high performers in and out of the classroom and therefore, highly esteemed among students, teachers, and the community in general.

With the exception of Darla—who was friendly with everyone—kids from the three groups didn't mix much. It was a strange dynamic. Derrick and I were both newcomers, but with Derrick's talent for sports and my association with Darla, we were quickly included among the jocks.

All the fuss about me being "new blood" caused me to pause one morning in front of my full-length mirror and take a comprehensive assessment of my physical assets. I examined my reflection closely and attempted to identify any noticeable positive traits. Despite my crippled hand, I came up with a short list of five.

First, I had long, well-toned legs (which my ex-boyfriend used to refer to as a set of very sexy "Popsicle sticks") that would do me absolutely no good during the six months of cold weather in Andersen. Second, I had a firm, flat stomach (good if you sport a belly ring, but again, not something anyone was likely to see). Third, I had a clear olive complexion and very soft skin (I had my mother to thank for that—she always told me I'd appreciate it someday). Fourth, I had long auburn hair that fell to my waist. It held a glossy shine and tended to change colors depending on the angle of the light. Sometimes it was brown with golden highlights; other times, particularly in the afternoon sun, it glistened in alternating shades of burnt copper and cinnamon. And finally, I had arching eyebrows and thick, dark eyelashes (a real plus because I hate mascara).

That summed up my "fab-five" list.

By the time school began, Darla and I had become good friends. We spent most of our free time together, but Darla had a definite agenda; she was determined to worm her way into Derrick's attention and that meant spending time with Eric, who I had to admit, had a growing appeal about him. When he was around, I always ended up in stitches. To me, he seemed perfectly harmless and genuine. If Darla had not warned me about him, I never would have guessed he was a player.

Whenever we hung out as a group, Eric would volunteer to give me a ride home. After the first couple of times, the others expected the two of us to leave together—code in force. According to Darla, it was all part of Eric's strategy to work his magic on me. She had warned him several times not to waste his time on me—that I wasn't "his type"—but Eric didn't lack for effort or confidence. He was obviously used to getting his way. It would have been unbearably irritating if it were not for the fact that he was so much fun to be around, not to mention devastatingly cute. Still, I kept Darla's warning in the forefront of my mind, guard up.

"Eric, you're wasting your time," I said when he brought me home from a volleyball game at the lake.

I sounded like a broken record. Night after night the routine was the same. Eric had made it a custom to walk me to the door whenever we got home after dark, but before I could reach for the door handle, he would whip around in front of me and block my path. Each night he became a little bolder—tonight he was in top form.

"I can wait." He raised an eyebrow and tilted his head tauntingly to the side.

"Seriously, Eric! Get out of my way."

"I don't think so." He flashed his smooth, cocky grin at me.

"You're making this very uncomfortable for me."

"That's all part of my plan," he winked.

I had to bite my lip to keep from blushing. "Fine. Plan all you want, but get out of my way."

Eric nodded proudly. "Face it, I'm getting under your skin."

"Yeah, sort of like lead poisoning." I tried to be stern, but I couldn't stop myself from smiling.

"Ah ha! You see? You like me. Admit it."

"Get-out-of-my-way! You stubborn br—"

"Now, now. Don't be calling me names." He locked eyes with mine and put his fingers against my lips.

I took an exasperated breath and gave him my most evil "warning look." Eric laughed—a contagious laugh that made it impossible to be mad at him. I rolled my eyes.

"All right . . . I'm going." He pranced backwards down the sidewalk to the street where his truck was parked. "But I'm getting to you, whether you admit it or not."

I shook my head as I watched him swing agilely into his truck. The truth was, if Darla had not warned me about him—and if he were not her ex-boyfriend—he would be impossible to resist.

Autumn arrived at the end of September, right on cue. The sky turned a milky shade of white with scattered hues of blue peeking through at random intervals. The sun dropped lower on the horizon, so when it managed to break through the cloud cover, its rays spread in beautiful streams that highlighted the foothills. I watched the light show from my bedroom window while I got ready for school. The foothills were spectacular and mysterious at the same time.

"Better wear a coat," Uncle Connor called when he heard me hurrying down the hall. "It's going to be cooler today."

I smiled to myself. He reminded me so much of my mom.

"She's a big girl, Connor," Marci warned him jokingly.

Marci and Uncle Connor's relationship was interesting, definitely not your traditional marriage. She spent at least three nights a week at her home in Jackson so she wouldn't have to drive so far to work. It seemed to work for them. I was still adjusting to the idea of him being married, but as far as I could tell, Marci was good for him— although she was nothing like I had expected. She had incredibly long hair which she usually wore in a loose braid or some sort of twist, and she never wore makeup; she didn't need it. She dressed in clothes that reminded me of what hippies wore in the sixties and seventies, but she pulled it off with an air of elegance and class. I'd never met anyone quite like her.

Marci kissed Uncle Connor on the mouth and held his face in her hands for several minutes before saying goodbye. He blushed. I pretended not to notice as I walked past them and made my way to the car.

Uncle Connor drove me to school on his way to work, just as he had every day for the past four weeks. It had rained during the night leaving large puddles of water along the roads and walkways. The leaves were transforming into brilliant shades of orange, yellow, and red, creating a three-dimensional canvas of luxuriously rich autumn colors in every direction. This was the first time I had ever experienced an actual fall season.

When Uncle Connor dropped me off, Darla and her friend Crystal greeted me at the main gate. They were chattering on about plans for Homecoming which was just around the corner. I gathered from their conversation that David Price had asked Crystal to go to the game but not to the dance the following night, so she was wondering if she should accept Brandon Jameson's offer to the dance or go solo in hopes of hooking up with David sometime during the night. A difficult dilemma indeed.

I don't know why, but I didn't care for Crystal. Maybe it was because she reminded me so much of my former best-friend-turned-traitor, Jolene. Crystal was an incessant flirt. Lots of boys seemed to like her, but she didn't have a steady boyfriend. By the time we arrived at our first class, Crystal had not reached a decision about Homecoming. She made Darla and me promise to help her decide before the day was over. I controlled the urge to roll my eyes at the thought of continuing the conversation later. I'd been working on the eye-rolling thing; Marci said it could lead to premature age lines and sagging eyelids.

After school, Darla met me by my locker and walked with me across the street to the Community Recreation Center, or the "CRC" as they called it. The CRC and the high school were in partnership to provide opportunities for students to participate in non-academic extra-curricular programs—something that was important on some university applications. The CRC offered self-defense classes, dance classes, music lessons, various art classes, and a monthly book club. Adjacent to the CRC was the public library, the police station, and the fire department. Together, the high school campus and the CRC made up a town square.

The public library was an extension of the school library, so it was a popular hangout for the brainiacs. My favorite part of the library was the lounge, where couches and over-sized chairs faced toward a floor-to-ceiling picture window that overlooked the town's central park. Darla and I often spent our afternoons there studying, but today we were going to complete our applications for a community service position. In order to graduate, seniors had to show proof of at least forty hours of volunteer service. The most coveted position was library assistant.

As we approached the library, we passed a hallway leading to the area designated for music instruction. In the distance, I heard the echo of classical music playing. Surprised, I paused to listen for a moment. I closed my eyes, and an instant longing flooded through me. In the past few weeks, I'd almost been able to forget. . . .

"What's the matter?" Darla asked as I stared down the long corridor.

"Shh," I whispered, "that's one of my favorite melodies."

"What is it?" she questioned, anxious to keep moving.

"Tristesse." I said the word with such reverence that Darla stopped to listen more carefully. "It's Chopin's Étude in E."

"What's an 'a-tude'?" she whispered.

"It's French for 'little study,'" I replied, shushing her again. I could tell by the look on her face that she was confused. "It's a music term," I explained, "describing exercises Chopin wrote to practice various points of technique. They're fairly short, but ridiculously complex."

Darla nodded, satisfied, and inclined her head to continue listening.

I turned to follow the sound which led toward a narrow hallway of practice rooms. Darla followed silently behind. As we continued along the path, I noticed that there were six practice rooms, three on each side of the corridor. Each had a door with a small window in the top half and a sign-up sheet for reserving the room. I started to peek through the window where the sound was coming from, but Darla grabbed my arm.

"What are you doing?" She struggled to keep her voice low.

"Shh," I hissed. "I want to see who's playing."

"Geez, Beth," she groaned, "we need to hurry." She moved to the side and waited impatiently while I satisfied my curiosity. I could tell by her tapping foot that she was annoyed.

Glancing through the window, I spied the back of a young man sitting at an old upright piano. From behind, I couldn't tell if he was a student or a young teacher. He wore a long-sleeved white shirt with the cuffs turned up exposing beautifully shaped hands. His long, curved fingers moved effortlessly across the ivory keys. His hair was dark and casual with a hint of wave that reflected the light from a small window on the far side of the room.

I watched his strong hands as the second half of the Étude began its climatic climb up the scale. Flawlessly, his fingers brought the melody to its peak where it hovered, anticipating a subtle decline. I stood mesmerized, enjoying each familiar progression, and marveled at his skill and the ease with which he played. Instinctively, I tightened my left hand and flinched when the pain reminded me that I could no longer make a complete fist and hold it tightly. I looked down, shooting a quick glance at my disabled hand and felt an instant sting of self-pity.

No, I scolded myself, forcing my attention back to the boy at the piano.

I listened, captivated, as the music asked a question and then answered in agitated response until it finally descended to a peaceful resolve. The level of emotion he put into the closing measures of the song moved me; it was so forlorn, so melancholy. He allowed his fingers to linger peacefully on the keys as he finished. Then he lowered his head slightly as if to listen more intently to the fading sound of the final chord.

"May I help you?" a deep voice from behind me asked.

"Oh!" I gasped, jumping quickly away from the window. Darla had seen it coming and giggled.

I caught a quick glimpse of the pianist's face as he swung around in response to my gasp. His eyes met mine for a brief instant, long enough for embarrassment to color my face. I turned away quickly and found myself face to face with the man who had startled me. Although he was gray-headed and sported wire-rimmed glasses, he was alarmingly handsome.

"Hello. I'm Mr. Laden, head of the community music program." His smile was pleasant as he held out his hand. I shook it tentatively.

"I'm sorry. I didn't mean to be nosy," I said. I sounded guilty, as if I'd been caught doing something wrong, but Mr. Laden seemed amused. Darla jumped in to bail me out.

"We're on our way to the library," she explained.

Mr. Laden nodded politely.

"This is Beth Arrington," she announced. "She's a new student here."

"Ahh, Miss Arrington," he said knowingly. "I heard you were coming to Andersen this year."

"You did?" I recalled what my uncle had said about small towns; there were no secrets.

"Indeed," he nodded. "I've been hoping to meet you. I read about your performance at the National Piano Player's Guild scholarship competition last year." He paused briefly, reading the confusion on my face. "I make it my business to follow the national competitions," he explained. "The reviews said your performance was . . . what was the word . . . 'inspiring.' Congratulations."

"Thank you," I replied. I hadn't realized reviews were published so widely. "I didn't mean to intrude, but I had to stop and listen. He plays the Étude so perfectly."

Mr. Laden nodded in agreement, and at that moment the fellow who had been playing stepped into the hallway. Something in his stature told me that he was definitely *not* a student. He must have been over 6 feet 2 inches tall and had a slender, though muscular, build.

His eyes were the first thing to catch my attention. They were so dark that from a distance they appeared almost black. But up close, I could see that they were a deep midnight blue—resembling two perfectly cut sapphires, each shimmering with a hint of emerald. They reminded me of a clear evening sky just before nightfall, when the sun has gone down but there is still light along the western horizon. His hair was a shimmery dark brown trimmed neatly around his neck and ears, but longer on the top. The relaxed highlights in each wave gave it a soft, touchable look. He had wide, prominent cheekbones that angled downward along his jawline framing a masculine, square chin.

"How's it going, Mr. Laden?"

"Hello, Jonathan," Mr. Laden replied, and then grinned teasingly, inclining his head in my direction. "It appears you have an audience."

The blush in my cheeks deepened. *Jonathan—I wonder what his last name is?*

"Hello," he said politely. "Do you play?"

"Yes," I said quickly, then shook my head in correction. "Er, actually, no. I used to," I stammered.

He looked puzzled as though waiting for an explanation, but I offered none.

"Do you like Chopin?" he asked.

"Yes, very much," I nodded. "I'm particularly fond of his Études—Étude in E is one of my favorites."

Darla cleared her throat and gestured toward the clock. "We should go," she insisted. "We have to get to the library before all the applications are gone. Sorry we interrupted you." She smiled thoughtfully, and then tugged on my arm, urging me down the corridor.

"It's no bother," Mr. Laden called after us. The two of them chuckled and then muttered something unintelligible as we exited through the double doors at the end of the hall.

Duets

CHAPTER 2

*B*y the end of September my circle of friends had widened, due in large part to Eric's efforts to win me over. Any friend of Eric's was a shoo-in with the popular crowd. During this time, I was so busy adjusting to my new situation that I hadn't been able to dwell on the unanswered questions surrounding my accident. My mother had always told me that the truth has a way of revealing itself over time. Like heat safely chambered in the center of the earth, the truth would eventually search for a path that permitted it to rise to the surface, taking advantage of any weakness in the hard, rocky crust where it lay trapped.

My mother had a peculiar way of turning just about everything into a science lesson. It was part of her charm and the reason I often found myself looking at things through a scientific lens.

The computer essentials test required for library assistant applicants was not difficult and it didn't take as long as the librarian anticipated, in spite of my disability. I was confident that I did well enough to meet the application requirements. When I left the testing center, I decided to wander through the music corridor instead of exiting through the main doors.

I was slightly relieved, yet admittedly disappointed, when I did not hear any music coming from the deserted practice rooms. I paused for a moment next to one of the open doors and although I knew it would be painful, I couldn't resist the lure of the piano.

I approached the old upright methodically and rested my right hand lightly on its shiny white keys. I let my fingers slide slowly across the keyboard without making a sound. It had been a year and a half since I'd felt the familiar ripple of smooth ivory beneath my fingers; it felt as natural as breathing.

I closed my eyes and breathed a deep sigh of longing as I relived a dream; it was a memory from a distant lifetime. I was on stage in the Performing Arts Center at the University of California Santa Barbara preparing for my performance at the National Piano Players Guild scholarship audition. Three judges—Dr. Reid, Dr. Nelson, and Dr. Smiley—sat staunchly in the front row of the theatre while graduate students and the performers' family members occupied the remainder of the seats. My mom and dad sat anxiously in the third row to the right of the stage, nervously anticipating my performance. The room smelled of musty old wood and stale floor wax. I took a deep breath and savored the odor—a familiar smell that I had grown to love.

The competition had required me to prepare three pieces from varying musical genres, so I had selected compositions from Bach, Beethoven, and my personal favorite, Chopin. I planned to open with a Bach Prelude and Fugue followed by all three movements of Beethoven's *Sonata Pathetique*, and then conclude with Chopin's Nocturne No. 2 in E-flat.

I sat resolutely at the intimidating grand piano situated near the center of the stage, closed my eyes, and began to envision the music in my mind as I lifted my hands slowly and rested them lightly on the keys. At the precise moment that my fingers made contact with the keys a subtle breeze glazed through me, empowering me with an unnatural sense of tranquility and composure. I graced through Bach with unprecedented ease and confidence, pausing at the end of the fugue to catch my breath. Before I knew it, my fingers began to hammer the dynamic opening of the *Pathetique*. Throughout the three movements, I had an uncanny sense that a greater power was playing through me. I never opened my eyes, not even between movements, afraid that if I did, I might break the magical spell.

As the final chord of the Nocturne resonated throughout the theatre, I opened my eyes and fixated on the hands that had played so flawlessly—my hands—and yet that night they were not mine alone. The audience hesitated briefly, creating a deafening silence, before breaking into spontaneous applause. The explosion of noise brought me to my senses, and I stood to take my bow. It was a triumphant moment, but I almost felt guilty taking all the credit, for even though it was irrational to believe that some phantasmic entity played through me, I could not deny the reality of the experience.

I realized I had won the approval of the three judges when they each stood and returned a bow. Judges at this event were not supposed to applaud a candidate; however, protocol permitted them to stand as a show of respect for a performance. Tears flowed in a steady stream down the sides of my face as I observed the emotion in my parent's eyes. Theirs was an expression of pure joy. It was a moment I never wanted to forget, even though it was painful now to remember.

Despairingly, I examined my left hand and peeled back my bent fingers, forcing them to straighten. I winced as the effort sent a stabbing jolt through the palm of my hand and along my forearm. The tips of my fingers tingled with numbness as I held them straight. My throat tightened as I stared at the puckered red scar that marked my palm. I released my fingers and observed as one by one they returned involuntarily to their permanently bent position.

For the next few days, I gave Darla every excuse possible for us to do our studying at the library. I kept my ears intently peeled every time we passed the tiled corridor that led to the practice rooms, hoping to hear the echo of classical music. Something about the way Jonathan had played the Étude intrigued me—I wanted very much to hear him play again.

Friday afternoon Darla left me to fend for myself after school. She had to pick her little brother up from the elementary school before getting ready for the football game. Without Darla there to distract me, the pull of the piano was too strong to resist, and I found myself once again wandering through the music hall. I slipped quietly into the practice room at the end of the corridor and sat down at the wooden upright. Like before, I traced the slick keys with my fingers. I thought about the shiny, black, baby grand piano that my father had bought for me the year I turned twelve—a piano presently locked in a storage garage where it sat idly collecting dust. I had tried to convince my father to get rid of it when he sold the house, but he refused. Selling the piano would mean he had accepted the painful reality that I would never play again.

As my fingers continued to slide pensively along the keys, my mind drifted aimlessly from memory to memory—like the morning of my first recital; I was only seven. I threw up repeatedly, insisting I had contracted a fatal illness. Or the evening of the school play, when I suddenly went blank and began playing the opening prelude in the wrong key. It wouldn't have been so bad if it weren't for the violinist who insisted on playing her part in the correct key; imagine that. I smiled at the memory and then my mind landed on another scene—our tight little family of three gathered around the instrument that I loved. It was an oft-repeated scene; my mom would watch admiringly as my dad and I sat at the piano, battling each other with invented versions of "Three Blind Mice." Dad was the master of random improvisation and was forever taunting me with it, always challenging me. He had an irritating way of blasting me off the keyboard with insane impromptu renditions of the simple melody.

Absentmindedly, I tapped the opening sequence of "Three Blind Mice." I got through the first line, and then froze, staring forlornly at the white keys that were beginning to yellow with age. The memory of my mother and father was so vivid that I sensed if I turned around, they would both be standing behind me—which probably explains my overreaction to the voice that suddenly spoke.

"Are you going to stare at it, or play it?"

"Ahh!" I jumped, whirling around and clutching my throat. There he stood, leaning against the doorway with his arms folded casually across his chest. He chuckled at my theatrics, but the amused expression on his face was neither smug nor condescending.

Thinking fast, I responded with as much poise as I could salvage. "I figured if I stared at it long enough, it would play itself." I worked at keeping a serious look on my face.

"I don't think it's working," he teased, inclining his head toward the piano.

"Of course not, you scared it," I replied. The thought made me laugh.

His eyes smiled, but he pulled his eyebrows together into a serious line. "I'll have to work on my approach."

He straightened and walked forward, extending his hand. "I'm Jonathan Rollings." The formality in his voice surprised me.

I stood and offered my hand in return. "I'm Beth," I replied coolly. I made a conscious effort to mirror his relaxed composure.

"I know." He rolled his eyes towards the floor. I followed his glance to my book bag where my name was colorfully tattooed across the shoulder strap. Darla's doing. "Are you studying music?"

"No. I used to," I grimaced, suddenly nervous. "But I can't—I don't play anymore."

"Really."

Though there was no questioning intonation in his tone, I sensed he was waiting for me to explain, just as he had the first time we met. I studied his demeanor carefully as I raised my hand, revealing my pitifully folded fingers. He reached for my hand but glanced at me before taking it, as if requesting permission. My eyes shifted from his gaze to my hand, and I shrugged. Carefully, he took my hand in his and unfolded my fingers, forcing them to rest against his wrist. I ignored the familiar pain that accompanied the movement. He examined my hand curiously, then turned it over uncovering the circular discoloration at the base of my fingers. He slid his finger over the deep red scar and sighed.

"What happened?"

"Accident." I discreetly pulled my hand away.

"Does it hurt?" His expression was sincere.

"Only when I forget . . ." I chuckled darkly, "or when I remember."

He watched me carefully and then nodded. He sat down on the piano bench, patting the spot next to him. "Sit for a minute?"

I stared at the seat beside him, suddenly uneasy. "I better go," I said quietly.

He waited for a moment, watching me carefully, and then shrugged. "All right."

I was half way down the corridor when I felt him pull gently against the top of my arm.

"Wait," he urged quietly, turning me to face him. "Can you come back Tuesday?"

"Why?" I answered. There was an embarrassing rise in the pitch of my voice that made me self-conscious.

He smiled politely. I couldn't help but notice the flawed symmetry of his lips; one side curved up more than the other. I fought the impulse to reach up and straighten them. I nearly laughed aloud at the absurdity of the thought.

"Come back Tuesday, if you can," he requested.

"You're not a student." I stated. It was *supposed* to be a question, but it came out more like an accusation.

"No," he chuckled, amused by my abruptness.

"Are you a teacher?" I had the odd feeling that he wanted to give me lessons.

He laughed heartily at the confused expression on my face and then scowled in feigned shock. "No," he said, trying not to smile. "I'm a student at the university in Jackson. I tutor music students here twice a week. It's part of a contract between the community and the high school. Students who can't afford private lessons come here."

"Oh," I declared. *That makes sense.*

The sudden vibration of my cell phone startled me and I jumped. Then I glanced at my watch and gasped.

"Oh my gosh! I need to go," I announced urgently, and hastily turned to leave. I was halfway to the end of the corridor before I realized he was speaking.

"Good to see you again, Beth," he called after me.

I hesitated for a moment, but there was no time for that now. I waved back at him and hurried on down the hall.

I was not surprised to discover that I had four missed calls on my cell phone, three from Darla and one from Eric. Eric had called to remind me that I was supposed to meet him for pizza after the football game tonight, and that there was still time if I changed my mind about going to the Homecoming dance with him in a few weeks. Darla had called, frantic, because I hadn't returned her phone calls. She was supposed to pick me up for tonight's game. I sent her a quick text message letting her know that everything was fine and I'd be ready as planned. It was less than a minute later when she called.

"Where have you been?" she demanded. "I've been calling you all afternoon."

"I went to the library after school," I said somewhat defensively.

"I checked there, the librarian said you hadn't been there."

"I went to check out the music rooms."

There was a long pause on the other end of the phone, then I heard her hiss. "You went to see that piano guy, didn't you?"

I didn't respond.

"Was he there?" She didn't miss a beat.

"Yes," I admitted.

"Did you talk to him?"

"Yes."

"You have to tell me everything!" she insisted.

"There's nothing to tell. Besides, I need to get ready for the game."

"Okay, I'll pick you up at five, but then I want details."

Because I had to walk, I didn't arrive home until four-thirty. I had to scramble to be ready on time. I quickly changed my clothes and searched for some warm blankets. Fall in Andersen was beautiful, but the evenings were bitterly cold—at least from the perspective of a native Californian. I couldn't imagine what the approaching winter nights would be like.

The evening proved to be even colder than anticipated. By the third quarter of the game, Darla, Crystal, and I were huddled together, shivering under our blankets on the icy metal bleachers. We were barely able to enjoy ourselves. Okay, the truth was *I* was the one who was uncomfortable. Everyone else seemed fine. They made fun of my thin California blood, and then took bets on whether I would survive a Wyoming winter.

Darla cornered me the first chance she got and needled me about my rendezvous at the music room. She wanted to know everything I had found out about Jonathan.

"What's he like? Is he nice?"

"I don't know. We barely spoke." For some reason, Darla's interest in Jonathan irritated me.

"Did you find out who is he?"

"His name is Jonathan Rollings—he's a music tutor."

"Seriously?" Then she spoke quietly, more to herself than to me, "that explains why I've never seen him before."

"He wants me to come back on Tuesday."

"Ohhhh," she sang knowingly.

"What?" I asked, suddenly suspicious.

"Poor Eric." She nudged my side with her elbow and giggled mischievously. I rolled my eyes in protest, but decided it would be wiser to simply laugh and let the topic drop—Eric was another story altogether.

I watched the remainder of the game through chattering teeth. Our team won by a narrow margin, so spirits ran high. The party at the Pizza Factory afterwards was loud, jubilant, and a lot of fun. I found myself in exceptionally high spirits and laughing easily. It was the first time I had felt this free in months.

That night, I dreamed about the accident—again.

By the time the following Tuesday arrived, I had decided to meet

Jonathan as he requested to let him know that I wasn't interested in tutoring lessons. Imagine, *me* needing a tutor! Absurd.

I slowed my pace when I heard music coming from the practice room at the end of the hall. I knew immediately that it was Jonathan; it wasn't difficult to recognize his style, even though I'd only heard him play once. I was careful not to make too much noise as I walked along the tile floor of the corridor; I feared he would stop if he heard my approach. He was just ending the middle movement of Beethoven's *Moonlight Sonata*. To my amazement—and utter delight—he broke immediately into the powerful opening of the final movement. It was a staggeringly difficult piece to play, yet he made it sound effortless. I slipped silently through the door and sat on the floor, resting my back against the wall. I closed my eyes and listened with quiet envy as he played. When he finished, I broke into a round of delighted applause.

"Hello," he said without turning around. I could tell by his voice that he was smiling.

"That was amazing!" I declared. "That's very difficult to play. I always have trouble . . . had trouble . . . with it."

"That's truly a compliment coming from you, Miss *Elizabeth* Arrington," he drawled, half-bowing as he turned around to look at me. "You might have mentioned you were a celebrity." He spoke as if to scold me, but his eyes smiled playfully.

"I'm not a celebrity," I replied, somewhat confused.

"You have quite a reputation from what I hear."

"Well, that's all history now." I couldn't help but wonder what he'd heard.

"Hmm," he nodded, glancing briefly at my hand.

Instinctively, I slid my hand behind my back out of his view.

Jonathan patted the piano bench next to him. "Join me for a minute."

I hesitated. Although I had come to let him know I wasn't interested in lessons, I felt compelled to hear what he had to say. He smiled graciously, then bent to retrieve something off the floor. When he turned around, he held a book in his hand.

"You might find this interesting," he offered, handing me the book.

"What is it?" I asked guardedly. He didn't reply; he simply made a gesture with his eyes. I read the title, *Popular Duets from Popular Composers*, and in smaller print, *for the advanced virtuoso*. I thumbed through the book and noticed there were several intricate arrangements of popular classical pieces. Jonathan reached over and flipped through the book to a page he had marked.

"I thought you might enjoy this one particularly." His eyes danced with childlike enthusiasm.

I recognized the music instantly; it was Chopin's Étude in E. I felt a wave of mixed emotions rush through me—the strongest of which was fear of his implied expectation. I turned to look at him; his expression caught me off guard.

"What?" he asked. His eyes flickered between the music and me. I couldn't respond. I just continued to stare.

"What?" he said again, this time quietly. His eyes searched mine.

"Why?" It was all I could manage.

"Isn't it obvious? This is where you belong," he replied, pointing to the piano.

"No. Not anymore. I—"

"Beth. . . ." His penetrating glance made me almost as uneasy as the lingering silence that followed.

"What's the use?" I finally murmured. My glance shifted to my crippled fingers. "I've only got one. . . ." I couldn't finish my sentence.

"That doesn't matter," he said softly.

"How can you say that? It's absurd . . . and . . . rude."

He shook his head. "No, I didn't mean it that way. I meant . . . let *me* be your other hand," he offered quickly. He glanced briefly at my hand, and then back at me. "Just for now."

His expression warmed and in spite of his presumptuous request, for some reason I didn't want to disappoint him. I hesitated for several moments before rolling my eyes (there went another eye wrinkle).

"Fine," I muttered begrudgingly, breathing a sigh of submission.

He ignored my obvious reluctance and turned toward the piano, positioning himself to play with his left hand. I raised my right hand to the keys and waited for his signal.

Jonathan played in exact time with me as we soared through the Étude. His interpretation of the dynamics and the way he anticipated my timing was uncanny. He retarded in the same places that I did, even though it wasn't noted in the music. My left hand twitched periodically out of habit; I had played the piece so often that my fingers knew exactly where his were, and they ached to take their place on the keys. Jonathan never looked at the music; his eyes focused intently on our hands.

As we finished the song, we both lingered on the final chord. I was afraid to look at him, afraid of the emotion my face might reveal.

"Well . . ." he took a deep breath, "let's see what else is in here." He gestured back to the music, and for the next hour we sat together at the piano playing song after song from the book of duets. We were about half way through the book when the janitor knocked against the open door.

"How late you kids gonna be?"

"We should probably go," Jonathan responded, glancing at me as he spoke.

"Yeah," I sighed reluctantly. I reached for my cell phone and discovered it was nearly five o'clock. "Oh no," I shrieked. "I need to get home."

"I'll walk you out," he offered as I gathered my things. "Where are you parked?"

"Um . . . I usually walk."

"Would you like a ride?"

"That's okay. I don't live far," I replied.

Jonathan rolled his eyes and then rephrased the question. "May I offer you a ride home?"

"Oh," I chuckled. "Sure. Thanks." Then as an afterthought, "You know, you really shouldn't do that."

"Do what?" he asked, raising his eyebrows.

"Roll your eyes . . . you're going to get wrinkles around your eyes."

He looked at me curiously for several moments and then chuckled.

The drive to Uncle Connor's house was a short one, barely more than a mile. Jonathan drove slowly while we talked, or rather while he asked questions and I responded.

"How do you like Andersen?"

"It's really pretty here."

"Wait until winter," he laughed. "Have you ever lived in cold weather before?"

"No," I shrugged. "I've always lived in California."

Jonathan nodded. "Hmm."

"But Andersen has always intrigued me," I added.

"Really? How so?"

"The whole 'vortex' thing, for one."

"You believe in the vortex theory?" He seemed surprised.

"I don't know. I don't really understand it, but my uncle sure believes in it. He has all sorts of rocks and crystals in his house. He claims they have unique properties that enlighten the mind."

"Interesting," he muttered.

"Oh. Sorry. Turn left at the road just past that row of trees." I had forgotten that Jonathan didn't know where I lived.

"It's the last house on the right, beyond the bridge."

He nodded. "You walk every day?"

"Only sometimes. My friend Darla usually gives me a ride."

Jonathan pulled into the driveway and put his car into park. "I tutor on Tuesdays and Fridays . . . that is, if you want to drop by the practice rooms again."

I climbed out of his car and glanced at him before shutting the door. "I don't think so . . . but thanks for today."

He smiled and nodded sideways. Then he backed out of the driveway and drove away.

"So . . . then what?" Darla whispered during English the next morning. "Is he *tutoring* you?"

"No!" I growled, but I wasn't offended. It was impossible to be offended by Darla.

"But he brought the book of duets," she argued.

"That was a coincidence."

"Sure," she smirked. "And he just happened to have one with your 'a-tude' in it . . . or whatever that word was."

"Étude." I shook my head in mock disgust.

"Whatever. He remembered you liked it; that's pretty cool."

"I guess, but it doesn't matter. There's not a big market for one-handed pianists." The painful reality of my situation really stung, and I blamed Jonathan for bringing that pain to the surface.

School finally ended, and although I'd said I would not be there, I made my way across the street to the practice rooms. The temptation to hear him play was too much to resist. My intention was merely to sit and listen without him knowing I was there. So I removed my shoes and snuck quietly down the hall. It didn't take long to determine which room Jonathan was in; pianists have their own unique style, and Jonathan's was unmistakable.

I sat in the hallway with my back against the wall so I could listen without disturbing him. He was in the middle of the first move-ment of Beethoven's *Pathetique*—the same sonata I had played in my competition. My heart ached with every chord progression; it was all so unfair.

The door at the end of the corridor opened and a young girl I didn't recognize stepped into the hallway followed by Mr. Laden. I stood at once not wanting to be recognized, but it was too late.

"Well hello, Miss Arrington. Good to see you again."

The music stopped and a moment later, Jonathan was at the door.

"Hey, Mr. Laden," Jonathan nodded, and then looked at me. "How long have you been here?"

"Looks like your admirer has returned." Mr. Laden grinned at Jonathan.

I didn't know what to say; I wished I hadn't come.

"Come on in," Jonathan urged. "I was hoping you'd come back."

"Don't let him give you a hard time." Mr. Laden winked at me and tilted his head in Jonathan's direction. "He loves a captive audience."

Mr. Laden turned and headed back to his room. Jonathan stepped aside, motioning for me to enter the practice room. He looked down at my feet and chuckled.

"No shoes?"

I shrugged.

"Must be a California thing," he teased. "How about we take another turn at the duets?"

"I didn't come to play. I came to . . . I just wanted . . ."

Jonathan raised his eyebrows. "Came to what, exactly?" There was a slight tone of accusation in his voice.

"Nothing." I shook my head. "I shouldn't have come." I turned for the door, but Jonathan got there first.

"I'm sorry," he smiled. "Stay for awhile. Please?" He gestured toward the piano and waited until I finally took my seat.

The remainder of the afternoon passed quickly. After relentless coaxing, Jonathan convinced me to play a duet with him. Once I started, I couldn't stop. We played through the remainder of the book, pausing at times to discuss the various composers of the pieces we were playing. Jonathan was amazing. He knew all sorts of trivia and obscure facts about several of the composers. I couldn't help wondering if he was making half of it up.

"How do you know this stuff?"

"Call it a hobby," he chuckled. "I suppose you could say it's in my blood." He flipped the page and stared blankly at the music for several moments, then turned to me. "What about you? What do *you* do for fun?"

"I dunno. Nothing really. It was always the piano for me."

An awkward silence hovered briefly, then Jonathan turned back to the piano. We continued playing the duets until the shadows on the wall revealed that it was getting dark outside. Jonathan offered to drive me home again and just like that, the afternoon was over.

"Tuesday," he said as I got out of his car. It wasn't a request. "I'll bring something new."

He was halfway down the driveway before I could respond.

I wandered absentmindedly into the house and was surprised to find Marci and Uncle Connor together on the couch. Whatever they were doing came to an abrupt halt when I walked through the door.

"I'm sorry," I said. "I didn't mean to interrupt."

"Isn't it kind of late?" Uncle Connor asked reproachfully. He didn't usually speak to me in such a harsh tone, so I wasn't sure how to react.

"I'm sorry. I should've called, but normally you aren't home yet so I didn't think it would matter," I explained.

"Normally?" he blurted. "This is when you *normally* get home?"

"Connor, don't." Marci shushed him.

"No, not normally." My alarmed gaze bounced between Marci and Uncle Connor. Marci put her hand on Uncle Connor's arm and shot him a look of warning; he pursed his lips and let out a frustrated sigh.

"Darla called," Marci said quickly. "She's apparently been trying to get ahold of you all afternoon . . . something about planning for a mock trial."

"I've been trying to call you too," Uncle Connor snapped. Again his cross tone surprised me. Part of me felt sorry for making him upset, but another part of me was angry. After all, I wasn't doing anything wrong. I reached into my bag to grab my phone, curious as to why it hadn't vibrated when he'd called me, but it wasn't there. I began to search more frantically, but I couldn't find it.

"My phone is gone," I gasped. I racked my brain trying to remember the last time I used it. I bit my lip and looked apologetically at Uncle Connor.

"I-I think I forgot my phone today," I confessed.

Uncle Connor glared at me for a moment and then his expression shifted. "Where have you been?"

"I was," I hesitated and looked down at the carpet, "playing the piano."

I thought I heard Marci gasp quietly, but neither she nor Uncle

Connor said anything. I finally looked up to find them both staring at me. I blinked at the sting of tears that threatened the corners of my eyes. Uncle Connor's gaze shifted slowly from my eyes to my crippled hand where he paused for a moment, and then his eyes met mine once again.

"I don't understand. How? Where? And who was that young man who dropped you off?"

I wasn't sure which question to answer first. I figured I would work backward.

"His name is Jonathan Rollings," I began. Uncle Connor flinched at the name, but Marci put her hand on his arm again and stopped him from interrupting. "He's a music tutor at the high school. He's been working with me." It all came out wrong and too quickly for me to stop and think about what I was saying.

"A music tutor." Uncle Connor spat the words with an obvious edge of sarcasm.

"That's not what I mean," I fretted, suddenly feeling cornered and defensive. I looked pleadingly at Marci, silently begging for an ally. She must have read my thoughts.

"Connor, why don't you call the restaurant and change our reservations to a later time." He threw her a bewildered look, but she motioned toward the kitchen. He let out a deep huff, like a child who had been reprimanded, and then he left the room.

"Your uncle was worried about you when Darla called, and then he couldn't reach you," Marci explained. She glanced toward the kitchen. "It's all that business with the attacks in Jackson that have him upset and worried."

"What attacks?"

"The string of assaults on teenage girls in Jackson . . . all of them were raped. Surely you've heard about it; it's all over the newspapers and television."

"Yeah, I know about those, but I thought they caught the guy who did it. Didn't two of the girls identify him?"

"That's the problem. They both identified a man whose body was found buried on a construction site last week."

"How's that a problem? He's dead, right? So there's nothing to worry about."

Marci shook her head. "According to forensics, he's been dead for over five months. There's no way he could be the one attacking the girls. The police think whoever it is must have somehow planted false evidence." She tapped the arm of the couch several times and then shrugged, changing the subject. "Your uncle will be fine, don't worry. Remember, having a teenage girl in the house is new to him." She smiled, glancing toward the kitchen where Uncle Connor had been exiled. "Just don't forget your phone again!"

Darla met me at the school gate the following Tuesday morning; Eric was nowhere in sight, which was unusual.

"Hey Darla," I said, greeting her as I passed through the gate. I had to step carefully to avoid what I referred to as 'puddle pools,' deceitful spots of water that appeared to be shallow puddles, but when you stepped in them they easily covered your entire foot. Twice I'd had to spend my day sloshing around school in water-soaked socks.

"Oh. Hey, Beth." Darla's eyes darted from side to side as though searching for someone.

"What's the matter?" I tried to follow her flitting glances. "Looking for Derrick?"

"No. I'm avoiding Crystal. She's driving me crazy about Homecoming."

"Oh," I snickered, helping her scout the area. Crystal, with her overdone eye makeup and high-pitched fickle laugh, had a way of making every conversation about her—and whatever boy was her flavor of the moment.

"Speaking of Homecoming," I asked casually, "who are you going with?"

"You," she replied quickly.

"Is Eric still planning to go?"

"As far as I know," she shrugged. Then she whirled around. "Why? Did you change your mind about going with him?" Her tone was casual, but her eyes betrayed her thoughts.

"Uh . . . no. Not exactly."

She eyed me suspiciously. "What's that supposed to mean?"

"Nothing . . . nothing that can't wait."

"Well, he's not here anyway. His family was out of town all weekend." She paused and then turned around to face me. "What's going on with you two, anyway?"

"Nothing. We're just friends."

"Maybe in *your* eyes, but I don't think Eric sees it that way."

"Eric has a tendency to exaggerate, as you well know."

"Well, the longer you put him off the more obsessed he'll become. Wretched Eric. He only wants what he can't have." Darla's icy sarcasm surprised me, and it cemented my suspicion that there was more to their history than either would admit.

When school finally ended, I hurried through the hallway toward the music department. As before, Jonathan was already playing in one of the practice rooms. He favored the room on the right at the far end of the hall; he claimed the acoustics were sharper.

I slowed my pace as I approached the door; he was playing something new. It sounded like a classical piece, yet the melody was free flowing—much less structured than music from the classical period.

He paused in the middle of the measure. "Hello, Beth," he said without turning.

One day, he's going to turn around, and find somebody else standing here. I chuckled at the thought, but kept it to myself.

"What are you playing?" I asked. "I don't recognize the composer."

"Don't you?" He turned around slowly, oddly curious.

A brief silence followed—then a thought suddenly occurred to me and my eyes widened. *"You* wrote it?"

He scrutinized my expression and after a few moments, shook his head slowly. He seemed disappointed.

"No. Not me," he half smiled. "It was written a long time ago."

"Would you play it again? Please?"

He nodded and turned to play. I closed my eyes and listened intently to the melody. It was like something from a dream. In my mind, I pictured a young debutant pining over her soldier who was off to war, a soldier who would return for her some day, but not for a very long time. She carried a parasol to protect her delicate skin from the sun's harsh rays and wandered aimlessly along a wooded path, pausing now and then to pick a wildflower or watch a bird. She carried a sketch pad and a set of charcoal pencils. I watched as she located a felled log in a clearing and gently sat down to sketch. She looked like an angel perched on a wooden cloud.

Jonathan stopped playing and a curtain fell on the scene abruptly. I opened my eyes and looked at him.

"Why did you stop?" I questioned.

"That's the end of the song."

I thought for a moment and shook my head. "No, there's more," I insisted.

"Nope," he replied, moving his head from side to side.

"There's something missing. There should be a bridge or something." Jonathan watched me with wonderment. "Play it again, please?"

"Why don't you play it this time?"

"Very funny," I replied scornfully.

"No, really." He began to pluck the melody line with his right hand. "This is the main theme; everything else builds around it. Listen."

I watched his hand, concentrating on the movement of the melody line. It was a beautifully simple piece.

"Here's another variation." He adjusted his hands and played the theme again, only this time in a minor key. The music was foreboding—as though inspired from the depths of tremendous sorrow. Instinctively, I began to hum the tune as he played. He turned to watch me but continued playing. I couldn't shake the gnawing feeling that the melody was incomplete.

Jonathan stopped and motioned for me to play the right hand. I placed my hand in the correct position and tapped out the melody, following Jonathan's lead as he played the same notes an octave lower. It only took a minute for me to learn the main theme. He began to play the accompaniment while I continued to play the melody. The muscles in my left hand twitched; I was overpowered by the urge to play the song with both hands.

Jonathan paused, watching me carefully. Without saying a word, he lifted my left hand and placed it on his. One by one he straightened my bent fingers so that they lay flat on top of his. Then he lifted both our hands to the keys, mine still resting on his. I glanced up at him, but he turned back to the piano and signaled for me to begin.

As we played, I could feel the movement of Jonathan's muscles in the palm of my left hand. I was intensely aware of his skin beneath my hand; but what took my breath away was the startling sensation that I was controlling the movement of the accompaniment myself. It was the first time since the accident that I had been this close to actually playing. A myriad of emotions rose within me—everything from regret to elation. I had to concentrate carefully to keep them from reaching the surface. I closed my eyes and allowed the melody to take hold of me as Jonathan's hand and mine played as one.

When the melody concluded I hesitated, not wanting to move. But I was afraid it might be awkward if I lingered too long, so I slid my hand slowly off his. I glanced up at Jonathan's face, but he was staring at our hands. The expression on his face was unreadable. He swallowed, and then reached down and lifted my hand. He eyed the red scar in the middle for several moments.

"Your hand—what kind of accident caused this?"

I wasn't ready for this conversation. "Does it matter?"

"What do the doctors say?"

"They say it's dead." I pulled my hand away from his.

"What about physical therapy?" He was still looking at my hand with obvious curiosity.

I sighed bitterly. Did he honestly think I hadn't tried everything? "There's too much nerve damage. Like I said, it's dead." I tucked my hand out of view.

"Is it?" He looked skeptical. "You don't feel anything?"

"Pain." I rubbed my scar. "I feel pain."

"That's good," he muttered, more to himself than to me.

"Excuse me?" I wasn't going to let that comment escape unnoticed. "Pain's good?" I said, eying him with skepticism.

"In my opinion, yes. It's good that you feel pain."

I started to protest, but he cut me off.

"Don't you see? That's proof that your hand is not dead. As long as there's pain, there's hope."

"Jonathan, stop." My dad had used the same logic to convince himself that I might play again someday. "The damage to my tendons and bones is irreparable. End of story."

He looked like he wanted to say something more, but changed his mind.

We gathered our things and walked quietly to the parking lot. The silence between us was not uncomfortable, but I felt uneasy as he drove down the path to Uncle Connor's house. I assumed he was still mulling over questions about my hand, a dead issue in my opinion, but I had another question.

"Jonathan?" My words broke the silence.

"Hmm?"

"You never told me who composed the music we were playing."

He bit his lip and cut his eyes at me. "Her name was Eleanor." He watched my reaction carefully.

"Who was she?"

He paused for a moment. Then very casually—as if it no longer mattered—he responded, "Someone who lived a long time ago."

Homecoming

CHAPTER 3

*H*omecoming in Andersen was an event that the entire town seemed to await with eager anticipation. Banners lined the main streets through town, store windows proudly displayed the school colors of forest green, golden yellow, and black, and tickets to the game could be purchased in most of the local businesses—while supplies lasted. The football game sold out almost as soon as the tickets arrived from the printer.

By Friday afternoon, spirits were high everywhere on campus. We held a pep rally for the football team, voted for the Homecoming king and queen (to be crowned during halftime), and adorned ourselves with tassels and bells to cheer our team on. Darla picked me up for the game at five o'clock—earlier than we would normally leave for a game. She insisted on arriving in time to secure the best seats possible. By now, I'd learned my lesson about outdoor events in October, so I gathered the warmest blankets I could find and put on a pair of thermal underwear. Darla laughed hysterically at me for bundling up so thoroughly, warning me that the *really* cold weather wouldn't officially arrive in Andersen until January.

"Thank goodness football season is over in December," she teased. "You'd never survive a game in January!"

"Yeah, good thing basketball's an *indoor* sport."

"Don't look now, but you're being summoned." Darla gestured toward the field. Eric was standing off to the side, away from the other players. As soon as I spotted him, he motioned for me to come down to the field. "Better not keep the star quarterback waiting," she said with joking sarcasm.

I gave Darla a disapproving look and then stepped carefully down the metal bleachers. I pushed through the incoming crowd and made my way down to the field. Eric was in especially good spirits.

"How 'bout we go to a movie tomorrow night and blow off the dance," he suggested, "just you and me."

"Eric," I started to protest.

"C'mon," he urged, reaching for my hand. "It'll be fun."

I marveled at the enormous size and strength of his hand as he weaved his rough fingers between mine. He pulled me closer to him, unleashing an irresistible smile. I had to remind myself of the code— and the fact that there were hundreds of eyes looking at us. A part of me wondered if his sudden public display was meant for my benefit or to entice the curiosity of on-lookers. Eric had many admiring fans.

"I already told Darla I would go to the dance with her." I knew it was the wrong argument as soon as I said it, but it was the first thing that came to my mind.

"She'll understand, trust me." Eric winked at me and squeezed my hand. The movement almost paralyzed me; his fingers felt like lead pipes between mine. I struggled to untangle my fingers from his.

"Eric, I *want* to go to the dance. I happen to like dancing."

"Fine. Then go with me."

"I'm going with Darla," I reminded him firmly.

"Whatever you say," he shrugged, "you're the boss."

I sighed. I hated it when he played the poor victim. Before I could retaliate, his mood switched gears.

"How about a kiss for good luck?" He raised his eyebrows hopefully. I'm not sure, but I think I blushed. I suddenly felt very awkward. "Could mean the difference between winning and losing our Homecoming game," he teased. He lowered his face to mine and tapped his fingers against his cheek. "C'mon, right here."

I felt as if the entire town of Andersen was watching this embarrassing exchange. Against my better judgment, I reached forward and kissed his cheek, then hurriedly pushed him away. He roared with laughter and took off jogging toward his teammates.

Surprisingly, the evening was warmer than we anticipated. By the third quarter of the game, I began to regret the fact that I was wrapped in thermal clothing underneath my jeans, sweatshirt, and down jacket. I discovered that I didn't need the blankets to stay warm, which made the evening far more enjoyable.

The game was a nail-biter from beginning to end. Our team would score and take the lead, turn the ball over to the other team, and then they would score. It kept us on the edge of our seats all evening. The intensity increased when the opposing team took a risk and went for a two-point conversion instead of the extra point in the fourth quarter. It was a gutsy decision by their coach, and it kept us on our feet for most of the quarter. The most aggravating part of the game was when our team went for the extra point and the kick was blocked. That meant we were down by two points going into the last two minutes of the game with the score 27–29. Then, as if in slow motion, the opposing team's quarterback threw a pass that was intercepted by one of our players, who then ran the ball forty-three yards before being tackled by our stunned rivals. Excitement exploded in the stands as our team took possession on the 18-yard line. It took three plays to score the final touchdown of the game, making the score 34–29. Confetti flew across the crowd as the students screamed and hugged. And Eric received the game ball—naturally!

As it turned out, Eric arranged things with Darla so that he could take me home after the game. I'm sure the fact that Derrick was hanging around helped. In Darla's mind, if she was okay with me hanging out with Eric, then Derrick should be okay about hanging out with her. She had it all worked out; sometimes she made me feel like the sacrificial lamb.

We chatted about the game on the way home and Eric did the "gentleman" thing and escorted me to the door.

"Thanks Eric," I said politely. "I appreciate the ride." I turned and reached for the doorknob, but Eric grabbed my hand and cradled it against his chest, forcing me to step in closer to him. He reached around my waist with his free arm and closed the gap between us. Again, I fixated on the strength of his hands.

"How about a victory kiss?" His eyes danced with unusual excitement.

I closed my eyes and sighed. "Eric, you know this isn't going to happen."

"Why not? You like me, you know you do." His confidence always seemed to catch me off guard.

"Eric, it's not right. We've been through this. Darla's my friend."

"She's cool with it." He tightened his arm around me and rested his lips against my ear.

I felt confused and strangely uneasy. "But I'm *not* cool with it," I replied, somewhat winded.

"It's just a kiss, Beth. It's not a marriage proposal," he murmured as he pressed his lips against my ear and along my cheekbone. His smug attitude annoyed me and brought me to my senses. I twisted away from his grasp.

"It's not going to happen, Eric."

Frustrated, he threw his hands in the air, palms forward. "Is this because there's someone else?" His words had a biting edge to them.

Ah, the victim was back. "What's that supposed to mean?" I threw the rhetorical question out as a defensive barrier, but I knew exactly what he meant.

"Your 'tutor' perhaps?" His fingers made mock quotes around the word "tutor."

"Good night, Eric," I said coldly. I stared him down until he finally gave up and left.

I was grateful that Darla had persuaded most of our friends to make the Homecoming dance a group affair. Eric was still pouting, but I pretended not to notice. He was obviously not used to rejection. I had to admit, a distant part of me wondered what it would be like to date him for real. Eric was everything a girl could ask for—hot, ripped, charismatic, and always the center of fun. He was the perfect guy—but the rest of me was not interested in the perfect guy. Adam, my ex-boyfriend, had been the perfect guy too. Thanks to my relationship with Adam, I had discovered that "perfect guys" often stand on counterfeit pedestals.

Eric squeezed my side gently. "Why are you so quiet tonight?"

I hadn't noticed how far my thoughts had drifted.

"Sorry," I smiled as Eric pulled me onto the dance floor.

By the middle of the night, I began to suspect that the number of girls who had shown up without dates distracted Eric. Either Darla was right about him or he was trying to make me jealous. It wasn't working. With a little bit of nudging, I managed to convince Eric to dance the next few dances with someone else.

Darla waited for the next set of slow dances to ask Derrick to dance. I watched her gaze adoringly into his eyes as they glided smoothly across the floor. I studied Derrick's expressions, looking for any clue that he might return her affection, but his face remained indifferent. I decided that the two of them made a perfect-looking couple, and that he was a jerk for not noticing what a terrific girl she was. Most boys in the school would consider themselves insanely lucky to have Darla's attention—especially to have her look at them as she did Derrick. I was watching the two of them carefully when a familiar voice startled me.

"Good evening, Beth."

I spun around quickly. "Jonathan," I stammered. "What are *you* doing here?"

"They needed chaperones, so I volunteered." He shrugged, grinning.

"You're *chaperoning?*"

"Yep," he replied, amused.

"And how's that going?" I tried not to laugh.

"Not much has changed," he smirked. "So, who's the guy you've been dancing with all night? Is he your boyfriend?"

His use of the word "boyfriend" struck a nerve. I felt instantly uncomfortable.

"Eric? No, he's just a friend."

"Does *he* know that?" Jonathan's eyes followed mine to Eric, who was dancing with Stephanie McKay—head cheerleader, naturally.

"If he doesn't, he's pretty dense," I grumbled. Then I started to chuckle. "Actually, he is *very* dense."

Jonathan eyed me with playful scorn, pretending to disapprove. "Well, he seems pretty into you, if you ask me."

"It's just because I'm the new girl in town." I was surprised by how uncomfortable this conversation was making me feel.

Jonathan shook his head in disagreement. "Don't sell yourself short."

I shrugged my shoulders.

"You look very pretty, by the way," he added.

"Thank you." I blushed, but he didn't notice; his eyes were focused on Darla.

"Hmm," he muttered after a moment.

"What?"

"Your friend, what did you say her name is?"

"Darla."

He nodded. "She's very obvious about her interest in—"

"—Derrick," I filled in the blank for him.

"She should try holding something back."

"I think she's tried just about every strategy imaginable. She's pretty crazy about him."

"She's a pretty girl."

"Yes, very pretty," I agreed, wondering where he was going with this. An unwelcome knot formed in the pit of my stomach and for the first time, I resented Darla's beauty.

He shook his head slightly, "If he hasn't noticed her by now, it isn't there."

The music ended and Darla and Eric made their way over to where Jonathan and I were standing. As they approached, I could tell by the look on Eric's face that he was not pleased to see Jonathan next to me. Darla looked at me with masked surprise.

"Eric, Darla, this is Jonathan." I introduced them quickly, and braced myself for the inevitable awkwardness.

"Hello," Jonathan smiled, extending his hand first to Darla and then to Eric. Jealousy reared its ugly, green head as I watched Jonathan clasp Darla's flawless hand. The power of the emotion surprised me. Fortunately, no one noticed.

"You must be the one Darla told me about." Eric's tone was abrasive, yet he tried to appear nonchalant. Jonathan chuckled.

"And you must be the guy that Darla *did not* tell me about," Jonathan retorted. He glanced at Darla and winked. She mistook the gesture as an invitation.

"Do you want to dance?" she asked Jonathan, casting her eyes toward mine questioningly as if seeking permission. The green-eyed demon in me coiled and then hissed. Could she hear it?

"Thank you, and I'd be honored . . ." he gave her a subtle bow, "but chaperones are not permitted to dance with students unless they're related," he explained humorously. Darla looked stunned; Eric huffed.

"Classic," Eric chuckled dryly. He looked up, pretending to recognize someone across the room. "Hey, I'll be back, okay?"

Darla and I peered at each other and shrugged our shoulders. She watched Eric suspiciously as he headed across the dance floor to the opposite side of the room where Derrick stood. Jonathan watched Darla—I watched Jonathan. He shook his head and then glanced at me as if we shared a common secret. He bent over and whispered something in Darla's ear while eyeing a group of boys huddled together in the back of the auditorium. The back of my ears burned. Darla's eyes furrowed together as she searched the crowd at the back of the room, but then widened as she spotted one of the boys in the group. She turned around and looked straight at Jonathan in amazement. He raised both his eyebrows, cut his eyes toward the back of the room at the huddle of boys, and then nodded discreetly at Darla. She looked at him quizzically and then smiled thoughtfully, tilting her head to one side. She reached over and took my arm, pulling me closer to her.

"I'll be right back," she spoke in my ear. "I'm going to the restroom."

I nodded, and Darla strode away in a light prance.

"What did you do to her?" I asked Jonathan when she was safely out of earshot.

"I gave her another option," he replied, watching as she scampered away. "She probably won't take advantage of it, but it's something for her to think about."

I was about to press him for more information, but he changed the subject. "So what's the story with you and this Eric guy?"

"I told you, he's a friend. We hang out sometimes." I followed Jonathan's eyes to where Eric stood. He and Derrick were looking in our direction.

"So he wouldn't mind if you and I hung out?" He looked at me slyly. I felt the previous uneasiness slip away and a new qualm take its place. "'Cuz I get the feeling he wouldn't like that too much," he added with a devilish smile.

I felt a warm flame of blush rise behind my ears. "No, I don't suppose he would," I chuckled, still watching Eric in the distance.

"What about you?" he asked.

"What about me?"

"Would *you* mind?" He glanced at me, and for a second he seemed nervous. I hesitated for a moment, wondering if I had heard him correctly. I replayed the conversation in my mind and decided I had.

"No. I wouldn't mind," I smiled, turning back toward the crowd.

"Speak of the devil," he muttered. "I'll see you later, okay?" He started to turn away, then leaned over and whispered into my ear. "You really do look pretty tonight."

I swung around to see what he had been looking at and noticed

Eric walking toward me. When I turned back around, Jonathan was gone.

"Where'd the piano pansy go?" Eric demanded.

"Nice, Eric," I replied, rolling my eyes. Darn, another wrinkle.

Eric smiled broadly and pulled me onto the dance floor. I didn't see Jonathan for the remainder of the dance, and Darla didn't resurface until the evening was nearly over. When I finally saw her again, she pulled me aside anxiously.

"What's up with Jonathan? I can't believe he was here."

"I'm as surprised as you are." I couldn't help myself, but I had to know. "What did he say to you?" I asked, trying not to let it show that it bothered me.

"He told me not to waste my time on Derrick, that Derrick was obviously not interested, but that there was somebody else who'd been eyeing me all night."

"Who?"

"Evan Bradley."

"Ahhh." That was no surprise to me; Evan had been eyeing Darla since the beginning of the school year.

"I know, huh," she snickered. "He told me I should look Evan's way a few times instead of wasting all my energy on Derrick."

"Maybe he's right," I whispered. Eric, noticing our exchange, cut in on the conversation.

"What's going on?"

"Girl talk," Darla and I said at the same time. She looked at me and we both laughed. The green-eyed monster slithered away silently.

When I awoke the following morning, my room was exceptionally bright. I crawled out of bed and stepped across the floor to pull back the curtains. I squealed with delight when I discovered that the sun was shining brightly—not a cloud in the sky. I could smell the mouth-watering aroma of bacon frying in the kitchen, so I speedily washed my face, brushed my teeth, and changed into a pair of shorts and a T-shirt before venturing out to the living room. I was surprised to find Uncle Connor already up, dressed, and watching football.

"Well, good morning!" he grinned. "Glad you finally decided to join us."

"I told you the bacon would wake her up!" Marci hollered victoriously from the kitchen.

"What time is it?" I tried unsuccessfully to suppress a yawn.

"Nearly ten o'clock," Uncle Connor replied.

"Seriously?"

"Must've been some dance," he teased.

Though I tried, I couldn't keep from smiling. It was a great dance, but it wasn't the memory of dancing that was making me smile. Marci appeared in the room with a tray of bacon, lettuce, and tomato sandwiches; a favorite of Uncle Connor's, especially during Sunday morning football games.

"Did something happen between you and Eric?" Marci asked.

"Eric?" I shook my head. "No!"

"What's wrong with Eric?" Uncle Connor interrupted. "He seems like a nice enough kid. Comes from a good family too."

"Nothing's wrong with Eric . . . he's a good *friend*." I raised my eyebrows and shot them both a reproachful warning.

"So, then," Marci prodded, "why the smiles this morning?"

"No reason," I replied innocently. When it was clear that I wasn't going to offer more, Uncle Connor grunted and changed the subject.

"What are your plans today?"

"I was hoping to get some sun . . . read, maybe," I replied.

"You obviously haven't been outside," he chuckled.

"No, but it's a gorgeous day."

"Ah, poor California girl," he chided. "Go ahead. Take a walk to the end of the driveway in your shorts and then tell me how you plan to 'get some sun.'"

"Fine." I knit my eyebrows together and walked stubbornly to the front door. I was tired of being teased about my "California thin" blood and not being able to handle Wyoming weather. I was determined to show everyone that I was just as thick-skinned as the next person. When I opened the door, however, a rush of cold air slapped me in the face. I was not about to give Uncle Connor the satisfaction of knowing I was a wimp, so I braced myself and marched to the end of the driveway. It probably would have been wise to put some shoes on first, but I was already out the door before the thought occurred to me. By the time I got to the end of the driveway I wanted to turn around and run back into the house, but I knew he would never let me live it down. So instead, I forced myself to meander slowly back up the driveway and into the house. It was all I could do to control the shivers that hammered my body, but I held firm. Uncle Connor laughed heartily when I walked smugly back into the living room.

"You're just like your mother," he chuckled.

That was as long as I could hold out. "Geez! Uncle Connor," I finally conceded, "It is *freakishly* cold out there!"

"Told you so," he laughed.

"How can it be so sunny and so cold at the same time?"

"You should see how red your cheeks are," he teased. "Such a sharp contrast to your blue face."

"All right, that's enough," Marci interjected. "Sunbathing is obviously out of the question Beth, so how about some hot chocolate instead?"

"Th-th-that w-w-would be gr-gr-great," I chattered jokingly, emphasizing each stutter for dramatic flair.

We watched most of the football game together while I did the laundry and finished my homework. Later, in spite of the brisk, frigid air, I bundled up in a warm, cozy blanket and took a book and a pad of paper outside to enjoy the sunshine. Even though there was a sharp chill in the air, the sun pierced through the cold and warmed my face. It even managed to penetrate the blanket that was wrapped around my body. Nestled snugly against the serene backdrop of the foothills, embraced by warmth and contentment, I relaxed into a peaceful slumber.

As I slept, in spirit-like fashion I was carried to the top of a high grassy hill overlooking a vast meadow of rolling green. From that vantage point, I was able to observe the events that were unfolding below me. I watched as one by one, forces gathered on each side of the rolling hills. Soldiers valiantly formed two lines, each facing the other, with approximately a thousand yards or more separating them. On both sides, the men were armed with swords and rifles, and spaced strategically among them was an occasional canon aimed pointedly at the opposition.

From where I sat, I could not see the soldiers' faces clearly, but I easily discerned from their body language that each awaited the call to advance with nervous anxiety. One particular young man, standing among the soldiers to my right, was examining the opposing army through an old-fashioned telescope. He appeared to be searching for something or some*one* in particular. After several moments, he lowered the lens and cast his eyes in my direction, seeming to search the hillside where I stood. His eyes fixed on something beyond me, and he bowed slightly as though addressing royalty. I turned my head, expecting to see what it was that had prompted this show of respect, but there was no one there. I cast my eyes back toward the row of aligned soldiers only to realize that his eyes were focused on *me*. He appeared to be waiting for me to give him a sign or a signal of some sort. Understanding dawned as I comprehended that *I* held the fate of all these soldiers within my power. One signal from me would launch both sides into a massive scene of bloodshed.

The setting was ominous. I didn't know what to do, and yet somehow I knew that to do nothing would yield a fate even worse than death. I sighed remorsefully, careful not to make any move that could be interpreted as a signal to advance. Immediately, I was aware that I held something in my left hand. I glanced down and noticed that the object was a golden scepter adorned with a stunning array of sapphires, emeralds, rubies, and diamonds arranged in a peculiar pattern. I held the scepter tightly and marveled that I had full use of my left hand—every muscle was strong and powerful—there was no sign of deformity.

Without thinking of the consequences, I stretched my hand out in front of me, holding the scepter horizontally so I could study its magnificence. As I did so, I caught another glimpse of the young soldier. He nodded in obeisance and turned to his fellow soldiers, giving them the command to advance. There was no way to take back the signal I had inadvertently given. Despairingly, I let go of the scepter and it fell to the ground.

"Beth." An out-of-place voice called my name from the distance.

"Beth." It called again, louder this time. My surroundings began to alter, and slowly the scene of advancing soldiers disappeared, replaced by the soft, rolling silhouette of the foothills.

"Beth!" This time I recognized Marci's voice. She stood next to me with a wide grin on her face.

"There's someone here who's very anxious to see you."

"Who?" I yawned as I attempted to stretch my legs.

"Hey, Bethy," a deep voice called from behind me. I recognized it instantly.

"Carl?" I gasped.

"Hello, cousin," he drawled in his most charming, gentleman-like manner.

"I can't believe you're here!"

I quickly tried to untangle myself from the blanket that now seemed to hold me hostage. As soon as I was free, Carl scooped me off the ground into an enormous bear hug. After a few moments he set me down and backed away, looking me over from head to toe.

"Ah, still the prettiest girl I ever laid eyes on!" he teased. "Dangerous brown eyes . . . lethal legs . . ."

"Sure, sure," I said, rolling my eyes and trying to look cool, but I could feel the blush rise in my cheeks. Carl noticed and chuckled.

"What the heck are you doing out here?" He eyed my chair, apparently humored by the idea that I was "sunbathing" while cocooned in a blanket. "California girls! Ya gotta love 'em!" He shook his head in mock reverence and winked at me. "By the way, when did you get so tall?" he grinned.

Without another word, he folded the chair, tossed my blanket over his shoulder, and started back to the house. "How 'bout some ice cream for the sun goddess, eh? Let's head to Jenkins Ice Cream Parlor."

The last time I had seen Carl was at his high school graduation four years earlier. I was fourteen and awkward—he was eighteen and gorgeous. Built like a professional athlete, Carl stood a towering six feet two; his coloring was the spitting image of his mother. He had her warm, golden blonde hair. It was thick and wavy when he wore it long, but even cut short I always felt an irresistible urge to run my fingers through it. He had the same bright hazel eyes as his father, but Carl's always sparkled with mischief. He used to tease me unmercifully whenever we came to visit, and he had a knack for practical jokes that got him into a lot of trouble.

At his graduation, Carl introduced me to a group of his friends and told them I had broken his heart when I up and left for California. I knew he was teasing, but I turned a deep shade of purple just the same, especially when he bent down and kissed my forehead. I didn't wash my forehead for weeks. The last I'd heard, he was "taking a break" from college so he could travel across Canada.

Carl and I spent the evening reminiscing over old times, times when my mom and I would visit during the summers while my father was away on assignment. He always seemed so much older than me back then, yet now that he was twenty-two the difference in our ages didn't seem so drastic. He was well aware of the fact that I'd had a huge crush on him when I was younger; he did his best to encourage that, and not very subtly I might add.

"Hmm," he mused as he finished his ice cream. "This is a sad night, indeed."

"Why?" I waited for his punch line; I never knew if he was serious or joking.

"Because you no longer look at me like I'm *the man*," he replied with feigned remorse. "I knew this day would come," he added, shaking his head, "but I didn't expect it to be so soon. So, give it up, who's the lucky guy?"

"What lucky guy? There's no guy," I insisted, but even as I uttered the words, I felt the color rise in my cheeks.

"You see? I'm right, aren't I?" Carl eyed me suspiciously but left it at that. "Well, whoever he is, he's a fortunate man in my book."

"No," I said, brushing off his comment. "It isn't like that." I couldn't help but think about the way Jonathan had watched Darla at the dance and how he'd readily admitted he thought she was pretty. "I'm not sure I'm his type," I sighed. "Not in that way."

Carl laughed. "You can't be serious."

"You wouldn't understand, Carl."

"Try me."

I shrugged my shoulder as I took the last bite of my ice cream. "There's this girl at school, she's like . . . perfect. I think she's more his type."

Carl waited, then shook his head and grinned. "You have no clue."

"No, really. She's amazing. She's—"

"Beth," Carl interrupted. "I know what you're going to say. This girl has the perfect smile, perfect hair, perfect shape. Right?" He raised one eyebrow and looked at me. "And let me guess, she's blonde too."

"Something like that," I grinned, suddenly embarrassed by how childish I sounded.

"I know the type. Trust me—they peak young. You, on the other hand," Carl placed his hand on my arm. "Your kind of beauty is far more . . ." he searched for the right word, "timeless."

I blushed again and realized that even now—after all this time—I still had a slight crush on my impetuous cousin. I couldn't help but laugh to myself.

"What?" Carl asked innocently.

"Nothing," I said, shaking my head.

He sat back in his chair and folded his arms across his chest. He watched me for several moments before he finally spoke again. "You know, I'm always intrigued by hot girls who don't know they're hot."

His comment caught me off guard. I looked away from him, flustered.

Carl gave me a teasing look of satisfaction. "Be right back," he smiled as he went to order some sodas. I watched him walk away, amazed by his flawless form and the way his biceps bulged beneath his T-shirt. I wondered what he did to stay in shape.

He returned with our drinks and handed me a straw. Then he sat down and scooted his chair next to me. He put his arm around my shoulders and squeezed me affectionately. "Now, tell me all about my new competition."

"Not a chance," I said, pushing against his side. It was like pushing against a brick wall. "Besides, that's enough about me. What about you? Last I heard you were wandering around Canada."

"Don't believe everything you hear. I've been doing a lot of things—traveling mostly."

His eyes shifted unnaturally as he got up and moved to the seat across from me. It was clear he wasn't going to be completely honest with me.

"I was wondering," he said, changing the subject, "have you heard anything from your father?"

"My dad? No. Why?"

"Just wondering," he replied, dismissing the question matter-of-factly at first, but then adding more earnestly. "You haven't heard *anything* from him?"

"No, there's no telling when he'll be able to contact me. Why do you ask?"

"No reason." He shook his head and changed directions. "You know, my dad is really happy you're here. He always wanted a daughter. In fact, I was relieved when you were born. I'm pretty sure he would have started dressing me in skirts and buying me dolls if it weren't for you." He winked at me and we both laughed. I was picturing Carl in a dress; the sight was hilariously disturbing.

"So, tell me," I leaned in and lowered my voice. "What do you think of Marci?"

Carl laughed. "She's interesting, isn't she?"

"She's nothing like I expected, I admit. I just can't get used to seeing your dad with someone. It's . . . weird."

"Yeah, I figured they would hit it off. That's why I introduced them. But I sure as heck didn't think they would run off and get married—"

"Where did you find her?" I interrupted.

Surprisingly, Carl blushed. I was pretty sure I'd never seen him do *that* before.

"She was my art teacher," he admitted.

"Your what?"

"You heard me," he joked.

"You took an art class?"

"Not just an art class, a sculpting class," he chuckled, pretending to be pleased with himself.

I looked at him skeptically; this had to be good. "Why would you do that?"

Carl shrugged. "A girl." He started to laugh. "And she wasn't even that cute."

I burst out laughing.

"You laugh, but hey, I got a B in the class." He pretended to be offended, but that just made me laugh even harder.

"Apparently, that's not all you got," I teased.

Carl raised his eyebrows.

"You got a new stepmom too."

Carl laughed and shot me a wicked grin. "Yeah, but you're the one who has to live with her."

When we left the ice cream parlor, Carl decided I needed a driving lesson. I informed him that I was a perfectly capable driver, but he insisted that until I'd driven a "real" car, my experience didn't count.

Carl still drove the car he'd rebuilt when he was in high school, an old 1974 Chevy Vega Wagon. He had tailored it specifically for drag racing.

"I installed a 327 Chevy V8 engine built to high performance," he said, "in place of the original engine."

I didn't know what any of that meant, but it was obviously something important among racers.

Carl had told me all about his car several years ago when he was still in high school. It had front wheel locking brakes that allowed him to spin the rear tires, getting them hot so they would grip the road better in a race. The car had special suspension specifically designed for race cars, and a modified transmission that could be shifted manually when he wanted.

Everyone in town was familiar with Carl's vehicle, particularly the local police.

We drove east along the main street of town until we reached an open patch of highway. Carl pulled the car over to the side of the road and got out. He walked around to the passenger side and opened the door, gesturing for me to scoot across to the driver's seat. I was about to get that driving lesson he had mentioned earlier—only this was a different type of driving than I was accustomed to. I adjusted the seat and looked over at Carl apprehensively.

"Are you sure about this?" I asked.

"Absolutely. Show me what you've got," he urged, shooting me a sly grin.

With that, I revved the engine. I had forgotten what he told me about the front lock brakes, and when I pressed on the accelerator, the back end lifted, allowing the back wheels to spin. I gasped in delight and Carl laughed.

"Let her rip!" he roared, and we were off.

The fine for drag racing in Wyoming is astonishingly steep. Luckily, there were no other vehicles involved in my little joy ride; so technically, the police officer couldn't write me up for racing. Instead, he cited me for "driving at a reckless speed." How much could the fine be for driving over a hundred miles an hour on the highway? I was sure it wouldn't be cheap. Secretly, I had to admit the exhilaration of driving that fast almost made it worth the cost—that is, until I discovered that Uncle Connor would have to accompany me to the courthouse when I paid my fine. I cringed at the thought. Carl tried to act remorseful, but I sensed a bit of pride in his voice when Uncle Connor confronted us about what we had done.

"*You* were driving?" Uncle Connor snarled at me incredulously.

"Yes," I bowed my head in shame. I glanced quickly at Carl who was fighting back a grin. I wanted to punch him in the stomach. Uncle Connor shook his head in disbelief.

"I don't know what to say. I thought you had more sense than that."

"I'm sorry, Uncle Connor. It was stupid," I admitted.

"Dad, this is totally my fault," Carl interrupted.

"Oh, I'm certain of that." Uncle Connor glowered at Carl, and then he turned his reproachful glare back at me, "I hope you know that the fine for this will be close to $300. Do you have that kind of money to throw away?" It was a rhetorical question.

I wondered how long Uncle Connor would continue his rebuke. Fortunately, his inexperience with raising girls paid off. He cut his reprimand short and sent me to my room to "think about" what I had done. He wanted to have a word with Carl, but I feared he wouldn't show as much restraint with Carl as he had with me. I shot Carl a sympathetic look which he returned with a look of smug confidence.

As I retreated to my bedroom, I could hear the volume of Uncle Connor's voice rise. The words "stupid," "idiotic," and "unbelievable," were shouted repeatedly over the next several minutes. Most of what Uncle Connor said was unintelligible, but it was clear he was raking Carl over the coals. When there was a pause in the conversation, I could hear the low rumblings of Carl's replies. His tone never sounded defensive; in fact, I wasn't certain, but he almost sounded amused.

Later, as I lay in bed mulling over the day's events, I couldn't help but chuckle. Carl was a troublemaker, no doubt, but he was charming and fun and I knew Uncle Connor would not be able to stay mad at him for long. I recalled the exhilarating feeling of driving Carl's car, speeding down the open highway, and I had to admit I liked it. In spite of Uncle Connor's obvious disappointment in me, that night I went to sleep with a smile on my face.

On Monday I turned nineteen. I was nineteen in body only; my brain was still missing a year. Except for a pineapple upside-down cake (compliments of Marci) and a trip to Pete's Steakhouse, my birthday went virtually unnoticed. My grandmother in San Diego sent me a card with a hundred-dollar bill inside, Marci and Uncle Connor bought me a new cell phone with all the bells and whistles on it, and Carl gave me an IOU with the promise of something very special forthcoming. There was nothing from my dad.

The piano music I heard coming from the practice rooms on

Tuesday afternoon was far too labored and forced to be Jonathan's. Curious, I peeked through the door to see who was playing. A young boy with sandy blonde hair, maybe a sophomore, sat stiffly at the piano. He was struggling through the scales of Schubert's Impromptu No. 2 in E-flat major. I recalled the year I'd learned the piece and laughed silently to myself. My instructor at the time, Professor Stydle, nearly threw my piano book across the room after his repeated attempts to correct my technique had failed. He was very German, and very strict, but he played the piano like a god. I felt a slight stab of pity for the young boy who was fighting a similar battle with the piece now, and wondered what Mr. Stydle would say if he were here. The thought made me cringe.

I waited patiently for him to finish the song, making a mental note of each mistake. In spite of his rude style, his attempt at the piece pleased me. Schubert was not an easy composer to master. The young boy was obviously unhappy with his performance because he slammed the book shut and huffed loudly. I couldn't help but laugh. He turned around quickly, startled by my undetected presence.

"I'm sorry," I smiled. "Don't be too hard on yourself—that actually wasn't half bad."

"Sure," he snorted. "It's the half that *was* bad that ticks me off. No matter how hard I try, it's always the same!"

"Ever think maybe you're trying *too* hard?" I suggested.

He shrugged and then sighed forcefully. "I dunno. It doesn't matter anyway. I'm no good at this kind of music."

"I disagree. You just need to relax a little; you're too focused on your technique."

"But the impromptus are all about technique," he argued.

"On the surface, maybe." I watched as his expression grew more perplexed. I glanced down at my hand for a brief second and then set my bag on the floor. "Mind if I show you something?"

"Go ahead," he shrugged, and started to get up.

"No, don't get up, just slide over. You play the left hand." I motioned for him to get ready and began the descending scale of the opening measures. He struggled to keep up for the first two lines, but eventually found the right groove. I stopped after the first page.

"Wow! You're really good!" His eyes lit with fire.

"Now, try it again. And this time, I want you to watch your right hand, not the music."

"I *have* to read the music," he insisted.

I shook my head. "No you don't. Your fingers already know what notes to hit. Watch your hand, and keep your forearm parallel to the floor—no vertical movement."

"Huh? How am I supposed to do that with scales?"

"The same way I just did—trust me."

"Okay, I'll try." He sounded skeptical.

"Don't think about the music; focus on keeping your arm parallel."

For the next several minutes he played the opening lines repeatedly. I held my arm cross-wise, slightly above his, to help him break his up and down habit. After several attempts, his fingers glided smoothly across the keys and his eyes sparkled with elation.

"That's amazing! You were right!" His gleeful satisfaction sparked an unfamiliar emotion in me.

"You've got it . . . now just keep practicing. You'll have the entire song nailed in no time."

"Hey, you're pretty cool. What's your name?"

I chuckled. "Beth. What's yours?"

"Justin." He glanced down at my hand and stared at my bent fingers. "What happened to your hand?"

"Car accident." Did I really think he wouldn't notice?

"Wow, that totally sucks." His response was refreshingly innocent.

"Well, Justin, hang in there. Okay?" I slid off the seat and turned to leave. To my surprise, Jonathan was standing in the doorway.

"Oh! Hey!" I reached down to grab my bag, but Jonathan got there first. He handed me my bag without saying anything. I didn't recognize the expression on his face.

"Thank you," I smiled. He stood aside so I could pass through the door. He didn't speak until we were several steps down the hall.

"That was pretty cool, what you did in there."

I raised one shoulder and shook my head. "How long were you standing there?"

"Long enough to watch you transform him from frustrated to confident."

I started to step into Jonathan's usual practice room, but he put his hand on my shoulder and stopped me. "Can we take a walk?" he asked.

"Sure." This was unusual. "Where do you want to go?"

"Nowhere in particular." He smiled an uncharacteristically forced smile. "Let's just walk."

As we entered the parking lot, Jonathan grabbed my bag and tossed it into the back seat of his car, leaving no question that he would drive me home later. This simple gesture pleased me more than I expected.

We walked down the street toward a park that was located behind the library. The water in a quaint duck pond lapped gently against its narrow shoreline and reflected the blue sky overhead. A meandering nature path wound through the park and around the pond. At one point we had to cross over a small stream and Jonathan took my hand to help me. Once across, he didn't let go. His hand was pleasantly warm.

We strolled silently hand-in-hand around the pond watching the ducks play in the rippling water until Jonathan motioned toward one of the park benches nestled cozily off the main path. He was quieter today than usual. As we sat down, he held my hand in his lap, interlocking our fingers and cupping his free hand around the back of mine. I noted the significant difference between his hands and Eric's. He traced the outline of my fingers with his, examining each of my fingers carefully.

"Is something wrong, Jonathan?"

He continued to stare at my hand. He was smiling, but this smile was different, almost guilty. He pressed his lips together and grinned.

"What?" I pleaded. The suspense was killing me, but it only made his smile widen. When he turned to look at me, he cocked his head to the side and sighed heavily.

"The dance Saturday," he began. I felt an unwelcome surge of panic form in my stomach. He wanted to take back what he'd said about us hanging out sometime. That would explain why he seemed uncomfortable.

"What about it?" I asked reluctantly.

His eyes bored into mine, eyebrows pulled together in a tight line. "When I saw you dancing with that guy. . . ." He spoke as though there was a bad taste in his mouth.

"Eric?"

"Yeah, him." He made a gesture with his head, as if to dismiss the mention of Eric's name, then he looked away.

"What about him?" My stomach twisted into a knot.

"I didn't like it," he finally said. He glanced over his shoulder at me, then shrugged and tossed a small rock into the pond.

"Oh," I said, confused. "He's just a friend. . . ."

His eyes seemed troubled. "I didn't like the way he looked at you."

"That's just Eric," I explained, trying to sound casual. "He looks at all the girls that way." I'm not sure why I added that last part, but Jonathan responded with a quick look of disapproval that would have put my mother, the queen of disapproving looks, to shame.

"That's not all." He cleared his throat. "I didn't like seeing his hands on you either." His sapphire eyes studied mine and I felt an anxious fluttering in my stomach.

"Yeah, Eric was—"

"It wouldn't matter who it was." Jonathan interrupted. His hand squeezed mine gently.

"Oh," I whispered.

I wasn't sure how to respond. This was new. I wanted to say something, do something, but what? The only thing I could think of was to rest my head against his shoulder. He sighed, and continued to caress the top of my hand with his thumb.

We sat in serene silence for what seemed like an hour while the surrounding trees transformed from their normal bright hues of green to a dull black green as the sun began to set behind the foothills. A crisp breeze ushered in the first signs of dusk. The brisk air blew gently against my face, sending a warning signal that it was time to go. I didn't want the day to end, but the last thing I needed was to have Uncle Connor upset with me—again.

We walked back to Jonathan's car; but before he opened the door for me, he pulled me close to him, wrapping his arms tightly around my shoulders. I leaned into his embrace and rested my head against his chest. I could hear his heart thud powerfully. The smell of his cotton shirt reminded me of freshly washed linens, and I closed my eyes to drink in the pleasant scent. After a moment he pulled away, opened the car door, and helped me inside.

When we arrived at Uncle Connor's I started to climb out of the car, but Jonathan stopped me, grabbing my arm before I could move.

"What are you doing on Saturday?" he asked.

"Nothing. Why?" I replied.

"Do you like horses?"

"Sure."

"You said you were interested in the vortex theories, right?"

I nodded expectantly.

"How would you like to see one of the most amazing sights in all of Wyoming?" His eyes reflected a youthful eagerness that I found irresistible. I raised both eyebrows in response.

"I want to take you to one of my favorite places, and it's right in the thick of Wyoming's vortex."

Palisades

CHAPTER 4

I was surprised when I received a note from Mr. Laden during my third period class on Thursday asking me to come to his office after school. Many thoughts passed through my mind, none of them very reasonable. I wondered in the back of my mind if he disapproved of Jonathan spending time with me.

"Mr. Laden?" I knocked on the side of his open door, and waited for him to invite me in.

"Miss Arrington, please . . . sit down." He gestured to the seat across from his desk. "Thank you for coming."

I sat down facing Mr. Laden with sudden apprehension. I waited for him to continue.

"Do you know why I called you in here?" he asked, raising his eyebrows.

My chest tightened. "No, not really." I shook my head slowly. "Does it have anything to do with Jonathan?"

"I suppose you could say that." He smiled a relaxed smile that looked like it was meant to put me at ease, but it didn't work. I stared stiffly at him. "Jonathan told me what you did with Justin the other day."

"I didn't do anything. I just helped him a little. . . ."

Mr. Laden shook his head. "That's not what I heard. Jonathan is not one who impresses easily. He said what you did was almost magical."

I sat back in my chair, confused. "I barely did anything—Jonathan must have—"

"It doesn't matter," he cut me off. "You know, we don't breed many classical pianists here; most of our students' interests lie in modern works, or creating their own compositions. The more serious students study privately. It's rare that we have a student who is classically trained, like Justin."

"He's rough," I noted, smiling, "but he's determined. He has potential."

"Which brings me to why I asked you to come. How would you like to work with Justin on a regular basis? We normally don't offer paid positions to students, but with your background, we'd be foolish not to make an exception."

"You want me to teach him?" I asked incredulously. I shook my head quickly. "Oh, no. No, I'm not a teacher."

"Just think about it," Mr. Laden requested. "You'd be doing Justin a huge favor."

"Mr. Laden . . ." I took a deep breath and sighed. "I'm sorry. I can't help you."

Mr. Laden let my resolve register for several seconds before responding. "Well," he forced a slight smile, "the offer is there if you change your mind."

"Thank you, but I won't."

I left Mr. Laden's office hurriedly. A familiar weight launched itself in my stomach as I cursed my injury repeatedly in my mind. I didn't want to help others play the classics; I wanted to play them myself. That had been my dream for as long as I could remember. I entered the practice room on the opposite side of the hallway and marched angrily to the upright piano. I pulled against my bent fingers, prying them straight and forcing them onto the keyboard. I used my right hand to press down on them, ordering them to play. I picked up my wrist and hammered my limp fingers against the keys—once, twice, three times.

"Play!" I sputtered the words. "Useless! Useless!" I used as much force as possible to slam my hand into the keys. My fingers crumbled lifelessly against the keys and folded. The movement shot an excruciating series of painful jabs through my palm and wrist and along my forearm. I grabbed my hand and pulled it firmly against my chest, then doubled over while I waited for the pain to subside. Tears streaked my cheeks; I breathed deeply, fighting the urge to give in to my emotions with each staggered breath. It took several minutes, but I finally managed to collect myself. Brushing the moisture from my face, I stood erect and headed out the door. Through the corner of my eye I spied Mr. Laden standing in the hallway just outside his office. I knew he was watching me; I'd probably shocked him with my little tantrum, but I didn't care.

I didn't go to the practice rooms on Friday. Instead, I took Eric up on his offer to go see a movie—without anyone else tagging along. I wanted nothing to do with Jonathan and his perfect hands, or Justin or pianos or duets or Mr. Laden or anything that might remind me of my broken dream.

It never occurred to me that by agreeing to go with Eric, I was sending him a mixed message. That fact became notably clear as the evening progressed. I held Eric's iron hand during the movie and I didn't protest when he put his arm around my shoulders and pulled me close to him; nor did I stop him when he played with my hair. But on the inside, I was cold as ice. I didn't care about anything or anyone.

When we arrived at the house after the movie, Uncle Connor and Marci were engrossed in a heated conversation in the living room. From what I could discern, they were arguing about the attacks on the girls in Jackson. There were no new leads, no new evidence, and no suspects. Uncle Connor was convinced it was the work of a serial rapist, an out-of-towner. He used the word "intruder." Neither Marci nor Uncle Connor acknowledged us when we arrived, so we left them to their debate and headed downstairs to the basement.

Normally, I'm afraid of basements. I don't like anything that puts me underground. There's no logical explanation for my phobia, I've just been that way since I was a small child. But Uncle Connor's basement isn't too bad. His house sits on an uneven lot that slopes downward behind the house, so he has a walkout basement that is light and airy.

The bottom of the staircase opens to a large, spacious room. Along the opposite wall, an oversized, sliding glass door opens to the back-yard, so it doesn't feel like you're underground. I recalled being sent to the basement to play when I was a child, and how thankful I was that at least part of the room was open to the outdoors.

With Carl and his big brother Nick both gone, the basement wasn't used much. A pool table sat to one side near a small couch and three over-sized barstools. When Carl was in high school, he and his friends hung out there often. When my mom and I visited, I used to sit on the floor and watch them, listening intently to their conversations like an annoying younger sibling. Behind the pool table there was a U-shaped mini kitchen with a double sink, refrigerator, built-in microwave oven, and a small stove top. Best I could tell, the kitchen and pool table area were directly beneath the garage and kitchen.

The area of the basement closest to the large, sliding glass door was completely open, void of any furnishing other than the plush carpet that set it apart from the rest of the room. To the far left, underneath the hallway and my bedroom, was an open playroom set up for the grandchildren. This was the side of the basement with no windows, so the area seemed particularly cold and dark. It was ghostly still without the noise of children's shrill voices, but it instantly came to life when Nick and his family visited.

"Cool," Eric nodded approvingly. "You got anything in that fridge?"

I reached in and grabbed two sodas, handed one to Eric, and

then motioned for him to sit down on one of the black, wooden barstools. But he was preoccupied with the pool table.

"Wanna play?" he asked, gathering the line of colored pool balls into the triangular rack.

"Sure," I shrugged. I stepped around the table and tossed Eric a cue stick, then popped open my soda and waited for him to break. He slid his stick smoothly against the white cue ball and blasted the neatly set balls into a flurry of directions. Surprisingly, none of the balls made it into a pocket. My turn.

I circled the table, using my cue stick as a crutch, and then decided on the best shot. I bent over the table and steadied the stick against my left hand when it suddenly occurred to me that I wouldn't be able to guide the stick without the use of my fingers. I growled in frustration as the cue stick flopped from side to side. Eric took quick advantage of the situation and offered to help—Eric style.

"Here," he said, moving around to where I lay bent across the table. In an instant he was hovering over me from behind, his breath hot against my cheek. He wrapped his ginormous hands around each of mine and helped me guide the cue stick to a solid strike. I started to straighten, but Eric didn't move.

"Okay, Eric," I said, feigning annoyance, "let me up."

In one smooth movement, he wrapped his arm around my waist and spun me around, pulling me up so we stood face to face, our bodies pressed together. By the smug grin on his face, I could tell he was very proud of himself. He used his free hand to brush the side of my face. I knew what he wanted. I watched his lips nervously, taking notice of their flawless shape. A mental image of Jonathan's mouth flashed through my mind, his uneven lips that turned up on one side more than the other. I tried to force the image from my mind, but all I could see was Jonathan's face.

"C'mon, Beth," he said huskily, "kiss me. It's obvious you want to." He shot me a victory wink that snapped me back to my senses.

"All right, that's enough, Eric. Game's over." I tried to wiggle free, but Eric laughed and pulled me closer. His face was mere inches from mine, and though I tried to lean away from him, his hold was iron strong. His eyes danced with eagerness as he examined the conflict in my face and anticipated my next move. He was a pro.

I was shocked by how readily my body was willing to betray my heart. I had no interest in a romantic relationship with Eric, no feelings beyond friendship; but a part of me was curious. We were alone. No one would ever have to know if we kissed. I even rationalized that it would be the best thing—because Eric would finally get what he wanted and lose interest in pursuing me. It all made logical sense, right?

But there was one very big problem.

Eric's hand cupped my cheek and nudged my mouth back to his. His hand was rough against my skin. I thought about how awkward it felt whenever he held my hand and twisted his monster fingers around mine. In an instant, another image flashed in my mind—the image of Jonathan's hands and the way I felt when he laced his fingers through mine and caressed the top of my hand.

Eric brushed his lips lightly against my chin, but before he could press his mouth to mine, I turned away. It took every bit of strength I had to convince him to release me.

"What is your problem?" Eric's patience had reached its limit.

"I'm sorry Eric. We can't do this . . . *I* can't do this."

"Do what, for Pete's sake? It's just a kiss!" he growled in frustration. "You make me crazy sometimes."

"You should probably leave," I said, half out of breath.

"This is about Darla and her damn 'code' isn't it?"

I chuckled loudly. For once, this was *not* about Darla—or the "code."

"No, actually," I said, shaking my head.

"Then what?" He paused for a moment, and then his eyes suddenly burned with understanding. "This is about that piano wuss, isn't it?"

My eyes filled with regret; I couldn't bring myself to answer him.

"Well? Isn't it?" he demanded.

I closed my eyes and sighed loudly. "Yes, I guess it is." I was admitting it as much to myself as I was to Eric. The realization made me suddenly nervous.

"Are you nuts? What is he to you anyway?" The thick blue vein in Eric's neck bulged.

"I don't know . . ." I looked down at my feet and shrugged, "but I need to find out."

"Beth, there's chemistry between us, I know you feel it."

I shook my head. Eric's definition of chemistry was a lot different from mine. "Admit it Eric, you're just looking for another score."

"Is that what you think?" He spoke with anger, but there was pain behind his eyes.

"It doesn't matter," I sighed. "This thing with Jonathan, it's—"

"Ah, bull!" Eric scoffed. "You wouldn't even notice him if he didn't play the piano." Eric's eyes were on fire; I'd never seen him like this.

I stared at Eric for a moment. "You better go," I said icily.

He stepped forward and grabbed my arm, "Beth, you haven't given *us* a chance," he pleaded.

"Eric, stop!" I yanked my arm away from him. "There *is* no us!"

"Whatever! I'm outta here." He turned to leave and started up the stairway, but he stopped halfway and glared back at me. "Don't bother coming to the barbecue they're planning after the game to-morrow night," he said bitterly.

I sighed. "Eric—"

"Believe me, Beth, there are plenty of willing women out there."

With that, he raced up the stairs and was gone. I felt the walls vibrate when he slammed the front door.

I awoke the next morning to several beams of sunlight streaming sideways across my bedroom. I watched as dust particles wandered weightlessly along drunken paths. I had apparently forgotten to close the shutters when I went to bed.

I stood and stretched, yawning noisily as I made my way to the bright window. I watched in wonderment as large, puffy white clouds rolled across the sky, casting dark shadows on the purple foothills in the distance. Everyone commented on the unusually warm weather we had been having; Andersen normally saw its first snowfall by mid-October. I was glad that winter was taking its time to arrive;

fall was my favorite time of year. I loved the vast array of colors that dotted the surrounding landscape, the sound of dead leaves crackling beneath my shoes, and the smell of heavy moisture in the air.

Two chimes let me know that I had a new text message.

I'll be there by nine. J.

I looked at the clock. Eight fifteen. I would need to hurry if I wanted to be ready on time.

I had heard Carl talk about the Upper Palisades Lakes, but I'd never seen them before. According to Carl's stories, the lakes were "magical," and the surrounding scenery would take my breath away. But nothing could prepare me for the real thing.

Jonathan arrived wearing a long-sleeved white T-shirt with the sleeves pushed up to his elbows and a baseball cap that somehow made him look very young. We chatted about school and music as we drove his horses to the trailhead, but he was content to enjoy the trail ride itself in silence so I could experience the full impact of the surrounding landscape without distraction. It was like something I had only seen in movies or picture books.

The trail meandered through a canopy of Douglas firs and other pine trees, then zigzagged in patterns across a gently flowing stream as the horses climbed. I occasionally caught a glimpse of the azure sky through the evergreen branches towering above me. It was laced with feathery white clouds that resembled oversized puffs of cotton. The rich brown tones of the soil complemented the bright greens of the low-growing shrubs and fused harmoniously with the dark hues of the majestic pine trees. An occasional deciduous tree brightened the landscape with splashes of gold, orange, and crimson, adding variety to the already picturesque scene. The stark contrast between earth and sky caused me to marvel. It was all too vivid to seem real.

The horses seemed unaware of the impressive beauty that surrounded them as they plodded their way along the familiar trail. I was surprisingly at ease on my horse; I couldn't resist the instinct to bend down and pat the side of his head, enjoying the feel of the soft hair which shimmered in the sun's rays.

As we reached the first clearing, I spied the first of two small lakes connected by a moving stream. The crystal water glowed fluorescent shades of turquoise each time the sun's rays peeked through the clouds, creating the illusion of a light source shining upwards from the bottom of the lake. The iridescent illumination of the water caused me to gape in awe. Jonathan watched me and smiled with satisfaction.

"It's pretty, isn't it?"

"I've never seen anything like this before!" My eyes were wide with excitement.

"It's a little different than the lakes you're used to."

"The only lakes I've ever seen are gray or green, and they usually stink. How can there be water like this?" I sounded like a child intrigued by a magic trick, dancing up and down to know the magician's secret.

"It's Wyoming water," he chuckled as if that should have been obvious. I wrinkled my nose at him and he broke into a hearty laugh.

"This is the most beautiful lake I've ever seen! And look, you can see so far down!" I glanced at Jonathan briefly, my face frozen with amazement, and he flashed me a gratified grin.

"Come on, there's more."

More than this? My eyes never left the water as we continued along the trail that curved around the lake. Sunlight danced along the top of the glistening water like diamonds shimmering in the sun, casting rainbows of color in all directions. I couldn't help but compare the sparkling water to Jonathan's eyes; both were the same deep shade of blue, and both were equally stunning.

My jaw dropped when we arrived at the second clearing; the view rendered me speechless. We had entered a heavenly garden surrounded by multiple hues of green, gold, orange, red, and brown; a rich palette including every color Mother Nature could create.

"I had no idea places this beautiful really existed," I muttered incredulously.

Jonathan beamed triumphantly, obviously pleased with my

reaction. I watched the water gently slap the shore as fish of various sizes and colors swam peacefully through the translucent pool, utterly unaware of their captive audience.

"Wow!" I managed to whisper.

Jonathan chuckled. "Impressed?"

"I'm more than impressed!" I replied, "I'm . . . I'm wow'd! I've never seen anything this beautiful. Have you?" I turned back to him and noticed that he wasn't watching the water; he was watching me.

"Yes, I have," he said softly.

"I—"

"Shhh." He put his finger to his lips and walked closer to me. He brushed the hair away from my face and slowly bent down and kissed my cheek. I took a short breath, closing my eyes—half in surprise, half expecting something more—until I felt him pull away. He smiled and then ran his finger softly over my cheek where he'd just kissed me.

"I'm glad you like it."

I wasn't sure if he meant the lake or the kiss.

He tied the horses to the branch of a nearby tree and took two brown sacks from his saddle pack.

"Lunch," he announced as he handed me one of the sacks.

We walked along the graveled edge of the lake toward the mouth of the stream and then veered off toward two large boulders nestled in the shade of the nearby trees. I watched as a bird hopped anxiously between two branches and wondered what business could be keeping it from heading south in time for winter.

Jonathan and I sat in silence for several minutes before breaking open our lunch sacks. I watched with fascination as he slowly surveyed our surroundings, arms folded with his elbows propped against his knees. In front of us was the glistening lake, the feathered horizon of the towering pines, and the blue canopy of the sky. He turned his face toward the sun, closed his eyes, and took a long, deep breath. I relaxed against the warm granite boulder and studied every subtle change in his expression, the peaceful pattern of his breathing, and the way his hair formed short twists that flipped away from his neck—a gentle rebellion against his baseball cap. After several minutes, he opened his eyes.

"Don't you love that sound?" He was still looking at the sky.

"What sound?" I turned my head to the side and listened intently.

"The sound of air moving through the trees. It's just like the sound the stream makes."

"How do you know which one you're hearing? They both sound the same to me."

Jonathan turned his head and grinned at me from beneath his cap. "How do you tell the difference between pianos?" He waited, letting me think about that. "It's the same concept, just different instruments."

"I never thought of it that way. I guess you're right."

Jonathan eyed me for several moments before chuckling.

"What?" I asked, suddenly suspicious.

He shook his head. He was obviously not going to tell me. "Let's eat," he said, changing the subject.

Our lunch consisted of peanut butter and jelly sandwiches, granola bars, trail mix, and apples. Jonathan called it "energy" food. He retrieved two cans of cola from his pack, drained the melted ice from a small thermos, and poured the contents of the first can inside. He crossed the river on some flat stones and wedged the second can between two large rocks that were conveniently submerged there in the icy, running water. He was very much at home in this setting.

Jonathan was unlike any guy I'd ever met. Eric and his friends were constantly pre-occupied with sports: who held what record, who was likely to make it to the playoffs, who might be drafted into the pros next year. When they weren't talking about sports they were playing them, or planning the next big sporting event. Jonathan was different. He was focused and serious, and at the same time confident and relaxed, but in a quiet way. He seemed to draw his strength from within, not from sports or weight lifting like Eric. Though Jonathan's strength was far less obvious, it was just as impressive.

I was lost in my thoughts when Jonathan broke the silence.

"Beth, will you tell me about your accident?"

He reached for my left hand as he asked. Instinctively, I pulled it away. He had seen my disfigured hand up close several times but for some reason, here in the open I felt self-conscious. I was keenly aware that my fingers were no longer graceful and elegant as they had once been. The sight of them, bent and useless, aroused the all too familiar stabbing ache in the pit of my stomach. Jonathan looked gently into my eyes as he reached across and cupped my hand in his.

"Tell me about the accident, Beth." He sensed my resistance. "Please," he whispered.

I pulled my hand away from him again and began instinctively rubbing my scar. Perhaps it was wishful thinking that if I rubbed my hand hard enough, it would come back to life. I felt Jonathan's fingertip on my chin as he nudged my face back toward his.

I hadn't talked about the accident since I'd been released from my fruitless stay at the trauma center. Perhaps that was why I relived it in my dreams so often. The truth was, I wanted to talk about it. My father preferred to pretend it had never happened, Uncle Connor usually found a way to avoid the topic, and even Carl refused to bring it up. Perhaps they feared it would be too painful for me, or maybe it was their own pain they wanted to avoid.

"Please tell me," Jonathan said more earnestly. There was an unusual plea in his voice that made me feel that knowing what happened that night was somehow important to him.

"Okay," I agreed, "but—"

"No," he interrupted, "no 'buts.' Tell me everything."

And I wanted to. I wanted him to hear the whole story; not just how my hand got hurt, but everything else. Then, if he thought I was nuts, he could go on his way and whatever was developing between us could end before either of us was in too deep. I sighed audibly and stood. It would be easier if I didn't have to look at him.

"It happened a year and a half ago . . . the night of my junior prom," I began. "I was a junior class officer, and it was the tradition at our school for the junior class officers to plan the prom as a sort of parting gift for the out-going seniors. I'd been seeing this guy named Adam off and on since the tenth grade, and during the year we'd put all our extra money into a piggy bank to save up for the prom. He was graduating, and he wanted it to be a night to remember."

I wasn't certain, but I thought I heard Jonathan sneer.

"We broke up three weeks before the prom," I continued.

"He broke up with you?"

"Technically no, but sort of."

"I don't understand." Jonathan sounded confused.

"He wanted something I wasn't ready to give," I explained, turning to face him.

"I see."

I couldn't read his expression. "Actually, we'd broken up twice before for the same reason, but he always came back after a few weeks and would convince me to give him another chance."

Jonathan pressed his lips together as if he was annoyed.

"I know. It sounds stupid to me too. But at the time . . ." I hesitated realizing how foolish I sounded.

"So what happened?" Jonathan asked.

"A few weeks before the prom, he began pressuring me again . . . for more. He insisted that if I truly cared about him, I would understand how strong his needs were. I was torn between doing what was right and not wanting to go through the pain of another breakup."

I watched the expression on Jonathan's face shift from troubled to something stronger. Anger perhaps?

"What did you decide?" He pulled his eyebrows into a tight line.

"I told him the same thing I always told him. No!"

"And then he broke up with you?"

"No. He brooded over it for awhile, and then he became bitter and cold. The friendship between us was rapidly deteriorating, so I convinced him it would be better if we took a break from each other. I didn't need to twist his arm."

"So how does this fit in with your accident?"

"I'm getting there. Since I no longer had a date for the prom, I volunteered to help serve refreshments during the dance and take care of the band if they needed anything. It never dawned on me that Adam would show up." I stopped and watched Jonathan's face carefully. His jaw tightened slightly.

"He brought a date!"

It was probably supposed to be a question, but it was clearly an insolent accusation. I nodded slowly. "Not just a date. He brought my best friend."

"What?" Jonathan snapped, and it made me jump. "Are you serious? They were . . . together?" He tapped his two index fingers together for emphasis.

"In every sense of the word—at least to the degree that's legal in public. I watched them grope each other all over the dance floor."

"And she was your friend?"

"Yes."

"What did you do?"

"I did what I could to save face. I stayed long enough to convince my friends that everything was fine, and then I quietly slipped out. I called my mom and she came to get me. I'd held it together as long as I could, and I started crying the minute I climbed into my mom's car. Nothing she said could console me. I was sobbing. I was bitter. I was fuming. And I blamed myself." I cut my eyes up at Jonathan.

"What do you mean, you blamed yourself?"

"If I was more like other girls—if I could have given him what he wanted—then I would have been the one dressed in the pretty dress and dancing at the prom."

I had to look down because I felt the flame of stupidity rise to the top of my cheeks. I shrugged to mask my embarrassment.

Jonathan made a low grumbling sound. "Do you really believe that?"

"I did that night," I answered honestly.

"My mom did everything in her power to try and convince me that I'd made the right choice. She begged me to promise her that I would never think less of myself for doing the 'right' thing. I figured she was just overreacting, like a typical mom. While she was lecturing me, I reached down to unbuckle my shoes. But the seat belt restrained me, so I unhooked it. My mom snapped at me, and that was it. That was the straw that broke the camel's back. I was furious. I ordered her to get off my case and leave me the hell alone." I glanced remorsefully at my feet. "Those were the last words I said to her."

Jonathan sat motionless. "Then what happened?"

"I never saw what actually happened. While I was rubbing my throbbing toes, my mom let out a horrible scream and slammed on the brakes. All I really remember is the sound of the screeching brakes and the feeling of pressure—as if I were being grabbed and thrown around by some violent force. I heard the screech of twisting metal and the brittle pop of cracking glass, and then I felt a sudden blow to my head. My mom was still screaming, and—"

I broke off and looked at Jonathan.

"And?" he urged.

"Well, this is the part that landed me in a psychiatric center." I studied his face carefully before I continued. "It was dark and I was hurt. I was pinned under something and I could feel my hand burning like it was on fire, but I was powerless to move. When I looked up at my mom, she had a horrified look on her face and she was reaching for me. I tried to respond to her, but I couldn't move. Then, just like that," I snapped my fingers and Jonathan flinched, "she was gone."

"Gone? You mean she died?"

"No. I mean she was gone," I said flatly. "She was snatched away before my eyes. From my angle, it looked like she was taken *up*."

Jonathan stared intently at me; there was no disbelief in his expression. "Do you remember anything else?"

"Not really," I lied.

"Beth?" he pressed.

I shrugged.

"Tell me *everything*."

"There's just, well . . ." I hesitated.

"Yes?"

"I swear there was someone else there."

"Like who, the paramedics?"

"No, before that." I said. "Somebody pulled me away from the burning car, and I heard voices. The one who grabbed me kept telling me to hold on. The other one was looking for something—or someone."

"Then what?"

"Then . . . nothing. Everything went black. The next conscious memory I have is when I woke up in the hospital seven months later. They told me my mom burned to death when the car's engine caught fire. They had already held a memorial service for her, and what was left of her remains had been cremated."

"I'm so sorry," Jonathan whispered regretfully.

"I tried to convince my father that there were other people involved, but when the police investigated the scene, they found no sign of any physical evidence to suggest another car was involved or that someone else was present. The authorities and the doctors determined that my brain had mixed up other memories as a defense to help me cope with the trauma of seeing my mother die."

Jonathan stood and stepped toward me. He took my shoulders firmly in his hands and looked me squarely in the eyes.

"Is that what *you* think?"

I paused. I could say yes, and he would think I was normal. Instead, I answered honestly.

"No. I remember everything clearly. There's no cloud, no fog, and no made up memory. I know what I saw, and I know what I heard."

I held Jonathan's intense gaze with confidence. After a moment, he nodded.

"Okay," he said, and he let go of my arms.

"Okay?" I asked. *Okay what? Okay I'm crazy? Okay you believe me?* I waited for him to say more; it upset me that he let it go at that.

"Please tell me what you're thinking," I asked quietly.

"I'm thinking you had one hell of an experience!"

"That's not what I meant," I murmured. He stepped closer and gently wrapped his arms around me.

"You mean do I believe you?" he asked.

"Yes."

"Does it matter?"

As he searched my eyes, I realized that it *did* matter. I desperately wanted him to believe all of it. I needed him to. I nodded once.

He pulled me closer and tucked my head under his chin. "Yes," he said quietly, "I believe you." He held me like that for a moment, stroking my hair. Then he slowly backed away.

"Let's walk," he said, taking my hand in his.

After a silent stroll along the stream that connected the two lakes, Jonathan gathered up the remains of our lunch and placed them in his pack. He tied the pouch and pulled the strap tight, then casually stroked his horse's neck.

"So, whatever happened with your best friend and that guy?"

"Adam," I clarified.

"Whatever." He dismissed the name with a brief wave of his hand. "Are they still together?"

"No. They broke up before he graduated."

"Interesting." He continued stroking the side of his horse.

"Why is that interesting?"

"I don't know," he shrugged. Then, as an afterthought, "Did you ever confront your friend?"

"Sort of. She tried to apologize, insisting that nothing had happened between her and Adam. But by that time, I no longer cared."

"I imagine not," Jonathan nodded.

"Because of the coma and the time I spent in the trauma center, I missed my entire senior year, so I lost touch with my friends."

Jonathan cocked his head to one side. "What about Adam? Didn't he come to see you?"

"No."

"Coward," Jonathan smirked.

"Well, actually, I think he came to the hospital once while I was in the coma, but I don't count that. We haven't spoken since before the accident."

Jonathan shook his head and released a humorless chuckle.

"What about you?" I asked.

"What about me?"

"Was there ever anyone for you?" I asked, and then flinched. Of course there were girls. Then an uncomfortable thought occurred to me. *"Is there someone?"*

He saw the path my mind was traveling and chuckled, but his eyes were tender.

"To answer your first question, yes. Once."

"What happened?"

He chewed on his bottom lip for a moment and stared at the distant horizon. I regretted asking, but I couldn't take it back. So I waited.

"She left," he replied after a long pause.

"Oh. I'm sorry," I said. But he shrugged it off.

"It's in the past. I'm good now." He threw me a sideways grin and his eyes lit up.

He offered me his arm and helped me mount my horse.

"Did you love her?"

He stopped and considered thoughtfully for a moment. He rubbed the bottom of his chin with his thumb and forefinger and then looked up at me.

"Did you love Adam?" It was a fair question, but it made me uncomfortable.

"Well . . ." I stalled. *I asked you first.* He was waiting for my answer.

"I thought I did at the time, but I would have to say no." The revelation came as a surprise to me.

Jonathan raised his eyebrows and nodded.

"Yeah, I know what you mean." He patted my horse's head and then flashed me a very boyish grin. "And to answer your second question, I'm working on that."

I was still trying to process that last part when he suddenly remembered something.

"I'll be right back," he announced hastily.

He darted back toward the boulders where we had eaten our lunch. He again crossed the river to the other side, trotting confidently across the large stones that provided a convenient path through the water. I took advantage of the opportunity to appreciate what I had refused to allow myself to scrutinize earlier—his muscular physique. I was lost in thought when I realized he'd turned around and caught me staring at him. His grin widened playfully as he reached into the water to retrieve a shiny, red object. It was the other can of cola left over from our lunch.

I don't know exactly what happened next—whether he lost his footing, or the rock he was standing on suddenly gave way—but one moment he was upright and the next minute he was sprawled out on the rocky bed of the river. He gasped as his upper body hit the icy water. I started to get off my horse to help him, but I hesitated when I saw that he was shaking, laughing hysterically. He held up the can of cola and gave me an enthusiastic "thumbs up." His grin was triumphant; I couldn't help but laugh, until I saw the steam of red trickling down his forearm.

I dismounted and began making my way toward him, following along the water's edge. He was already up and half way across the river when he motioned for me to stop. He was soaked from head to toe. I knew he must be cold, yet he showed no signs of discomfort. *Male ego* I figured. I stared as the water on his skin glistened in the setting sun and a steady stream of red blood trailed down his arm and into the river.

Something wasn't right.

"I saved the cola!" he boasted proudly, and took a short, humble bow. He was either unaware or unconcerned about his bleeding arm.

"Good thing," I replied, and then pointed. "Look at your arm!"

"Ugh," he grunted. He bent down casually, allowing the river water to run over his injury as he handed me the soda can.

"Grab a rag from my pack, would you?" he asked matter-of-factly.

I hurried to his horse, pulled a rag from the pack on his saddle, and began folding it into a long, narrow band of cloth. I stood in front of him holding the rag, but I couldn't take my eyes off his arm. When he pulled it out of the water, I gasped sharply. There appeared to be two distinct fluids oozing from the wound. One of the fluids was normal blood, but the other looked clear like water, only thicker. I bent forward to examine the strange liquid more carefully, but he took the rag from my hand and covered the wound, holding the cloth firmly in place. After a few moments I lifted my eyes and realized that he was watching me quizzically. My mind was still trying to make sense of what I'd seen.

"What was . . . ? I-I've never seen anything like that before. What *was* that?" I asked. I was trying not to panic, but the cut was obviously more serious than he realized.

"It's fine, really." He was trying to keep me calm, but it wasn't working. "Trust me, Beth." His gentle tone was disarming, particularly under the circumstances, but for a second I felt like I might lose my footing and stumble. "It's okay," he assured me as he grabbed my arm to steady me.

"But, what—"

"No, Beth, really—it's fine," he interrupted, then he shook his head. "Grab my first aid kit, would you? It's in the side pouch of my pack." He motioned with his head toward his horse.

I retrieved the kit and located a large bandage. I was doubtful it would be enough, but maybe it would hold until we got back to the ranch. A dark shadow passed over the river making it suddenly appear cold and unfriendly. I glanced up at the clouds and watched them roll rapidly across the sky; they were heavier and much darker than they had been earlier. I marveled at how quickly Wyoming skies could change.

Jonathan removed the blood-drenched cloth from his wound, finally allowing me to examine the cut.

I stood gawking at his wound, unable to formulate a coherent sentence. My eyes could not make sense of what they were seeing; his wound had not only stopped bleeding, it appeared to be healing—right before my eyes.

He scrutinized my expression carefully. He wasn't surprised by my reaction. What I found inconceivable was that he was behaving as though everything was normal. His face was blank as my gaping stare moved from the wound to his eyes and back again. He nudged my arm, gesturing toward the bandage I had brought from the first aid kit. Nervously, I fastened the bandage tightly against his arm and held it in place until I was certain it would hold. He covered my hand with his and squeezed gently.

"Perfect," he smiled.

He submerged the cloth into the river and wrung it until the water ran clear, then he led the way to our horses. I followed, dumbfounded, trying to reason through what I had just witnessed. Jonathan offered his bandaged arm to help me mount as if nothing at all had happened.

"That's it?" I asked, annoyed.

"What?" he said innocently.

"You're not going to explain what just happened to your arm?"

"There's nothing to explain. The cut wasn't that deep."

"I saw it—it was gushing clear fluid from it. It—"

"Beth, things are not always as they seem. Will you just trust me on that?"

"But, Jonathan, it—"

"Please Beth, whatever it was, you can see for yourself . . ." he held his arm up to me, bandage and all. "It's fine now."

I stared at him, dissatisfied with his lack of explanation. But I could tell by the determination on his face that the subject was closed. I dropped it for the moment. I knew about people who bled profusely at the smallest cut; maybe Jonathan's blood had a similar disorder, only in reverse. I let my mind peruse all possible scientific explanations as my horse followed docilely behind Jonathan's mount.

The sky continued to darken as we made our way toward the ranch; there was no way we were going to get there before dark. Jonathan remained quiet. He seemed uneasy. I wasn't paying attention to the trail, still too distracted by the bandage that covered a third of Jonathan's forearm and brooding about the fluid that oozed from his wound to notice when the first drops of rain began to fall. An unexpected, violent roar of thunder shook the sky and the ground around me, and my horse reared up, knocking me off balance. It was very awkward for me to hold the reigns in my right hand, nothing about it felt natural, so when my horse suddenly lurched forward it threw me to the side. Instinctively, I grabbed for the reigns with my left hand. The tension shot a sharp pain through my hand that penetrated through every tendon along my forearm. Without thinking,

I let go of the reigns to stop the fiery pain in my hand and lost my grip. The horse jerked again and down I went, bouncing awkwardly down the side of the horse and landing flat on my backside with a thud. I groaned. Part of me wanted to laugh knowing full well I'd made a spectacle of myself, but when Jonathan pulled his horse around, he wasn't laughing. My horse took off and before I could catch my breath, Jonathan lit off his horse and dropped to my side.

"Are you okay? What happened?" he asked anxiously.

"I'm fine," I answered through embarrassed laughs. *I love making a fool of myself.*

"Are you hurt?" he asked as he pursed his lips, respectfully stifling a chuckle.

I shook my head. Watching him try so hard *not* to laugh made me burst out in hysterics. The rain had begun to fall steadily, so the ground around me was rapidly turning to a slimy mixture of pine needles, dead leaves, and mud. Jonathan watched me through clenched lips, and then his shoulders started to shake. I slugged him in the shoulder with my right arm, and that was it. He burst out laughing and plopped himself onto the ground next to me. Soon we were both drenched in a chaotic mixture of rain and mud.

Once he composed himself, he scooped me into his arms and carried me to his horse. I didn't protest. Instead, I concentrated on the solidity of the muscles that supported me with effortless ease. When he put me down, he pulled me against his chest with one arm.

"What am I going to do with you?" he asked, still chuckling.

"Stick around. There's another show in about an hour," I replied with the most ardent grin I could muster.

"I would hate to miss that," he joked, and squeezed his arm tighter around my shoulders.

I pressed my face into his chest and he held me close to him long enough for my resolve to waver. I was supposed to be annoyed with him, but suddenly I was no longer thinking about blood, bandages, the fall, the rain, or the mud. Instead, I focused on the firmness of his chest beneath his rain-soaked shirt, the pressure of the arm that pulled me against him, and the natural scent of his wet skin.

"Here," he said, moving me to the side of his horse. "Let's get you up."

He guided my foot into the stirrup and helped me onto the horse. Then he climbed up behind me and reached around to take the reins in his left hand. He folded his right arm around my waist and held me against him. I grabbed onto the horn of the saddle, but as soon as he urged the horse to move forward, he covered the top of my hand with his, and then folded both of our arms securely around my waist. He had no difficulty cupping my entire hand beneath his own and after a few moments, he began to caress the top of my hand gently with his thumb. I was acutely aware, once again, of the difference between his hands and Eric's.

The rain continued to fall sporadically as the night sky turned black. A brilliant display of stars peaked randomly through the breaking clouds. We were wet and it was cold but I couldn't imagine feeling warmer or more content than I did at that moment. I wanted the ride to last forever.

The Ranch

CHAPTER 5

When we got back to the trailhead, my horse was already there, waiting patiently. Jonathan loaded the tired horses into the trailer and we drove straight to the Rollings' ranch, arriving shortly after eight o'clock. He gently helped me out of the truck and was maneuvering the horses out of the trailer when a husky man wearing a thick flannel shirt and a baseball cap approached and greeted us with a pleasant yet concerned smile.

"What the heck happened to you two? It's late." He patted the horses firmly as Jonathan handed him the reins. "What . . . ?"

He stopped short when he spotted the bandage on Jonathan's arm and looked at him quizzically. Jonathan glanced at me reassuringly and brushed a lock of wet hair away from my face.

"The thunder spooked her horse and he bucked. Threw her pretty good," he explained. "It's my fault. I should have brought us back before the storm began."

Jonathan spoke to the man without looking away from my

eyes. His reply was generous, all things considered. Being "thrown" off a horse was perfectly respectable, but I had bounced off the horse like a rubber ball bouncing down a flight of stairs. There had been nothing graceful about it.

"Are you hurt, honey?" the man asked.

"She's fine, just a little shaky," Jonathan answered for me.

I was shaky?

"That's because she's soaked to the bone," the man commented, eyeing me curiously. "Better get her inside."

"Pardon my manners, Beth," Jonathan said with exaggerated charm. "Allow me to introduce you. Mason Tyler, may I present Miss Elizabeth Arrington. Mason lives in the guest house just beyond our stables. He basically runs everything around here. We'd be lost without him.

"Pay him no mind, Miss. Jonathan has a tendency to exaggerate." Mr. Tyler winked as he reached for my hand.

"I'm pleased to meet you," I smiled as I offered my hand in return. "Please call me Beth."

"Fair enough, and you can call me Mason . . . right after you call your uncle. He's called three times in the past two hours."

"Oh," I moaned.

"Go on, get inside," he ordered, grinning. "I'll take care of your horses."

Jonathan took my hand and led me along the walkway to the front door which opened into a spacious entryway. On the right was a door leading into a small room that appeared to be an office. The left opened into an over-sized "great" room, and straight ahead was a large dining room with the kitchen just visible beyond. Jonathan guided me into the office and handed me the telephone.

"Here. Use the landline," he suggested. "Cell service is unreliable here, too close to the canyon."

"Thank you." I dialed Uncle Connor's number and waited for it to ring. Jonathan heard a noise, then perked up and smiled.

"That must be the girls. I'll be right back," he whispered as he darted quickly toward the door.

"Hello?" Uncle Connor's voice sounded calmer than I had anticipated.

"Hi, Uncle Connor. I'm sorry it's so late." My mouth suddenly went dry.

"What happened?" he asked.

"The storm. It started to thunder and I was thrown from my horse."

"Are you okay?" he interrupted.

"I'm fine," I reassured him.

"Anything hurt?" he said. I detected a slight bit of humor in his tone.

"Only my ego," I murmured under my breath. "Mr. Tyler said you called three times. Is something wrong?" I paused, not wanting to open a can of worms. "Are you mad at me?"

"No. Nothing like that," he replied. "I was calling because there's a fire across the canyon and it jumped the highway. They closed the road between the Rollings' ranch and the main highway."

"Are you serious? How can there be a fire when it's raining?" Before he could answer, the implication of his words suddenly struck me. "Wait a minute, if the road is closed, how do I get home?"

A silent pause followed, and then, "Let me speak to Jonathan."

Oh no. Uncle Connor, don't do that.

"Beth?"

"Why do you want to talk to Jonathan?"

"Just get him for me, please."

He was trying to sound patient, but I could tell he was not going to explain himself to me.

"All right. Hold on a minute."

I set the phone down and went outside to find Jonathan. I didn't see anybody at first, but I followed the sound of voices and found Jonathan standing next to two girls by the side of the house. I assumed they were his sisters. The three of them were engaged in a conversation about Jonathan's bandaged arm; something he said must have been funny because they were laughing. I approached hesitantly so I wouldn't appear rude, even though I was anxious about keeping Uncle Connor waiting.

Jonathan saw me and immediately motioned me over and introduced me to his sisters. Grace was the oldest. She was taller than me by two or three inches and had a slender build. Her light brown hair was pinned on top of her head in a casual bun with wisps of subtle waves dangling free. Her eyes sparkled green and lit up when she smiled, similar to the way Jonathan's did. It was easy to recognize them as brother and sister. Without reservation, she held out both of her hands to me, palms up, waiting for me to place my hands in hers.

"I'm glad to finally meet you," she said warmly.

Without thinking, I offered her both my hands. Her hands were delicate and warm and so soft that I had to look down at them to make sure they were real. They felt like hands that had been protected by wearing gloves and had never been exposed to weather or sun. I couldn't help but grimace when she gently squeezed my hands in hers. She looked down at my left hand quizzically.

"Hmm," she commented, "how very interesting."

I wasn't accustomed to having people notice my handicap openly. Her reaction caught me off guard and I withdrew my hand from hers.

"Forgive me, please," she said. "I don't mean to be rude."

"No, it's okay," I replied, shaking my head. "Most people pretend they don't notice. I actually appreciate an honest reaction for a change."

The younger sister, Janine, was definitely the more reserved of the two girls. She was stunning, with a petite figure that reminded me of a fragile princess. She blushed easily, revealing evenly spaced dimples on either side of her smile, when Jonathan chided her for worrying. Apparently she had run off to find us when we didn't return on time. Her hair was golden brown and cascaded in waves to the middle of her back. She eyed her older brother worshipfully, and by his reaction, I concluded that he was very protective of her.

I remembered that Uncle Connor was still waiting on the phone and my feeling of anxiety returned. Jonathan noticed the change in my demeanor and raised his eyebrows.

"Excuse me," I said to the three of them. I turned to Jonathan and lowered my voice. "My uncle wants to talk to you."

"He does?" he asked, grinning. "This ought to be fun."

I cringed and followed him back into the house.

The conversation was one-sided. Jonathan's replies were "Yes, sir." "No, sir." "No, I hadn't." "Really?" "I understand." "I see what you mean." "No, they're out of the country but both of my sisters are here." "Yes, of course." And then finally, "I'll make sure she is."

"What the heck was that all about?" I prodded as he hung up the phone.

"There's a fire on the west end, so the highway between the base of the canyon and the junction to Andersen is closed," he explained. "We can't get through until the road opens and that might be sometime in the middle of the night."

"What does he want you to do?" I asked, confused.

"You'll need to stay here tonight," he said grinning. "Your uncle isn't happy about that, but there's no other option."

"Oh," I nodded. The full impact of what he'd just said didn't sink in for several minutes. My mind was on the fire. "How can there be a fire when it's raining?"

"It happens frequently here. Lightning strikes the arid areas of the canyon and the fires take off. Often the rain is heavy in the mountains, but the canyon stays pretty dry."

"So, what happens now?" I asked.

"First thing we need to do is get you into the shower," he chuckled. "You're a mess!"

"Gee, thanks," I responded. "You don't look so good yourself." Actually, I was lying. Even covered in dry mud, he looked amazing. I watched his smug expression as he looked himself over and pretended to be offended.

"Come on," he said, "I'll have Grace take you upstairs so you can clean up. I'm sure she can find something for you to wear while your clothes are washing."

Grace was the perfect host. She brought me a clean pair of sweat pants, a T-shirt, and some clean towels before she escorted me to her bathroom.

"Take as long as you need," she insisted. "I'll get the guest room ready. It's been a long time since we've had a visitor. It'll be fun!"

The hot shower felt wonderful. My legs were sore from the horseback ride, my tailbone ached, and there was a three-inch scrape atop a black and blue bruise forming on the side of my thigh. None of that mattered though. As I studied the scrape, I thought about the cut on Jonathan's arm and the clear fluid that had seeped from his wound. How could it heal so quickly? Was there some special healing power in the river water? *Very scientific, Beth,* I chided myself.

These questions, though unsettling, failed to detract me from memories of the day's activities. I had told Jonathan everything about the night of my accident and he had believed me. He had listened without judgment, never questioning that the evidence did not support my version of the truth. I reached up and stroked the spot on my cheek where Jonathan had kissed me. The sweet memory of his closeness put all my questions aside for the moment.

After I finished my shower, Grace escorted me to the guest room. It was decorated in late nineteenth century antiques with a rustic, hardwood floor; a mahogany, four-poster bed; and lace curtains that flowed delicately to the floor. A portrait of a stunning young woman hung on the wall opposite the window. Her beautiful emerald eyes were shaded by a demure, old-fashioned bonnet. Her likeness added to the femininity of the room. Something about her seemed familiar. Was it her eyes? I got the feeling that I knew her from somewhere, which of course was impossible. I decided it had to be the painting itself that was familiar. I had probably come across it in an art book or museum somewhere. I continued to stare at the painting until I heard Grace's gentle tap on the open door.

Grace allowed me time to settle in and then tapped gently on the open door.

"Janine made sandwiches; are you hungry?" she asked.

"Famished," I replied. "I'll be right down."

She shut the door softly and I took a long glance in the vanity mirror. *Yikes!* I thought to myself when I saw my sunburned face and mat of wet, tangled hair. After a quick study I used the bottle of lotion sitting on the vanity to smooth my skin and struggled to pull a large-tooth comb through my hair.

It's the best I can do, I thought, and headed downstairs.

I followed the long hallway from the guest room to the stairs, passing three other bedrooms along the way. One of them was set up like a hotel suite with a sitting room off to one side and an opening into what I figured was the master bathroom. The other bedroom was smaller and decorated completely in creamy white tones. I guessed this was Janine's room. Grace's bedroom was the one closest to the staircase.

As I descended the stairs, Janine caught my eye and broke into a shy smile. Jonathan was sitting opposite Janine with his back to me. He turned around, following Janine's gaze, and immediately stood. He walked forward but stopped at the base of the stairs and smiled up at me. He folded his arms smugly across his chest.

"What?" I asked suspiciously.

"Nothing." He shook his head, his smile broadening.

"What!" I demanded.

"You look adorable," he laughed. "But it's a little unsettling seeing you dressed in my sister's clothes."

"Jonathan! Don't be rude!" Janine reproached.

We both chuckled as Jonathan climbed the stairs to meet me. "You really do look adorable," he whispered in my ear. He offered me his arm in a truely chivalrous fashion. "Shall we?"

There was an old-style charm to the ranch, particularly in the large living room which Jonathan referred to as the "great room." Decorated in rich browns, deep greens, and subtle gold, it matched the era of the guest room. The only thing out of place was the sixty-inch plasma screen mounted on the wall above the fireplace. Before the fireplace was a rustic brown leather sofa, matching easy chairs, and a round coffee table. Along the far wall was a large picture window where a very comfortable looking lounge chair sat next to a reading table and a Tiffany-style floor lamp. The true focal point of the room, a deep mahogany, full-sized grand piano, was strategically placed in the corner. The elegance of the instrument nearly took my breath away.

Jonathan squeezed my elbow as he followed my gaze. Then Grace entered carrying a tray of mugs.

"How about some hot chocolate with our sandwiches?"

"Thanks, Grace." Jonathan took the tray from her hands and set it on the coffee table.

The four of us sat around the table eating sandwiches and drinking hot chocolate while a fire in the fireplace sent a permeating glow through the room. The warmth and magic of the fire created an ambiance of intimacy. I had the feeling I had known them all for years.

Eventually, Grace invited Janine to help her clear the dishes and the two of them excused themselves. Jonathan chuckled at Grace's obvious scheme to give us some privacy.

"Shouldn't we offer to help?" I asked, wanting to be polite.

"That would sort of spoil her plot to leave us alone, don't you think?" Jonathan grinned and stood up to stretch. He reached for my hand and helped me to my feet, then led me over to the piano.

"What do you think?" he asked, stroking the cover with affection. He lifted the lid and propped it into place.

"It's gorgeous. I bet it sounds amazing." It was my way of asking him to play.

Jonathan sat on the bench and patted the spot next to him, the same way he always did when we met in the practice rooms.

"What are you in the mood for?" He tickled a loose chain of chords spanning the width of the keyboard.

I considered my options, and then I was struck with a sudden whim. "How familiar are you with 'Three Blind Mice?'"

Jonathan looked confused, but he caught on when he realized I was challenging him to a one-handed dual. For the next half hour we battled each other playfully, laughing with each skillfully performed arrangement of the simple tune. He was a much more formidable opponent than my father used to be; I had to crank it up a notch to beat him. He finally relented when he realized I wasn't going to quit until I'd won. I was the champ, after all.

"You win." He pretended to tip his hat to me, but something in his smug smile told me I'd just been duped.

"You let me win!" I accused him. "I demand a replay."

Jonathan laughed. "I may have let you win, but it was only because I couldn't beat you."

I had to think about that. I still felt duped.

"Can I ask you a question?" Jonathan's face was instantly serious.

"Sure." Something told me this had nothing to do with "Three Blind Mice."

"Why did you turn down Mr. Laden's offer?"

My face fell instantly; this was not a conversation I wanted to have.

"Beth?" Jonathan reached for my left hand, but I tucked it against my stomach.

"I'm not a teacher," I said flatly.

"You have a God-given talent for the piano. Don't you think you should use it?"

"Ha!" I snorted bitterly. "If there really is a God, then why did he give me a talent and then snatch it away so thoughtlessly?"

"God didn't snatch your talent from you—"

I cut him off abruptly. "No, he left the talent, he just obliterated my hand. Yeah, there's a loving God for you." The icy cynicism in my words didn't seem to faze Jonathan.

"It wasn't God that caused your accident, Beth."

"He might not have caused it, but if he's so all powerful, then why didn't he stop it?" I looked pleadingly at Jonathan.

"I don't have the answer to that." He reached again for my hand; this time I didn't pull it away. "I do know this; you have a gift. I saw it when you were with Justin. And even though you can't use your talent the way you planned, the way you dreamed, you owe it to yourself not to let it die. Beth, you owe it to the world."

"I can't do it," I whispered. Emotion lodged in my throat.

"Why not?" He searched my eyes for understanding.

Moisture gathered in the corners of my eyes. I struggled to blink it away but it was too late. "Because it hurts too much." Streams of tears slid in perfect unison down each of my cheeks. Jonathan drew a sharp breath and wrapped his arms around me, pulling my face to his chest.

"It hurts," I repeated, my voice muffled by his shirt.

"I'm sorry." He stroked my hair. "I'm truly sorry."

"Every time I hear a piano, every time I. . . ." A strangled sob escaped my throat, dislodging the lump that I had hoped to keep down.

"Shhh. I know." He continued stroking my hair and held me while I struggled in vain to stop my tears. "I know."

"Sorry," I muttered.

He bent and gently kissed my forehead. "You've had quite the day, haven't you?" His sympathetic smile moved me. "How 'bout we go see what Grace is up to?" he offered softly, wiping my face with the bottom of his shirt.

Although it was getting late and I was tired, I was disappointed when Jonathan finally announced that he had to leave.

"Why do you have to leave?" I asked too hastily.

"I sort of made your uncle a promise tonight."

"What promise?"

"Let's just say he's not comfortable with the idea of us sleeping in the same house."

"Are you serious?"

"He's old fashioned," he said calmly. "And he's protecting you."

"Protecting me from what?"

"From me, apparently," he laughed.

"Where are you going?" Janine cut in.

"To stay with Mason," he said. "Have no fear ladies, I'll be back in the morning." He winked as he pulled on his jacket.

"Well," Grace began, "it looks like the party's over until morning." She yawned. "If you need anything, Beth, I'm just down the hall."

"Thank you," I replied.

We said our good nights as the last of the fire's embers slowed to a mellow glow of orange and red, and I retired to my room. I climbed into the oversize bed and snuggled beneath a white, goose down comforter that contrasted sharply with the rich wood trim of the bed frame.

As I lay there, embraced by the memories of the day, I soon slipped into a deep sleep and started dreaming—once again carried away to the grassy hillside overlooking a large field surrounded by rolling hills covered with flowing grass and bright orange and yellow wildflowers. The hill where I sat was steep enough that I could not see over its edge, but I could gaze beyond to the vast spaciousness of the horizon before me. A feeling of despair and intense loneliness overcame me and I stood, desperate to make my presence known. Where were the soldiers? Why was I left behind? I tried to call for someone, to find some evidence that I had not been abandoned, but as I opened my mouth there was nothing but silence.

I was becoming despondent when I caught a glimpse of someone approaching.

A woman dressed in a creamy, antique white dress made her way to the top of the hill. She carried a candle in one hand, but its light was far above the glow of a normal flame. In the other hand she held a scepter, the same scepter I recognized from my earlier dream. I glanced down, suddenly aware that I, too, held a candle. But mine was not illuminated.

The woman approached me gracefully, smiling, yet there was apprehension in her eyes. She continued advancing until she stood directly in front of me. She held out her candle to me; the glow nearly blinded me. Then she motioned with her eyes for me to raise my candle to hers. When I did, my candle ignited into a brilliant, glorious light. She stepped away from me and as she did, her flame gradually dimmed until it went out, leaving a thin trail of pure, white smoke in its place. Then she floated away.

I felt a warm sensation along the side of my head and within seconds I was back in the four-poster bed. The sun's early morning rays streamed through the lacy curtains and caressed my face. I turned away from the light, and as I did so I found myself staring into the face of the woman in the painting that hung on the wall. Those eyes. Her piercing green eyes seem to gaze directly into mine. Again, I had a feeling I had seen the painting before, but where?

The woman in the painting was not the same woman as the one in my dream, although they appeared to be from the same era judging by the way they were dressed. However, the girl in the painting was more fragile than the one from my dream. Normally, I didn't recall my dreams easily, which was why the dreams of the grassy hillside were so puzzling. The details remained vivid long after I awoke.

I slid off the bed lazily and made my way down the hallway to the stairs. The house was quiet, no sign of stirring from either Grace's or Janine's bedrooms. I decided to wander downstairs and look for something to distract me while I waited for some sign of activity. As I entered the great room, I was able to see it for the first time in the light of the early morning sun. Funny how our perspective changes when we see things in a different light.

I noticed some sheet music spread across the top of the piano and my curiosity got the best of me. I was sure it wasn't there last night and the lid was now closed. Who could have been there? Was Jonathan back already?

I picked up several pages of the music; it was hand composed. I followed the melody in my mind and recognized it as the theme Jonathan had played for me, the one he had taught me. The piece appeared to be a work in progress with several of the pages written in a different pen, which made no sense; Jonathan had said it was composed a long time ago.

I returned the music to the piano and meandered around the room. Its size and charm was even more impressive in the daylight. I followed a long hallway from the great room to a large bedroom. The door was open so I wandered inside. This room was more modern than the other rooms in the house with very eclectic furnishings and wall art. Some of the artwork was impressionist, some modern, and some baroque. There was no apparent theme, at least none that I could discern. An entertainment center stood along the wall adjacent to the door. It stood proudly demanding attention and housed a stereo, Bose speakers, and a turntable inside. A computer with a wide, flat screen monitor sat on a desk beside the window.

The room was masculine except for an old Elizabethan chest of drawers that stood angled in the corner, vying with the window and the entertainment center as the room's focal point. Atop the

chest were two old photographs in simple baroque frames, one of a
man and the other a woman. The pictures appeared to be from the
mid 1800s because the man was dressed as a Union soldier from the
Civil War. It was a full-body shot, so it was difficult to see his face
clearly, but from what I could tell, he was the spitting image of Jonathan. The resemblance was so obvious that I knew it had to be one
of his ancestors. I was so intrigued by the photo of the soldier that
I didn't pay much attention to the other photo. When I picked up
the frame holding the woman's picture, I had to do a double take. I
gasped when I saw her face and nearly dropped the picture. The girl
in the frame was the same woman from my dream. I was sure of it.

Impossible! I had never seen this picture before.

My hand began to tremble as I stared at her angelic features.

"Beth?" Grace's voice came from the doorway. I jumped, losing
my hold on the picture. It fell to the floor with a tinkling crash as
broken glass shattered in all directions.

"Oh!"

"I'm sorry, Beth," Grace apologized. "I shouldn't have startled
you that way."

"No, I'm sorry. I was snooping," I admitted.

"Please, don't worry about it," she replied.

"Where can I find a broom?" I asked, embarrassed.

"Jonathan will take care of it later," she tried to assure me but it
made me even more anxious.

"Please," I cringed. "I don't want him to know—"

"Don't be silly," she cut me off. "He won't mind that you were
in his room."

"His room?"

"Can't you tell by the look of it? Nothing matches," she snickered.

"Ugh!" I sighed. Could it get any worse?

Grace recognized how upset I was and mercifully tried to distract
me by walking over to Jonathan's entertainment center. "This stereo
is his pride and joy," she said. "He has it wired to surround sound
speakers hidden throughout the entire house. Well, on the bottom
floor, anyway. It was a massive undertaking and, I must admit, it's

pretty impressive. You'll have to ask him to demonstrate it for you later. He'd love that," she grinned. "Come on, let's go start the coffee."

She must have noticed my hesitation because her grin softened to an understanding smile.

"All right, wait here. I'll be right back," she conceded.

She returned shortly and handed me a dustpan, a broom, and a small bag. I bent down to sweep up the pieces of broken glass and handed her the frame and the picture.

"Who is she?" I asked, pointing to the woman in the picture.

"Eleanor Hastings. Why?"

"Because I dreamed about her last night."

The astonished look in Grace's eyes startled me. "You mean you dreamed of someone who *looks* like her."

"No, it was *her*."

"The mind is a tricky thing. . . ." Her voice trailed off as she reached down to hand me the bag so I could drop the glass fragments inside.

"Is this the same Eleanor that wrote the theme that Jonathan plays?"

"The very same. She was beautiful, wasn't she?"

"Very," I agreed. A sudden chill ran through my veins and the hair on my arms stood at attention. How could I dream about a woman I'd never seen before? It was impossible, yet it had happened.

"That soldier looks a lot like Jonathan, doesn't he?" Grace's question interrupted my thoughts and I turned to get a better look at the man in uniform.

"Is that who Jonathan was named after?"

"You . . . could say that," she smiled as she funneled the remainder of the broken glass into the bag. "Now, let's go start breakfast. I am the world's greatest waffle maker," she said as I followed her into the kitchen to help.

I was laboring over a pan of sizzling bacon when I felt an energetic jab in my ribs. I jerked, nearly sending hot bacon grease flying across the room.

"Good morning," Jonathan announced as he strolled away to swipe a waffle from Grace's stack. She punched him in the arm as he took a bite, but she didn't protest. I watched the expressions of endearment that passed between them. Being an only child, I felt envious of their relationship.

"Janine up yet?" Jonathan asked Grace.

"Nope, the sleeping dead have not arisen," she said jokingly as she handed Jonathan the plate of hot waffles. "Make sure those make it to the table, okay?" she ordered, trying to look stern.

"Grace makes the best pumpkin waffles in the history of . . . of waffles," he grinned.

Oh, so that was her secret. Pumpkin! I would have to remember that just in case I ever made breakfast for Jonathan. I chuckled to myself at the presumptuous notion and Jonathan noticed.

"What are you laughing at?" he chided, but as he did so I realized he was no longer wearing the bandage on his arm. I looked closely at his forearm where the wound should be but all that remained was a faint red streak about four inches long.

"Wow!" I exclaimed.

"What?"

"Your arm!" I pointed. "That's . . . amazing!"

"Hmm," he replied, shrugging.

"H-how did it . . . ?" I stammered. "That cut was deep."

"Things are not always as they seem." He winked at me as he placed two waffles on my plate. "Now, try these. I promise you're going to love them."

I stared at him, expecting some reasonable explanation for his arm but it was clear there would be none. He gave me his naughty, sideways grin as he took a bite of waffle and closed his eyes to savor the taste. When he opened them again, my brows were knit together in a scowl which only made his smile broaden. He reached over and cut a small piece of waffle from my plate, dipped it in syrup, and held it to my mouth. I rolled my eyes, but opened my mouth obediently. The flavor succeeded in distracting me; they were the best waffles I'd ever tasted.

Janine came downstairs to join us when the smell of pumpkin spice and bacon finally woke her. She moved slowly and didn't have much to say until breakfast was over and we started clearing the table. She wasn't grumpy or sour, just strangely quiet and slow. The doorbell rang as we were finishing up the dishes.

Jonathan excused himself to answer the door and moments later we were all surprised to hear Uncle Connor's voice coming from the entrance. He seemed annoyed to see Jonathan and spoke rather coldly to him, which was uncharacteristic of Uncle Connor. No doubt he'd jumped to the wrong conclusion.

"Good morning, Connor," Jonathan said pleasantly. I was startled by his use of Uncle Connor's first name. It seemed rather familiar and unconventional given the fact they didn't know each other very well, but Uncle Connor either didn't notice or didn't care.

"Where's Beth?" he demanded flatly.

I quickly made an appearance.

"Good morning," I said brightly. He smiled and I stepped through the door to give him a hug. "What are you doing here?"

I realized my question sounded rude, so I quickly added, "I mean, you didn't need to drive all the way out here." He glanced briefly at Jonathan.

"They opened the canyon road around four. I figured I'd save Jonathan a trip."

I glanced briefly at Jonathan and he rolled his eyes. Luckily, Uncle Connor didn't see.

"I could have driven her home," Jonathan said, trying to sound polite. "It wouldn't have been any trouble."

Grace and Janine appeared from the kitchen and Grace immediately became the hospitable hostess.

"Good morning, Mr. Lee," she said, glancing from Uncle Connor to Jonathan.

I was completely dumbfounded to discover they knew each other.

"Won't you come in and have some breakfast?" Grace said as she offered Uncle Connor her hand. "I made pumpkin waffles and if I do say so myself, they're quite legendary." She flashed him a generous smile and curtsied briefly as he shook her hand. Uncle Connor was flattered by her charming manner and blushed when she smiled at him.

"Appreciate the offer," he responded, "but I just came to get Beth." He turned to me, suddenly looking a little embarrassed. "Are you ready to go home?"

I excused myself and hurried upstairs to gather my things. Janine retrieved my clothes from the dryer and placed them in a bag.

"Just hang on to Grace's sweats. You can get them back to her later," she insisted.

"Thanks," I replied hastily. "I'd better not keep my uncle waiting."

I gave her a quick hug and hurried downstairs. Jonathan met me at the bottom of the stairs just like the previous evening when he'd whispered in my ear. The memory of him so close to me made my pulse race. But there was no adoring whisper this morning and no hand-holding. He simply took the bag from my hand and walked with me to where Uncle Connor was sitting. Grace had poured him a cup of coffee while he waited for me. When he saw me, he stood and quickly took one last sip.

"Thanks," he said to Grace. "It was a pleasure seeing you and your sister again."

I noticed the absence of Jonathan's name in his statement.

"You're welcome here any time, Mr. Lee," Grace replied. She'd definitely mastered the art of charming older men. I made a mental note to learn her technique some day.

"Please, call me Connor," he said, lowering his head briefly. Then he smiled and turned to me. "Are you ready?"

"I think so," I lied. I wasn't ready to leave this house, or the people who lived in it.

Jonathan walked me out and tossed my bag in the back seat of Uncle Connor's truck. My uncle drove one of those mid-sized trucks with four doors, and he was very proud of it. I couldn't tell one make from another, but I knew it was something special because whenever he drove me into town, men would stop and ask him about it.

Uncle Connor walked around to the driver's side and got in, allowing Jonathan to get my door for me. As he reached around me to open the door, he placed his free hand on my back and gave me a gentle squeeze.

"I'll see you later," he said quietly. His hand tightened momentarily on my waist and he grinned conspiratorially as he helped me into the car.

"Bye, Beth," he smiled, and then he looked through the window at Uncle Connor. "See you, Connor."

They exchanged a brief look, but I was aware that something unspoken had passed between them.

Senior Tradition
CHAPTER 6

*U*ncle Connor was silent for the first two miles of the trip home and then he started mumbling under his breath. He kept his eyes fixed on the road, ignoring me, but every once in awhile I could make sense of his grumblings.

"Should've known . . . never should have . . . stupid!"

From his mutterings, I gathered that he'd jumped to the erroneous conclusion that Jonathan had stayed at the ranch last night after promising he wouldn't. I wasn't sure if I should remain silent until he calmed down or speak up. When my dad got this way, Mom would lay low and ride it out before trying to talk to him. I wasn't that patient.

"Uncle Connor?" My words sliced through the thick mood.

He released an annoyed sigh and looked over at me. His lips were pulled together in a tight line.

"What?" he grumbled.

"I know you're upset—"

"Darn right I am! I should never have trusted—"

"He didn't break his promise," I interrupted before he could finish. He relaxed his shoulders slightly but didn't respond. "He spent the night with Mr. Tyler at the guest house. He came back this morning for breakfast." I waited, hoping he'd process the information before exploding.

"He left?"

"Yes."

"Humph! Well, that's something." He eyed me for a moment before looking back at the road. I waited for him to relax before saying anything further. It took awhile but eventually his countenance softened.

"I get the feeling that you and Jonathan know each other," I stated pendulously.

Uncle Connor cut his eyes at me and shrugged. "I had dealings with his family back when they ran a working ranch."

"You know his family?" I asked, shocked.

"Not well, but yes."

"Did something happen that made you not like them?"

"Not at all," he responded. "His family was always very cordial. I was sorry they shut down the ranch."

"Why did they?"

"Don't know for sure. Reckon they wanted the freedom to travel. They spend a lot of time away. Doesn't seem fair to the young girl."

"Janine?"

Uncle Connor nodded. "She's not technically their daughter. She came to live with them a few years ago. I don't know the whole story—just that within a couple of months after she arrived, they shut down the ranch. They've been traveling on and off ever since."

"How strange," I said, half under my breath. Uncle Connor raised his shoulders and shook his head. He was much calmer now, so I decided it was safe to ask him the question that was really on my mind. "Why don't you like Jonathan?"

"It's not that I don't like him, I just don't trust him. I suspect he has a bit of a wild streak."

"A wild streak?" There were many descriptions of Jonathan in my mind. "Wild" certainly wasn't one of them.

"Perhaps wild isn't the right word, but he's always struck me as a kid with an agenda." He looked at me briefly, probably to check my reaction. My expression was blank. I didn't know how to respond. Uncle Connor was usually very intuitive when it came to reading people, but his perception of Jonathan was way off the mark.

"To be honest," he chuckled under his breath, "it would be difficult for me to like any boy who affects you the way he does." He grinned and nudged me with his elbow.

I blushed and averted my eyes. It made him laugh.

"You like him, don't you?"

The flame in my cheeks deepened and I wondered just how far he planned to take this conversation.

"He's nice." It was a safe answer.

"Mm hmm," he responded, "and . . . ?"

"And what?" I cringed.

"And you're . . . attracted to him."

My face exploded with color; I could no longer look in Uncle Connor's direction. He'd been right when he said he had *no clue* about teenage girls. He was easy to talk to about normal things, but this was excruciatingly awkward. "I guess," I squirmed.

"Okay," he chuckled. "We don't have to talk about it right now."

"Thanks." I breathed a deep sigh of relief and relaxed into my seat.

We drove in silence through the canyon and onto the highway that led back to Andersen. I pondered our conversation. I couldn't imagine why Uncle Connor would question Jonathan's character. Jonathan was always a perfect gentleman. But it was true; the more time I spent with him, the more he occupied my thoughts. I thought about my mom. I wished desperately I could talk to her. A wave of emotion brought tears to my eyes, but I blinked them away before Uncle Connor noticed.

I had several assignments to finish before school the next morning and a string of missed calls on my cell phone. There were two calls from Eric, two text messages from Darla, one call from Uncle Connor, and one from a number I didn't recognize. Eric had been trying to find out if I was going to the barbecue after all, even though he'd told me not to. His next message asked why I didn't show up at the game, what was I doing last night, and why wasn't I responding to his text messages!? Geez! He'd obviously decided he wasn't mad at me anymore. Darla left me similar messages. I didn't feel like explaining, so I sent them both a brief e-mail and then started to tackle my mountain of homework.

The effort was fruitless; I continued to battle with my thoughts. There was no way I was going to be able to focus on U.S. Government, calculus, or psychology. I finally gave up, slipped on my jacket, and headed outdoors.

As I walked down the driveway, I was surprised to see the garage door open. Carl's car was up on blocks and Uncle Connor was doing something underneath it. I grimaced as I recalled the previous weekend and the trouble that Carl and I had gotten into when he let me drive his car. Carl had left early Tuesday morning; I had no idea when I would hear from him again.

"Uncle Connor?" I bent down so I could see him better. "What are you doing?"

"Surgery," he hollered from beneath the car.

"What do you mean?"

"Didn't Carl tell you?"

"Tell me what?"

He scooted out from under the car. He was completely covered in grime, his face streaked with grease and his hands filthy.

"Good grief!" I shrieked. "What happened to you?"

He grumbled, but he was in good spirits. "Carl wants you to have his car," he announced. "He said to tell you 'Happy birthday.'"

"What? Are you serious? Is he crazy?"

"Do I really need to answer that question?" Uncle Connor said sarcastically.

"I can't drive that car!" I declared.

"Well, I've got a date with the county courthouse that says

otherwise," he said, smirking. I flinched, but at least he was no longer upset about my ticket.

"But, that's . . . not . . . a normal car," I insisted.

"Hence the surgery," he said smugly. He gestured to whatever it was he was doing under the car. "I'm trying to turn it into something a little less conspicuous and a little more safe."

"It's a 1974 Vega. It's going to be conspicuous no matter what you do to it."

"Hmm . . . Carl was sure you'd be happier about this than you apparently are," Uncle Connor laughed as he rolled himself back under the car.

"Does he know what you're doing to his car?" I shouted.

"Whose idea do you think it was?" he shouted back. I tapped his leg several times, signaling for him to roll out again where I could see him. He obliged but with a look of amused annoyance.

"This was Carl's idea?" I asked. "But this is his . . ." I couldn't think of the right word. The car was definitely Carl's pride and joy several years ago. I suppose there were more important things on his mind these days. But the car was a piece of his history, and I couldn't imagine him wanting it disabled.

"Beth," Uncle Connor said kindly, "Carl wants you to have his car. He believes you'll treat it well. I just want to make it a little quieter and safer before you drive it."

By *safer* he meant *slower*.

"Are we done here?" Uncle Connor asked. He pretended to be annoyed, but I could tell he was having fun.

"Yeah, sure," I replied, still stunned.

Even though the thought of taking the Vega to school was embarrassing, it meant that Uncle Connor wouldn't have to drive me every morning. I liked knowing that this would help him. Then the thought occurred to me that if I had my own car, Jonathan wouldn't be able to bring me home on the days we met after school. I wondered if that was the reason behind Uncle Connor's eagerness to fix the car.

As I walked along the trails behind the street where Uncle Connor lived, I retraced the events of the weekend with Jonathan. I was still troubled by his wound and the thick, clear liquid in his blood. How had it healed so rapidly? And what was Jonathan's connection with Eleanor? Why did he have her picture in his room? Most importantly, why did I dream about her before I'd even seen her picture or heard about her?

I allowed several possibilities to pass through my mind but none of them seemed satisfactory. If my mom were alive, she would undoubtedly suggest that I view the facts from a more spiritual angle. She believed everything could be explained, if not by science then by faith. She would likely say, "Things are not always what they appear to be." Jonathan had said that same thing to me. In my experience, that was just the type of cliché people used when things are *exactly* as they appear.

That was as far as my mind could go. I had no answers. I had no theories. Try as I might to make sense of things, no explanation seemed plausible. In the end, I had to admit to myself that there was only one question that mattered: where do I go from here?

The next week proved to be exceedingly frustrating. Darla flirted shamelessly with Evan Bradley which was too bad because I could tell he was legitimately interested in her and I was convinced that her only motivation was to try to make Derrick jealous. Evan was by far the better choice for Darla in my opinion. He was intelligent, tall, muscular, and striking in appearance; but he was shy, and therefore lacked the larger-than-life persona that some of the other boys possessed. Darla invited Evan and his friends to sit with us at lunch, and I had to admit that having them around was an improvement. It seemed to subdue the drama that Crystal and her friends usually subjected us to for the hour.

Eric, on the other hand, was a different story. He pretended as if the conversation between us in my basement had never taken place. I did my best to be friendly and polite while maintaining a more defined distance between us, but Eric was a pro at ignoring boundaries.

The discussions at lunch during the week mostly centered on the upcoming weekend. It was a long-standing tradition for the seniors to invite the juniors to a bonfire at the summit of one of the mountains in the area the Saturday evening before Halloween. At midnight the seniors told chilling stories of local legends combined, of course, with sensational ghost stories and cryptic tales of the supernatural. It had originally begun as a rite of passage for juniors and a way to keep the local legends alive. But over the years, the stories had taken on a new flare with the intent to terrorize the participants. It was all in good fun as it was explained to me and this year the event would be extra special because Halloween happened to fall on Saturday, so the seniors were planning an all-out "ghostathon." It sounded fascinating and I was sure it would be fun. I was grateful, however, that I was a senior and not a junior.

As the week passed, my anxieties about Jonathan increased. I hadn't heard anything from him. Nothing at all! I went to the practice rooms on Tuesday after school, but he wasn't there. I figured he would call or text or send me an e-mail or something but there were no messages from him. Nothing. No explanation. It caused me to second-guess everything that had transpired between us. As each afternoon passed without a call or a message, my doubts gave way to a stronger, more powerful emotion—anger.

By Friday afternoon, I was painfully conflicted about Jonathan. Disappointment overwhelmed me and it frustrated me that I was allowing my emotions to rule me so completely. Memories of Adam and old emotions from the night of my junior prom surfaced, and I had to fight to keep from succumbing to a fit of depression. I knew it was irrational to feel this way. I fought a constant, inward battle to stay positive.

How unnerving to realize that just one week of silence on Jonathan's part could completely unravel me. Fortunately, I had a great deal of homework to distract me. By eight o'clock Friday evening, I'd finished my calculus, U.S. Government, and physics homework. The only subjects remaining were English and psychology. Uncle Connor was working late and Marci wasn't around, so the house was disturbingly quiet and lonely. Our next novel in English was *The Jungle*, which I'd already read in the first semester of my junior year. I detested it. I resented having to read it again. I decided to tackle psychology first but after reading the same page three times, I gave up. I had no idea what the author was saying. I pushed the book aside and stood to stretch my legs.

"Hey, what's going on?" Uncle Connor appeared in the doorway.

"Hi, Uncle Connor," I yawned, "just doing homework."

"What are you working on?

"Nothing, really. I can't concentrate."

"Have you eaten yet?"

"Nope. Do you think I could order us a pizza? Is Marci coming?"

"Yes, let's order pizza. And no, Marci won't be here tonight. It's just you and me." He reflected on that for a moment and then raised his eyebrows. "Why aren't you out with Darla or Eric tonight?"

"Darla went to Jackson with her family," I informed him. I ignored the Eric part.

"Ah," he nodded.

"Uncle Connor?" I glanced up at him and decided to take a stab in the dark. "Have you ever heard of a wound healing abnormally fast?"

His face was expressionless. "Why do you ask?"

"Just curious," I said casually.

"Is that something you're studying?" he questioned, gesturing toward the pile of books on my desk.

"No, I'm just curious."

He studied my eyes for a moment before responding. "I suppose it happens sometimes. It doesn't seem like such a stretch that some people heal quicker than others." His answer was deliberately evasive.

"What about this," I continued, "a liquid that's clear like water, only thicker, and is mixed with the blood that comes out of a wound?"

"Beth, what's going on? Has something happened to you?"

"No, it's nothing." I tried to sound as if I'd lost interest but something in his choice of words confused me. I filed it away.

"Are you sure you're okay? You've been moping around the house all week. Even Marci noticed there was something wrong."

I was so transparent.

"Beth, if there's something you want to tell me, I hope you know you can trust me."

"I know. It's nothing." I shook my head and forced a smile.

He started to leave but then turned around suddenly. "I almost forgot. You have a message on the machine, something about a senior spook-out, whatever that is."

"Oh wow. I forgot." I explained to Uncle Connor how it was traditional for the seniors to take a group of juniors to a mountain summit for a bonfire and sleep out, and how they told spooky stories at midnight. I couldn't help but notice the skepticism in his expression.

"Yes, I remember this when Carl was in school," he muttered.

"Darla invited me to go."

"Absolutely not!" He scowled; his tone caught me off guard. "You're not about to go on an overnighter with a bunch of teenagers—I don't care what the tradition is." Uncle Connor nearly spit out the word *tradition*. His outburst annoyed me.

"These are my friends, they're harmless!" I argued.

"Is this a school-sponsored activity with adult chaperones?" he asked with smug sarcasm.

"N-no," I stammered, "it's just for fun. I don't see the big deal. Don't you trust me?"

"It's not a matter of trusting you. It's a matter of responsibility. And, no, I do not trust an unsupervised group of seventeen- and eighteen-year-olds at an all-night party. Do you think I'm crazy?"

"Wow," I said coldly, "you're usually so cool about things." I was hoping my last comment would guilt him into letting me go.

"Not when it comes to my sister's daughter." He spoke apologetically. "Besides, do you think your mother would approve of you going?"

I was going to lose this one. My mother would *not* approve of an all-nighter. *However,* I considered slyly, *she* might *be willing to negotiate.*

"What about a compromise?" I suggested. He raised his eyebrows and waited for me to continue. "What if I promise to come home at two? Then I can be there for the stories without staying all night."

He knit his brows together. "You can go if you're home by midnight. That's the best I can do." He spoke with finality, and I knew that arguing further would be fruitless.

"All right," I conceded. It would be awkward to leave just when the stories began, but at least I wouldn't be sitting around the house "moping" as Uncle Connor had put it.

I heard the signal alerting me that I had a new e-mail. I opened the window to my e-mail account and saw a message from Jonathan. I felt a sudden stab of anxiety. When I opened his e-mail, I was furious.

Hey Beth, how was your week? Are you busy tomorrow?

I growled at the computer loudly and stood up to keep from smacking the screen.

Uncle Connor glared at me, a shocked expression on his face. "What's wrong?" he asked cautiously.

"*Ugh!* All week he ignores me, and then he acts like everything is normal!" I stood there glaring at the e-mail as if by doing so Jonathan would feel my anger. "Jerk!" I scowled.

"Who's a jerk?"

"Jonathan," I bellowed, "who else?"

"Ohhh," Uncle Connor nodded knowingly and if I didn't know better, I would say he was trying not to smile. "I see."

I quickly sat down at the computer and hit the "reply" button. I sent a quick, one-word response. As soon as I could think straight, I was going to give him a real piece of my mind.

Uncle Connor cleared his throat. "Um, Beth, do you mind if I give you a little advice?"

"What!" I snapped. He raised one eyebrow at me disapprovingly. I relaxed and corrected my tone. "What?" I repeated, this time calmly.

"I may not have any experience with teenage girls but I have a world of experience with teenage boys. I would suggest that you think first, before you respond."

"What?" I seethed, "I'm supposed to act like nothing is wrong?"

Uncle Connor tilted his head to one side and shrugged. "That's my suggestion."

I stared at him in disbelief. Jonathan was a jerk for acting this way. And I thought Uncle Connor disapproved of him, anyway.

"Why should I act as if everything is okay?"

"Just hear me out," Uncle Connor said quietly. I let out an exaggerated sigh and moved away from the computer to give him my complete attention.

"First of all, do you believe that Jonathan has feelings for you?"

I reflected on his question carefully. "I don't know." I chose the cowardly response.

"Really? How would he react if he heard you say that?"

I shrugged my shoulders.

"Well?" he prodded.

"I guess he wouldn't like it," I admitted.

"So I'll ask you again. Do you believe he has feelings for you?"

"Yes," I sighed, "but why did he ignore me all week? If he really cared, wouldn't he *want* to talk to me, or see me?"

"I can guarantee you that he has no clue you're upset right now."

"Well, that's just ridiculous. How could any guy with half a brain not figure that out?" I asked rudely.

"That's part of the grand mystery between men and women. We *don't* figure each other out," he declared. "That's why there's so much passion when you fall in love."

Love?

"Who said anything about love?" I asked incredulously.

Uncle Connor grinned and shook his head. "I'll leave that for you to figure out." He chuckled when he saw my expression. "I will tell you this much," he offered, "you should probably give him the benefit of the doubt."

"Oh please. Last week you were ready to kill him," I said sarcastically.

"Well, let's just say that I care about *you* more than I dislike *him*." He nudged my arm and smiled. His Irish eyes sparkled with mischief.

"Then I probably shouldn't have sent that e-mail," I sighed.

"You already sent a reply?"

"Sort of," I cringed.

"What did it say?"

"It said, 'Fine!'" I admitted sheepishly. "Should I send him another one?"

"You won't have to," Uncle Connor laughed heartily. "My guess is that one way or another, he'll figure out a way to see you."

I considered that for a moment, but decided not to get my hopes up. However, that didn't stop my heart from leaping when the doorbell rang about thirty minutes later. I wasn't surprised when Uncle Connor announced that the pizza had arrived, but I admit I was disappointed. As it turned out, Jonathan did not come by that evening, but he did respond to my e-mail.

Are you okay? ??? ??? ???

I snickered at his use of so many question marks. My talk with Uncle Connor had softened my anger to the point that all I could think about was how glad I was to hear from him—finally!

I'm fine. Busy week. How about you?

I tried to keep my tone friendly; I wondered if that would transfer across internet lines. It only took a few minutes for him to reply.

Can I see you tomorrow?

I was still miffed about him ignoring me all week but the thought of seeing him. . . .

Sure. What do you have in mind?

Not that I cared much.

Bike ride. Dress warm. Pick you up at nine.

A bike ride? Was he kidding? The days were hovering in the high fifties. Who rides a bike when it's that cold? Before I could respond, he sent another message.

Okay, ten :)

I couldn't help but laugh. I was definitely not a morning person; he seemed to have figured that out.

See you then, I replied.

A few minutes passed before I heard the e-mail signal again.

I bet you look adorable right now. See you in the morning. G'nite :)

By the time I wandered out for dinner, the pizza was cold, but I didn't care. It was the best tasting slice of pizza I'd ever eaten. Uncle Connor eyed me from his chair and grinned.

"Well, your mood has certainly changed. Must have heard from Prince Charming, eh?"

I nodded, and I didn't even care that I was blushing. "We're going on a bike ride tomorrow morning."

"Dress warm," he chuckled.

When I went back to my room to get ready for bed, I had another e-mail message waiting. I hurriedly opened the window, but I didn't recognize the sender. I was about to delete the message thinking it was probably spam but the name in the subject box caught my eye. *Bethyanne.* My mother used to call me *Beth Anne* when she was upset with me, but there was only one person who ever called me Bethy. I quickly opened the e-mail.

Hey, kiddo. Did you like the gift I left for you? Wish it could have been a convertible sports car but let's face it, who drives a convertible in the winter in Wyoming? I'm sure Dad has already dismantled some of my handiwork, but don't let him take all the fun out of it for you. Try to stay out of the courthouse 'till I get back, okay? Dad tells me you hooked up with Jonathan Rollings. I should have figured that one out on my own. He's cool . . . just keep an open mind :)

Carl.

P.S. If you hear from your father, let him know things are on schedule. And smile, Cuz!

I stared at the e-mail, not quite certain what to make of it. Carl knew Jonathan too? Why hadn't Jonathan mentioned that before? And why was Carl sending a message to my father through me?

As I climbed sleepily between the crisp cotton sheets of my bed and pulled the down comforter securely around me, I was about to drift into a contented slumber when an unexpected draft of air hummed softly through the shutters. I sighed, crawled out of bed, and shuffled to the window; everything appeared solid. I double-checked the locks and ran my hands along the edge of the pane to make sure the seal was tight. I was just about to pull the shutters closed when something in the shadows outside caught my eye. I stood still, watching, waiting for another sign of movement, but there was none. It must have been an animal of some kind I finally determined; either that or my eyes were playing tricks on me.

Intruder

CHAPTER 7

*J*onathan arrived promptly at ten the following morning. I was still in my bedroom trying to decide if I should wear my red button-down blouse or my blue pullover sweater. I decided it didn't matter since I would be bundled in a jacket for most of the day. I was still adjusting to the cooler temperatures even though the locals considered temperatures in the fifties and sixties reasonably warm.

From my bedroom, I could hear the low murmur of voices and though I was unable to discern what they were saying, I knew the voices belonged to Uncle Connor and Jonathan. I crept down the hall not wanting to interrupt them. I was secretly hoping to hear what they were saying, accidentally, of course, but when I reached the living room, the conversation ended abruptly. Uncle Connor had said something about it being "too soon" and "you should have given her more time."

"More time for what?" I asked casually. Jonathan and Uncle Connor exchanged a quick glance and instantly their expressions changed.

"More time for you to sleep in," Uncle Connor replied. His smile was forced.

"She looks rested enough to me." Jonathan's smile was not forced and it changed the room from dull to bright in an instant. He was wearing a long-sleeved blue and red rugby shirt with the sleeves pushed up on his forearms. His eyes were sheltered under the brim of a red baseball cap but even in the shadows they twinkled when he looked at me. I reminded myself that I was supposed to be mad at him.

"Hi, Jonathan," I said, blushing the moment his name rolled from my lips. Uncle Connor made a gesture as though he were batting away an annoying fly.

"Good morning," Jonathan replied cheerfully. "You ready?"

"I guess so." The hesitation in my answer had nothing to do with Jonathan; I was anxious to be with him. It was the thought of spending the day on a bicycle that bothered me. I knew that even though the sun was shining brightly, when I walked outdoors I would be slapped with a blast of cold air. I still found it a mystery that the sun could be so bright and yet the air so cold.

"Where are you headed?" Uncle Connor directed his question at Jonathan.

"Thought I'd take her on the river trail that leads to the falls beyond Fisherman's Creek."

"Hmph," Uncle Connor grunted.

"I don't know though, it's probably too cold for her thin blood," Jonathan added with an ornery grin. He nudged me in the arm jokingly as we started to leave.

As soon as he opened the door, I spotted two bicycles strapped to the bed of an old, noticeably well-used truck. "Whose truck?" I asked as we reached the driveway.

"Mine," he replied, making a face as though that should have been obvious.

"You have a car *and* a truck?"

He shrugged and then opened the door for me and helped me inside. He drove about twenty miles outside of town before pulling onto a dirt path that led toward the foothills. The narrow road wound around the hills, twisting and turning in tight curves. My stomach began to feel queasy the further we went, lurching and churning with each swerve of the truck.

"How much farther?" I groaned through my tightly clenched jaw. I focused on breathing deeply as I clutched the handle next to the passenger's seat. Jonathan glanced at me and then quickly spun back for a second look.

"Beth, you're pale as a ghost!" he exclaimed, utterly surprised by the look of agony on my face.

"Green might be a better description," I moaned.

He pulled the car to the side of the road and walked around to open the door for me. I turned around and started to get out, but he rested his hand on my shoulder to keep me seated.

"Maybe you should sit still for a minute," he suggested, steadying me.

"I'd rather walk, if that's okay."

"Sure," he replied, and lifted me down. He curled his arm around my shoulder, supporting my weight against his side as we walked along the dirt path.

"Better?" he asked after several minutes.

I nodded and then breathed a heavy sigh of relief.

Jonathan chuckled softly. He turned to face me, resting both of his hands on my shoulders. He bent his head down so he could look squarely into my eyes. "Tell me something." His crystal eyes looked concerned.

"What?"

"Were you mad at me last night?" He tilted his head slightly and watched my reaction. I turned my head away, embarrassed by the accusation, but he put his hand under my chin and gently forced me to face him. His face was only inches from mine. "You were," he confirmed. He studied my eyes, searching for something.

"Maybe . . . a little," I half admitted. I tried to shrug and look away, but the tug of his hand under my chin redirected my eyes back to his.

"Why?"

"I . . . it was nothing, really."

"Why?" he repeated softly. He brushed a strand of hair away from my face. My eyes closed, reacting to the tenderness of his touch. I sighed quietly, afraid that if I opened my eyes he would read the truth in them. All at once, I felt the warmth of his lips against mine, lightly at first, then more firmly. Caught completely by surprise, I gasped. By the time I realized what was happening, his lips were gone and so was the moment.

My eyes flashed open wide. Jonathan was watching me carefully. His mouth twitched as he fought to restrain a smile. He examined my eyes for a moment, and then burst out laughing.

"What?" I demanded.

I hadn't kissed many boys; in fact, Adam was the only one I'd ever kissed on the mouth. But even with my limited experience, I knew that laughing was not a good sign. Besides, Jonathan *stole* that kiss—our first kiss, the kiss I had been waiting for—and I'd missed it. It wasn't fair. I could feel my eyebrows pull together as I grasped the full measure of what had just happened. Jonathan continued to study my face and it only made him laugh harder, in spite of the fact that he was pressing his lips together. His sapphire eyes danced victoriously.

"Tell me why you were mad at me," he urged again, chuckling through the words.

The realization that he had just stolen our first kiss made it easier for me to admit that I *was* angry with him last night. "You ignored me all week. Then last night your e-mail was so, 'how was your week?'" I sneered, imitating his voice.

Jonathan continued to look amused, but I could tell by the way his eyes moved from side to side that he was searching for something. Slowly the humor in his expression faded.

"You thought I was ignoring you?"

"What else would I think? You didn't show up after school. You didn't call or text or even send an e-mail all week." The words sounded childish and irrational, and part of me wished I'd kept my mouth shut.

"I'm . . . sorry." He paused briefly, then added, "I didn't know. I was looking for—"

"How could you *not* know?" I interrupted. "We spent the whole day together at the lake and then the night at the ranch. It was so great and you were so sweet and then . . . nothing." I made an animated gesture with my arm to emphasize my frustration. The German in me had surfaced; I could tell because my chin shot forward just like my dad's did when he was angry.

"Last weekend was great for me as well." His voice was tender and sincere and to my surprise, not defensive. "I thought about you all week. It never occurred to me that you would doubt that."

I sighed, looking apprehensively into his perfectly sincere eyes.

"I'm sorry, Beth. Truly."

"It's okay now," I shrugged.

"Come here. I have something to show you." He reached for my hand and we walked back to his truck. He helped me inside, then walked around to the driver's door. Once he was seated, he shot a sidelong glance at me and his face broke into a boyish grin.

"What now?" I sighed, self-conscious that I amused him so much.

He reached across me and opened the glove compartment. Inside was a shiny, navy blue box. "I got you something while I was . . . traveling this week."

A wave of regret washed over my face as he handed me the box. I suddenly felt like an idiot.

"Go on, open it," he urged.

The weight of the box surprised me; it was quite heavy. I pulled the laminated lid off the box and unfolded several layers of blue tissue paper. Tucked snugly in a blue, felt-covered case was a solid crystal prism. Jonathan pulled the prism from its place and held it up to the window.

"Look at this," he said, rotating the prism in the sunlight.

Embedded in the center of the crystal was a treble clef insignia. Colorful beams of light shot in all directions as the symbol refracted the sun's rays.

"Oh, Jonathan!" I whispered. "It's beautiful!"

"You see? I really was thinking about you this week."

He winked at me and I felt instantly small. I breathed a deep, repentant sigh. Could I possibly feel any more foolish?

Jonathan sat back in his seat and folded his hands behind his head. He looked very pleased with himself. "I just realized something," he chuckled smugly.

"What?" I was almost afraid to ask.

"I guess you could say we just had our first fight . . . only I missed most of it." His grin turned into a smirk.

I considered that for a moment. Then I thought about the way he'd snuck that kiss from me earlier, and I glared at him with feigned reproach. "I guess that makes us even," I said, mirroring his smugness.

"How's that?"

"I guess you could say we just had our first kiss . . . only I missed most of it," I sneered jokingly. But then I blushed shamelessly. Jonathan burst out laughing again and this time I joined him.

"Okay, we're even," he chided. "But . . ."

I looked at him questioningly, waiting for him to complete his sentence.

"I wouldn't take it back," he chuckled. "I wish you could have seen the look on your face. I wouldn't have missed that for anything. *That* was priceless."

I pursed my lips and rolled my eyes at him. "Would you give me a little warning next time you plan to kiss me?" I asked, hopeful that he *was* planning to kiss me again.

"I'll work on my approach," he nodded and winked at me, still chuckling.

The bike ride turned out to be much more enjoyable than I originally anticipated. The air was surprisingly warm. The thermometer claimed the temperature reached a whopping high of sixty-two degrees. The waterfalls were beautiful—unlike any I had seen—and even though I was unable to clasp the handlebars with my left hand, I found I could use my wrist for balance. Riding the bike was not as difficult as I had feared it would be.

When we arrived back in town, we stopped for hamburgers and a milk shake before returning to Uncle Connor's house. Uncle Connor had gone to Jackson Hole again with Marci, so Jonathan and I had the house to ourselves. We sat comfortably together on the couch with our feet propped up on the coffee table and our fingers loosely clasped, resting on his leg.

I stared absentmindedly at the crystal prism now sitting on the end table where it reflected the sun's rays. The treble clef emblem reminded me of the duets I'd played with Jonathan. My part was always the right hand except for the day he'd placed my left hand on his, the day I heard Eleanor's theme for the first time.

"Jonathan," I spoke softly, breaking the comfortable silence.

"Hmm," he replied lazily.

"Will you tell me about Eleanor?"

Jonathan stiffened slightly, but quickly relaxed. "What do you want to know?"

"Who was she? You said she lived a long time ago."

"Yes."

"Was she a relative of yours?" I glanced up to watch Jonathan's expression. He appeared to be deep in thought but confused at the same time.

"No. Why would you think that?"

"You have a . . ." I stopped short. I wasn't ready to confess that I'd been in his room. "It's just a guess."

Jonathan began to rub his fingers lightly back and forth across mine. "No, she wasn't a relative," he said thoughtfully. "She was sort of a friend of the family."

"Hmmm. Then what about her composition? Who'd she write it for?"

Jonathan bit his lips and stared thoughtfully at his shoes. "She wrote it for a soldier during the Civil War. He was away at the time."

"And he never came back?" I asked, trying to fill in the blanks.

"He came back . . . but fate had other plans for the two of them." Jonathan noticed the question in my eyes. "Fate can be cruelly ironic sometimes," he added.

I understood the cruel irony of fate all too well. "How sad. Is that why she never finished the piece?"

"Perhaps," Jonathan said thoughtfully. "It never occurred to me that it was incomplete until you mentioned it."

Jonathan let go of my hand and put his arm around me, pulling me close so I could rest my head on his shoulder. He gently stroked my cheek with his free hand, letting the back of his fingers trace the side of my face and along my jawbone. He turned my face toward his and stared warmly into my eyes. His gaze trailed slowly downward until his eyes rested on my lips. My heart fluttered unwittingly.

"Beth," he whispered, "there's something you should know. . . ." Before he could finish his thought, there was a rattling sound at the front door and I backed away from him with a sudden jerk. Uncle Connor and Marci had returned earlier than I anticipated. Their timing couldn't have been worse.

"Hello, Beth," Marci spoke first as her eyes flickered from me to Jonathan.

"Hi, Marci. This is Jonathan Rollings. Jonathan . . . Marci."

"I figured as much," she said smiling. "It's good to see you, Jonathan."

Marci's choice of words seemed odd to me, but I dismissed them when Uncle Connor came through the door.

"Hey kids," he said, his eyes taking in the scene of Jonathan and me sitting together on the couch. "What time is your shindig tonight?"

I had completely forgotten about my plans for the evening and I suddenly felt uneasy that Uncle Connor had brought it up in front of Jonathan.

"They're picking me up at eight," I reported, careful not to mention any names. Eric had backed off finally, but I wasn't sure how Jonathan would react if he knew Eric would be there tonight. I caught a glimpse of Jonathan through the corner of my eye, his eyebrows raised slightly. I turned to face him as an idea quickly formed in my mind. "Do you want to come with us to hear some ghost stories?"

"Tonight?"

"Yeah."

"Sorry," he replied. "I promised Grace I'd be home to help her with some unfinished business."

"Oh," I said, pouting. My disappointment was obvious.

"Where will you be?" he asked.

"I don't know exactly, somewhere up the canyon east of town along the summit. We're building a bonfire for the juniors."

"Ahhhhh," he muttered knowingly, "the senior tradition." He nodded once and then glanced at Uncle Connor before he turned back to me. "Are you staying the night?"

"You know about the tradition?" I asked, surprised.

"Beth," Uncle Connor interrupted, "everyone in Andersen knows about it." Then he glanced at Jonathan. "She's only staying until midnight."

"I wish you could come with us," I said, turning back to Jonathan.

"I would," he hesitated, "but I don't know how long Grace will need me. In fact, I should probably head back now." He peered at the antique clock on the wall and then stood to leave. I walked with him to his truck, hoping to say goodbye in private. He climbed in and rolled down his window.

"Will you call me when you get home?" he asked.

"That late?"

He raised one eyebrow and tilted his head to the side, waiting for me to answer his question.

"Sure."

"Thank you." He pulled on his seat belt, started the engine, and shifted into reverse. "Don't let the stories scare you back to California," he joked, winking as he pulled away.

Eric arrived just before eight. Uncle Connor was still skeptical about me attending the bonfire but he remained silent as I gathered my coat and scarf. When I got to Eric's truck, I noticed there were several carved pumpkins in the back.

"Are those for tonight?" I asked.

"Yup."

"Very cool," I replied.

We were supposed to pick up Darla, Evan, and Crystal, but as Eric drove along the main road, he didn't take the turn to Darla's house. Instead, he continued toward the main highway.

"What about Darla?" I asked.

"What about her?"

"Aren't we picking her and the others up?"

"Nope. Darla's hanging out with Evan. Crystal got another ride."

"They're meeting us there?" An uneasy feeling formed in the pit of my stomach.

"I don't know. They don't report to me," he retorted. Then he reached across his seat, put his hand on my leg, and squeezed my thigh just above the knee. I stiffened like stone and jerked my leg out from under his hand. He glanced in my direction briefly and chuckled. "What's up with you? Relax, would you? Why so tense?"

Overconfident, cocky Eric had returned.

"Cut it out, Eric," I demanded, "or you can take me home." I turned my body away from his and tapped the floor of his truck nervously with my foot.

"Geez, it's no big deal, you know." He rolled his eyes and spoke as if I'd made some outrageous presumption.

Eric ignored my uneasiness, but he was obviously annoyed by my defensive posture. His behavior was unusual tonight; he seemed aggressive, almost hostile. I began to plan my exit strategy; I decided I'd ditch Eric sometime during the evening and ask Darla and Evan for a ride home.

We parked in a clearing at the base of the summit and waited for the rest of our friends to arrive. One by one more cars showed up, each with one boy and one girl inside. Naively, I wondered why more people weren't carpooling. Crystal arrived with Tom Stewart, which surprised me because I'd heard they were an item last year but went through a horrible breakup over the summer. Marta Simpson showed up with Jack Zimmerman. That was no surprise. They'd been glued together ever since Homecoming. Other couples arrived. Some I recognized, but they weren't from the group we normally hung out with at school. Two-by-two, they gathered at the tailgate of Eric's truck, each preparing to carry a carved pumpkin up the hill.

By nine o'clock, Darla and Evan had not arrived. I questioned Eric about them and he admitted that they might not make it because Evan planned to take Darla to some infamous spook alley in Jackson Hole.

"Are you kidding me?" I glared at Eric. I was seething. Jonathan had told me that he didn't like the idea of Eric and me together, yet here I was and now it was out of my control. I couldn't shake the feeling that this would upset Jonathan.

The hike from the clearing to the summit was only about half a mile, but in the frosty night air it felt much farther. It was a cloudless, moonless night and in spite of the massive array of stars that glimmered above us, it was especially dark. The walk along the narrow trail of switchbacks was an eerie sight—nothing but the flickering orange glow of ghoulish pumpkins lighted the path before us. Even the pumpkins with happy faces carved in them appeared ominous and hauntingly deceitful. I'm normally not a person who freaks out easily, but it reminded me of a procession of unsuspecting victims in a scene from an old black and white horror movie.

We finally reached the summit where a large, flat clearing overlooked Andersen. Lights from the town sparkled in the distance. Towering fir trees surrounded us on three sides and as they swayed robotically in the wind, they looked like giant, black creatures slowly coming to life.

We lined the perimeter of the clearing with the glowing jack-o'-lanterns and began building the bonfire in the center. The popping flames of the fire licked the night air, providing warm relief against the cold. I checked the zipper on my coat, pulling it as high as it would go.

The crowd was much smaller than I'd anticipated. I was under the impression that about a hundred kids would show up—but as I counted heads, there were only twenty of us, evenly paired. *How convenient.*

After the bonfire was securely blazing, two of the boys hiked down the trail to get the food and a cooler of drinks. About an hour later, they returned and began passing around cans of beer. My stomach tightened as I heard can after can pop open and watched heads tilt back to guzzle the contents in one breath. Eric passed several cans to me, but I refused them. A couple of the guys began to give Eric a hard time about his "girlfriend" being a little uptight.

"Nah, she's cool," I heard Eric say several times. "She just has a weak stomach."

The scene before me was one I never dreamed I'd be part of—the kind of scene I would hear about and roll my eyes because it sounded so far-fetched. I wanted to go home, but I didn't want to make a spectacle of myself or be the goody-girl that everyone would make fun of at school the following week, so I sat quietly, nervously waiting for midnight when Eric would take me home.

The party was jubilant as couples recounted stories of different outings they'd been on or teachers they'd harassed in the past. But around eleven the mood shifted, putting every nerve in my body on alert. Tom and Crystal were the first couple to disappear into the trees. They were followed by Marta and Jack who disappeared into a different area. By eleven thirty, it was clear there would be no stories of local legends or ghosts. Feeling utterly foolish, it dawned on me that the tradition here was not to induct juniors through some rite of passage, at least not by scaring them with tales of terror. The only purpose of *this* evening was to drink—and participate in a group make-out marathon.

I had left my phone in Eric's truck. I wondered if I could find my way down the path to call Uncle Connor without getting lost or being noticed, but Eric made sure I stayed next to him all evening. His speech became more slurred and lewd as the evening progressed. When he put his arm around me and used forcible strength to pull me next to him, I made my stand—cool or not.

"Eric, take me home. Now!" I demanded.

"It's not midnight yet." His sloppy speech turned my stomach.

"I don't care, I want to go home," I insisted.

"Ah, c'mon . . . just a little longer," he whined. "Besides," he slurred, "I can't drive, so you'll have to wait." His eyes were not his own—they were a glazed over, hazier version of the friendly boy I knew.

The wind stirred, casting ash flurries around the bonfire. The brisk mountain air which had smelled of burning wood earlier in the evening now reeked with the combined odors of alcohol and cigarette smoke.

"Give me the keys!" I ordered. "I'll drive." I spoke louder this time and several heads snapped around to stare at us.

"You'll just have to come and get them," he sputtered in sickening mockery.

I'm not sure what my plan was, but at that moment the only thing I could think of was to get away. I didn't care that Eric had the keys; I'd break his truck's window if necessary to retrieve my phone. I stood up angrily and brushed the loose dirt and pine needles from the seat of my pants. As I started to leave, Eric grabbed my ankle and yanked me back.

"Where do you think you're going?" he scowled. The other couples broke out in hideous bellows of laughter.

"Let go of me, Eric!" I snarled. "Now!"

I yanked my foot free and marched toward an opening beneath the monster trees that led to the trail.

"Oooooh, Eric, you've been told," a voice from the group jeered.

"Yeah, Eric, maybe you should let someone more experienced handle her," another volunteered suggestively.

"Shut up!" Eric growled. I heard the crackling sound of pine needles and swung around nervously. Eric was coming after me. His determined expression frightened me so I turned toward the black forest and started running.

"Damn it, Beth!" Eric ranted as he stormed after me. "Stop!"

I ran in the opposite direction of Eric's voice, but I had no idea where I was or where I was going. A sharp succession of branches and pine needles scraped against my face and coat as I pushed my way through the darkness, clutching at rough tree trunks to maintain my balance. Fallen branches and roots tore relentlessly against my pant legs while my hands battled tangled webs of sharp twigs. Soon

I could feel the warm sensation of blood oozing across the backs of my hands.

Stumbling recklessly along the uneven terrain, I flung my arms out blindly in front of me in an attempt to shield my face from the low-hanging branches. But I lost my footing when I tripped over a fallen tree. Fortunately, my coat padded the fall and I was able to quickly get back on my feet. I only had one thing in mind as I plowed through the black obstacle course—escape.

I could hear Eric yelling, angrily spewing a string of swear words as he pursued me through the trees. It didn't take long for him to catch up and I felt the force of his large hand on the back of my shoulder as he shoved me to the ground. Instinctively, my hands flew up in front of me to break my fall, but the minute my left hand hit the ground it folded, sending tremors of pain exploding up my arm as my face smashed into a bed of dead leaves and sharp pine needles.

Eric's body towered over mine in the dim starlight. He flipped me over onto my back so that I was looking up into his eyes, eyes that were now wild and unrecognizable. In a matter of seconds he was on top of me, pinning my shoulders to the ground with his massive arm.

Tears spilled down the sides of my face. The pain in my hand was excruciating, but I was so overcome with fear that adrenaline took over. I reached for Eric's jacket in an attempt to claw my way free from his grasp. He growled furiously and shoved my shoulders sharply against the ground. I tried twisting my hips and legs but his violent strength was too much for me. In one effortless move, he yanked my arms over my head and clutched both of my wrists in one hand, pinning them to the ground. Then he pressed his elbow against my chest, holding me down with such force that it was difficult to breathe. Using his legs and torso, he forced my knees to the ground so I couldn't move beneath him.

I shook my head back and forth furiously. "Please, Eric . . . please. Please don't do this," I whimpered, but he didn't budge. He used his free hand to grab my face and turn it toward him, holding it firmly in front of him. His hot breath stung my icy cheeks. He reeked of beer and cigarettes and the smell of burning wood.

"Beth . . ." he breathed, his voice coarse and raspy against my ear. He rested his face against mine, panting heavily, the weight of his body pressed firmly against mine. Then his breathing began to change from winded and staggered to aroused and heavy.

He slowly lifted his face off mine but didn't ease his iron grip. "Beth," he moaned, his eyes full of unbridled hunger as he focused on my lips.

"Eric. No! Please, don't!" I struggled for breath under his stone-heavy weight.

His eyes lifted to mine and he released a deep, tortured groan. I could tell by his breathing and the way his body was positioned over mine that he had no intention of stopping.

"Eric, please!" I pleaded. I began to sob.

"Beth . . ." his voice choked and he started to shake. "I-I can't—"

The words stuck in his throat. His face twisted and became distorted and another low, tortured groan escaped his lips.

Suddenly, his eyes glazed over, turning a milky yellow; then they slowly rolled backwards into his eye sockets, leaving nothing but the whites. At first I thought he was having some sort of seizure. But no seizure could explain what happened next. The whites of his eyes began to glow like two bright lights and then his eyes slowly rolled downward, locking into their normal position. But the eyes that stared at me were not Eric's; they were bright yellow, ringed with black.

The golden eyes smiled down at me lustfully and a brief flash of recognition raced through my mind. A scream of pure panic formed in my throat, but when I opened my trembling mouth, no sound escaped. I fought, wild-eyed and frightened, gasping for enough breath to unleash my voice; but a high, shrill screech was all I could force from my paralyzed lungs. He quickly clasped his over-sized hand tightly over my mouth, blocking out my anguished cries.

"Hello, Beth Anne," he said smoothly in a mocking, exaggerated tone. It was Eric's voice, but it wasn't Eric who was speaking. Somewhere deep within me a memory stirred, but the details that lay entombed and inaccessible were neither comforting nor reassuring.

Overcome by fear, I resorted to the only defense I had left. With great effort, I relaxed the muscles in my face and allowed his fingers to push inward against my lips. At the precise moment his fingers relaxed, I clamped down on them as hard as I could with my teeth. He yanked his hand away with a sputtered jerk, shaking it and clenching his fist. His glowering, ferocious eyes bored into mine with full intensity. As soon as I could suck in enough air to fill my burning lungs, I screamed with every ounce of strength I could muster. He raised his hand into the air, palm open, to strike me. I closed my eyes and scrunched my face tight, bracing myself for the inevitable blow.

Suddenly, the heavy weight of Eric's body was gone, sending a tingling rush of blood through my flattened veins. He hissed violently as his body flew backward, away from where I lay frozen in shock. A dark figure lifted Eric off the ground and hurled him into a nearby tree. As his body slammed against the massive tree trunk, the air rushed from his lungs and he fell to the ground in a crumpled heap.

Torn between gratitude and terror, I wrapped my body into a tight ball and rolled onto my side in a fetal position of self-defense. I began to hyperventilate, afraid that whatever force had thrown Eric off me would come for me next and finish what Eric had started. I gasped uncontrollably for air as I scrambled to my knees in an effort to stand. I wound my arms tightly around my waist as I tried to regain my footing, but my knees were too weak to support my weight. Collapsing onto the ground, I buried my face in a tangled bed of debris, sobbing hopelessly in self-defeat.

"Beth," a voice called urgently. "Beth, can you hear me?"

My mind instantly recognized Jonathan's voice but my body couldn't respond. My arms locked tightly across my chest and I rocked back and forth, afraid that if I let go I would fall apart. In an instant his arms were around me, pulling me to him.

"Beth," he said again in a reassuring whisper. "It's okay."

Jonathan propped my weight against the lower portion of his thighs and pulled me to my feet. Carefully, he steadied me until he was sure my legs were firmly planted. He wrapped his arm around my waist and led me away from the place where Eric still lay limply against the tree.

"Hang on, Beth, the path isn't too far—just beyond this cluster of trees." Jonathan's voice was reassuring but I wasn't comforted. My brain couldn't make sense of what had just happened. I trembled, too stunned by what I had seen in Eric's eyes—the vicious eyes that were clearly not his own. Eric was many things, but he was not evil or violent. He was aggressive on the football field, understandably so, but his basic nature was carefree and happy.

I shuddered and Jonathan tightened his grip as we made our way along the winding switchbacks. Through the trees I began to make out the slight glint of a shiny object ahead of us. Jonathan squeezed my side gently and pointed forward.

"My truck is just beyond this last row of trees. It's not much farth—"

The last word hung in the air, interrupted by a horrific "thud" followed by a blood curdling "snap." Jonathan suddenly went rigid, dropping his hand from my side. I whirled around to face him. His eyes were wide with shock and his mouth gaped open. His breath flew from his lungs in an agonizing moan as he dropped to his knees. He tumbled awkwardly to one side, gasping for air as he sprawled out on the ground writing in pain. Eric stood, triumphant, over Jonathan's fallen body. He was holding what looked like a large limb from a tree in both his hands, clutched as though he were swinging a baseball bat. He tossed the limb to the side and lunged toward me.

I froze.

The nearby trees swirled around me as my legs crumbled. In one fluid movement, Eric snatched me mid-fall and cradled my body against his as though he were running with a football. But instead of running forward he jerked sideways, heading toward the thickness of the trees.

"Time to finish what we began," he snarled, his breath hot against my face.

"Eric!" Jonathan bellowed indignantly from behind us. "Put her down!" His voice was icy cold, forceful, and laced with fury. Eric sputtered a mocking laugh and then tossed me across the pathway as if he were discarding some unwanted trash. I was terrified by his abnormal strength. He threw me as easily as he had thrown the limb a moment earlier. I hit the ground and skidded to an abrupt stop as I slammed against a nearby tree, gasping and sputtering as I struggled for control.

Eric spun around to face Jonathan who was still sprawled on the ground holding his right leg. I could still see the evil smirk on Eric's face as he gazed scornfully at Jonathan's crooked body. Jonathan glowered ferociously at Eric. And then, to my utter disbelief, with a steady, determined movement he stood, firmly planting his weight on his good leg and rising to his full height. His right leg was bent grotesquely away from his body just above the knee. As he stood, he closed his eyes and inhaled deeply. He held his breath for a moment and then opened his eyes slowly. His eyes were cold and glorious, emitting a stifling, determined confidence. Eric watched with curious pleasure as Jonathan teetered to retain his footing.

What happened next washed the amusement from Eric's face. If I hadn't seen it myself, I would not have believed it.

Jonathan's broken leg began to shift itself, twisting at peculiar angles until, increment by increment, it was completely set in place—whole. He adjusted his body and exhaled a ferocious sigh that set every hair on my body on edge. Then in one graceful, lion-like movement, Jonathan pounced forward knocking Eric onto his back.

Eric gazed up at him, disabled by shock. He tried weakly to scramble to his feet but Jonathan stretched back his leg and swung it around, heaving it into Eric's chest with such force that Eric flew back several feet and crumpled to the ground, gasping for air. Jonathan stalked forward and reached down, clutching Eric's upper arms. He drew in a deep breath and flung Eric forward, sending him face first into the dirt. Eric clutched desperately at the ground, clambering to regain his footing. He managed to wiggle himself to one knee but Jonathan lunged forward with his arms cocked back to his side, hands clasped together, and swung with fearsome force at the side of Eric's face. The movement was smooth and solid, similar to a skilled tennis player hitting a backhand shot from the baseline of a tennis court. Eric's head snapped back and then sideways. His eyes rolled back into his head and his body dropped limply to the ground.

Jonathan stood over Eric's motionless body, panting heavily, as he watched for signs of movement. He bent down, resting his hands on his thighs and inhaled deeply until he regained control of his breathing. Then he turned to face me.

I was wide-eyed and frozen, my body still trembling, unable to move, speak, or process what I had just witnessed. The world around me began to spin and my body wavered as I struggled to focus. I wanted desperately to find something solid to hold on to, but everything around me was moving too quickly—trees, branches, stars, pine needles, dirt, each spiraling in circles around me. My stomach knotted and heaved. I wanted to throw up but my brain could not send the message. I felt my head flop backwards just before everything faded into total blackness.

There's a place in my mind where I am neither conscious nor unconscious but safely at rest, free from fear, pain, and choice. In this state, I pass through various levels of awareness. The hypnotist who treated me after the car accident suggested that this was a form of self-hypnosis fashioned by my mind as a coping mechanism for the severe emotional and physical pain that I had experienced.

It was in this state of mind that I found myself now—only this time, I wasn't able to slip peacefully into a comatose state of emotional reprieve. This time I found myself face to face with the memory of a night even more terrifying and disturbing than the one I'd just experienced. Tonight I would watch my mother die—again. And I would view it in vivid detail.

The vision began with the realization that I was pinned by something extremely heavy, the weight of which made it impossible for me to inhale fully. I could see the suspended wheel of my mother's car through the corner of my eye and I could smell the odor of hot, rancid oil mixed with singed flesh. The image of my mother's face flashed like snapshots before me: first smiling, then angry, then horror-struck, and finally desperate as she was pulled away by some force with power greater than her own. These images flashed quickly like an old-fashioned animation flip-book, each time ending with her desperate face pleading for me to take her hand. As the images flipped page by page before me, I noticed that her lips moved with desperate determination and her eyes grew wide with panic. She was trying to communicate something urgent, but I couldn't discern the words her lips were forming.

This scene repeated itself several times before I noticed that just before my mother's face disappeared, she slowly turned her head to the side as if directing me to follow her eyes. Each time the flip-book repeated its animation, my mother's face grew more intense and terrified as she turned her head. I tried earnestly to follow her gaze but I was powerless to move. Then in an instantaneous flash of light, I saw a set of yellow eyes encircled by bold, black lines just above my mother's head. The eyes glowed wickedly, framed in a victorious expression of satisfaction. Almost as quickly as they appeared the eyes disappeared, replaced by complete blackness.

In the distance, I heard a faint whisper.

"Hold on, Beth. Hold on."

Warm fingers pinched my nose together and a determined mouth covered mine, filling me with breath and life. My lungs rose and held, and then a weight on my chest pushed the air from them into the blackness. I felt the breath of life flow through me again, lifting me up and releasing me slowly. A dark weight pushed heavily on my chest and then he was gone.

No, don't go. I fought desperately to utter the words but there was no air inside me. I searched frantically for my voice but it was buried under the weight on my chest.

No, no, no. I tried to shake my head. *Please don't pin me down.* I struggled to open my eyes, focusing every ounce of my strength on my eyelids, commanding them to move; my efforts were in vain.

God, help me, I prayed silently into the darkness. In my mind, I pictured Eric's face just inches away from mine. I watched his eyes roll back into his head and return burning bright yellow. Slowly, the bold black line traced the circumference of his eyes until they were fully encircled. The eyes intensified their aim until the burning was so severe I had to turn away, sliding back into the darkness.

"Hold on, Beth." The voice of life returned. "Just hold on."

He was so close that his breath warmed the side of my face; the security of his arms cradled me. His arms were strong and comforting, and . . . real.

"Beth." The arms loosened their hold on me, and the voice grew louder, more demanding. "Beth. Look at me!" He ordered.

I felt the sensation of air moving around me. A haze lifted from my eyes as I drifted closer to the sound of the voice. Slowly, awareness set in. Someone was carrying me. It was Saturday night, Halloween. Jonathan was here. It was safe to open my eyes.

"Beth," Jonathan whispered in relief when my eyes met his.

"Where are we?" I muttered. My voice was raspy and jagged.

"Home, honey," he whispered. He tightened his arms around me and held me close. "You're home."

Revelation

CHAPTER 8

*T*he whimsical rhythm of a crackling fire hissed and popped as I lay on the familiar sofa covered with heavy blankets. The flames cast warm shadows that danced freely along the walls. I had no idea how long I had been there, but judging from the dark picture window it was sometime in the middle of the night. My heart beat evenly, no longer defending itself against the stifling fear that had overcome me earlier. In the safety of Uncle Connor's living room, I allowed my mind to retrace the unfathomable events of the evening, searching for some plausible explanation. My mind could not accept what I had witnessed with my own eyes.

In the kitchen, low murmurings seemed to be escalating into an argument, but both Uncle Connor and Jonathan held their voices to an animated whisper. I listened intently to every utterance, attempting to decipher their words.

"It's too soon," Uncle Connor whispered harshly.

"How can you say that? They've already made contact."

"You should have stayed away. . . ."

"That's absurd!"

"Let me finish," Uncle Connor insisted. "You should have waited. . . ."

"She needs to know something!" Jonathan hissed, emphasizing each word. "One of them attacked her, for heaven's sake."

"You can't be sure of that." There was a hint of doubt in Uncle Connor's voice.

"I've fought them before, or have you forgotten?"

"Of course not, but Eric is unnaturally strong," Uncle Connor challenged.

"Not strong enough to break my leg with a single swing." Jonathan spoke with exasperation. It sounded like he was gritting his teeth. "Do you realize how much strength that requires?"

"You could be mistaken, he might have—"

"He snapped it in two! There's no mistake."

"And Beth saw this?" Uncle Connor asked, unbelieving.

"More than that," Jonathan replied. "She watched it mend itself." There was a long, silent pause.

"This is most unfortunate," Uncle Connor finally said.

"Why?" Jonathan's whisper was strained. "You planned to tell her anyway."

"That was before, before her mother . . . She can't handle any more!"

I heard a loud, exasperated sigh that sounded almost like a frustrated growl. I assumed it belonged to Jonathan.

"She can handle more than you think."

"No."

"She'll want answers," Jonathan argued, "and I refuse to lie to her."

"It's not your decision, Jonathan."

"I don't care. Either *you* say something or I will."

A loud THUMP followed. I wasn't sure, but it sounded like one of them had slammed his fist on the table. Probably Uncle Connor.

"You don't have the authority." Uncle Connor's whisper had turned icy.

"I'm not afraid to act on my own." Jonathan's response was low and decided.

"Damn it, Jonathan!" Uncle Connor's voice was forceful, but desperate.

"Shh! You're going to wake her." Jonathan's tone hushed. "We can argue later."

A chair slid across the kitchen floor followed by the sound of deliberately quiet footsteps. In less than a minute, Jonathan stood next to the couch. I met his eyes as he peered down at me.

"You're awake." He forced a smile.

I lay motionless on the couch, confused and full of mixed emotions. He started to reach for me but pulled back, his face torn between uncertainty and a genuine desire to comfort me. Images of his blood, his broken leg, his ability to heal before my eyes flooded my mind, searching for an explanation that my mind would accept. Steroids, perhaps? The evidence suggested the obvious— Jonathan was not normal. Yet here he was, kneeling by my side, seeming every bit normal.

A gush of tears burst from my eyes. At that moment, I didn't care about answers; all I knew was that I was frightened and confused. In an act of sheer desperation, I reached for him. Jonathan folded his arms around me and held me tightly, rocking me gently back and forth.

"I'm so sorry," he whispered. "I'm so sorry."

When I woke the next morning, I was in my own bed. I was wearing one of Uncle Connor's T-shirts but I had no memory of changing my clothes. My eyes felt heavy and raw with a burning, almost bruised feeling behind them. I stumbled to my feet and teetered my way to the bathroom sink. The cold water felt refreshing as I splashed it on my face. I gazed up into the mirror and almost didn't recognize the face staring back at me. My eyelids had swollen to double their usual size and the skin around them was rough and red. My body felt sore; every joint ached. Had I not known better, I would have sworn I'd been in another car accident.

I moistened a washcloth with cold water and folded it into thirds so I could hold it against my eyes. The cold was instantly soothing. After a few minutes it relieved the pain enough that I began to notice the rancid taste in my mouth. I retrieved a bottle of mouthwash from the cabinet and gargled, then brushed my teeth. As I waited for the water in the shower to heat, I removed my clothes and surveyed the damage. The aching around my shoulders and thighs felt as if I'd been lifting extremely heavy weights. Yet even with all the discomfort, except for a line of four small bruises along each of my wrists, there were no noticeable marks on my body.

I studied the bruises on my arms, turning my wrists from side to side, and determined that Eric's fingers must have made them when he pinned me against the ground.

Eric, Eric, Eric! His name echoed in my mind. A sense of panic washed through me as I recalled seeing him motionless on the ground. I needed to know if he was okay, to understand what had happened to him. There were so many questions, and today I was determined to get some answers. Last night would not remain a mystery the way the night of my accident had; I would not allow it. And this time I knew exactly where to begin.

I half expected to find the house empty when I emerged from my bedroom. Instead, I found Uncle Connor sitting in his chair holding a thick three-ring binder on his lap. His eyes were bloodshot and tired. He watched with apprehension as I approached and then motioned for me to sit in the chair opposite him.

"Are you all right?" I asked reluctantly.

He chuckled without smiling. "Shouldn't I be the one asking that question?"

"I need to know what's going on," I replied calmly but firmly.

Again he nodded, and then handed me the binder. I examined it carefully before opening it to the first page. There in bold print was the title: ***Immortality: The Eternal Nature of Man.***

Immortality . . . immortality . . . immortality. The word seemed to blink on and off as if powered by a neon light, but it was my eyes that were blinking, blinking to see if the letters would somehow rearrange themselves if I continued to open and close my eyes. I raised my head slowly and turned to face Uncle Connor. He looked away.

"I . . . don't understand," I muttered.

"This is what your mother was working on before she . . . before the accident," he said somberly. "There are half a dozen more binders like this in the basement."

"She was writing about life after death?" I asked, puzzled.

Uncle Connor folded his hands together and rested his chin on them. He eyed me for a moment before speaking again.

"Do you believe in God, Beth?"

I had no idea where this question came from but I went along.

"I don't know," I said, shrugging my shoulders. "I suppose I believe in *some* kind of all-knowing power or being."

"What do you know about the story of Adam and Eve?"

I sat back, trying to connect the dots. "You mean from the Bible?"

Uncle Connor nodded. "In the Book of Genesis."

"Not that much. They ate some fruit and got into trouble."

My family was not religious so my knowledge of the Bible was limited, but I knew my mom had read it often. She believed she needed a balance of both science *and* religion in order to understand the laws governing the universe.

"It's not that they got in trouble; when Adam and Eve ate the forbidden fruit they . . . changed." Uncle Connor watched my expression, waiting for some sign of enlightenment or understanding. "They *became* mortal." He spoke the words slowly and precisely.

"So?"

"Don't you see, Beth? They weren't *created* as mortals; they *became* mortal because of the choice they made."

I shook my head slowly, trying to understand what he was implying.

"God's first creations were *im*mortal." He paused, allowing that to sink in.

"So what? God made immortals. How does that have anything to do with what happened last night?"

"What if Adam and Eve were not the *only* immortals God created? What if there were others? What if there were immortals that did *not* change when Adam and Eve did? And what if those immortals were still here, trapped in this world?" He let his string of questions hang in the air as I absorbed them and considered their ramifications.

"But that's impossible . . . isn't it?"

"No, it's not impossible," he replied unequivocally. "If God has the power to create both mortals and immortals, is it such a stretch to consider the possibility that *both* might exist in our world? Those who were created at the same time as Adam and Eve remained immortal after the earth changed to a mortal sphere. They wouldn't have known what was happening. Because of mixed marriages between mortals and immortals, the genetic make-up of immortal children underwent a form of mutation, and the result was a race of beings that were . . . special."

My mouth hung open in disbelief. *Was it possible?*

"Just suppose," I said, thinking aloud, "that I don't believe in God. How would science explain what you're suggesting?"

The corner of Uncle Connor's mouth hinted at a half smile and he nodded. "You are so like your mother." He gestured to the binder in my lap. "As a scientist, I invite you to examine the evidence."

"Are you suggesting there's scientific proof that these immortals exist?"

"In a manner of speaking, yes. But research only confirms that immortality is *possible.*"

"But how?"

"Several years ago a group of genetic researchers discovered that human cells have a memory. When scientists altered specific genetic codes in certain humans, the cells 'reverted' to an immortal state, a state that prevented them from dying. It was as if the cells were 'reclaiming' their original, immortal properties. The reclamation proved to be irreversible."

I started putting the puzzle pieces together. "Are you suggesting that Jonathan is somehow a product of this reclamation?"

Uncle Connor took a deep breath. "There are different types of immortals, Beth. They're limited to some degree because they exist within a mortal realm. There are those whose genetic codes have been manually manipulated through scientific advancements and experimentation; then there are those who are literal descendents of the immortals created at the time of Adam and Eve. Jonathan belongs to the latter group."

Uncle Connor watched me carefully, studying every change in my expression. What he saw was confusion, doubt, and utter bewilderment.

"Beth, honey," his eyes searched mine, "you're the daughter of one of the most renowned and respected scientists in this field of research."

I pressed my fingers against my forehead. "You . . . you can't be . . . serious about all this." I kept shaking my head, repelling the thought that my mom could have kept something so colossal from me.

"All I'm asking you to do is keep an open mind."

Keep an open mind. Where had I heard that phrase recently? I attempted to access the archives of my brain, retracing my steps over the past week moment by moment. Suddenly, Carl's e-mail flashed into my mind with abrupt clarity.

He's cool . . . just keep an open mind.

"Jonathan," I whispered slowly. "Jonathan is . . . immortal?" I felt a fluttering in the pit of my stomach and my entire body slumped resignedly onto the couch.

Uncle Connor stared at me understandingly. "Not in the purest sense of the word but to a lesser degree, yes." He paused, noticing the disbelief in my face. "I know how this must sound but Beth, this is not something I'd make up. It was just a matter of time before you figured out the truth about Jonathan."

"How long have you known about this?" I asked softly.

"Does it matter?"

"You've known . . . all this time?" My voice rose a little.

Uncle Connor nodded slowly. "When you asked about clear fluid in someone's blood, I thought maybe you were suspicious or that something specific had happened."

"But, how could you . . . ?" I shook my head in disbelief. I wasn't sure how to phrase the question. I watched Uncle Connor's face carefully and judging by his expression, he wasn't through.

"Jonathan is not the only one, Beth. There are others who are—special." He took a deep breath and peered into my eyes with unnatural intensity. "There are a few of . . . us." His voice broke on the last word.

Us?!

"You? You're one of them?" My words stung like an icy accusation. "That's crazy! How is that even possible?"

Uncle Connor stared at me for a moment without speaking while the wheels in my brain spun at warp speed. My mind raced through a myriad of questions and theories. He and my mom were twins—but she was dead—so what he was suggesting was impossible, right?

I pressed my wrists against the side of my head. *Think like a scientist,* I told myself. *There has to be some other explanation for all this, some freak of nature maybe, or some adaptation or mutation in the evolutionary process. Could humans evolve to such an extent? Could that explain why Jonathan's blood is different, or why he healed so quickly?* It was unfathomable, and yet, barring the theory of evolution, if what Uncle Connor had said about God creating other immortals besides Adam and Eve were somehow true, then—

"Jonathan?" I whispered to myself. "Is it really possible?"

Uncle Connor seemed content to sit quietly while my brain worked overtime. After several minutes of contemplation, my body stiffened and suddenly my mind shifted directions. Eric! Uncle Connor often referred to him as having unnatural strength.

"Eric? Is he . . . special too?"

"No." Uncle Connor quickly shook his head.

I recalled the fierce anger in Jonathan's eyes last night as he fought Eric.

"Is Eric . . . dead?" I could hardly bring myself to say the word.

"Of course not. I'm sure he'll be fine. He's a strong kid."

"Where is he now?" I asked.

"I assume he's at home," Uncle Connor said, looking down at the floor. "Beth, if Jonathan hadn't shown up . . . well, I could never forgive myself if something happened to you." Uncle Connor's eyes misted over as he forced the words from his mouth.

A light rap at the door interrupted our conversation. I waited as Uncle Connor greeted Jonathan and brought him to the living room. He looked surprised to find me sitting there, and he looked every bit mortal. My eyes traced his body from head to toe, then stopped and rested on his arm. He was wearing a long-sleeved T-shirt so I couldn't see the place where he'd cut himself just a week earlier.

"You're up," he said, half smiling. "How do you feel?"

"Sore," I answered. I moved to the side, clearing a place for him to sit next to me on the couch. Before he could say another word I reached for his arm and pushed up his shirtsleeve. He watched in silence as I ran my fingers along his forearm. There was no trace of his wounds. Nothing! My focus shifted next to his pant leg. I ran the palm of my hand along the side of his knee and down his calf, feeling for any evidence of swelling or soreness. Again, nothing. I looked up at him quizzically. He reached down and covered my hand with his and glanced at Uncle Connor who returned his glance with a slight nod.

Jonathan lifted my hand and laid it gently in my lap. Then he got up and walked over to the fireplace. He stood with his back to me and stared into the flickering flames. It was Uncle Connor who finally broke the uneasy silence.

"How's Eric?" he asked.

Jonathan turned around and looked at me before answering. "He'll be okay in a couple of days," he said coolly.

I'm not sure why I said what I did next. Maybe it was because I was looking for something concrete to grasp on to. Regardless, it didn't come out right when I said, "I want to see him." When I saw the anguish in Jonathan's face, I instantly regretted saying it.

Jonathan's eyes turned cold and he shot Uncle Connor a quick glance.

"It won't do you any good," Uncle Connor cut in. "He has no memory of last night."

"Is that true?" I looked to Jonathan for confirmation. "He doesn't remember any of it?"

"Pretty much. What he does recall is shaky; he has no idea how he ended up with a broken nose and four cracked ribs." There was a subtle smugness in Jonathan's tone.

I winced, remembering the blows Eric's body had endured. I was sure Jonathan had killed him.

"How did you know where we were?" I asked Jonathan.

"Your friend, Darla."

"When did you see Darla?" Even in the midst of all the craziness, the jealousy demon managed to open an eye.

"I finished with Grace early, so I decided to take you up on your offer. I went to the summit where the bonfires usually take place but couldn't find you anywhere in the crowd. I figured you'd changed your mind about going. I was heading back to the parking lot when your friend Darla stopped me."

"So Darla didn't go to Jackson," I reasoned quietly, "and she *knew* where I'd be?" This infuriated me.

"If it's any consolation, she didn't seem happy about it," he said reassuringly. "She didn't know exactly where you and Eric were, her directions were sketchy, but I knew the area she was referring to. I just had to locate the bonfire. I was below you on the path when I heard voices and an unusual rustling in the trees."

A cold chill shuddered through me at the memory.

"When I saw him on top of you like that. . . ." Jonathan shot a nervous glance in Uncle Connor's direction, then blew the air out of his mouth in a huff. I could tell he was reluctant to continue. "I, well, I wasn't sure what to think at first. When I realized he was, what he. . . ." He exhaled sharply, his eyes icy cold. "I wanted to kill him. Nothing else mattered. I just wanted to kill him." He bit his lips together.

I was silent for a moment, reliving the nightmare, then I shuddered. "His eyes," Jonathan, "I keep seeing those bright yellow eyes. What happened to Eric last night? What came over him?"

Jonathan and Uncle Connor eyed each other for several moments but remained silent.

"Jonathan!?" I wasn't going to back down. "I want answers!"

Jonathan waited for some sort of signal from Uncle Connor, but Uncle Connor just shook his head. Jonathan breathed a sigh of frustration.

"We think Eric was the victim of a unique kind of attack. That an . . . entity took hold of his mind."

"We don't know that for sure!" Uncle Connor interjected. "We need more information."

"Beth," Jonathan peered quickly at Uncle Connor, "if you feel up to it, it would help if you could tell us everything you remember about last night." His eyes studied me carefully.

"You were there, you saw what happened," I replied.

"Not everything," he corrected. "We need to know what happened *before* I got there. I know it's uncomfortable, but try not to leave anything out."

Jonathan and Uncle Connor listened sympathetically as I recounted everything I could remember. I told them about Eric's unusual behavior during the drive to the summit, how surprised I was that there were only a few kids at the bonfire, and how they were paired off in couples.

"That's because Eric and his friends were participating in a different kind of *tradition,*" Jonathan grumbled bitterly. He pursed his lips and averted his eyes. I could sense that he was uneasy but I waited for him to explain.

"You weren't at the senior-junior bonfire." He paused, and then turned to face me again. He studied my eyes carefully as if he expected them to reveal something, but all he saw was confusion. This seemed to satisfy him.

"I had no idea," I explained. "When I figured out what was going on, I demanded that Eric take me home—but he refused. That's when I decided to take off by myself."

"Do you have any idea how dangerous that was?" Uncle Connor scowled. "You could have easily gotten lost in those woods, Beth!"

"And that would be worse than being attacked by a 220 pound football player possessed by some, some, what? An evil spirit?" I snapped sarcastically. Uncle Connor frowned and then motioned for me to proceed.

"Eric's friends started to tease him about me leaving so he came after me. He was furious. He had a wild look in his eyes that frightened me. And he was drinking. I know people sometimes act crazy when they drink so I just started running. At that point I didn't care what direction I was headed, but I didn't get very far before Eric grabbed me from behind and threw me to the ground. I tried to get away from him but he was too strong, too heavy . . ." I paused to get control of my emotions.

Uncle Connor squirmed uncomfortably in his chair. Jonathan paced nervously, shifting his eyes from me to Uncle Connor to the floor and then back to me as I continued.

"I wanted to scream, I kept trying to force sound from my lungs but the pressure on my chest was too constricting. Something inside me told me not to give up, to fight, but then his eyes changed and. . . .

"Oh, Jonathan, I was sure he was going to kill me—or worse." Now I was really fighting hysteria.

Jonathan and Uncle Connor glanced at each other suddenly and another non-verbal communication passed between them.

"Can you describe his eyes?" Uncle Connor asked quietly, calming me.

I took a deep breath to control myself and tried to concentrate. "They were bright yellow, like they were glowing, but there was a ring of black around them. They were evil and terrifying, yet hypnotic at the same time; I couldn't look away from them. Then he said my name."

Jonathan's head snapped up instantly. "He spoke to you?"

"Yes. But it wasn't really Eric," I replied.

Uncle Connor looked as though he were going to be sick. "Beth, what were his exact words?"

"He said, 'Hello Beth Anne.' Uncle Connor . . . nobody calls me that except for my mom. I had the feeling that he knew me."

The room became silent. It was stifling.

"Impossible!" Uncle Connor hissed.

Jonathan sat back down next to me on the couch, staring straight ahead.

I released a dark laugh. "Oh, *that's* impossible?" I said, looking at Jonathan's leg. The heavy sarcasm in my tone didn't go unnoticed. Jonathan flashed Uncle Connor a questioning look.

"That's not all," I continued. "Whoever or whatever it was that overpowered Eric was there the night of my accident as well."

"It makes sense," Jonathan whispered. Uncle Connor nodded in reluctant agreement.

"They weren't after Hattie—they were after Beth," Uncle Connor concluded.

"They've made contact," Jonathan said to himself.

They were driving me crazy. "Who? Who made contact? Some of your *alleged* immortals?" I snapped.

"They . . ." Jonathan began, then he stopped short. I'm not sure if it was because he caught the word "immortals" or because he was interrupted.

"We don't know," Uncle Connor threw him a sharp look and shook his head, "but we won't rest until we find out." His eyes softened. Something in his expression told me he was finished with this conversation. "Honey, last night was terrifying for you; you're going to need time to recover . . . time to absorb all this."

"I agree," Jonathan said quickly. I started to argue but Jonathan changed the subject, looking at Uncle Connor for approval. "How 'bout we go for a drive and take your mind off last night for awhile."

"Do you feel up to that?" Uncle Connor asked, watching me carefully.

I knew they were trying to protect me from something, but I also knew I had a better chance of getting more answers if Uncle Connor wasn't around, so I agreed.

Jonathan drove slowly through town and turned off the main highway onto a dirt road that wove itself neatly through the forest to a small lake. When we arrived at the clearing that served as a parking lot, instead of getting out, Jonathan let the car continue running.

"Jonathan?" I asked. "Is something wrong?"

He shook his head, but didn't say anything.

"Tell me what you're thinking," I prodded. He reached his arm across the seat and began to twist his fingers through my hair and massage the back of my neck. He pulled gently on my neck, turning me toward him so that we faced each other.

"Beth, did your uncle tell you everything? I mean . . . the part about me?"

I nodded.

"Are you okay with it?" His voice was uneven.

"I don't know," I answered honestly. "It's all so unbelievable."

"Yes, I'm sure it is." His eyes dropped for a moment then flashed up at mine. "We're not that different, you and me, not really, not when you look at the big picture."

"Jonathan . . ." I shook my head. I wanted to believe him, to believe that the differences between us didn't matter. After all, he was the same person today that he was yesterday. "I seriously don't know what to think. My mind is reeling with questions." Jonathan dropped his eyes again and nodded knowingly.

"Don't get me wrong—I'm not saying that's a bad thing." I reached across and touched the side of his face with the back of my hand; it was the first time I'd ever touched him like that. "It's just that it's so unbelievable. It's like I left the real world behind when I went up that mountain last night. I came back to a world of make-believe. Maybe I never really came down. Maybe I'm trapped on the mountain slowly freezing to death and this has all been a wild hallucination."

Jonathan chuckled. "Would that story really be easier for you to swallow?"

"In some ways, yes. But something my mother used to tell me keeps gnawing at the back of my brain."

"What's that?"

"She always insisted that I have an open mind, that I never dismiss the unlikely or the improbable simply because it doesn't fit my definition of the truth. She said that physics is all about redefining truths and that the greatest advancements in science have come as a result of somebody's belief in the impossible."

"That's often true."

"She also taught me that the greatest scientists are those who aren't afraid to rely on faith when hard, cold evidence contradicts scientific laws. She said sometimes it takes science time to catch up to the truths that govern the Universe."

"She sounds like an amazing woman. I wish I could have met her."

"You know, the part of me that wants to believe in God has no problem accepting that immortals could exist. It's sort of like having angels on the earth. There were angels in the Bible, why not now? But logic tells me there's a scientific explanation for why you're . . . so different . . . and that Uncle Connor and my mother are whimsical fools who have a few of their nuts and bolts missing."

Even as I said it, I knew I didn't believe it. I shook my head. My mother was a bit flamboyant at times but she was insanely intelligent. "It's definitely going to take me awhile to process all this."

Jonathan reached over and took my hand in his, bent fingers and all. Warmth stirred inside me.

"Uncle Connor said you aren't immortal in the 'pure' sense," I continued. "What does that mean?"

"Pure immortals can phase in and out of this world at will, like those angels you just mentioned, and they can never be destroyed. Those of us with a mixture of fluids in our veins don't have those luxuries."

"So, you're a mixed breed?" I quipped.

Jonathan chuckled. "I suppose in a very loose sense of the word that's true. Technically, we're an alternate race of immortals with limitations that vary depending on the degree of immortal fluid that runs through our bodies. The two fluids—the thick clear liquid you saw when I cut my arm and human blood—cannot mix. Each works independent of the other. The higher the percentage of immortal fluids, the fewer the mortal limitations."

"I see." I was only half-fibbing. I'd seen Jonathan's blood first hand; there was no denying the two distinct fluids.

Jonathan sat quietly for a moment and then smiled.

"What?" I eyed him suspiciously.

"You're amazing." He had a surprised look of awe in his expression. "You're much calmer about this than I anticipated."

I shook my head. "No. I'm not amazing. I'm the daughter of a scientist."

He let that sink in for a moment.

"Beth . . . ?" His eyes slowly focused on my lips as he reached across and began to trace the contour of my cheek with his thumb. "I'm going to kiss you now," he whispered. "I just thought I'd warn you this time." His eyes narrowed with exaggerated seriousness but his mouth twitched as he tried to stifle a grin.

The heat inside me burst into flame, burning out all the conflicting thoughts in my mind as he leaned in and pressed his lips gently against my cheek. He pulled away slightly so that his mouth was just inches from mine. Then he did something I wasn't expecting. He beamed, his sapphire eyes twinkling with mischief.

"What?" I asked suspiciously.

"I just want to make sure you're ready this time," he chuckled.

I wanted to slug him. Instead, I reached over and pulled him to me. He brushed his mouth lightly against mine, flirting, still grinning. Then he wrapped his arm firmly around my neck and kissed me passionately. We relaxed into each other and the rest of the world melted away: theories forgotten, questions tossed by the wayside, all uncertainty banished.

When he pulled away, he rested his forehead against mine and twisted his fingers in my hair gently cupping my head with his hand. After a moment, he cleared his throat.

"What?" I asked, slightly out of breath.

"What would you say to a picnic?"

Eric

CHAPTER 9

I looked around us, there were no restaurants. I looked over my shoulder and surveyed his back seat, there was no picnic basket filled with food.

"Jonathan, next you're going to tell me that immortals, or half-breeds or hybrids or whatever they are, have some super power that allows them to magically make food appear out of thin air!"

Jonathan looked at me with mock disgust. "Now you're just being mean," he teased.

He pulled the car into reverse and sped around in a circle, stirring up a cloud of dust as he headed back to town. He pulled into the nearest drive-thru, a fried chicken joint. He ordered each of us a meal and a drink and just as quickly as we'd left, we were back at the lake. He parked the car, grabbed a thick blanket from his trunk, and opened my door.

Except for a few lonely fishermen and a healthy population of ducks, the lake was all but deserted. Jonathan handed me the bag of food and our drinks and spread the blanket on the sandy beach. He looked me over and frowned, then headed back to his car. In a moment he reappeared carrying my coat.

"You're probably going to need this in a few minutes," he grinned.

Smart aleck. He was right though; my blood still hadn't adapted to the deceiving Wyoming weather.

Jonathan lay back on the blanket with his arms folded behind his head, our food forgotten for the moment. The scientist in me had gained a second wind (no doubt thanks to the way he had kissed me earlier). I was flying. I had the feeling I could handle anything. Suddenly, the idea of immortality—whether pure or partial—seemed quite plausible. It fascinated me.

"Well, let's hear it," he said, grinning. "I can see the questions in your eyes."

He looked positively at ease. Little did he know he was up against the queen of questions.

"The strangest part of this," I began, "is that in my mind, if immortals exist at all, they do so as humans who have died. But you're not dead . . . you're a normal person. If I hadn't seen your leg move back into place on its own, which, by the way, is the freakiest thing I've ever seen, I would never—"

Jonathan chuckled, interrupting my verbose attempt to make sense of things.

"Even freakier than watching someone's eyes change to bright yellow?" he challenged.

"Absolutely. I could have convinced myself that I was hysterical and imagined the whole eye thing, but your leg, *that* was over the top."

"You saw my arm heal itself, you saw my blood. You had to suspect there was something *different* about me."

"Well, yeah. I figured that much. But I convinced myself that it was something in your blood cells or maybe in your plasma. Whatever it was, I figured it was unique to *you*. But I've known Uncle Connor my whole life. How is it that I never noticed there was something odd about him?" I immediately sensed the irony of what I'd just said.

"Haven't I heard you describe him as eccentric?" Jonathan suggested.

"Eccentric, yeah, but not . . . mythical."

"The word 'immortal' is not synonymous with 'mythical.' True immortals, the pure ones, never taste death. 'Mortal,' on the other hand, means death. It's that simple." He cocked his head to one side and studied my expression before he continued. "But you were half right about what you saw coming out of the cut on my arm; both fluids play an intricate role."

"How are the fluids so different?"

"Blood carries within it elements necessary to sustain life, but it also carries with it the potential to end life."

"I don't follow." I shook my head, trying to comprehend.

"Disease, degeneration, decay, mutations, etcetera. Although blood is necessary for mortals to exist, it's also the element that ultimately leads to death."

"And pure immortals don't have any blood."

"Precisely. The fluid that runs through a true immortal is clear, pure. It pumps through the body exactly the way blood pumps through the body of a mortal being, but it carries only life sustaining properties. There is nothing degenerative in the fluid of a true immortal."

"And you have both clear fluid and blood in your body because one of your parents is mortal?"

"Well, no. Both my parents are immortal."

"How does that work?"

"There are a couple of considerations. Obviously, through mixed marriages the fluids became contaminated. But adaptation is a key factor too. Our bodies have experienced an evolution of sorts over the past several generations. Those of faith maintain that when the earth became mortal, the physical laws that govern this realm," Jonathan gestured around him, "also changed in order to support mortal life. Immortals had to adapt—carry the components of blood in their body—in order to survive in a mortal realm. In doing so, they became subject to some of the limitations of mortality."

"This is mind boggling," I said, shaking my head. Here we were, talking about something one would only expect to hear in a science fiction movie, yet Jonathan made it all seem so clinical . . . so scientifically sensible . . . so intellectually sound.

"How were you . . . made?" I couldn't think of a better term. Jonathan laughed at my struggle for the right words.

"How were you *made?*" he countered.

"My parents, I suppose. Wait—" I held up my hand before he could throw that back in my face. "If humans are here through evolution, how, then, would you explain your existence?"

"Whether you believe in God or look at scientific evidence, it still comes back to adaptation."

"Meaning?"

"Meaning immortals have a superior ability to adapt to their environment. Their bodies have progressed to a higher level than others who are less . . . 'adaptatious.'" He smiled smugly, satisfied with his scientific rhetoric.

"Is that even a real word?" I questioned.

Jonathan chuckled and shrugged his shoulders. "I just made it one."

I rolled my eyes at him; I'd worry about eye wrinkles later. I tried to look annoyed but I had to admit, his explanations seemed reasonable. I couldn't help but think of my mom. I wished she were present to join in on this conversation. She would love this.

I reached over and took a drink of my soda. I watched the clear liquid rise and fall in the straw and I thought of the fluid running through Jonathan's veins.

As soon as the soda reached my stomach, I realized that I was famished. I thought back, trying to remember the last time I'd eaten. Distracted by the sudden realization that I was hungry, I reached into the bag and grabbed my box of fried chicken and french fries. I inhaled deeply, savoring the smell. I loved fried chicken; it made my mouth water. I was suddenly torn between my need for more answers and the monster hunger that rumbled in my stomach. I breathed deeply again, fanning the aroma toward my nose. I looked over at Jonathan who was now propped up on one elbow watching me with a quizzical look on his face.

"What?" I asked, frowning.

He continued to watch my hands then raised his eyes to meet mine. But he didn't say anything.

"What?" I repeated.

He remained quiet for a moment, his expression inscrutable.

"Jonathan?"

"It's just . . ." he shook his head and smiled. "It's just that I've never seen anyone so enamored with their food. Do you always sniff your food before you eat it?"

I looked down at my food and suddenly felt self-conscious. "Smarty pants," I grumbled. Jonathan laughed.

"Guess we'd better eat," he said enthusiastically. He reached his hand out, waiting for me to hand him his box of food. But I still had questions. I moved the bag away from his reach.

Jonathan let out a pitiful groan and rolled onto his back. I ignored his theatrics.

"When did you first know you were . . . different from other humans?"

"It's hard to say." He folded his hands behind his head and stared up at the sky. I could tell he was trying not to smile. "The process was gradual."

"What's the process like?"

"In the beginning, when we're children, we're pretty much the same as mortals. Then a sort of transformation takes place in our blood; it usually occurs around a person's prime. It's sort of comparable to what happens to a butterfly during metamorphosis. The change is pre-programmed to take place once our cells reach a specific level of maturity. At that point, the cells reclaim their innate immortal properties and from that time forward instead of *aging* we *progress*."

"There's a difference?" I asked.

"A huge difference," he said as he sat up. He reached over, pulled my face to his, and kissed me just long enough to shut me up. "Now, may I please have my food—before it gets any colder?"

As soon as the sun neared the foothills, the afternoon breeze kicked up making the air uncomfortably cool even with my coat on. We packed up our picnic and drove slowly back to Uncle Connor's house. Jonathan held my hand cupped in his and stroked the top of my bent fingers. As we pulled onto my street, he suddenly tensed.

"Hmm, looks like you're going to have your chance to see Eric tonight after all," he murmured. He gestured toward the driveway where Eric's truck was parked.

"He's able to drive?" I blurted.

"Give me a little credit, Beth. I broke some ribs; I didn't permanently damage the guy."

"No, I just mean—geez, Jonathan," I stumbled through the words, "he was unconscious."

"I disabled him, that's all. He'll mend," Jonathan said reassuringly. But the cold edge in his voice had returned.

He approached the house slowly. The moment Eric's truck was in full view I panicked. I was frozen to my seat. I was anxious to see Eric in theory, but seeing his truck caused a wave of apprehension to wash over me. Maybe Uncle Connor was right; maybe it was too soon.

When we walked into the living room, Eric was sitting on the couch with his back to the door. He was speaking to Uncle Connor who was seated in his usual spot, the chair closest to the fireplace. Eric heard us come in and stood slowly, turning to face us. I gasped when I saw his face and had to steady myself against Jonathan's arm to maintain my composure.

Two emotions flashed through my mind simultaneously—compassion and fear. Eric was my friend, someone I cared for. But he was also the boy who less than twenty-four hours ago had chased me down in the forest, thrown me to ground, and nearly suffocated me with his massive weight as he tried to force himself on me. The conflicting emotions confused me and weakened my earlier resolve. Part of me wanted to run toward him and make sure he was okay. The other part of me wanted to recoil into Jonathan's protective arms.

I suppose if I were completely honest, there was a third part of me that wanted to slap Eric as hard as I could. That urge was immediately suppressed when I caught a glimpse of his face. Deep purple bruises ringed his eyes making him look like a sickly raccoon. His cheeks were swollen and red, and his left eyelid was nearly double its normal size. He stood carefully. I could tell it took a great deal of effort for him not to wince as he moved. I assumed that was for my benefit, but maybe he was just trying to save face in front of Jonathan. All I could do was stare at him, stunned.

"Hi, Beth," Eric said meekly.

"Eric," I whispered.

"I was wondering if I could talk to you." His eyes flickered between Jonathan and me.

"Okay." I forced the words, still unable to break my frozen stare.

"Alone," he clarified, cutting his eyes briefly at Jonathan.

Uncle Connor stood and cleared his throat. "Jonathan, why don't we give them a few minutes to talk?" He nodded sideways in the direction of the kitchen.

The intonation in Uncle Connor's voice indicated that he wanted a chance to speak with Jonathan alone and that this was an opportune moment to do so without raising my suspicions. Too late. I was well aware that Jonathan and Uncle Connor knew far more than they were telling me. If Uncle Connor knew me at all, he must have already surmised that I would not rest as long as I sensed he was hiding things from me.

Jonathan bent down and kissed me lightly, sending a clear message to Eric.

"I'll be in the other room if you need me," he whispered. He glanced at Eric and then reluctantly dropped his hand from my waist. I watched as he followed Uncle Connor into the kitchen.

I wasn't surprised when I finally turned around to find Eric's eyes boring into me.

"So, that's how it is?" Eric asked. He glanced toward the kitchen. I nodded affirmatively.

Eric's shoulders slumped. He sighed, acknowledging defeat.

"I'm sorry, Eric," I said softly. "I told you how I felt."

"I figured, hoped actually, that things might be different." He shrugged and the side of his mouth turned up into a half smile, but it wasn't a happy smile.

"I know you did," I murmured.

Eric's vulnerability made him seem much younger than he was and my sense of compassion toward him prevailed over my sense of fear. I moved cautiously toward him until I was close enough to reach out and touch his arm. I hesitated—I was uncomfortable standing so close to him—but he closed his eyes and sighed as I softly brushed the side of his arm with my hand. It was a remorseful, pitiful sigh.

"Is that what last night was all about?" I asked.

Eric shook his head. "I don't know *what* last night was all about," he replied, sincerely confused.

I tugged at his hand, attempting to lead him to the couch; but in a gutsy move, he abruptly caught me in his arms and pulled me roughly to his chest.

"All I wanted was a fair shot," he said hoarsely. His tight hold on me immediately aroused flashes of memory from the previous night—the odor of mountain pine and bonfire smoke still emanated from his skin. I stiffened, half-frozen in place, until I found the strength to push away from him.

"I'm sorry," he said, relaxing his arms.

"Eric, there will never be more than friendship between us," I said angrily. "I wouldn't do that to Darla. You're her ex. Friends don't date their friends' exes. Believe me, I know how it feels to be betrayed by a friend." The picture of Adam and my former best friend groping each other on the dance floor flashed into my mind.

"Darla . . . ?" Eric murmured. "This is about Darla?"

"You know it's not—but she is my friend. That's just the way it is."

"I think I know better than anyone *how it is* with Darla," he said bitterly.

"What happened between you two?" I asked. "I know you cheated on her but that's ancient history. Why is she still so bitter where you're concerned? It isn't normal."

"She has good reason to be." He lowered his face again and began to rub his forehead in frustration.

"What did you do to her?" I asked.

He shook his head back and forth remorsefully. "It's a long story."

I sat down and rested my back against the couch, making an exaggerated effort to look comfortable. I gestured for him to continue. He watched me for several seconds and little by little resolve formed in his eyes.

"Darla and I used to date a couple of years ago. Actually, it started before that, when we were kids. We were inseparable back then."

I smiled halfheartedly. This information was nothing new.

"She's always been gorgeous, you know." Eric paused as if he expected that piece of information to surprise me. It didn't. "Everyone in town talked about her beauty but it never went to her head. She never saw herself as anything more than 'adequately handsome' as she expressed it." He paused. "She was my first kiss—did you know that?"

Oddly enough, Darla had never mentioned that before. Eric grinned recalling the memory, his adoration for her reflected in his eyes.

"We were in fourth grade," he chuckled. "We wanted to see how long we could hold a kiss, so we put our lips together and I counted by raising one finger at a time. We thought we were so cool when I got through all ten fingers. It was totally lame." Eric looked up at me; his swollen eyes were full of life.

"So what happened?" I prodded.

"We had just gotten our driver's licenses and we thought we owned the world. We used to take turns driving each other all over the place just so we could experience the freedom of being able to go anywhere we wanted. One night—I guess it was a year ago last summer—I knocked on her bedroom window around midnight and dared her to take off with me for a midnight drive. We thought we were Bonnie and Clyde, sneaking off in the middle of the night without telling anyone. There was a sort of thrill to it, you know?"

Eric smirked as he looked at me. I nodded.

"Anyhow, I drove her across the border into Idaho. We snuck into Soda Hot Springs and dared each other to go skinny dipping. Heck, it didn't seem like a big deal at the time; we always went skinny-dipping when we were little. We were giggling like two kids stealing a box of Oreos from the kitchen cupboard."

Eric glanced up at me then bit his lips together and shook his head regretfully. A heavy weight suddenly dropped to the pit of my stomach.

"There we were, two stupid idiots swimming in the moonlight. One minute we were dunking each other and horsing around and the next we were kissing, only not like we did in fourth grade if you know what I mean. I kept thinking she'd stop me but she didn't, so I kept going. One thing led to another . . . and then I couldn't stop . . . and hell, things just went too far."

Eric studied my expression quietly which I assume was one of shock and surprise and sadness all rolled into one. He lowered his gaze, jabbing his foot against the floor nervously. "The drive back was the most awkward hour of my life." He paused for several moments and then chuckled darkly. "I figured by the next day things would be back to normal and we'd just go on—life as usual, you know?"

I lowered my head and pinched the top of my nose between my fingers. "But things didn't go back to normal, did they?" It was a rhetorical question. Eric shook his head regretfully.

"No. In Darla's mind, we were as good as engaged. Not that I blame her. I felt terrible. I didn't want to hurt her so I went along with it for several months. She never let *that* happen between us again but . . . I just wasn't ready for what she wanted. I wanted to experience other girls before I settled down with one person. I didn't know how to 'break up' with her without destroying our friendship. I was damned either way. The worst part of it all is that I really did . . . do care about her. I still love her; I just can't be what she wants me to be."

Eric searched my face for some sign of emotion: condemnation, understanding, sympathy, something! But all I could do was shake my head.

"So, that's when you cheated on her?"

Eric nodded. "I became a total jerk. I figured she'd break up with me—but in the end, I really hurt her. That's how I got the reputation of being a womanizer. I started ditching her so I could be with a different girl every couple of weeks and . . . well, it didn't take long for people to talk. It's a small town, you know? The rumors were exaggerated, but I never tried to refute them. I *wanted* Darla to think I was a dirt bag. It finally worked and she broke up with me."

"Ah, geez, Eric," I said reproachfully.

"That's not the worst of it." Eric exhaled a deep sigh. "I sort of told Tom Stewart what happened at the hot springs."

"Oh, no! Eric, you didn't!"

"Tom thought maybe he could have a shot at her too. When she shot him down, he retaliated by spreading the word that she was an easy sack."

My stomach twisted into a painful knot. Poor Darla.

Eric shifted his weight awkwardly and then hobbled over to stoke the fire. "You know the ironic thing?" he asked after a long pause. "When we were kids, I just assumed that one day we'd end up married. Even after we broke up, I kind of felt that someday, after we'd both dated around, that we'd get back together." Eric's expression suddenly changed. "But then I met you."

"Me?"

"Yeah," he chuckled. "I saw you sitting on the bleachers with Darla and my knees buckled beneath me. I knew Darla would warn you about me, but I figured if you got to know the real me that I'd have a chance. It seemed like it was working too—at least, until your piano buddy showed up."

"Jonathan," I corrected him.

"Whatever. I wasn't surprised when I saw how he looked at you the night of homecoming. But it was the way *you* looked at *him* that upset me—it was the way I wanted you to look at *me*. It took all my reserve not to pick a fight with him that night," Eric snarled jokingly, but I could tell there was truth behind his words.

"Then, after what happened in your basement, I figured I better move quickly before he got his hooks into you too deeply. I wanted to prove to you that this was real. It was never about scoring. I wanted to kiss you—I mean *really* kiss you."

Eric closed his eyes and shook his head. "I've never wanted to kiss anybody the way I wanted to kiss you." He opened his eyes and looked at me longingly. "And I wanted you to kiss me in return. Then you'd know how good it could be between us. I still don't know how it all went wrong or how I ended up like this." He waved his hands towards his body and smirked. "I hope the other guy looks as bad as I do."

I couldn't control my reaction; I let out a dark chuckle.

"What?" he demanded, offended by my sudden outburst.

"Nothing," I mused, shaking my head. I figured I'd better change the subject before I said something really hurtful. "Tell me what you remember about last night."

"I remember everything fine up until you left and then it gets blurry. I saw you take off through the trees; you weren't even close to the path and I knew you'd get lost. I called for you to come back, but you ignored me. Then my friends started harassing me and I got angry—not with you, with them. When I started to follow you, you turned around and hightailed it into the trees. All I could think of was that I needed to stop you before you got too far in to find your way out, but you wouldn't stop. As soon as I got close enough I tried to grab you, but ended up pushing you to the ground. You went berserk—screaming and fighting and twisting around like a crazy person. It was like trying to tackle an angry mountain lion. I remember thinking, *I need to calm her down.* Then, when I was so close to you, when I felt your body under mine . . . I don't know, there just wasn't an off switch. One minute I was about to kiss you and the next moment I felt a ripping pain shoot through my head. Somebody must have hit me or something. Everything's hazy after that. The next thing I remember, I was propped up against a tree next to the main path a good hundred yards away from where we'd been. That's when your piano boy showed up and took me home." He chuckled. "I was so out of it I didn't care that it was him helping me—I was just happy to get out of there."

"His name is Jonathan," I corrected him again, trying not to sound annoyed.

"So you've said." He flashed his famous, sarcastic grin. "I figured you must have said something to him and that's why he came looking for me."

"Ah, Eric," I muttered. "Last night was a ridiculously idiotic idea. You can catapult it to the number one spot on your list of the top ten most stupid moments. Did you really think that all I needed was some alcohol and a kiss, and then bang, we'd be an item?"

"Something like that, yeah." He shrugged. His face was so pathetic that I pursed my lips, trying hard not to laugh. Nothing he'd revealed tonight was funny but I didn't know what else to do. In spite of the fact that he'd been a total jerk to Darla, I sensed that beneath his tough-guy exterior, he felt truly sorry for hurting her.

"Go ahead and laugh," he said sarcastically. "I know you want to."

This was the side of Eric that was so charming. I stifled a chuckle and he mocked me by mimicking my every move, making it impossible not to smile. He started to laugh but instantly winced and grabbed his ribs. Even though I knew he was in pain, I burst into a roar of laughter.

"Stop! Stop! Please! You're killing me!" he grimaced through gritted teeth, but his eyes were smiling in spite of their swelling and his obvious discomfort.

"You are the most insane person I've ever met!" I said, frustrated that he'd gotten me to laugh.

"Does that mean you forgive me?"

"I'll think about it," I replied.

I walked Eric to the door and watched him leave. Before his truck was out of the driveway, Jonathan was at my side.

"You're right," I said watching Eric drive away. "He doesn't remember anything about attacking me, and he has no clue that it was you who pulled him off me."

Jonathan moved behind me and wrapped his arms around my waist. He rested his chin on the top of my head and I could feel that he was nodding. I laid my arms across his and pulled them tighter around me.

"Does he need to know what really happened to him?" I asked.

"He'll have to know, eventually."

"Why?" I wasn't disagreeing with him, but I was curious as to why Jonathan's response was so absolute.

"Because he needs to be prepared for the next time it happens."

"Next time?" I gasped. "This will happen again?"

"It's very likely." Jonathan turned me around to face him. His gaze was fixed and serious. "You need to be very careful around him, Beth."

"I can't go through that again," I complained. "What if you aren't there next time?"

"I've been worrying about that all day," he muttered.

"You're going to have to teach her how to recognize them and how to fight them," Uncle Connor interrupted from behind.

"Who?" I questioned.

"The intruders," Jonathan replied. "That's what we call entities that take over a person's mind or body."

"Also known as possessors," Uncle Connor added. "Beth, you'll need to learn all you can about them. Knowing them—understanding them—will help you prepare to face them. They caught you off guard last night. We won't let that happen again."

Before I climbed into bed, I turned on my computer to check my e-mail. There were two messages, one from Darla and one from Eric. I opened the one from Eric first.

I'll be around if he screws it up, just wanted you to know.

I hit the reply button:

Thanks for the warning :)

Then I opened Darla's.

Hi Beth. How was your weekend? Did Jonathan find you last night? I bet that was awkward. Sorry if I caused a problem.

I chuckled as I hit the reply button. If she only knew! How should I respond? Should I tell her that I had my first—and second—kiss from Jonathan this weekend? That the second kiss was much more amazing than the first kiss, but no less memorable? Should I tell her that some paranormal entity possessed Eric and tried to "disable" me, and I didn't know why? Should I tell her that Jonathan broke Eric's ribs? Perhaps I should explain to her that Jonathan—and my uncle for that matter—belongs to a realm of immortal humans who apparently have been mingling with mortals since the days of Adam and Eve. And on a more personal note, should I tell her that I now know what happened between her and Eric?

My mind wandered back to my relationship with Adam. I shuddered at the realization that I'd actually questioned whether I made the right decision about my physical relationship with him. I'd kept him at arm's length, and it cost me the relationship. At the time I was devastated, but now I felt grateful. On the other hand, in a playful, fleeting moment of passion, Darla had given a part of herself away that she could never get back. I wondered if she would ever truly get over the emotional trauma of it all, or would she secretly regret it every day for the rest of her life? I couldn't help but ache for her.

I hit the reply button:

Not much to report, everything's cool. How about you? Did you have fun with Evan? Can't wait to hear. G'nite.

The Vortex Cellar
CHAPTER 10

The annoying buzz of my alarm startled me from a very pleasant dream. In vain, I struggled to hang on to the images as they flickered into dust. The dark gray light that filtered into my room made me question if my clock was working correctly. I rolled over lazily and grabbed my cell phone from the nightstand. It took several blinks for my eyes to focus enough to see the display. Yep, my clock was right. I groaned, pulled back my warm comforter, and slid my feet to the floor. In defiance of my phone and clock, I shuffled to the window to see if it was still nighttime. Thick, heavy clouds hung low on the horizon blocking any hope of sunshine and it was raining—violently. Streams of water blew sideways across the landscape, forcing the trees to bow in protest beneath the persistent hammering. It was going to be one of those days.

In spite of the dismal weather, I welcomed the arrival of a new week, glad to put the trauma of the weekend behind me. I stumbled into the bathroom and ran the water for a hot shower. The bruises on my body had faded from dark blue to pale green and yellow and I studied them quizzically. I'd been certain the marks would remain for several days before beginning to disappear. I noticed, also, that it no longer hurt when I moved; in fact, my previously sore joints felt amazingly loose and strong. I wondered about Eric, if he was better today too.

Darla called offering to drive me to school. I was still self-conscious about driving Carl's car to school and I absolutely dreaded the idea of driving in bad weather, so I accepted her offer readily. Just as I figured, she was prepared—loaded with questions. Before she began needling me for details, she apologized for her role in setting me up with Eric.

"I'm really sorry, Beth," she began. "I warned Eric that you'd be furious but he wouldn't listen. He had this idiotic notion that if he could be alone with you—you know, without me around to protect you—you wouldn't resist him. He claimed it had almost worked before . . . once."

"Don't worry about it." I ignored the implied question in the last part of her statement. Instead, I scanned her face for any clue of intended betrayal, but honestly, there wasn't any. She seemed genuinely sincere. "Anyhow, go on," I urged, "what happened when Jonathan got there?"

"He asked if I knew where you were. I wasn't going to tell him at first but when I looked into his eyes, I couldn't help myself. He looked so concerned. He was not happy when I told him about Eric's scheme to take you somewhere unexpected." Darla looked regretful. "I never should've let Eric do that. I'm so sorry, Beth."

"Like I said, it's not your fault. Then what happened?"

"Jonathan took off in a hurry." She raised her eyebrows and leaned in closer to me. "I wish I could've been there when he showed up. I would love to have seen the look on Eric's face."

"Hmm," I muttered under my breath.

"What happened when he found you guys?" She obviously hadn't seen Eric since the weekend.

"Eric and the others had started drinking. I wanted Eric to take me home, but he wouldn't listen to me. I was on my way to sit in the car when Jonathan showed up and took me home." I left out the rest of the details.

"Good thing he found you," Darla commented.

"That's an understatement," I grumbled under my breath. "So, tell me how it went with you and Evan?" I asked, anxious to change the subject.

"It was fun, actually," she shrugged, grinning. "Evan is really nice. . . ."

She left the word dangling, hesitant to add more.

"But?" I nudged her arm.

"But," she sighed, "he's no Derrick Miles."

I couldn't help but scoff in exasperation even though I knew it would put Darla on the defensive. Derrick wasn't even in the same league with Evan as far as I was concerned. Derrick had no personality. He was what I referred to as an emotional flat-liner.

"You know, that might be Evan's greatest asset," I chuckled, hoping she'd find humor in my subtle sarcasm.

Then Darla did something that completely took me by surprise, she blushed—and not the pretty pink shade that she reserved for Derrick. Her face turned a deep shade of crimson, and she couldn't refrain from smiling. I wondered how long it would take her to realize that she liked Evan; seeing her blush so deeply convinced me that it was inevitable.

School was uneventful. Eric didn't show up—no surprise there. Judging by what I'd seen, he'd need several days to recover. I wondered if he'd ever remember the truth about Saturday night in its entirety and if so, how he'd react knowing Jonathan was the one who stopped him from really hurting me.

When school ended, I turned on my cell phone and saw a text message from Jonathan.

Went to Jackson Hole. Call you later.

I smiled. This was a new level for us and that pleased me.

"Beth?" Darla interrupted my thoughts. I looked up at her questioningly and waited for her to finish. "Do you mind hanging out for awhile? I need to finish my science lab and Mr. Kavanaugh only does makeups once a week. It shouldn't take too long."

"No problem," I replied. I had plenty to keep myself occupied.

My plan was to hang out at the library and work on my homework, but instead I found myself standing in the doorway of the practice room where Justin was hard at work on the same Schubert Impromptu he'd been working on the day I first met him. I frowned, remembering Mr. Laden's offer. I started to leave, but I couldn't ignore the subtle tendency Justin had of accenting every third note in the scales. It was a common bad habit with that piece of music. Perhaps I should just mention it to him—in passing, of course.

Before I could talk myself out of it, I set my bag down and crept to Justin's side. He noticed me at once and quickly stopped.

"Hi, Beth," he beamed.

"Hey, Justin. How's it going?"

"Better, I think. I still can't get the chords down in the middle section but the opening is better, thanks to you. Wanna hear?"

How could I resist? His youthful innocence endeared him to me instantly, yet he looked so serious. I didn't bother to confess that I'd already heard it a moment earlier.

"Of course I do. Please . . ." I motioned for him to begin, but he didn't make it past the first line before I stopped him. "Wait. Hang on a second."

Justin looked up at me quizzically. "What'd I do wrong?"

"Nothing . . . wrong exactly. Let me show you something—then you tell me if you hear the difference."

I gestured for him to slide over; he eagerly obliged. I played the first few lines twice, right hand only, of course. The first time, I accented every third note; the second time, I left off the accent. I stopped and looked at Justin who appeared rather perplexed.

"What I am listening for?"

"Listen again. This time, close your eyes."

I repeated the exercise, emphasizing the accent slightly more. This time Justin heard it right away.

"Wow! There's a huge difference."

I inclined my head in agreement. "You're accenting every third note; it's very subtle, but noticeable. Are you keeping your forearms parallel to the floor like I suggested?"

"I'm trying to," he replied, slightly frustrated.

"I want you to try it with your eyes closed—and I want you to picture your hand 'falling' from the top of the keyboard to the bottom. Don't accent anything along the way until you reach the turn at the bottom."

For the next hour, Justin played and I offered suggestions. I had no idea how much time had passed until Darla showed up.

"Beth! I've been looking all over for you! I thought you were going to the library."

"I started to—I got a little side-tracked. Sorry."

"It's fine," she eyed Justin questioningly, "but I need to hurry—I was supposed to pick up my little brother ten minutes ago. He's probably flipping out right now."

I grabbed my bag hurriedly and said goodbye to Justin, encouraging him to work on the techniques I'd shown him. He thanked me and then went back to work. His dedication to the instrument was admirable—and one I recognized all too well.

Darla dropped me off after swinging by Andersen Elementary to retrieve her very agitated little brother. I was surprised to discover that Uncle Connor had already arrived home from work. He was in the kitchen chopping onions, preparing a garnish for a large pot of chili. Apparently, there was going to be a good game on tonight. We usually ordered pizza on Mondays, unless Uncle Connor was particularly excited about a game or was expecting company.

"Is Marci coming home tonight?" I tried to sound casual but picturing the two of them together still made me laugh. I couldn't help but chuckle.

"What's so funny?" Uncle Connor demanded suspiciously. He

pulled his eyebrows together scornfully. "And yes, Marci will be here, but not until later."

"Cool," I said nonchalantly, letting the subject drop. "Need some help?" I asked, eyeing the mess he'd made in the kitchen. He looked around the room sheepishly and grinned.

"Pretty obvious, huh?"

I tossed my bag aside, washed my hands, and grabbed the cheese from the refrigerator. The odors from the onions struck my eyes causing them to burn even though I was standing at least three feet away from them.

Uncle Connor smiled and handed me the cheese grater; his eyes were moist with tears—I assumed from the onions—and he started to sniffle, pretending to cry. Then he opened the freezer door and stuck his head inside. He opened his eyes widely, allowing the frosty air to beat on his face.

"What in the heck are you doing?" I snorted playfully.

"Getting rid of the onion fumes, obviously." He pretended to be disgusted by my obvious ignorance.

"That is the most ridiculous thing I've ever seen," I giggled.

"You laugh, but it works every time. See? No more tears."

"I'll keep that in mind the next time I have onion duty," I teased. Surprisingly, though, his eyes had actually cleared.

We worked silently side by side for the next several minutes, getting the chili ready to serve and cleaning up the mess he'd made. I cocked my head to one side and watched him furtively through the corner of my eye. It had always puzzled me that he never seemed to change. *Immortals don't age,* I remembered Jonathan saying, *they progress.* He'd never had the chance to explain what he meant by that.

"Can I ask you something?" I asked hesitantly.

"I was wondering why it was taking you so long." Uncle Connor grinned smugly, but his eyes didn't leave the simmering pot of chili as he stirred. "I figured you'd hammer me with questions the moment you walked through the door. I even came home early so I wouldn't have to miss the game while you interrogated me."

I pressed my lips together and scowled. "Well, it's not every day you find out someone you know has immortal fluid in his veins," I reminded him.

"Granted," he acquiesced. He removed the wooden spoon from the chili and turned down the flame. Then he reached for the hand towel and began wiping down the stove. "Fire away."

"Jonathan said immortals don't age, they progress. I don't understand the difference." I watched Uncle Connor's expression as he considered my question. He turned toward me with the towel still in his hand and rested his back against the counter.

"Immortals age . . . but at such a slow rate it's undetectable. Remember, age is connected to time, and time for immortals is not the same as it is for mortals." He checked my expression for some sign of comprehension. Finding none, he scratched his head and sighed.

"Beth, time as you know it only exists on this planet. Elsewhere in the universe, time is different—relative, if you will. Mortal beings on earth age because finite units of measure—applicable only to earth—determine the length of their lives. From the time they're born, both mortals and immortals grow and change. Their bodies regenerate themselves until they reach a certain level of development, or 'progression.' But at a certain age, a mortal's body begins to *de*generate. Aging, in the sense you're referring to, is part of that degenerative process."

"If the reclamation in immortals happens when they reach the age of maturity, then why are you older than Jonathan?" I asked.

"I'll try to explain," he said, pausing for a moment to consider. "An immortal progresses in order to fulfill a purpose. Like all species, humans—both mortal and immortal—have a compelling drive to procreate. But with an immortal man, the drive is even stronger. A married immortal, one who has created offspring, will continue to progress because he is fulfilling his procreative purpose."

"So Jonathan won't progress any further until he's married?"

"That's part of it, yes."

"What's the other part?"

"Jonathan comes from a long line of travelers—" He stopped short. "I think it would be better if he explained that part himself. As for his progression, it didn't stop; it just slowed down, preserving his chance to produce offspring."

I thought about that for a moment. Jonathan as a father . . .

"Don't you see?" Uncle Connor continued. "That's why there's so much research being done to perfect the science of biological immortality." He wiped down the last of the countertop and folded the dish towel, setting it next to the sink. Then he motioned for me to sit down at the kitchen table.

"Humankind has sought the fountain of youth for centuries. There are numerous stories, myths, and legends. There always have been, ever since the dawn of time. Researchers, experts in the fields of biology and physics, have discovered knowledge that makes them confident they can stop aging in humans, creating a race of biological immortals."

"And my mom was involved in that research?"

"Your mother was right in the thick of it. It's all in her binders. According to scientists, when we're born, our cellular membranes are perfect . . . strong . . . sort of like the plastic tip on a new shoelace. Over time, the plastic tip weakens, and the shoelace frays. That's what human cells do. Researchers believe that all they need to do is figure out how to keep the cells from fraying, and they'll be able to stop aging."

For nearly an hour, Uncle Connor attempted to explain the scientific complexities of immortality; but as near as I could tell, it was all based on theory. I spewed questions so rapidly I was certain he felt he was under attack by machine-gun fire. His patience impressed me, but when he heard a car pull into the driveway, he leapt up eagerly to answer the door. I think I detected a glimpse of welcome relief in his expression.

"Marci's early, I'll go help her. You stir the chili," he ordered as he hastily left the kitchen. I laughed silently at his abruptness.

I lifted the lid from the pot of simmering chili and began to stir slowly. The odor of fresh basil, onions, tomatoes, and garlic floated upward from the pan and lingered in the air. I drew in a deep breath, savoring the aroma as I circled the wooden spoon around the perimeter of the pan. As I watched the spoon, I thought about the many cycles of science—the water cycle, the rock cycle, the nitrogen cycle, the life cycle, and the matter cycle—all of them required a power source. Was God that source? Was it logical to believe that it all happened by chance?

I was lost in thought as I pondered these questions, hypnotized by the circular pattern of the spoon's wake in the chili. I lifted the spoon from the pot and rapped it firmly on the edge of the pan. The circular flow ceased to exist, as if it had never been there . . . like the death of a mortal. I quickly returned the spoon to the pot, anxious to recreate the circular wake. Just then, two warm arms wrapped around my waist, startling me from my thoughts.

"Ahh!" I jumped, but the arms around me only tightened and pulled me closer.

"Hi there," Jonathan's voice vibrated softly in my ear. I relaxed immediately, resting my back against his chest.

"I thought you were in Jackson Hole."

"I was. I finished earlier than expected. I can go back if you like," he joked.

"Uh uh," I shook my head. He turned me around to face him and started to say something but instead he laughed.

"What?" I demanded, suddenly self-conscious.

"Your face," he chuckled. "What were you doing, giving yourself a steam bath?"

I started to turn toward the counter to reach for a towel, but he wouldn't loosen his grip on my waist so I did the next best thing. I leaned forward and rubbed my face against his sweater.

"Nice," he drawled sarcastically. But he took advantage of the closeness and tightened his hold even more. I tried to pull my face away from his sweater, but I didn't get far before I felt his lips on mine. An electric charge ran through me as I raised my arms and folded them around his neck, pulling myself into his kiss.

"Eh hmm," Uncle Connor cleared his throat loudly.

Jonathan and I broke apart instantly and I turned several shades of scarlet.

Uncle Connor glared at us both without saying a word. I couldn't tell if he was upset or just trying to make me squirm for the fun of it.

"Hmph," he grunted. "I need to stir the chili."

Jonathan and I moved out of his way and sat down at the kitchen table.

"Good thing you came over," Uncle Connor said as he stirred. "Beth, here, has been interrogating me all afternoon."

Jonathan chuckled and brushed his hand along the length of my arm, sending chills up my spine. He lifted my crippled hand slightly and cupped his fingers around it, softly stroking the side of my thumb with his. He seemed to favor my hurt hand. I couldn't wrap my fingers around his or even clasp his hand; all I could do was allow my folded fingers to rest in the protective cup of his palm. He seemed to like that.

Jonathan winked at me. "And I thought I was just coming over to watch the football game."

Uncle Connor turned toward us. I could see the wheels spinning in his head as he gazed at me thoughtfully. He cut his eyes over to Jonathan and peered back at me without speaking. I glanced at Jonathan, but he just looked at me and shrugged his shoulders. When I turned my focus back to Uncle Connor, he was looking at the ceiling, moving his head slightly back and forth. He was obviously working through something in his mind.

"What, for heaven's sake?" I finally blurted. My curiosity couldn't stand the uneasy silence any longer.

"There's something I want to show you," he said resolutely; then he glanced at Jonathan. "I might as well show both of you."

Jonathan and I looked at each other, shrugged, and turned back to Uncle Connor in one fluid movement. Uncle Connor reached down and checked the burner, setting it on the lowest possible flame. He covered the pot and set the spoon carefully on its spoon rest.

"Come with me."

We followed him through the laundry room and down to the basement. When we reached the bottom, Uncle Connor turned toward the area behind the staircase. I knew there were rooms there, but that part of the basement was usually off limits. The first room contained several pieces of old, well-worn furniture. There were also several boxes stacked along the walls.

The next room was lined floor-to-ceiling with deep-set bookshelves along three of its four walls. A dark mahogany desk spanned nearly the entire width of the room. Opposite the desk was a large easy chair resting next to an old fashioned floor lamp, the sort of lamp that required candles instead of light bulbs. The style and furnishings of the room didn't fit with anything else in the house; it was a room transported from another time. There were no modern amenities—no phone, no computer, no stereo, no track lighting—nothing common to a modern study. But it wasn't to either of these rooms that Uncle Connor was leading us.

We followed him around the back of the staircase to a small door. I assumed it led to an oversized storage area underneath the stairs. When Uncle Connor opened the door and pulled the light chain, I could see that the area went back far beyond the stairway. We had to duck our heads to walk through the door and follow the narrow passageway. Anxiety suddenly erupted in the pit of my stomach. Uncle Connor obviously wasn't aware that I had claustrophobia. Any tightly enclosed space made me extremely fearful.

Down the center of the passage was a long carpet runner that covered most of the concrete floor. Uncle Connor reached down and flipped the rug back, revealing what I could only describe as a trap door. A picture suddenly flashed through my mind—a picture of a safe house where slaves hid during the time of the Underground Railroad.

"Whoa," Jonathan nodded approvingly. "Very cool!"

The anxiety in my stomach twisted into a painful knot as I realized Uncle Connor's expectation. My heart began to race and my breathing escalated rapidly. I struggled to breathe evenly. I could feel a full-blown panic attack coming on.

Uncle Connor lifted the door. It creaked, protesting loudly as he removed it from its resting place. He secured a rope attached to the inside of the door around a large eye hook in the floor so the door couldn't close. He climbed down a wooden ladder, leaping abruptly to the floor below as he neared the last three rungs, and disappeared into the darkness. He reappeared a moment later after switching on a light that illuminated the area below us. He beckoned to us to follow him.

"I-I don't . . . I can't," I stuttered. My eyes widened and I stared desperately at Jonathan.

"It's okay," he assured me, suddenly comprehending my phobia. "I'll help you." He waited for me to respond but I was frozen, my feet planted like two fence posts cemented to the ground. I breathed deeply, focusing on taking long breaths and holding them before exhaling. I knew it wouldn't be long before I began to hyperventilate. It was all I could do to maintain control.

"Don't worry, Beth, I'll be right next to you."

Still oblivious to my discomfort, Uncle Connor called up to me, "This was one of your mother's favorite rooms." He again held his hand up and motioned for us to climb down the ladder. Jonathan didn't hesitate. As soon as he was a few rungs down, he reached up for me.

I sat down on the cement floor, swung my legs into the door opening, and reached down to grab hold of the top rung of the ladder. I grasped the rung tightly with my right hand and secretly cursed my deformed left hand because I was unable to wrap it around the ladder for security. I knew if I kept my eyes open I'd see myself going under the ground and panic. I closed my eyes tightly and tried to visualize myself in a large, spacious field—a wide open expanse of green grass and wild flowers. I forced my legs to move down the rungs of the ladder, keeping my mind focused on the open meadow. I felt the security of Jonathan's hand on my back as I stepped downward, but I refused to open my eyes until my feet were safely on the ground and I felt his arms snugly around my waist. I quickly turned to him and buried my face in his chest, panting heavily into his thick cotton sweater.

"Are you okay?" he asked, cupping the back of my head gently with his large hand. I shook my head back and forth, not looking away from his chest. His shoulders shook, and I realized he was laughing.

"You think this is funny?" I wailed. "This is like being buried alive!"

"I'm sorry." He continued to chuckle, but did his best to steady me.

Eventually I pulled away from him, but kept my eyes focused on his sweater. I was suddenly aware of a strange noise. It was the sound of water dripping but the sound was magnified, each drip ringing across the surrounding walls like a canyon echo. The cool air smelled of rich minerals, like soil after a fresh rain.

I dropped my head to peer down at the floor and discovered I was standing on a large, flat slab of glistening granite. Slowly, one inch at a time, I turned my body to the side and lifted my eyes. Uncle Connor stood a few feet away with his arms folded across his chest, waiting patiently for me to get hold of myself. I gasped as I beheld the walls of the room, sucking in a lungful of brisk air that smelled like a combination of calcite and salt. It was pleasant and fresh, not at all musty or moldy as I would have expected a cellar to smell. The light globe that hung loosely from the ceiling reflected off the granite floor, casting shimmers of light in all directions. It looked like a floor carpeted with silver, white, and black glitter. I looked closely at the walls surrounding us; they were glistening limestone draped with glowing moisture that revealed a subtle rainbow of colors when the light hit them. The room was unlike anything I'd ever seen.

In sharp contrast to the natural floor and walls, a large metal table surrounded by four black stools with tall backs sat in the center of the room. The table was covered with three ring binders, books, scrolls, drawings, and more binders, all arranged in a sort of organized mess. I got the feeling that whoever sat here knew exactly where everything was.

It took me several moments to grasp the reality that we were standing in a large hole beneath the basement of Uncle Connor's house. It seemed impossible. It was as if we'd stepped off the last rung of the ladder and landed in a completely different world. My jaw dropped as my eyes surveyed the room, examining every detail, and committing as much to memory as possible.

"Wow!" I whispered to Jonathan. "Wow!"

Uncle Connor smiled approvingly. "Remarkable, isn't it?" His voice echoed softly in the chamber as he spoke. "You asked me about Andersen being one of the vortexes of the earth. Well, here you are. This room is located very near the heart of the Andersen vortex. The energy emanating from the minerals imbedded in the floor and walls surpasses anything I've ever witnessed. I built my house on this spot for that very reason."

"Cool," Jonathan nodded admiringly.

Although I was intrigued by this amazing chamber, I was confused as to why he'd decided to show it to me. Then it hit me.

"My mom knew about this, didn't she?" I exclaimed.

Uncle Connor nodded; there was a hint of sadness behind his smile. "She believed that in the heart of a vortex, science and faith united harmoniously. She was convinced that in here her mind opened to an influx of inspiration, melding the seemingly contradictory laws of reason and religion. She described it once as receiving pure light and knowledge from heaven leading to new perspectives on old ideas. In her opinion, the energy in this room enabled her to comprehend the complexities of scientific laws on a higher plane."

Uncle Connor walked slowly to the center of the room and brushed his hand along the top of the table, pausing each time his hand passed over a binder or book. "This is where you'll find answers to many of your questions about immortals," he said resolutely. "As you can see, the binder I gave you is one of many." One by one, he lifted each binder and read its title aloud: "*Birth and Destruction of Immortals, Immortality and the Creation of Man, Adam and Eve, The Age of the Earth.*" He paused before picking up the next one—it was clearly the most worn: "*Biological Immortality.*" He read the title slowly as he flipped pensively through the pages. "This is the one she was working on before the accident."

I approached the table, humbled; there was so much about my mother I didn't know. I'd always considered her eccentric and strange in a spacey kind of way. I suddenly felt guilty; I'd underestimated just how intelligent she'd been.

"I wanted you to know . . . to know your mom better." He paused, setting the binder carefully back in its place. "I don't have one tenth of the knowledge she had." He spoke so softly that it sounded like he was talking to himself. He gazed at me quizzically for a moment, pulling his eyebrows into a tight frown.

"What?" I asked, suddenly self-conscious. Jonathan squeezed my waist, pulling me snugly to his side.

"With all your questions, how can it be that you haven't asked the most obvious one?"

He cocked his head to the side and studied me carefully, as if searching my face for something he couldn't find. I felt uneasy under his silent gaze. The echo of the moisture falling on the walls was deafening in contrast to the suddenly quiet room. I searched my brain for the question I was obviously missing.

"I don't understand," I said, confused.

"You haven't asked the one question that I've dreaded the most."

Uncle Connor continued to stare at me for a moment, then he slowly shifted his gaze to the table and then back to me. He gestured with his eyes and a slight nod of his head to the table, and my eyes followed his movement, searching for some hint of what he was trying to communicate without saying it outright. It was supposed to be obvious whatever it was, and I was frustrated that I couldn't grasp his meaning. I looked at the titles of the binders on the table several times, each time taking note of the direction my mother's research was taking her.

Then like a jolt of electricity, comprehension came. My eyes widened and my mouth fell open, stunned by the revelation that surged through me. It was so obvious, and yet at the same time, so unfathomable.

"Mom!" I whispered. Uncle Connor concentrated his gaze, peering sharply into my eyes as if trying to telepathically transfer information from his mind to mine. I clutched my stomach and the room began to swirl around me. Black specks shot like dancing stars across the white of the limestone walls as my knees weakened like soft rubber—no longer able to support my weight. Instantly, I felt Jonathan grab me under my arms and set me down on one of the stools. He held my shoulders firmly, steadying me until I could regain my composure. I began to breathe deeply, too deeply and too rapidly.

"Beth, slow down," Jonathan said calmly. "Breathe slowly. Watch me," he said, pulling my chin up so that his eyes held mine. I bit my lips together and concentrated on following his breathing pattern. After several moments my heart rate slowed and my breathing returned to normal.

"That's better," he said, satisfied. "You okay?"

I nodded, still biting my lips. I placed my hand over my chest and took several deep breaths before speaking.

"She was . . . like you." I gaped wild-eyed at Jonathan. "And you," I said, turning to look at Uncle Connor.

Uncle Connor acknowledged my statement with a single nod.

"And like Marci," he added quietly.

Marci's one of them? It took a minute to process this information. A million questions soared in my mind, but something wasn't making sense.

"But if Mom was immortal—"

Emotion suddenly burned like a smoldering flame in my throat. "I don't understand, Uncle Connor. How could she die?"

"She didn't die, Beth, she was destroyed by another immortal."

Jonathan watched me carefully, ready to act if I lost control again.

"It was immortals who were there that night, wasn't it!" I searched Jonathan's face for confirmation.

"Only another immortal could have disabled her and destroyed her body," Jonathan explained. He could see the confusion in my eyes as I considered what he was suggesting. It didn't make sense that an immortal's body could be destroyed. Wasn't that the same thing as death?

"An immortal body is made of flesh and bone, just like a mortal body," Uncle Connor began to explain. "It's the fluids that flow through an immortal's body that carry the elements of immortality—the elements that keep us from aging, suffering from disease, or dying. Unfortunately, because we share the blood of the mortal realm, we're limited."

"But why would someone want to destroy my mom?" My voice cracked as I sputtered the question. Tears spilled over and ran down the sides of my face. I brushed them away quickly, trying to stay focused on Uncle Connor. Jonathan rubbed my shoulders sympathetically.

"We aren't sure. The most obvious explanation is that she had information others didn't want her to have."

"Others?"

"Yes. Just like humans, some immortals live by a darker law."

I tightened my arms around my stomach.

"There's something else, Beth," Uncle Connor added, exchanging a quick glance with Jonathan. "Immortality passes in the genes. The alleles are recessive. They pass down, sometimes skipping several generations, then suddenly show up if partnered with another carrier. Like me, your mother only had immortal alleles to pass to . . . her offspring."

He paused, allowing me to absorb this information. It didn't make sense.

"But I'm not immortal . . . am I?" I said, questioningly. Uncle Connor shot Jonathan a determined look before he continued.

"We don't know yet. . . ." His voice clung to the last word.

"Yet?"

"Your mother and I both breached the most important code of the Lebas." I raised my eyebrows, but he held out his hand to stop me from interrupting. "The Lebas is the high council of the immortals. One of the 'expectations' is that immortals will not interfere or intervene in the natural lives of mortals—unless authorized to do so. Marriage to a mortal is forbidden."

"Not always," Jonathan interrupted.

"The exceptions are rare." Uncle Connor shot a warning glance at Jonathan. "Procreation in mixed marriages dilutes the flow of immortal fluids and taints the bloodline permanently. Your mother and I married mortals and produced offspring—it didn't sit well with the Lebas.

Uncle Connor paused again, searching my face for signs of an impending meltdown, but I was beyond that point. I had detached myself from the sensationalism of his words and slid into the emotionless, safe role of scientist. I was vaguely aware of Jonathan's arm resting on my shoulders, but my concentration was fully focused on gathering information and categorizing it without internalizing any of it.

"What did they do when you violated their rules?" I asked.

"We lost our standing with the council—we were 'demoted' you could say. That's how I ended up in Wyoming." Uncle Connor chuckled darkly. "No one on the council was surprised when your mother ended up marrying your father; she had always been fascinated with mortals. It was inevitable she would eventually fall in love with one of them."

Uncle Connor smiled warmly. "And she fell hard for your father! I never saw anything like it." '

A lump lodged in my throat. I thought of the many times I'd watched my mom wrap her arms around my father. She practically idolized him.

Uncle Connor continued. "The offspring," he gestured toward me, "of a mortal/immortal marriage are usually mortal because mortal genes dominate. However, some mortals carry the recessive gene and if passed to a child, signs of reclamation usually manifest themselves around the time a child reaches biological adulthood—seventeen to twenty for females and somewhere between nineteen and twenty-two for males."

Jonathan squeezed my side again.

"I haven't manifested any signs," I said, sounding remorseful. I was suddenly aware that the thought of being immortal—even to a small degree—intrigued me. Jonathan reached for my hand and lifted it, holding it gently in his.

"Your hand," he said softly, "it should have—" he hesitated, then sighed.

"—healed," I said sadly.

Jonathan nodded.

"But it's still too soon to know," Uncle Connor added reass-uringly.

"You just barely turned nineteen, and . . . well, the fact that you were in a coma for so long may have affected the timing."

I nodded. "And your sons—Carl? Nick? What about them?" I asked.

"Carl yes. Nick . . ." he shook his head, "there are no signs in Nick. He doesn't know about any of this. Carl, on the other hand, began to manifest the signs early. As you can imagine, he embraced the idea enthusiastically." He grinned, rolling his eyes as he spoke, but I sensed there was pride behind his smile. "But your situation may prove more . . ." he paused, searching for the right word, "*unique* . . . than you know."

"How so?"

"Your father is mortal, but he's the descendent of an immortal. Not only that, he's a direct descendent of the royal family of the Lebas." I felt Jonathan stiffen slightly as he controlled a low gasp. Uncle Connor continued, "Their bloodline was all but destroyed in the mid-eighteen.hundreds by a clan of immortals seeking the throne of the Lebas. If your father passed an immortal gene to you . . . well . . . you can imagine that your mother would have guarded that information—at any cost."

Uncle Connor looked at Jonathan briefly and then turned back to me. "If, indeed, you begin to manifest signs of immortality, *both* sides of the immortal realm will want you. Your mother knew this and searched desperately for some way to shield you from the manifestation of any immortal traits. She was determined to find a way to keep you mortal. That's one of the reasons she immersed herself so passionately into the research on biological immortality. She figured if there was a way to make a mortal immortal, then by reversing the process, an immortal could become mortal."

"She wanted to keep me mortal?" The prospect saddened me.

"She was willing to risk everything to protect you from our world."

No one in the room spoke for several minutes. I half expected to wake up and discover that all of this was a dream. There was no secret room under Uncle Connor's basement, my mother was just a normal mom who died in a tragic car accident, and I was merely an average teenager in her senior year of high school. I tried to hold onto those thoughts, but my futile attempt was comparable to harnessing a windstorm. And blaring in my mind was the inescapable realization that this world my mother died to keep me from was also Jonathan's world. Would being part of Jonathan's world somehow make my mother's death meaningless?

"May I take some of these books upstairs to my room?" I asked, turning to Uncle Connor.

"Yes . . . except for this one," he said, picking up the binder entitled *Biological Immortality*. "This binder would be exceedingly valuable to the Niaces—"

He broke off his sentence, interrupted by the awareness that I didn't know what he was talking about. "Those who rebelled against the Lebas are called Niaces," he explained. "They're loathsome beings who seek to control the mortal world. They strive endlessly to usurp the authority of the Lebas and destroy those who support them."

Jonathan stiffened and then reached over and picked up a couple of the binders. "Enough for one day?" he asked.

I nodded, ignoring the slight catch in Jonathan's voice as he spoke.

"Then how about some of your uncle's great chili and Monday Night Football?" He smiled, but it seemed forced.

"For what it's worth, Beth," Uncle Connor chimed in, "you've assimilated an enormous amount of information in the past few days with a tremendous amount of grace. Your mother hoped you'd never need to know all this, but I suspect . . . well . . . I *know* she'd be proud of your willingness to maintain an open mind."

"Thank you." I didn't know what else to say. That was the highest compliment he could have given me.

Uncle Connor led the way up the ladder to the trap door. It was an eerie feeling to be climbing *up* to a basement, and my heart began to pound relentlessly—again—as I approached the top of the ladder. Uncle Connor reached down and lifted me through the opening. Once grounded, I was anxious to get out of the closet and back upstairs to the main level. Jonathan followed behind me as Uncle

Connor secured the trap door and replaced the carpet that concealed it. He locked the closet door on the way out and stuffed the key into his pants pocket. I sensed that I was not welcome to return to the secret room without him present—not that I could imagine myself ever going down there alone. I chilled at the thought.

In the kitchen, the chili still sat simmering on the burner. It smelled wonderful. I lifted the lid and stirred the spicy mixture, a simple, automatic motion that I found comforting. Uncle Connor went straight to the television set in the family room, allowing Jonathan and me some privacy. I watched the spoon make circular patterns in the chili while Jonathan stood behind me, his arms wrapped tightly around my waist. I sighed. It was as if the last two hours had never happened—but my life would never be the same.

Boundaries

CHAPTER 11

*S*everal nights later, an e-mail came in from my dad.

Beth,

Finally received clearance to write. Hope all is going well for you at school. I miss you every day and wish I could see you. Still no word on how long they will need me here. I'm sure your uncle is taking good care of you.

I have to keep this brief as time is limited. If things have gone as planned, you can expect a couple of deliveries soon. One of them is quite peculiar; you might need help with it. The other is a Christmas present. I'm sorry I can't be with you for the holidays. I'll miss you shaking all the gifts.

This is important. We are fairly confident that the mail we send is secure; however, we can't be sure that the mail we receive won't be intercepted. Write when you can, but be aware that others may read the mail you send me.

I love you always,

Dad

P.S. Tell Carl thanks for me.

I read the e-mail from my father several times before closing the screen. A wave of emotion rose within me as I thought of him alone during the upcoming holidays. This would be the second Christmas since my mom died, and I knew it would be extra hard and lonely for him. I was fortunate, surrounded by people I loved; but who would be there for my dad?

I plucked out a reply to his e-mail, cursing the bent fingers on my left hand that prevented me from typing quickly.

Dad,

It's great to finally hear from you. I think about you every day and hope you are okay. I miss you tons and wish we could be together. Uncle Connor has been great, and his new wife is cool. I'm learning a lot from her, and I'm making new friends that keep me busy. You'll be happy to know that I'm kind of playing the piano again, at least halfway. I met a boy who plays very well, and he plays duets with me. It reminds me of when you and I used to play together.

Guess what? Carl gave me his car. Don't worry, Uncle Connor made some alterations first. Better go.

Love you lots,

Beth

Almost forgot, Carl said to tell you that things are on schedule.

I hit the send button and buried my face in my hands, holding back the tears that would inevitably come as I thought about my father. I hadn't realized how much I missed him until I read his message.

I thought about the "peculiar" delivery that was arriving and wondered why I would need help with it. It was just like my dad to keep me guessing. He always made a game out of giving me gifts—hoping to throw me off guard so I wouldn't guess what he'd bought for me. This was probably just his way of trying to fool me. I always got in trouble at Christmastime for shaking my presents to predict what was inside, so dad became very creative when packaging my gifts. The memories of his ingenious and often ridiculous attempts to stump me made me chuckle. The subtle release of emotion was just enough to send tears streaming down my cheeks. I didn't try to stop them; instead, I curled up on my bed, wrapped my arms around my pillow, and cried openly.

"Beth," a faint whisper hissed behind me. My eyes flashed open and I turned toward the sound, but my room was dark and I couldn't tell if there was anybody there.

"Uncle Connor?" I called into the darkness. "Marci?"

My room suddenly seemed unusually quiet, and the silence unnerved me. I felt a slight breeze pass next to me, giving me the eerie sensation that I wasn't alone. I spun around and noticed my curtains swaying gently along the floor. I could see through the patterned lace that the window was open slightly. I slid off my bed and moved cautiously toward the window, unable to exhale as I approached. My fingers searched for the split in the free dangling curtains and pulled them aside. I surveyed the moonlit scene outside the window, carefully scrutinizing every tree and shadow. The moon hung low in the sky, casting long shadows across the yard. But there was no perceivable movement other than the gentle ruffling of fir trees in the distance.

I reached up to clasp the edge of the window so I could slide it shut. As I did so, another gentle breeze swept by me. The breeze came from inside the room and passed through the narrow opening in the window to the darkness outside. I gasped, startled by the unnatural flow of energy, and quickly heaved the window shut and secured the lock. I wasn't easily frightened as a rule, yet I couldn't shake the feeling that someone or something had been inside my room.

I turned around and moved slowly away from the window. Backing myself up against the wall, I inched my way toward my bathroom. When I finally reached the opening, I quickly flipped on the light switch. Light flooded across the bedroom, revealing nothing unusual or out of place. My computer was still on, but sleeping. The covers on my bed were wrinkled where I had been lying. The curtains hung softly, undisturbed, against the floor. I breathed a deep sigh of relief and chuckled quietly at my overactive imagination.

I went to the bathroom sink and turned on the water, allowing it to run a few minutes as it heated. The warm water running across the tops of my hands made my arms fall limply along the edge of the sink and my body relaxed. I bent my head toward the bowl and splashed the warm water on my face, then reached blindly for the soap. After I finished rinsing, I grabbed a hand towel from the towel rack and pressed its softness to my face; but when I opened my eyes, I caught the reflection of a dark shadow hovering behind me.

"Ahhg!" I gasped, sucking in too much air. I let out a high-pitched shriek and my flailing arms threw water all over the mirror.

My eyes flashed open wildly—then I suddenly realized I was no longer standing in the bathroom; I was lying on my bed, curled up as I had been after reading my father's e-mail. My heart pounded fiercely against my chest as I surveyed my surroundings and realized that I had been dreaming. I stared sharply at the window and then moved my eyes slowly toward the bathroom door. The room was quiet and warm—normal. I pressed my hand to my chest and breathed deeply, calming my heart rate each time I exhaled.

I wonder if immortals have nightmares?

I turned over and peered at the clock next to the computer on my desk—3:54 a.m.— too early to get up, but I was afraid to go back to sleep. I slid off the side of the bed and strolled sleepily to the computer, searching for a track of classical music. I finally decided on *Beethoven Beloved*, a series of Beethoven's most beautiful melodies. The first on the track was *Moonlight Sonata*. I lay quietly and as I drifted into sleep, a vision painted itself in my mind of Jonathan and I sitting together at a shiny grand piano, my left hand on top of his, and my head nestled contentedly against his shoulder.

The next day dragged: seconds turned into minutes and minutes to hours. Eric returned, still blue under both eyes but in reasonably good spirits. I overheard several people inquiring about the fight he'd been involved in, but he deflected their questions by admitting that he had very little memory of what happened. All the hype seemed to make him even more popular than ever.

Eric walked with me between classes as usual, but he was careful not to overstep the invisible boundaries I'd drawn between us. His humble demeanor and the childlike pain in his eyes made it easy for me to feel a growing sense of compassion towards him. It angered me when I heard his friends harass him about me.

I don't know what prompted me to do it, but after lunch, just before Eric walked away, I reached up on my toes and kissed him on the cheek.

"What was that for?"

"For them," I said, cutting my eyes toward his group of friends who stood several yards away analyzing Eric's every move.

"Hmph," Eric snorted, rustling the hair across the top of my head. "Did you seriously just give me a mercy kiss?"

"I-I just . . ." I was perplexed by his reaction.

"Ah, geez, Beth, you're killing me!" Eric shook his head incredulously. He started to walk away but stopped and turned back to face me. For a moment he looked as though he wanted to say something, but he just shook his head again and turned around to join his friends.

As I approached the music hall after school, several of the rooms buzzed with the sounds of various instruments. I wondered at the sudden increase in activity. I was relieved to find the last room in the hall vacant and I quickly took my place at the piano, securing the room before anyone else arrived.

The last piece of classical music I'd heard was Beethoven's *Moonlight Sonata* last night in my room, so it was the melody in my mind as I stared at the keys. I began to play the right hand of the sonata, suddenly aware that the entire melody was based on a right hand solo. I played the first few measures and a thought occurred to me. The bass could be played with one note if I left off the octave. I lifted my left hand to the piano and positioned it so that my knuckles aimed directly at the keys. I tapped out the bass notes with one knuckle and began playing the right hand. I knew the music by heart, so I closed my eyes and played, improvising the left hand where necessary. The feeling of playing with two hands—rough as it was—elated me, and I couldn't help but experience a sense of satisfaction as I played through the entire sonata. As I neared the end of the song, I was aware that I was no longer alone. But I couldn't bring myself to stop playing until I finished the piece. I sensed Jonathan's quiet presence behind me as I softly struck the final chord.

"Hi." I greeted him without turning around. He ghosted closer to me, so close that his breath softly grazed my neck, causing goose bumps to rise on my arms.

"Hey," he answered.

"Oh!" I snapped my head around abruptly, startled because the sound of his voice had come from so far away. He stood casually by the entrance, several feet from where I sat. Confused and a little freaked out, I raised my hand and rubbed it against my neck where I'd felt his breath just a moment earlier.

"I could have sworn you were standing right here," I said, patting my shoulder with the palm of my hand. Jonathan seemed perplexed for a second, but then he chuckled warmly.

"You were daydreaming about me, huh?" he teased.

"No," I blushed. "I'm serious. You were right here." I pointed to the area immediately behind me.

Jonathan moved across the room and stood next to me. "I'm here now," he said, gently rubbing my shoulders. I shook my head as if to dismiss the obvious flaw in my sense of depth perception.

"That was so weird," I hissed as a cold shudder raced down my spine. Perhaps my imagination was playing tricks on me, like in my dream last night.

Jonathan set a book on the piano book rest. It was the complete collection of Chopin's Études.

"A book of Études . . . for the étude," he grinned, gesturing toward me.

"Excuse me?" I questioned, amused by his smug smile. "Are you implying that I'm a difficult exercise?"

"Hmm," he teased, pinching his lips together. "More like a beautiful and intriguing composition that increases in depth and value with every turn of the page—definitely worthy of study." He bowed his head in a mock gesture as if addressing royalty.

I pretended to gag. Jonathan laughed.

"I decided we don't need the duet book anymore," he declared.

"What do you mean?" I asked as he opened the book and turned to the third number, the Étude in E.

"Together, we should be able to play just about any piece of music." He picked up the book and fanned through page after page of selections, then placed the book back on the piano.

"Are you kidding? Have you tried to play some of those Études?"

"A couple of them. Why?"

I reached for the book, opened it to one of the pieces towards the back, and set it in front of him. Études generally become more complicated and difficult the higher their number in a sequence. I purposely chose one of the most tedious pieces to make my point, the Étude in A minor.

"Impress me," I challenged, directing my eyes from his to the music.

"Eh . . . hum." Jonathan cleared his throat and rolled his eyes. "I really don't think this is necessary. . . ."

I raised my eyebrows in protest and Jonathan shrugged.

"If you insist—but you might want to move. This could get messy."

"I'll take my chances," I insisted, nudging him to begin.

To my delight and utter amazement, Jonathan placed his hands in position and began to play the Étude without the slightest hint of a struggle. He was completely relaxed. He played the piece flawlessly. I watched in total disbelief, stunned by his expertise and the ease with which his fingers flew across the keys. I'm certain my mouth hung open during the entire piece, and I continued to gape at him for several moments after he finished.

"Wow," I finally managed to mutter. "I *am* impressed."

"Well, I might have cheated," he winked.

"I can barely stumble through that one," I confessed.

I stared down at my deformed left hand and sighed regretfully. I didn't need to say anything; Jonathan quickly cupped my hand in his and raised it to his lips, lightly kissing the circular, red scar that I tried so hard to ignore.

"Beth," he said quietly, "what do you regret the most about losing the use of your hand—I mean, apart from the obvious?"

I considered his question carefully. "I regret that I never had a chance to make my mark, to rise to the highest level of achievement possible."

He thought about that and nodded.

"And . . ." I added, "I never had the chance to master the Hungarian Rhapsodies. That's what I was working on before the accident." I smiled resignedly.

Without saying anything more, Jonathan flipped the music back to Étude in E, placed his left hand on the keyboard, and motioned for me to begin playing. As we played, he continued to hold my left hand in his palm. His skin was unusually hot as he stroked the top of my hand with his fingers. After a moment, he released my hand and twisted his arm upward, laying the palm of his hand against my right cheek. He stroked my cheek with his thumb as he pulled me toward him so that my cheek rested against his shoulder. The warmth of his hand slowly caressing my face distracted me and I lost my place in the music, my fingers suspended mid-measure. A fire was slowly building inside of me.

"Let's get out of here," he whispered huskily.

We gathered our things and headed for the parking lot. Jonathan opened the door for me and tossed my things into the back seat, the same thing he'd done many times before. But this time there was a sense of urgency in his actions. He climbed into the driver's seat and sped out of the parking lot.

"What's the matter?" I asked, a little alarmed.

"I had to get out of there." He shrugged his shoulders, eyes intent on the road.

"Where are we going?"

"I don't know," he grinned. "I just couldn't stand sitting there a moment longer."

"I don't get it," I said, confused. "Was there a problem?"

"Definitely," he replied, biting his lips together, "Especially if you knew what was going through my mind—definitely a violation of my community contract." He grinned and looked at me intently. I blushed at what he was implying.

He chuckled grimly and turned his eyes back to the road. He drove beyond the town limits toward the foothills and stopped at a spot overlooking the valley. There was a breathtaking view of the Teton Mountains in the distance. A blanket of snow that didn't quite reach the valley floor covered the surrounding mountains and hills. The sun was low enough on the horizon that it cast an orange shadow against the white treetops, a perfect complement to the azure blue sky.

"Wow." I was momentarily overcome by the beauty of the scene. "It's like a postcard," I whispered.

Jonathan didn't let go of the steering wheel for a moment. He just sat there, staring through the windshield, undecided. Finally, he sighed and got out of the car, moving around the back to my side. He opened my door and extended his hand to help me out. He pulled me close to him, closed the door, and backed me against the car. The fire smoldering inside me burst into flame—I barely had time to catch my breath before he folded my arms around his neck and crushed his body to mine in a demanding embrace. His lips hunted for mine and he moaned softly as our lips met. He kissed me with an unfamiliar urgency that left us both gasping for air. He opened his mouth, moving my lips apart. My tongue willingly met his as I pulled myself into his kiss.

When our lips finally parted, Jonathan didn't back away as I expected. Instead, his strong arms pulled me even closer to him, holding me in a tight embrace even more passionate than his kiss. I was beginning to feel light-headed, but I didn't want him to let me go. I could feel his breath against my neck. His hands trembled as he slid them beneath my sweatshirt and along my back. I tightened my arms around him, wanting him closer still. The outside air was cool, but his body felt amazingly warm, and I melted into his warmth and shared his passion.

After several long minutes, Jonathan sighed and pulled his chin up, resting it on top of my head as he so often did. But he didn't release his hold on me. I nestled my face snugly against the base of his throat and concentrated on the path of his wandering hands.

"I've been thinking about you all day," he sighed, still breathing heavily. "About being with you . . . like this."

I couldn't find the words to respond so I said nothing, content to stroke the back of his neck with my fingers.

"It's a good thing we left," I finally mumbled against his neck.

"That's an understatement," he agreed, chuckling under his breath.

"This is nice," I whispered.

"You have no idea," he groaned softly. "I could hold you like this forever."

Finally, I gently pushed him away so I could study his face more closely. He pouted, confused by the sudden change in my demeanor.

"How long have you been immortal?" I asked softly.

He hesitated a moment. "I told you, I've always been immortal." His gaze narrowed as he scrutinized my expression.

"How long?" I insisted.

"Does it matter?" he asked, frowning.

I thought about it carefully before answering. "I need to know, Jonathan."

"Beth, it doesn't work like that," he said slowly, still studying my expression. "As I said before, immortals don't really age."

"I know what you said . . . and I get it . . . but how old would you be if you *did* age?"

"I can't answer that." He shook his head.

"Can't? Or won't?"

Jonathan looked hurt. "My family . . . we're known as travelers."

"Yes, Uncle Connor mentioned that, but he said you would have to explain it to me."

"Traveling is a special calling among immortals. Those who travel progress . . . *differently* . . . than those who don't."

"Why would traveling from place to place affect someone's progression?"

"Not from place to place . . ." Jonathan eyed me cautiously. "From time to time."

I stared at him blankly, utterly perplexed.

"I'll try to explain," he offered. He walked around the car, opened the trunk, and searched through the contents. He discarded several items until he found what he was looking for—a spool of rope. He began to unwind it, handing me one end and then backing away with the other end.

"Have you ever read the book *A Wrinkle in Time*?" he asked.

"Yeah, like in fifth grade," I scoffed.

"Well, it's sort of like that. Here . . ." he laid his end of the rope on the ground, then walked back to me. He took my end and set it on the ground too, then pulled the rope so that it formed a straight line across the ground.

"Mortals exist in linear time. A baby is born here . . ." he reached down and picked up a stone and placed it at one point on the rope. "Let's call this point 1847, just for example." Something in his eyes told me that the date was somehow significant to him. "Every point on the rope, before this rock, represents a time period leading up to 1847. The rest of the rope," he gestured to the part on the opposite side of the stone, "represents the years following 1847, chronologically speaking."

"Okay," I shrugged. That was simple enough.

"Mortals live their lives on this rope. They age by slowly sliding forward from the moment they're born until they die, and then their forward movement stops. They always move in a straight line and they never leave the rope—ever."

"Linear time," I confirmed. This was nothing new to me.

"Travelers don't slide on the rope . . . not technically." He reached down and pinched a spot on the rope between his thumb and index finger. "There are two schools of thought when it comes to travelers. The first theory is that we're connected to the rope at one given point—the point of conception—and we never leave that point on the rope."

I looked at him quizzically.

He pointed to the rope. "Pinch any spot on the rope."

I bent down and followed his instruction.

"Travelers experience linear time by bringing the rope—" he motioned for me to walk toward him, the rope still between my fingers, "—to them, creating a fold in the rope."

"Like *A Wrinkle in Time*," I muttered quietly.

"Well," he picked up the rope, "I admit it's a crude model, but yes."

"What's the second theory?"

"The second theory, and the one I favor, involves circular time." Jonathan gathered the rope and laid it out again, this time in a large circle. He set the stone on the edge of the circle.

"According to this theory, in order to stay on the rope, you have to move in a circular pattern. Any *linear* movement would throw you off the line of the circle. No matter where one begins on the circle, there is no end; time, in this scenario, is defined as an eternal round."

"Why do you prefer this theory?"

"Because it's reasonable. And because so much in nature is patterned after circles."

His answer made me think again about the water cycle, the nitrogen cycle—all the cycles of nature. I contemplated the concept for a moment.

"So, either way, age—"

"—doesn't exist." Jonathan finished my sentence for me. "Because for travelers, linear time—"

"—doesn't exist," I finished.

"The problem for most mortals is that they can't think beyond finite, linear patterns. Ironically, mortals are the ones who actually travel *through* time. For immortals, it's the other way around—time travels through us."

He gathered the rope and began weaving it around the spool until it formed a ball. Then he tossed it in the trunk and slammed the lid shut. He brushed his hands off as he walked back to me, gathering my waist in his hands. "Satisfied?" he asked hopefully.

"Hardly," I chuckled sarcastically. "I'm going to have to think about this."

I frowned as I pressed my wrists to the side of my head. I'd found myself doing this a lot lately. Knowing my luck, it would lead to premature wrinkling—same as with eye rolling.

Jonathan's face fell. I pressed my lips together, fighting back the urge to laugh as I watched him try to conceal an agonized sigh.

"You know this opens up a whole new line of questions for me, don't you?" I stated hesitantly.

"Yeah, I figured as much." Jonathan started to say something else then stopped. A playful grin lit up his face. He grabbed my sides and squeezed my ribs with his fingers, causing me to twist violently against his chest. Before I could protest, I was firmly in his arms.

"Go ahead, ask me another question." He smiled a naughty, daring smile.

It took some effort but I managed to think of something. "How does the—" but he cut me off mid sentence when he pressed his lips lightly against mine, teasing me.

I couldn't possibly win this one, so I decided to lose graciously and enjoy myself. I wrapped my arms around his neck and pulled myself as close to him as I could.

"You win," I muttered against his lips, trying to shake my head without breaking the kiss. "No more questions."

Next thing I knew, we were pinned against the car again, pressed against each other and staggering to catch our breath. His mouth never left mine. His hands moved firmly down my sides and slid under my shirt again, pulling on the small of my back. Butterflies flurried in my stomach. I sensed we were about to cross a dangerous line, dangerous because I wasn't sure how to stop him, and even more dangerous because I didn't *want* to stop him.

Then a picture flashed in my mind, a vivid picture of Eric and

Darla, and I heard Eric's words in my mind: *"I kept thinking she'd stop me, but she didn't, so I kept going. One thing led to another, and well, things went too far."*

And then I remembered the words that followed. *"The drive back was the most awkward hour of my life—"*

I wasn't ready to cross this line—not yet.

It required every bit of resolve I could muster, but I forced myself to pull out of the kiss, resting my forehead against Jonathan's lips. I slid the palms of my hands down his shoulders and against his chest, forcing a subtle, yet defined distance between us.

"I'm sorry," he gasped, panting heavily against my hair.

"Don't apologize," I whispered. My breathing was as heavy as his. "I need to stop . . . but I don't want to."

A mental image of Adam flashed across my mind. This was usually the point where Adam would lose his temper and accuse me of not understanding his needs. This was where he would leave, seeking "understanding" elsewhere with another, more "mature," girl as he put it. This was the part where I would get my heart broken, again. A nervous anticipation rumbled in the pit of my stomach as I awaited Jonathan's reproof for stopping him.

That reproof never came. He stroked my hair and nodded. He was still holding me, but his embrace had switched from passionate to protective.

"Do you want me to take you home?"

I shook my head, not ready to leave him yet.

"Then we better walk," he suggested. He reached up and gently took my hands away from his chest.

We walked in silence along a path that followed the ridgeline of the road. The air was crisp and thick with the heavy smell of moisture. I sensed there would be another storm soon. The sun rested comfortably on the horizon, preparing for its final bow behind the mountains. Soon it would be dusk when light hovered indecisively between afternoon and night—night always winning the tug-of-war in the end.

I thought about time and the things Uncle Connor had said about time being relative, and about Jonathan's analogy of the wrinkle in the rope. I tried to picture him as a little boy, growing up as naturally as any other boy, and then changing suddenly, suspended indefinitely on the rope.

"Beth?" I felt a gentle tug on my hand.

"Hmm?"

"You didn't answer me." Jonathan paused, waiting for a response to a question or a comment that I hadn't heard. "What are you thinking about so intently?"

"Time."

Jonathan raised his eyebrows and released an exasperated sigh. "Really? Still on the time thing?" Then his sapphire eyes flashed a mischievous threat. "Don't make me kiss you again," he warned playfully.

"Sorry." I conceded.

"It's funny, you seem so obsessed with the time thing; but for me, time has never mattered—until now."

"Why now?" I asked.

"Well," he shrugged, "time moves much more slowly when we're apart."

"I know what you mean."

I couldn't control my next thought. I pictured myself as a pebble on Jonathan's rope, and wondered how many other girls might have been pebbles before me. Surely he hadn't always been alone; he'd even told me there had been someone else. Jonathan read the consternation in my face and cocked his head to one side, pulling his eyebrows together.

"Now what?" He was trying so hard to be patient.

"It's nothing."

"You're obviously troubled by something. Tell me."

"It's embarrassing," I muttered, looking down at the ground.

Jonathan lifted my chin with his fingers, and studied my face. "What is it?"

"That day, at the lake, you told me there was somebody you loved once."

"Yes, a long time ago."

"Was it like . . ." I bit my lips together and turned away, searching for the courage to ask him what I desperately needed to know. "Was it . . ." I couldn't finish my thought aloud, but Jonathan understood immediately.

"Like us?"

I nodded timidly and he pulled my face around to meet his gaze.

"No," he said, shaking his head slowly from side to side. "It was a different time."

"Oh," I said, trying to sound satisfied. I wasn't. Jonathan sensed the insecurity in my voice and raised his eyebrows.

"What is it that really troubles you?" he prodded.

"It's just that, well, at the lake, when you spoke about it, you seemed so sad. There must have been strong feelings . . . at some point."

He raised his eyes as if recalling the conversation and nodded, finally comprehending the source of my concern. He closed his eyes and pulled me to him, wrapping one arm around my shoulders and bending to rest his cheek against the side of my head.

"It was the nearest thing to being in love I had experienced, until now," he whispered in my ear.

I'd never heard him use the *L* word before. I couldn't respond—I just stood there dumbfounded.

Jonathan chuckled. "What? No questions? You mean the scientist's daughter hasn't figured out that I'm passionately in love with her?" He seemed sincerely shocked by the notion.

I felt an odd ache in my chest as he said the words. I could feel the heat rise in my cheeks and I turned away shyly, but he caught my face with his hand, forcing me to look at him. His eyes were smiling, reflecting the last of the sun's glow. I watched in awe as they twinkled against the sunset.

He bent his face toward mine and kissed me softly on the lips. Then he flashed an unnerving grin—the kind that told me he was hiding something. "Now, isn't there something you'd like to say to me?" he said as he caressed my lips tenderly with his fingertips and raised one of his eyebrows.

I'd never said "I love you" before, at least not to a boy. The simple declaration formed in the base of my throat but the words wouldn't come out. In a few moments, Jonathan chuckled.

"Well," he smiled knowingly, "you may not be ready to say the words right now, but the look on your face that first time I kissed you . . ." his grin widened. "It told me everything I need to know."

I pursed my lips together and wrinkled my nose.

He bent down and kissed my cheek before pulling me into a warm hug. He held me quietly for a minute before speaking again.

"I should probably get you home."

I looked around and noticed that it was getting dark. It must have been later than I thought. I nodded in agreement, and Jonathan led me back to the car.

He started the engine and turned on the heater. I hadn't realized how cool the air had become until I sat down on the cold leather seats. Jonathan reached behind him, grabbed a blanket from the back seat, and handed it to me. I snuggled under the blanket and sighed contentedly.

"Can I ask you something?"

"What a shock, more questions," he laughed. But then he noticed I was serious and his face sobered. "Of course."

"What was her name?"

He placed his hands on the steering wheel and stared out through the windshield for several moments before he turned to look at me. He studied my eyes, his lips in a tight line, before turning away from me.

"It's okay," I murmured, "I shouldn't have asked. I—"

"Eleanor," he sighed, interrupting me before I could continue. "Her name was Eleanor."

A heavy uneasiness plunged to the pit of my stomach and for a moment I thought I was going to be sick. I hadn't seen that coming—yet how could I have missed it? It was so obvious. The queasiness in my stomach unnerved me as I recalled the picture of Eleanor sitting prominently on Jonathan's dresser. The ugly green jealousy demon roared to life.

"Of course!" I whispered. "The picture."

Jonathan looked confused.

"I saw the picture when I stayed at the ranch that night."

"Picture?"

"I'm sorry. I just happened to wander into your room; I didn't even know it was your room until Grace told me."

Comprehension crossed Jonathan's face. "Beth, it's okay. You don't have to explain. I'm just surprised you didn't ask me about it." He watched me carefully for a few moments and then suddenly broke into a smug grin. "Is that what happened to the glass that used to be in the frame?"

"Oh, crud. I totally forgot about that. I meant to tell you that morning, but Uncle Connor showed up, and then . . . I just forgot."

"Tell me what?" His curiosity deepened.

"It was the weirdest thing. When I saw Eleanor's picture, I was instantly drawn to her because I'd dreamed about her during the night."

"You what?" His head snapped around abruptly.

"I saw her picture—"

"No, not that. You *dreamed* about Eleanor?"

"Yeah, I dreamed about her that night," I replied, anxious to continue my explanation. But Jonathan cut me off again.

"But . . ." He shook his head, his face full of doubt.

"Anyhow, I was holding the picture in my hand when Grace walked in. She startled me and I dropped the frame and the glass shattered everywhere. I'm so sorry. I meant to replace it for you."

"It's not important. I should have put the picture away but I didn't see the need."

"She was very beautiful," I stammered, feeling a little intimidated and insecure.

"She was," he agreed.

His reply definitely didn't build my self-esteem. The green demon hissed.

Sensing my discomfort, Jonathan pulled to the side of the road and put the car in park. He turned to me and brushed the hair away from my face.

"Beth . . ." he hesitated, "you are the most beautiful woman I know. Your eyes hypnotize me, and I swear, sometimes the way you look at me makes me feel like I've known you forever. Your touch makes me burn with a desire unsurpassed by any I've ever known. And the way it feels to kiss you . . ." he sighed heavily, "it makes me absolutely insane, and I forget all about being good."

I sat staring at him for a moment, speechless. The green demon should have melted away, but for some unexplained reason it hovered silently in the shadows.

"How long have you been rehearsing those lines?" I finally asked, holding back a smile.

"Totally impromptu." He shook his head and grinned.

I reached across the seat and pulled his face to mine, pressing my lips firmly against his.

This time it was Jonathan who broke away first.

"We *really* need to go," he said, breathless, "or I'm going to do something we'll both regret."

He held my hand as he drove. It was completely dark now and I knew Uncle Connor was probably worried. I checked my cell phone; there were no messages or missed calls, so I was hopeful he wouldn't be angry. I quickly dialed his number but got his voice mail instead. I left him a brief message explaining that I was with Jonathan and was on my way home and was sorry for not calling him sooner. I hoped it would be enough to pacify him. I could tell that Jonathan was chuckling. As we pulled up to the house, his face turned serious again.

"I was wondering," he began.

"Yes?"

"You said you dreamed about Eleanor—"

"Actually, I've dreamed about her a few times," I admitted.

"Can I ask what the dreams were about?"

"You can *ask* me anything you want," I chided. He pursed his lips and rolled his eyes at me.

"*Will* you tell me?" he pressed.

I paused a moment to gather my thoughts. "It's pretty much the same dream every time with only a few minor variations. We're both holding a candle—hers is lit, mine is not. She glides towards me and reaches out her candle to light mine. Her flame ignites mine and our candles burn together as one flame."

"Interesting." Jonathan was pensive.

"In the last dream, she handed me a rolled up sheet of paper tied with string. When I unrolled it, I noticed it was sheet music—handwritten. I recognized the melody line as the theme she wrote for her . . ."

My words stopped short as the truth struck with unexpected force.

"Y-you!" I stammered. "*You* were her soldier. She wrote it for *you!*"

Jonathan swallowed hard and bit his bottom lip. He nodded sideways, reluctant to acknowledge the truth, yet unable to deny it.

I sat gaping at him, stunned. I pressed my wrists hard against my forehead, fighting the emotions that threatened to expose my insecurities about Eleanor. As ridiculous as it seemed, out of everything that had been revealed to me, this was the revelation that broke me.

"Are you okay?" Jonathan asked warily.

"No," I answered honestly. "I need to be alone right now."

"Beth, I never meant to—"

"Jonathan, please. I need some time to think."

Jonathan took a deep breath and then nodded. "I understand."

We got out of the car and walked in silence to the front porch. He bent down, resting his lips against my ear.

"I love you," he whispered. He kissed me tenderly on the cheek, lingering for a moment before he turned and walked back to his car. I wanted desperately to call him back but the words wouldn't come. I stood frozen—a statue on the porch—as he drove away.

I turned slowly and entered the house, suffering from the pain I'd seen on Jonathan's face as he left. Why did the knowledge that Jonathan was the object of Eleanor's affection bother me so much? I was not only jealous of her but of Jonathan's feelings for her—feelings that had remained with him for who knows how long.

Hah! Time doesn't exist for Jonathan, I thought, letting sarcasm cushion my pain. But the logical part of my brain knew that I was being irrational.

"Hi, Beth."

I jumped, startled by the sound of Marci's voice coming from the living room. I wasn't expecting to find anybody home.

"Oh, hey Marci," I replied, catching my breath.

"You seem troubled . . . is everything okay?"

"Yeah, I guess so," I shrugged.

"Was that Jonathan?" she asked.

"Yeah."

"Did you two have a fight?"

"No, nothing like that."

She was silent a moment. "Do you want to talk about it?"

"I-I . . . wouldn't know where to begin," I stammered, suddenly full of emotion.

"Oh, dear," she replied, aware that I was on the verge of tears. She walked over to me and put her arm around my shoulders.

"Come here," she said, giving my back a gentle pat. "I think it's time you and I had a talk."

Visitors

CHAPTER 12

I tossed my book bag on the floor, plopped down next to Marci
on the couch, and began to explain everything to her—leaving out the part about Eleanor being more than a hundred and fifty
years old.

Marci was able to offer a clear perspective on my feelings without
sounding judgmental or condescending, and I realized while listening to her how much I needed someone like her around—someone
older and more experienced. I guess that's why I wasn't upset when
the conversation took an unexpected turn.

"How serious are the two of you?" Marci questioned.

"Well . . ." Marci raised one eyebrow and waited patiently for me
to continue, scrutinizing my expression carefully.

"We like each other a lot," I finally admitted.

"How much is 'a lot'?" she pressed, refusing to accept any ambi-
guity in my response.

I shrugged my shoulders and felt my face begin to burn.

"I see," she nodded. "Do you love each other?"

I chewed my lips nervously. Marci assumed the answer by the way I squirmed and by the way my cheeks flushed, burning to the point of being painful.

"Beth," Marci probed my eyes, "love is a very powerful emotion—it can make it difficult to think clearly. And the emotion is especially potent in first love. It's no wonder you're a bit bemused and disjointed."

I nodded, but secretly cringed on the inside when she said the words *first love;* I would never be Jonathan's *first* love, and that realization bothered me. It was ridiculous for me to feel that way—he'd said himself that what he felt for Eleanor wasn't the same as what he felt for me—but I couldn't shake from my mind the image of them together.

"Sometimes it feels like I can't even breathe when I'm with him," I admitted.

"I know what you mean," she smiled. Her eyes revealed that she was thinking about someone else at the moment. "Can I ask you something very personal?" she continued.

"I guess," I shrugged. *What could be more personal than asking me if I loved Jonathan?*

"How far have things gone between you?"

The burn on my face intensified and I couldn't look her in the eyes.

"I see."

"No," I said quickly, "nothing like *that.*" I realized she'd jumped to the wrong conclusion.

"Oh?"

"But—" I couldn't say the words.

"But you want it to be like *that.*" She finished my sentence for me. I shrugged my shoulders nervously. When I lifted my face to meet her gaze I expected to see disapproval, but her eyes were expressionless.

"That is, I think I do, but," I sighed, "I just don't know if . . ." I hesitated, searching for the right words. Finally, I just blurted out my question. "How do you *know* when it's right?"

Marci stared at me, very unemotional and very businesslike and very *not* like my mother.

"Let me make sure we're on the same page. We're talking about sex, right?"

Her forthright question caught me off guard. I'd never had an in-depth conversation about boys with an adult before. I doubt my mom's prudish lectures would count as an actual conversation. My mother was very old fashioned about sex—at least where I was concerned. She always put a moral spin on the topic which made me feel guilty for even thinking about it before I was married. I'm sure that had a lot to do with why I couldn't go there with Adam; although in retrospect, I was glad about that. Even though the topic of sex made me feel squeamish and awkward, I wanted desperately to talk to someone about it—but I wanted advice, not values.

"Yes," I said, finally answering Marci's question. I looked her squarely in the eyes as I spoke.

"Okay," she said, nodding. "Have you and Jonathan discussed it?"

Marci's question confused me. *Discuss sex with Jonathan?* The idea made my stomach twist uncomfortably.

"Of course not," I grimaced.

"Well, then . . ." she chuckled, not at my words but at my physical response to her question, "that's probably a sure sign that you're *not* ready."

"But it's supposed to be spontaneous, isn't it?" I argued.

"Only in romance novels and movies," she sighed. "Not in real life—especially not the first time."

I knew my reaction was childish, but I couldn't help but roll my eyes.

"Beth, when the time is right, you and Jonathan will need to talk about it. You're talking about an entirely new level of commitment in your relationship. Leaving the decision to some spontaneous whim could easily lead to regret. And remember, once you've gone there, you can never take it back—it's non-renewable."

I sat still for a moment. My mother had often referred to my virginity as a non-renewable resource. Science teachers!

Part of me wanted to run from the room with my ears covered, but another part of me appreciated the fact that Marci was talking to me as an equal—not as a child. Her words made me think about Darla and Eric; how one moment of spontaneity had had such a lasting impact on both of them.

"I wouldn't know how to talk to Jonathan about this," I admitted.

"You will . . . when the time comes." She reached across and lifted my chin with her fingers. "The important thing is . . . no, the *most* important thing is that you know yourself—know what *you* want—before you have the conversation with him."

"What if I don't know for sure, but he does? What if he's ready?"

"*You* decide when your first time will be. Nobody can make that decision for you, and you should never allow someone to pressure you into it."

"He would never do that," I replied defensively. Marci smiled.

"He may not mean to, but desire, like love, can be overwhelmingly powerful. You need to set clear limits—that part is up to you."

"Why is it up to me? That's not fair," I complained.

"It just is. Boys . . . heck, men in general . . . don't think when it comes to sex. Their bodies take over and they just keep going until someone stops them."

I considered her words carefully and nodded slowly. I thought about what Eric had said: *I kept thinking she'd stop me, but she didn't, so I kept going.*

"You have a lot to think about," Marci concluded, "but there's one more thing you need to consider—and you *will* need to discuss it with Jonathan."

More? What more could there possibly be? It was going to be hard enough for me to look Jonathan in the eyes after this.

"Precautions," she said flatly. "The two of you will have to discuss birth—"

"Stop!" I blurted. "No!"

"That's the real world, Beth." Her tone was soft, but unapologetic. She watched me carefully for several moments. "Okay." She patted my knee, signaling her willingness to drop the subject. "But if you need me to help you with that, I'm here."

"Thanks," I muttered uncomfortably.

"Beth, you're a beautiful, intelligent, amazing young woman. You'll know what's best for you, and you'll be amazed at how much clearer things seem once you've made your choice—and once you've discussed it with Jonathan."

I didn't see Jonathan and me having that discussion anytime soon.

I caught the glow of my computer as I entered my bedroom after dinner. I was sure I'd turned it off before leaving that morning. Darla's phone call must have side-tracked me. Actually—no, I distinctly remembered feeling impatient as I waited for the screen to shut off. I had been irritable because I was running later than usual. How odd. Maybe Uncle Connor or Marci had turned it back on, although I couldn't imagine why. Uncle Connor had his own computer and there was another one, an older model, in Carl's bedroom.

I flipped on the screen and to my surprise, not only was the computer on, the cursor was flashing on the Google search bar. The words *biological immortality* appeared in the browser. It was obvious that someone had been in my room; I had never done a search on this topic. It was one of the subjects of my mother's research. I thought about the binder hidden in the cellar and Uncle Connor's caution that it remain under lock and key.

I couldn't resist the temptation to hit the enter button. To my surprise, there were nearly two million hits for the topic. I scrolled through the results, looking for credible website domains. I clicked on several sites with papers written by graduate students and university professors. One caught my attention immediately. It was written by a Harvard graduate who claimed that cells were like shoelaces. I immediately thought of the conversation I'd had with Uncle Connor about this. The assertion in the Harvard paper was that cells fray with age, and scientists believe they've figured out how to put a new "cap" on aging cells. Apparently, a true immortal's cells never fray.

I continued skimming through various abstracts and although some of the articles were interesting, they offered little beyond what

I'd read in my mother's binder. I spent several minutes perusing the search results; I was about to close the screen when another hit caught my eye: *BIVenture.mil*. I recognized the domain ".mil" as a military page. Clicking on the website, I skimmed through several links before pausing on a specific abstract. I immediately recognized the author, Malcolm Schweigger, from letters included in my mother's binder. A portion of the abstract read:

In a recent interview with Malcolm Jonias Schweigger, Dr. Anthon Svengia revealed that research leading to the actualization of biological immortality is closer than previously thought. In his opinion, scientists are within twenty years of perfecting the science of the cessation of aging and the regeneration of not only limbs, but muscle tissue and organs as well. Tests are currently being conducted at undisclosed locations of southeastern Europe and northern Africa. When asked specifically about the nature of the tests, Dr. Svengia would not comment, but according to an abstract from a recent lecture, the tests use human subjects and the results have been astounding. "It basically stems from a thorough understanding of the nature of the elements. Once we were able to manipulate the individual components, the science took on a life of its own," Dr. Svengia stated. According to Schweigger, the problem facing the BIVenture's advancements is an organization doing business as Project Mortality. The organization is fighting adamantly against further developments of the technology and chemistry advancements necessary to stop and/ or reverse the aging process. According to one source, the fear is that death is a natural part of all human cultures, and our planet cannot sustain the impact of eliminating mortality.

Before closing the browser window, I decided to bookmark the military website so I could ask Uncle Connor about it later. When I hit the bookmark button, an error message appeared on the screen and the computer froze. I waited several minutes, hoping it might unfreeze, but it never did. Finally, I had to shut it down and restart it. When the internet browser came up, I typed the same words into the browser bar and got the same one million seven hundred ninety-nine thousand hits; only this time, I couldn't locate the military site I'd been viewing previously. I clicked on Advance Search and refined my search to military sites only; there were over two hundred results. I searched through endless pages of URL addresses, finally giving up.

Before shutting the computer down, I checked my e-mail. My countenance fell when I clicked on my mailbox and there was nothing from Jonathan. I felt a sinking weight anchor solidly in my stomach. Should I call him? Text him? Apologize? Send him an e-mail? I battled with myself for several minutes before throwing my hands in the air and growling in frustration.

I wandered into the living room and asked Marci and Uncle Connor about my computer being on, but neither of them knew anything about it. Both claimed they'd never entered my room, nor would they without first asking me.

"You must have inadvertently left it on this morning," Marci suggested.

"No . . . that's just it. I clearly remember waiting for it to shut down," I insisted.

"Sometimes, instead of shutting down, a computer will restart. It's not—"

"I know," I interrupted, "but this morning I watched it shut down."

"Connor?" A quizzical expression crossed Marci's face as she stared at Uncle Connor.

Uncle Connor rested his chin in his hands and didn't say anything.

"Is it possible there was somebody else in the house?" Marci prodded. Several moments passed before Uncle Connor responded.

"I doubt it," he said, tapping his thumb against his chin.

"Then how do you explain it?" I asked.

Uncle Connor thought for a minute.

"There is a possibility . . . but it's a stretch."

"What's that?" Marci and I asked in unison.

"If your father was trying to get a message to you without risk of being intercepted, it's possible he may have accessed your computer remotely." Uncle Connor raised his eyebrows and wrinkled the corner of his mouth as if to imply his explanation held little validity.

"He can do that?"

"As I said, it's a stretch . . . but yes. The military, and even our government for that matter, have the uncanny ability to tap into our computer systems. Your father's high level clearances might enable him to run a remote access program on a domestic system, provided he has the right equipment."

"But why would he do that? Why would he want me to look at sites about biological immortality?" I asked, confused.

"It may not be that literal," Uncle Connor thought aloud. "It's possible he was sending some sort of coded message."

"If that were the case, why not simply e-mail me? He sent me one this morning so I know he has the ability."

"I don't know, Beth. We can't be certain it was your father who turned on your computer." He shook his head and frowned. I could sense he was as troubled by this as I was, but he was in protective mode and didn't want me to worry.

"Well, then, if not him, who else would have access to my computer?"

Uncle Connor continued to shake his head slowly back and forth. "I don't know honey. I honestly don't know."

I debated whether I should tell Marci and Uncle Connor about the strange feelings I'd experienced recently—sensing that someone was in my room last night or that someone had been next to me in the practice room earlier today—but I determined it was better not to say anything. The last thing I wanted, or needed, was to sound like a paranoid teenager.

It was getting late, so I decided to get started on my homework. With all the turmoil over the weekend, I'd neglected reading the assignments for my English class and had fallen behind in calculus—not a good thing. I plopped down in the center of my bed, spread my books around me, and settled in for a long evening of catch up and study. I struggled through the calculus homework first because it was the most difficult.

As I finished the last of my assignments, I realized I'd been humming Eleanor's theme through most of calculus—the song she had composed for Jonathan, *her* love. I wondered why Jonathan had chosen to share her theme with me. I contemplated this question for awhile, and the only logical explanation I could come up with was that Eleanor and I shared something besides Jonathan in common. I recalled my dreams about her. In each dream sequence, she held a glowing candle that she used to light mine; and in the most recent dreams, she handed me her unfinished composition. Were these more than just dreams? What message was she trying to force across the veil between life and death? Another question crossed my mind, but I dismissed it as quickly as it came, refusing to entertain any further dappling with the metaphysical.

A low vibrating noise shook me from my thoughts. A welcome relief washed over me when I flipped open the phone and saw who was calling.

"Hi." I spoke calmly into the phone, hoping he couldn't hear the elation in my voice.

"Hi," his smooth voice echoed.

I sighed involuntarily. "What are you doing?"

"I've been thinking."

"What about?" I fished.

"Two things, actually. First, I wanted to know how you're doing, and second, I wanted to apologize."

That last part surprised me.

"Apologize for what?"

"I should have told you about Eleanor before today. Actually, I tried to once, but we were interrupted. Before that, it just seemed crazy."

"Crazy?" I questioned.

"What was I suppose to say? 'Hi, my name is Jonathan. I used to like someone who lived in the 1800s, but now I've moved on.' Face it, that's not something you hear every day."

I snickered at the absurdity in his tone.

"I'm glad you think it's funny," he said defensively, but I could hear the humor in his voice.

"When you put it that way, I'm the one who should apologize," I admitted.

"You have nothing to apologize for," he replied. "Your reaction was normal. In fact, I'm surprised you aren't mad at me."

"I could never be mad at you," I muttered.

Now it was Jonathan who laughed.

"I'm sure there'll be plenty of times that I make you angry. The question is, *when* I do, will you forgive me?"

"Always," I assured him.

Jonathan was quiet for a moment, then he changed the subject. "How's the homework going?"

Things were back to normal. We talked for a long time about everything and about nothing. Eventually, I told him about the strange occurrence with my computer this evening, and about the feelings I had experienced about not being alone. He seemed neither mystified nor troubled by what I told him. Maybe there really was nothing for me to be concerned about.

We talked so long that my ear started to burn and I had to turn on the speakerphone so I could set the phone down. I lay down comfortably on my bed; I didn't want to hang up and break the connection between us. I liked the idea of the line staying open between us all night long. I never tired of hearing his voice. However, in spite of my effort to stay awake, my mind began to drift during our conversation.

"I think we'd better hang up," he chuckled.

"Why?" I yawned.

"Because you just told me not to turn on the heater."

"Huh? Oh. Sorry. I guess I dozed off for a minute."

"I should let you go." There was finality in his tone.

"No," I responded abruptly. "Don't hang up."

"Don't you think we've burned up enough cells for one night? What else is there to talk about that can't wait until tomorrow . . . that is, later today?"

I rolled over and looked at the clock; it was 2:22 a.m. *Good grief!* He was right; I was going to have a problem staying awake in my classes later—but I didn't care.

"What are you going to do when we hang up?" I asked.

"I'm going to play the piano and then go to sleep."

"You're going to play the piano at this hour?"

"I always play before I go to bed," he explained. "It helps me unwind and sleep better. Some people watch television, I play piano."

I wanted to ask him what he played before going to sleep, but I was afraid he'd stir up my insecurities by telling me it was Eleanor's theme. I decided on another question instead.

"Can I ask you something?"

"Sure, you're the question queen, after all."

I ignored his playful sarcasm. "Why did you play Eleanor's theme for me?"

"I suppose because you and Eleanor share a connection with music and with me. It's been years since I played it—in a very real sense, you're the one responsible for resurrecting her theme."

In a brief flash, I saw the image of Eleanor in my dream, lighting my candle with hers and handing me the music from her composition. Was Jonathan right? Did Eleanor and I share a metaphysical connection?

"Beth . . ." Jonathan lowered his voice. "I love you."

The familiar heat ran through me, but all I could mumble was, "Thank you."

I heard him chuckle softly and somewhere, perhaps closer than I imagined, I could sense Eleanor's presence. But now I wasn't afraid.

I don't recall saying goodbye. The next thing I knew, I was standing at the bottom of a narrow metal staircase. It led to a door off a small landing. A golden-haired man dressed in a very official looking gray uniform stood between me and the door, and as I climbed the stairs and approached him, he turned to face me. His eyes glowed bright yellow and were framed with a thick black outline. Oddly, they didn't radiate light; rather, they were dull and flat like the eyes of a dead man. A shudder raced down my spine, yet something compelled me forward.

I reached for the door, but the man quickly grabbed hold of the handle before I could grasp it. His threatening glare pierced through the fog-like haze that permeated the air around us. I took a step backward—paralyzed.

"You cannot pass through this door," he warned. His voice was icy and deliberate. "It is not for people like *you*."

My natural instinct was to step away, but the force that pulled me closer to the door wouldn't allow me to retreat. Resigned, I reached for the handle again; the man snatched his hand away abruptly to avoid contact with me.

"Hah," he droned wickedly. "You won't make it. You'll be lost, unable to return."

I hesitated, frozen. Yet somehow I knew I must pass through that door—something important depended on it.

Reluctant yet determined, I stepped through the narrow opening that led to the base of a spiral staircase. It wound upward into thick blackness. With my left hand, I reached for the iron railing. As my hand gripped the rail, the sliver of light from the open door folded away, leaving me in total darkness. Before the light dissipated, I caught a glimpse at the hand that grasped the stair rail. It was not *my* hand. This hand was perfectly formed, without blemish or scar.

As though resigned to a predestined fate, I placed my foot on the first stair. Screeching protests pealed in the distance, and the moment I stepped forward a sudden dampness misted my face. Flying debris whizzed past me; I could feel the air currents from its chaotic movement. Loud crashes and clangs echoed up the shaft as the debris smashed into a solid surface somewhere below me. I hesitated, feet planted on the first rung of the staircase, clutching the rail with an iron-firm grip—something my own left hand would never be able to do.

"You can do this," a soft voice whispered in my ear.

"Mother!" I spun in the darkness, expecting to find her next to me.

"No, Beth, you must do this on your own," she instructed.

"I don't think I can," I murmured, my voice cracking with fear.

"You will," she insisted. "You must."

Her voice faded into the distance and I sensed her presence disappearing.

"Wait!" I pleaded.

"Hold on to the rail, Beth. No matter what, do not let go of the rail!"

"I can't."

"Step forward," her voice commanded, although it was a mere whisper, and then it was gone.

The atmosphere around me was suddenly thick with moisture and unbearable cold. I wanted to bend into a huddle, pressing my arms to my chest in a protective stance, but my hand held firmly to the railing. I took a step upward and a thick blanket of cold pressed against me, forcing me back. I heaved my head forward, and the rest of my body followed. I was determined to press through the icy wall of darkness that pushed against me.

All at once a piercing scream assailed my ears, deadening my senses. I reached out defensively with my right hand and pushed ineffectively against the noise. A ghastly odor assaulted my nose, causing me to recoil; the smell blasted into my face with such a violent impact that I nearly lost my grip. It was piercing and hideous, and although I'd never experienced it before, I instinctively knew that what I was smelling was the odor of pure evil.

The repelling smell of death caused a vile, nauseating taste to form in my mouth. I spit and sputtered in angry convulsions. Then my face went taut as the rancid scent of evil crept through my mouth like thick, black oil. It rolled slowly along my tongue, down my throat, and into the pit of my stomach, catapulting my gut into violent heaves.

The stair rail became as frigid as a block of dry ice. The severe cold sent shooting daggers of pain through my hand and along my arm, but my frozen muscles were unable to react. I winced in pain, wanting desperately to free my hand from its iron grip on the rail, but my fingers seemed welded in place.

Suddenly, the high-pitched screeching stopped and my left hand and arm went numb. A blanket of dense weight bore down on me as if a heavy cloak had been placed on my shoulders. The weight pressed against my chest, forcing the air from my lungs. I felt like I was being overcome. I wanted desperately to forfeit all resistance and succumb, to let the compelling force overtake me. Maybe then

I would be free from pain and the evil presence that threatened to destroy me.

This must be what it's like to die, I thought.

"Fight!" a whisper hissed urgently in my ear.

I can't, I answered silently, unable to command my mouth to move.

"Fight!" This time the whisper was louder and more forceful.

How?

The unwieldy weight squeezing my chest grew heavier; somehow, I understood that if I relinquished my grip on the rail, my life would end.

The fingers in my left hand began to tingle and twitch sporadically, but I was still able to hold on to the railing. This knowledge gave me a glimmer of courage. Using every ounce of strength I could muster, I opened my mouth to speak.

"Aurhgh!" A strangled growl bellowed from my throat, defying the blackness around me. My legs folded, faltering beneath the weight of darkness.

"I told you," evil spoke. "You are no match for me, Beth Anne!"

Panic jolted through my body, and in a flash, I was lying on top of my bed, screaming wildly into the night.

It was probably several minutes before Uncle Connor bolted through my bedroom door; I wasn't sure. I couldn't control the wailing screams that rocketed from my mouth in constant succession. My uncle's face twisted in terror when he saw me flipping violently from side to side on top of my bed, eyes wild with fury. He sprinted to the bed and pinned my shoulders against my pillow. Fixing his knees on either side of me, he held me firmly against the bed until the convulsions subsided. My eyes were still wide, but my screams transformed into heavy sobs. At once, I was in Uncle Connor's arms, cradled against his chest, his arms locked around me like an iron barrier.

"Hold on!" he panted. "Hold on, Beth."

He reached across my bed, flipped open my cell phone, and punched in a series of buttons before hitting "send." There must have been a quick reaction on the other side of the line, because instantly Uncle Connor barked an order into the phone.

"Get over here. Now!"

Conquering Darkness
CHAPTER 13

*O*nce I'd stopped sobbing, Uncle Connor carried me from my bedroom to the living room and built a fire in the fireplace. He didn't turn on any lights.

"It's better that you stay in darkness for now," he explained. "Don't let it become your enemy."

He continued to "shush" me and insisted that I needed sleep because I was in shock, but I refused to close my eyes. I feared that the moment I closed them, the dense blackness would overpower me again.

I was lying on the couch near the fireplace when Jonathan arrived. I'm not sure how long it took him to get to Uncle Connor's house and I don't remember Uncle Connor leaving my side to let him in the front door—I only know that he came. He took one look at me and his countenance fell.

In one swift movement he was at my side, lifting me onto his lap as he took my place on the couch. He folded me into his arms and held me, brushing his fingers through my hair. I felt nothing, other than the involuntary shudders that quaked though my body every few seconds. Uncle Connor sat motionless in the chair opposite the couch and stared ominously at Jonathan.

"Has she said anything?" Jonathan spoke quietly, as if I wasn't there. But I didn't care. I wasn't there, not really.

Uncle Connor shook his head. "Look at her!"

Jonathan pulled a blanket from the back of the couch and wrapped it around me, tucking it firmly in place. I didn't move; he maneuvered me around like a limp rag doll.

"The intruder must have been a powerful one," Jonathan said quietly.

"Yes," Uncle Connor agreed.

Jonathan shifted his weight under me so that he was looking squarely into my eyes. He flinched when he looked at my face, but he didn't turn away. He studied my eyes for a long time. I stared blankly in return.

"Beth, can you hear me?" He placed his hand gently against my cheek.

I heard him fine, but I couldn't respond. All I could do was stare blindly at him. Another tremor flittered through my body, and Jonathan tucked the blanket tighter around me.

Uncle Connor slid from his chair and knelt on the floor beside me.

"Honey?" Uncle Connor whispered. He laid his hand lightly on my shoulder.

"Beth!" he repeated sharply. "Look at me!"

Without turning my head, I cut my eyes and glared at Uncle Connor.

"Honey, I want you to close your eyes."

More tremors shook my body.

Uncle Connor sighed heavily. "That's how she's been ever since I found her screaming uncontrollably on her bed."

"She's scared to death," Jonathan muttered.

"Do something," Uncle Connor pleaded.

Jonathan nodded and lowered his face so that his eyes were level with mine.

"Beth, I want you to close your eyes."

My eyes widened in response to his demand.

"Honey, listen to me. You're frightened and that's okay, but you have to battle that fear. It's the first lesson in fighting an intruder. They can't exercise any power over you unless you give it to them." He paused, caressing my cheek softly. "Do you trust me?"

I blinked, and using every ounce of willpower I could muster, I nodded once.

"Okay," he continued. "I'm going to count to two, and then I want you to close your eyes and hold them shut while I count to five. You'll begin to feel a heavy weight press against your lungs, but you're going to ignore it. You're going to focus only on the sound of my voice. Do you understand?"

I nodded. I could focus on his voice. I could do that.

"Are you ready?" His eyes narrowed as he waited for my response. I nodded again.

"Okay. One . . . two . . . close your eyes."

I shut my eyes and immediately felt the pressure. It was like a thousand bricks pushing down on my chest.

"One . . . two . . ." Jonathan began counting slowly. The weight of the bricks increased with each increment.

"Three . . ."

Ignore the pressure.

"Four . . ."

The weight—it's too heavy.

"Five. . . ." Jonathan sighed. "Good. Now open your eyes."

No. Keep counting. Please. It feels so good to sink.

"No, Beth," he ordered. He cupped my chin in the palm of his hand and shook my face gently. My eyes snapped open with the jerking motion. I glowered angrily into his eyes, but he ignored my glare.

"Good. Now do it again, but this time, I want you to open your eyes the moment I say 'five,' understand?" I blinked, and he nodded.

We repeated this exercise several times; each time he changed the command in a subtle way, giving me something else to concentrate on before opening my eyes. With each attempt, it became easier to ignore the engulfing weight that felt like an anchor dragging me to the depths of some abyss.

My breathing became deeper and heavier each time Jonathan told me to close my eyes. The last thing I remember was waiting for him to count to twenty.

"Eleven . . . twelve . . . thirteen. . . ." His voice faded into the darkness, and in an instant, I was transported to the spiral staircase, surrounded in blackness.

I clutched blindly in front of me, frantically reaching, grasping, searching for anything familiar. My left hand hit the cold staircase railing. My right hand followed the left, grabbing hold of the rail. I clutched it tightly, and then dropped to my knees.

"Jonathan," I whimpered despairingly. "You tricked me! Why?"

"Beth," Jonathan's pained voice was clear, but distant.

"How could you send me back here?" I cried, defeated.

"Tell me where you are." His voice echoed, making it difficult to distinguish the individual words.

"It's dark and cold and heavy."

"Can you see anything?"

"No—it's black," I bellowed.

The piercing peal of metal on metal screeched above me and the staircase began to vibrate unsteadily.

"Ahhg!" I howled into the darkness.

The movement of the staircase caused me to lose my balance and I stumbled. My legs sprawled out behind me, but I didn't lose my grip on the railing.

"Beth, I need you to tell me where you are so I can help you."

"Why did you send me back?" I growled. "I trusted you!"

"Where are you?" he demanded, ignoring my question.

"On a staircase."

"Okay . . . good."

"It's s-so dark and s-s-so cold!" The cold, humid air pierced through me, right to my bones.

"You're doing fine. Can you tell what step you're on?"

"N-n-no," I sputtered through clenched teeth. "T-t-too . . . c-c-cold."

"Are you closer to the top or the bottom of the stairs?"

I hesitated.

"I'm c-c-closer t-t-to the b-b-bottom," I chattered. The icy air whipped against my cheeks like daggers of freezing rain. The temperature was so unbearable I couldn't control the clamoring snap of my teeth.

"Beth, I want you to take a long, deep breath, sucking in all the cold air. It will hurt, but when you exhale, the air will be warm, and you'll be comfortable."

In an involuntary gasp, I drew in as much air as possible. Stabbing icicles sliced at my throat as the air worked its way down. As the biting chill penetrated my lungs, every muscle in my chest constricted. It took several seconds to remind myself how to exhale. When I did, the air around me changed; it became warm and soothing, just as Jonathan said it would.

"Are you warmer now?" He sounded closer to me than he had a few moments earlier. I started to reach for him.

"No," he snapped sharply. "Don't let go of the rail."

"Get me out of here!" I demanded through gritted teeth.

"Listen carefully—you have do this on your own."

"I can't!" I sobbed.

"Yes. You. Can!"

There I hung, completely engulfed in darkness, clutching to an unseen railing, lying limply across the stairs. What was the use? The man with the yellow eyes was right; I was no match for him. Instantly, the heavy weight returned, pressing tightly against my chest. I fought the urge to relax and give in to the pressure, knowing that in one moment of release I could allow the weight to overcome me and it would all be over. It would be so easy to let go. *So easy.* I felt myself sinking as I relaxed. It felt so good to—

"Beth!" Jonathan's voice was harsh. "Knock it off, damn it!"

"No!" I cried. "My arms hurt . . . the weight is too heavy."

"Get up—now!" he ordered.

"I hate you!" I cried.

"Good! Now get up!"

"I HATE you!" I screamed.

"GET UP!"

"Damn you!" I hissed bitterly, but as the anger embraced me I climbed to my feet.

"Now," Jonathan's voice was stern, but calmer, "close your eyes and start climbing. No matter what happens, keep your eyes closed. Keep your feet firmly on the stairs—and do *not* let go of that handrail. Do you understand me?"

Jonathan's commands sounded like those given by a parent to a disobedient child. I wanted to lash out at him. How dare he! I wanted to see him so I could yell at him. No, I didn't want to yell at him, I wanted to hurt him!

I bowed my head in determination and began climbing, advancing step by step up the staircase, hand over hand along the railing: one . . . two . . . three . . . four . . .

The screeching sound of twisting metal hammered above me again, and the staircase began to sway back and forth violently, heaving me into a forward lunge.

"Hah, hah, hah," an icy voice chuckled. The pungent smell of death returned and my breathing grew shallow. With each exhale, I attempted to repel the hideous odor.

"Jonathan!" I screamed.

"I'm here," he said reassuringly. "I'm right here. Keep climbing."

"There's s-someone . . . in here," I stammered.

"Tell him to leave," he replied matter-of-factly.

I pressed my foot onto the next step and slid my hand further up the rail. My eyes remained closed as I strengthened my death grip on the railing.

"You are lost," the voice sneered at me. "You cannot go back."

I panicked and my body began to tremble, first in small quivers and then in uncontrollable shudders. I struggled to hang on through each shaking tremor.

"Beth, tell him to leave—now!" Jonathan ordered.

I hesitated, afraid to speak. I had to make the fear go away—everything depended on it.

"Leave," I ordered, but the command rebounded back into my throat. It was as though an invisible force had stopped the sound waves before they could travel beyond my mouth. A dark, low laugh echoed behind me.

"Leave," I uttered again, more loudly.

The presence did not respond.

"Say it, and *mean* it!" Jonathan demanded sharply.

"Leave! Now!" I snarled into the blackness.

"Order him to leave!" Jonathan's voice was harsh, and I detected a slight edge of panic in his tone.

"I ORDER you to leave!" I screamed, this time with conviction. "NOW!"

The swaying motion of the staircase ceased. Immediately a brush of cold air swept past me and the stench of death disappeared. It grew quiet, and although my eyes were tightly closed, a pale orange glow of light warmed my eyelids. I froze in place, listening for the evil laughter to return. It didn't.

"Open your eyes, Beth."

The voice, a male voice, was one I didn't recognize.

"You're here," the man said.

My eyes were so tightly cemented shut that I had to pry them open. The light was bright. I blinked several times in order to see clearly while my eyes adjusted. I'd made it to the top of the staircase, and standing next to me was a man in a white suit; everything he wore was white—his shirt, his tie, his shoes—everything. But it wasn't his clothes that surprised me, it was his face. He had the most pleasant face I'd ever seen. He wasn't very tall, only a couple of inches taller than me. His hair was a shimmering gray, as if he were very old, yet his skin appeared young—perfectly smooth and even. His eyes danced as he smiled warmly at me. They had the same twinkle in them that Jonathan's eyes had when he smiled. His grin widened as I focused my gaze on him.

"Welcome," he said politely. "We're so glad you made it."

"She made it," Jonathan's voice echoed in the distance, but the man in the white suit didn't seem to hear him.

"Would you like me to show you around?" the man asked as he gestured for me to walk beside him.

"Yes," I replied. My voice was clear and normal again, and I smiled at the familiar sound of it.

"Beth, open your eyes," Jonathan's voice sounded in my ear, but I shook my head no; I wanted to walk with the man in the white suit.

"On the count of three, I'm going to snap my fingers and you'll open your eyes."

"No," I protested.

"One . . ."

"No, please! Wait," I pleaded.

"Two . . ."

The man in the white suit gently squeezed my arm.

"Another time," he smiled.

"Three . . ."

The snap of Jonathan's fingers cracked loudly in my ear and my eyes slowly began to open, but this time there wasn't a dreamlike quality to the movement. Awareness struck as I surveyed my surroundings. Jonathan sat angled in front of me on Uncle Connor's couch. Uncle Connor was still kneeling beside me. The fire crackled and popped in the fireplace.

Nothing in the room had changed since . . . since I—

I looked up at Jonathan and glared. My breathing suddenly became fast and heavy as a rush of anger flooded through me. I pulled my fingers into fists, and though the darting pain in my left hand caused me to grimace, I began flinging both fists against him. I hit his arm and his chest and was aiming for his head when he took hold of my arms and pinned them firmly against his chest with one hand. He wrapped his free arm around me and pulled me to him, rocking me back and forth.

"You did it, Beth, you beat him."

"Why did you send me back?" I whimpered my voice barely audible against his chest.

"He had no choice—" Uncle Connor interrupted as Jonathan pulled me closer.

"But why?" I moaned. Tears spilled down my face, soaking the front of Jonathan's shirt.

"You were still under his influence," Uncle Connor replied.

"I don't understand," I muttered.

"You must have let go of the rail the first time," Jonathan explained, "and that brought you back, but the possessor . . . the intruder . . . was still with you, or rather his influence was."

"I don't remember letting go—I don't remember anything. I only remember being afraid."

"We need you to try to remember, Beth. The more information we have, the better prepared we'll be." Jonathan rested his chin on top of my head as he spoke. Uncle Connor moved back to his chair, giving us some room.

"Prepared for what?" I asked, exhausted.

"Nothing you need to worry about right now," Uncle Connor cut in, and Jonathan moved his head awkwardly. It felt like he was rolling his eyes at Uncle Connor.

"Can you tell me what you remember?" Jonathan asked quietly.

I recounted the experience in as much detail as I could, trembling as I described the sensation of sinking lower and lower and the certainty that I was dying. Logically, I tried to convince myself that it was only a nightmare, but deep down I knew better—it was more vivid—and I was more aware of my senses than in a normal dream. I struggled to describe the sounds and to explain the awful taste and the hideous smell of death. Uncle Connor and Jonathan seemed especially interested in those details.

"He tapped into all five senses," Uncle Connor murmured, his eyes focused intently on Jonathan. Jonathan nodded.

"Is there anything else you can tell us?"

"Not really," I replied. "Except, well . . . I don't know if it matters."

"What?"

"I think it was the same . . ." I struggled for the right word, "entity . . . that overcame Eric."

"What makes you think so?" Jonathan asked.

"The eyes. I mean . . . I didn't actually see the eyes while I was in the dark, but before, when I was by the door, they were the same."

I pulled away from Jonathan, watching his expression as I spoke.

"What else reminded you of Eric?"

"He said my name, just like that night. He called me 'Beth Anne.'"

Jonathan flashed a sharp look at Uncle Connor who sat expressionless in his chair. He met Jonathan's gaze with flat eyes. They stared at each other without speaking for several moments. The silence made me uneasy.

"What?" I demanded.

Uncle Connor shook his head. "You must have been terrified." I could tell he was holding something back.

"The important thing is that you went back," Jonathan added. "You faced him. That took an amazing amount of courage."

"I wasn't courageous at all," I insisted. "I wanted to let go."

"But you didn't."

"But I would have if . . . if . . ."

"If Jonathan hadn't made you angry," Uncle Connor finished.

I paused for several moments and then realized he was right. My anger had given me the stubborn determination to climb, in spite of my fear.

"How did you know?" I whispered. I searched Jonathan's eyes and what I saw surprised me. It was relief.

"I didn't know," he admitted. "I hoped it would be enough."

"Jonathan is trained to deal with possessors—or intruders as we call them," Uncle Connor said, throwing a swift glance at Jonathan. "That's how he knew how to handle Eric, and that's how he knew what to do with you."

"But why me?" I asked, struggling to understand.

"We're not sure," Jonathan answered.

"But you have an idea?"

"We think . . ." Uncle Connor began, but his eyes flickered to Jonathan and he hesitated.

"We think he's been watching you for some time now," Jonathan explained.

"Because?"

"Because you've reached the age of adulthood," he explained. "Both sides are studying you."

The words struck with powerful force. I knew instantly that what he was saying was true. I'd felt it on several occasions, but hearing the words pulled a wretched knot in my stomach.

"What do they want?" I choked, fighting the emotion in my throat.

"They're waiting for your genes to begin the process of reclamation. Possessors gain the most power if they can influence an immortal when the alléles first reach maturity."

"That's right," Uncle Connor confirmed.

"But why attack Eric? He's not going through reclamation."

"Intruders will take any body they can. They prefer an immortal body because the senses are heightened, but they'll use mortals in the interim. They have the most influence on older teenagers and young adults. When they're finished using a mortal, however, they dispose of their bodies like common waste. Most humans don't recover."

"But Eric survived."

"Yes," Uncle Connor explained, "because Jonathan fought off the possessor. Like I said before, he's specially trained to fight them. Eric's mind was weak—I'm sure alcohol had something to do with that—but he must have retained some strength of mind or the possessor wouldn't have fled."

"And these possessors—they can have power over an immortal?"

"That's correct . . . if the immortal allows it," Uncle Connor confirmed.

"Why would anyone knowingly allow a possessor to control them?" I asked, horrified.

"Human nature," Uncle Connor said coldly. "They're promised power, wealth, success—whatever things they desire most. Once turned, they provide powerful tabernacles for possessors. And they're natural allies of the Niaces."

"You said both sides are watching me?" I looked at Jonathan and then at Uncle Connor.

"Yes, it's routine to study the progress of immortal offspring," Uncle Connor continued. "The Lebas, unlike the Niaces, however, don't interfere with the offspring's agency or right to direct his or her own life. Most of the time, the Lebas presence remains undetected."

"An étude," I murmured, releasing a huff of air as I said the word.

"What's that?" Uncle Connor asked.

"An étude," Jonathan repeated. "It means 'a little study.'"

The night faded and the first light of dawn sent a bluish glow through the room as I sat bundled in Jonathan's arms. The calming purr of his breathing relaxed me as his chest rose and fell in peaceful rhythms. I listened contentedly to the crackling of the wood as it popped in the fireplace. Uncle Connor had slumped in his chair and drifted off to sleep, but his face didn't look young and peaceful as it usually did, it was creased with lines of worry.

The bluish glow of the room began to brighten and change with each passing moment. The walls gradually came to life with shades of purple and pink as the sun neared the horizon. Jonathan sat in trance-like silence, twirling strands of my hair between his fingers. I knew he was seriously contemplating something—he was troubled. I could also sense that he wasn't going to share his thoughts with me. My focus bounced between Uncle Connor's face and Jonathan's methodic movements.

As morning arrived, the room took on brilliant hues of orange and yellow as the first rays of the sun peeked through the narrow slits of the shutters. I watched the rays paint horizontal lines along the walls and the furniture. Then, in perfect synchronicity, understanding emerged as dawn broke and the light of the sun permeated the room.

"He'll be back, won't he," I stated.

Jonathan pressed his lips against my hair and nodded his head.

"Yes," he whispered. "He'll be back."

Hours slowly turned into days and days drifted into weeks. Jonathan came often to pick me up from school—even on days when he wasn't tutoring. He stayed on those afternoons well into the evening, until Uncle Connor or Marci made him go home. He was surprisingly patient, entertaining himself while I completed my homework. I was preparing for semester finals, so some evenings he helped me study. Other nights he would peruse the books in Uncle Connor's private study. Jonathan seemed to enjoy the ambience of that room as much as Uncle Connor did, and eventually, I chose to do my reading in there as well so I could be closer to him. I felt more at peace reading next to Jonathan during those quiet evenings than I'd felt in a long time, but I knew it couldn't last forever. Jonathan had obligations that he'd placed on hold to take care of me. Soon, he would have to resume the regular routine of his life—and that included traveling.

Sleep was another issue altogether. For the first couple of nights, I had a hard time allowing myself to fall asleep. In spite of Jonathan's efforts to prepare me against further encounters with an intruder, as soon as I closed my eyes I'd feel pressure on my chest and imagine I was sinking into despair. I feared that falling asleep would allow the sinking sensation to overcome me and I might never awaken.

Marci sat with me during those nights, stroking my hair and forehead until I could no longer fight and my eyelids would finally close. Her touch was hypnotic and comforting, but I knew that eventually I'd have to be on my own.

I discovered that music helped, so each night I went to bed listening to my CD of Hungarian Rhapsodies. They were not the most peaceful and relaxing choice of music, but they were a great distraction. I focused on the intricate complexities of the music and my mind would eventually give in and let go, releasing me into slumber.

Most nights my dreams were normal, filled with images that made little sense, and I would forget them the moment I woke. But every couple of nights, Eleanor would appear in my dreams. I began to expect her companionship and as odd as it may sound, I welcomed it.

At school, things continued as usual. Evan and Darla hadn't gone public with their relationship, but I knew it had progressed beyond mere friendship. Eric and I had more classes together than Darla and I did, so we saw each other often during the day. I'd developed a special kind of bond with Eric, one that he had no clue existed. He and I had shared a common visitor and like it or not, that created a connection between us that was unique.

I wondered why Eric had no memory of his encounter with the possessor whereas mine was so vividly detailed. Jonathan seemed to think it was because he'd been drinking that night, but it was difficult for me to believe that a few drinks could impair the mind to such a degree. I'd both *hoped* and *feared* that Eric's memory would return. I hoped for it because I wanted to talk to someone who could understand what I'd experienced. I feared, however, that Eric would find out it was Jonathan who broke his ribs. I didn't want to see a confrontation between the two of them—not that Jonathan couldn't beat Eric in a fight, but it would be an ugly battle.

Through all of this, I found solace in the least likely place imaginable—the piano. On the days that Jonathan didn't come for me, I found myself across the street at the recreation center looking for Justin, often waiting for him at the practice rooms until the janitor rolled through and announced he'd be locking up the building soon.

When Justin didn't show, I practiced drills with my right hand. I paid no attention to the level of difficulty, choosing instead to focus on the purpose of the exercise until I mastered it. I repeated this through Hanon, Bach, Schubert, and the Chopin Études. Periodically, I'd lift my left hand to the keyboard and rest it there, pretending to play in my mind—for in my mind's eye I saw my hand as it used to be, before the accident.

More than once, I found myself pulling my bent fingers straight and holding them to the keys, trying to will them to move at my command. The exercise always resulted in pain. I recalled Jonathan's words: "As long as there's pain, there's hope." I clung to those words—not that I really believed them, just that it gave me something concrete to cling to in the wake of so much that was ambiguous and surreal. Once or twice, I even convinced myself that I felt something. On occasion, my mind entertained a wild whim. If biological immortality were possible, then maybe. . . .

On days when Justin came, I sat at his side, guiding him through the intricacies of whatever piece of music he was working on. He had long since mastered the Schubert Impromptu and had graduated to more sophisticated selections. Periodically, Mr. Laden would join us. He never brought up the topic of me working as a tutor again, but he kept a close eye on my interaction with Justin. Sometimes he would stand at the doorway and just watch; other times, he would pull up a chair and interject criticism. I wondered sometimes if Jonathan had warned Mr. Laden not to mention tutoring; but I didn't ask, and Jonathan didn't tell.

Justin was preparing for the upcoming annual Bach Festival. Winners of the local competitions would advance to the state finals and then perform in a nationwide celebration of Bach's life and music. Bach wasn't my favorite composer; he was too structured for my taste. With the exception of my favorite composer, Chopin, I preferred the passion and emotion of the romantic era. Nevertheless, Bach was a composer that all classically trained pianists were required to master—it was an unwritten rule among performers—so I poured my efforts into helping Justin do just that. After awhile, I began to feel myself playing vicariously through Justin, and that gave me a profound sense of satisfaction.

During those weeks, Jonathan had a chance to study much of my mother's research. He would share her ideas with me periodically, sometimes resulting in a lengthy discussion involving science and religion—my mom's pet subjects. Jonathan was particularly fascinated with her philosophies regarding the age of the earth. My mom believed that God created the Earth in seven creative periods, but that He used matter that was already in existence. Scientific law states that matter cannot be created or destroyed—it can only change forms. Mom's theory was that God organized existing matter to form the Earth as we know it today. According to her, carbon dating revealed the age of the *matter,* not the age of the Earth in its present form.

"It's a fascinating philosophy," Jonathan suggested one night while we sat in Uncle Connor's study. "I can see how her ideas would interest both the world of science and that of religion."

"Yeah, she always tried to marry the two," I replied.

"She had some interesting ideas about that as well," he grinned.

"About what?"

"Marriage." Something in my expression humored him. "Have you ever read her beliefs about it?"

"No, but I've heard her talk about it with Uncle Connor. They used to argue about it all the time," I said, rolling my eyes.

Jonathan chuckled. "I wish I could have known her."

"Yeah, she would've loved you," I grinned. "You would have become her next project."

"Her project?"

"Yeah," I laughed. "She would've needled you until she pinned down *your* beliefs—especially when it comes to God." I gestured toward the binder with my eyes.

"I'm not that complicated," he mused, a look of feigned disappointment in his eyes.

"What I mean is you don't seem to have a strong opinion either way."

"Then you haven't been listening," he said, raising his eyebrow.

"So, you *do* believe in God?" I asked reluctantly.

"Oh, I believe in God . . . we just don't always see eye-to-eye. Sometimes, I'm downright angry with him."

Jonathan's words surprised me. Most people who believed in God would never question Him or doubt Him, and here Jonathan was admitting that he not only questioned God, he actually got mad at Him. That seemed almost sacrilegious, and yet it was refreshingly honest.

"What's the matter," he smiled, "does that make you uncomfortable?"

"I don't know," I answered. "Maybe."

"What about you? Do you believe in God?"

I shook my head no. "My mother did her best to expose me to as many beliefs and philosophies as possible, but I think it confused me more than anything. I believe in something—I just don't know how to define it. And with everything I've learned during the past two months, I'm more confused than ever. There are days when

I'm sure I'll find out this was all someone's idea of an elaborate practical joke."

"That would be one cruel jokester, don't you think?" Jonathan laughed.

"Yeah," I scoffed. "It's not like I wasn't already messed up when I got here."

Jonathan crumpled a piece of paper into a tight ball and threw it at me in response.

"Ohhhh," I sighed, shaking my head, "you have no idea what you just started."

As fast as I could, I tore pages from my notebook, wadded them up, and heaved them at his face. Before I knew it, we were both on our knees batting paper balls ferociously at each other and laughing hysterically. I crawled behind the wing chair that sat across from the desk to barricade myself while I made several balls—which I threw all at once. Jonathan crawled after me, chasing me across the room until he caught me by the leg, and began hurling paper balls at the back of my head. I was laughing so hard it was difficult to react quickly enough to thwart his efforts, but I tried anyway. My face was hot and red and my stomach hurt from laughing so hard, but it was great therapy.

When Uncle Connor appeared in the doorway, our laughter ceased abruptly. He was leaning reproachfully against the doorjamb with his arms folded across his chest.

There we were, sprawled out on the floor, surrounded by a swarm of paper balls, and cackling like unruly children. Uncle Connor didn't say anything. He simply stared at us with pursed lips and nodded his head slowly up and down. After a few moments, which seemed like an eternity, he turned around and disappeared up the stairs.

Jonathan and I stared at each other, trying not to laugh. It probably wouldn't have been so bad if we'd been out in the open area of the basement, but we had desecrated Uncle Connor's private study.

"Oh crap!" I whispered, still red in the face from laughing. "I bet he's ticked at me."

"You mean *us*," Jonathan corrected. "I think we're *both* in trouble."

We were both still struggling to stifle our laughter as we waited for Uncle Connor to return. I figured by the prolonged silence that we'd better put the study back in order and head upstairs.

We cleaned up our mess and straightened the room, still snickering under our breath. I grabbed my books and blew out the candles in the study before we made our way in the dark to the bottom of the staircase. We were halfway up the stairs when Uncle Connor and Marci appeared at the top holding a bucket, their faces ripe with mischief.

"Ah, geez," Jonathan drawled from behind me.

Before I knew it, paper snowballs flew down the stairs in quick succession, hitting me in the chest, face, and head so fast I couldn't comprehend what was happening. I tried to shield myself with my books, but the shock of seeing Uncle Connor and Marci involved in such a childish game rendered me useless. Jonathan pulled on my arm from behind and I finally dropped my books and hightailed it down the stairs behind him. He gathered paper balls as quickly as he could and handed several to me. We took our places, hiding behind the walls in the basement, waiting for our attackers to approach.

In no time at all, it was all out war. A frenzy of flying paper snowballs erupted in the basement. There were no prisoners and no mercy.

I'd never seen Jonathan so completely relaxed. He was an ageless child, glowing with joy. Uncle Connor and Marci looked every bit as young as Jonathan did, and for the remainder of the evening, the four of us embraced the innocence of youth.

Special Delivery

CHAPTER 14

One of the deliveries my father had written me about arrived two weeks before Christmas—actually, two packages arrived. It was a Saturday morning. I was relaxing by the fire enjoying a cup of hot cocoa and a book when I heard a loud clanging commotion above my head. It felt like the entire house was shaking with each noisy clump . . . *galumph* . . . *clang* . . . *clump* . . .

"What the heck?" I grumbled, staring at the ceiling. I closed my book and went upstairs. I peeked into each of the bedrooms, but no one was home—Uncle Connor and Marci had gone Christmas shopping in Jackson. The clattering and thumping ruckus appeared to be coming from the roof.

I trotted back downstairs in time to see sparks flying from the flue in the fireplace. I cautiously stepped closer to the hearth and paused. Just then, a large white clump of something came crashing down the chimney. *Szzzzzz* . . . *thumph!* It looked like a perfectly formed snowball.

"Ho! Ho! Ho!" a deep, muffled voice roared down the chimney. "Bethy, have you been a good little girl?" It wasn't difficult to figure out what was going on—Santa Claus had come!

I sprinted to the door and ran outside. The glare of the sun hitting the snow on the roof made it difficult to see clearly; nevertheless, there, donned in a bright red hat trimmed with white fur, stood Santa Claus.

"You idiot!" I wailed. "What are you doing up there, trying to burn down the house?"

"I came to deliver your present, what else?" Santa shouted. The mock innocence was easy to detect, even from two stories below.

"Get down here you dork!" I giggled. "You'll break your neck." The excitement of seeing Carl again made me dance with glee; I was practically jumping up and down waiting for him to climb off the roof. I knew what was coming next, so I braced myself. He approached me enthusiastically and scooped me up into an enormous bear hug, nearly squeezing the breath out of me.

"Ooof!" I huffed helplessly. "Enough, Santa!"

Carl set me down, but he didn't let me go. He pushed me away from him and looked me over from head to toe, shaking his head.

"What?"

"Still prettier every time I see you," he winked. My face turned a bright shade of pink. It didn't matter how old I was, he still had the ability to make me blush profusely. Carl pinched my chin between his thumb and fingers. "And you have the prettiest rose-colored cheeks in town," he added.

"You're ridiculous," I mumbled, trying not to laugh.

I can't explain what happened next or where it came from, but a sudden rush of emotion overcame me. Tears welled up in my eyes and I threw my arms around his neck and started to cry.

"Bethy!" he gasped. "What? What is it?" His arms reached around me and patted my back hesitantly. "What's the matter?"

I shook my head against his chest, wiping my wet eyes on his shirt. He chuckled, and the shaking of his shoulders made me pull away from him, embarrassed.

"Whoa," he smiled, wiping away one of the tears I'd missed. "That's quite a reception."

I laughed hoarsely. "I'm sorry, I—"

"No, I like it," he interrupted. "In fact, I'm going to climb back on the roof so we can do this again." He grinned mischievously and raised his eyebrows; all I could do was slug him in the arm. He grabbed his arm and let out an exaggerated cry of pain that set us both roaring with laughter.

One thing about Carl, he knew how to make an entrance.

"So, where's the package you're suppose to be delivering?" I asked playfully. "Or did you throw that down the chimney too?"

"Come on, I'll show you." He nudged my arm and motioned for me to follow him. His eyes held a certain gleam which made me more than a little curious. He led me into the house, meandered casually through the kitchen, and then went down the basement stairs.

Nestled comfortably on top of a plush white area carpet near the far window sat my present. It looked natural in its new location—as if it had always belonged in that very spot. Black, shiny, and grand sat my piano, the one that had been locked away in storage for nearly nine months.

"Oh, Carl!" I gasped. My knees turned weak and I clutched hold of the stair rail to keep my balance. All I could do was stare at the piano through tear-filled eyes, unable to speak. Carl watched my reaction with satisfaction.

"Apparently, *some*body thinks Beth has been a good girl this year," he smirked.

And for the second time that morning, I threw my arms around his neck and cried.

He chuckled. "I've been home for five minutes and I've already made you cry twice. If you're not careful, Dad's going to send me away again."

"I-I'm sorry," I stuttered. "It's just . . ." I searched in vain for the right words. "Thank you," I finally said.

"Well, in all honesty, I can't take credit for this. It was your father's idea."

"My dad?" I sniffled.

"Mm hmm."

I walked slowly toward the piano and brushed my fingertips across the top. So much of my life had been centered on this instrument, many of my happiest memories. The moment was bittersweet as a stabbing ache of regret began to needle its way to the surface. As if programmed to do so, I flexed the muscles in my left wrist and attempted to pull my deformed fingers straight; but as usual, the effort was painfully unsuccessful. I couldn't allow *either* pain to linger—the emotional longing for what might have been or the physical pain in my hand. Instead, I focused on the promise of a new companionship with the instrument I'd loved for so long.

Carl joined me at the piano. He lifted the bench lid and reached inside the storage compartment to retrieve a very old book of piano music.

"This part was my idea," he said, suddenly more serious. He placed the music on the piano. "It's nobody you're familiar with, and it's been out of print for decades, but I thought you'd like it."

The title read, *Frydric Khuammerle's Compositions for the Right Hand.*

I opened the book and thumbed through the delicate, faded pages. The compositions were written at an advanced level, but solely for the right hand.

Carl explained. "Khuammerle lost the use of his left hand after suffering from a severe fever in the early eighteen hundreds. Rather than give up his love for playing the piano, he began creating complex compositions solely for the right hand. He never expected his work to be printed, but a few years after his death, his daughter compiled the compositions into a book and had them published. There were only a hundred copies sold."

"How . . ." I shook my head in disbelief. "How did you get this?"

Carl raised one eyebrow and pulled his lips together in a tight line. As I expected, he was not going to answer.

"It doesn't matter," I sighed, "I love it. I love you for thinking of it. Thank you."

"You're not going to cry again, are you? 'Cuz I don't think I could take more of that," he teased.

I slugged him in the arm again.

"I don't think I can take any more of *that* either," he said, rubbing the spot where I hit him. Carl's playful grin slowly faded and his eyes became serious.

"I believe the past two months have been quite eventful for you," he said sympathetically.

"Phfff," I snorted. "That's an understatement."

"Do you want to talk about it?"

"Thanks, but for the past few weeks, that's all I've done—ask questions and talk, then ask more questions. I'm trying desperately to make sense of everything. I think I'm driving your dad and Jonathan crazy. I'm just pathetic."

"Not pathetic," he disagreed, reassuringly.

He disappeared for a moment into the small kitchenette then reappeared with two sodas. He sat in the middle of the floor, opened the cans, and motioned me over to join him.

After drinking the sodas, we sprawled out on the basement floor and talked. I started from the beginning, describing the afternoon at the lake when I first noticed there was something unusual about Jonathan's blood and the speed with which he healed from his wound. I told him about Eric and Halloween and about the possessor. I told him how Jonathan fought that night with a broken leg and how it had mended on the spot. Carl listened patiently while I recounted each event in detail.

"Then there was *that* room," I said, pointing toward the door of the closet under the staircase.

"Yeah," Carl chuckled. "I wish I could've been here for that. I missed *all* the good stuff."

I kicked my foot playfully against his leg in protest and then continued to relate the events leading up to the present. I paused for a minute and rolled over onto my side to look at Carl, shaking my head slowly as he turned to meet my gaze.

"You know, I thought I was handling everything well," I

continued. "I didn't freak out when Jonathan and your dad told me about immortals; I tried to process the information like a scientist—with an open mind, you know—examine the evidence and develop my own hypothesis. But it's . . . it's just too much for me to maintain my grip on reality. The night I dreamed, or whatever you call it, about the possessor, *that* was more than I could handle."

"Not from what I heard," Carl interjected. "According to Dad, you handled it perfectly."

"No, Jonathan handled it perfectly. I was a wreck."

"You'd be surprised, Beth, how many people never get over that type of encounter. You were strong, and you allowed Jonathan to help. Don't underestimate the implications of that."

"Did it ever happen to you?" I asked.

"You mean, did a possessor ever try to get to me?"

"Yeah."

"No," he shook his head. "I've never had that experience. But the stories I've heard are all similar."

"So why did it happen to me? What do they want from me?"

"That's obvious. It's in your blood—or at least it will be once the change takes place."

"But that's just it . . . nothing has changed in me. I'm still mortal."

"That doesn't matter to them right now. You have the potential to become immortal very soon, and once the immortal fluid flows through your veins, it'll be too difficult for the intruders or the possessors to influence you."

"Speaking of that, what's the difference between an intruder and a possessor?" I asked.

"Not much, really. A possessor takes over the body—an intruder takes over the mind. But in reality, one usually precedes the other."

His eyes flickered to mine and he shrugged, then he made it clear why the Niaces might want me. "If they can pull you to their side now," he explained, "you'll be a powerful weapon for them."

"A weapon?"

"Mm hmm."

"Weapon for what?"

"To fight against the Lebas, I suspect."

I was frustrated. "You see, that's the kind of stuff I'm talking about. I don't have a clue what that's supposed to mean."

Carl tried to explain. "Basically, immortals aren't supposed to be here. This world belongs to mortals—at least for the time being. Yet here we are. As a result, we're subject to the physical laws of this realm. That's why we sometimes get sick and why our senses aren't as keenly developed as they would be if the laws of an immortal universe governed us. It also explains why our bodies can be destroyed—they're made of mortal elements that are constantly regenerated by the immortal fluids that flow through them. Take away that fluid and the body becomes corrupt."

"So, if something happens to an immortal, the Lebas will intervene?" I asked.

"Usually."

"Then why didn't they intervene when my mom died?" I asked bitterly.

"They did, Beth. Haven't you figured that out by now?" His eyes narrowed as he spoke and he raised himself onto one elbow. "You've maintained all along that there was someone else there that night."

I stared at Carl incredulously. "What are you saying, exactly?"

"I'm saying that the Niaces got there first, before the Lebas had a chance to intervene."

"Why didn't you tell me this before?"

"It's not that simple," he said defensively. "Immortals, as a rule, don't interfere with mortals."

"But Jonathan intervened when Eric attacked me."

"Jonathan breaks the rules," Carl said, cutting me off abruptly. "Or rather, he rewrites them to suit his own purposes."

My mouth dropped as I started to say something, but Carl quickly continued. "Not that I blame him—I would've done the same thing in his shoes—but technically, you shouldn't know about any of this, not yet."

"Because I'm not immortal."

"Not immortal *yet,*" he corrected me.

"And what happens to me if I never change, if I stay mortal like your brother Nick?"

He paused for several seconds and then began to shake his head slowly back and forth.

"I don't know," he finally answered.

"You said I would be a powerful weapon for the Niaces if a possessor gained control over me." I looked at Carl and he nodded. "Why is that?"

"Once immortal, you'll carry the fluids of a royal line that was destroyed a long time ago. That makes you a natural heir to the executive and legislative powers of the Lebas. Imagine the possibilities if you claimed your birthright under the influence of the Niaces."

Carl stopped, allowing the magnitude of his words to sink in.

"You're not the only one, Beth. The Lebas recently discovered an obscure line of natural descendents. The undetected gene had passed through recessive alleles for centuries."

"How was it discovered?" I asked. "I mean, if it weren't for my mom, no one would have known that my dad was a carrier, right?"

"Probably not. It first occurred to the Lebas when they suddenly discovered that immortal offspring were being born of mortal parents. The possibility of that happening had never been considered before."

Carl studied my expression closely, perhaps wondering how much I understood about genetics. He must have been satisfied with what he saw because he continued his explanation.

"Until a few decades ago, the science of genetics and the technological advances in chemistry had not progressed far enough for anyone to understand recessive alleles. Once understood, the Lebas became acutely aware that there could be numerous immortals wandering on the planet with no clue of who—or what—they were. The Niaces also have this information, and that threat has the Lebas urgently trying to identify what they call 'first generation immortals' so they can be adequately empowered against the influence of the Niaces."

Carl sat up and looked me squarely in the eye. "You asked me why the Niaces want you. My theory is that they found out about your father's bloodline, and that they came to disable you on the night of your accident."

"Disable me?" Carl's words carved a hole in the pit of my stomach. Had my mom given her life to spare mine? I recalled the words that passed between us that night; we had been arguing and I was angry with her for imposing her values on me—values that made me different from every other girl in school, at least that's how it seemed at the time. I thought about the horror I'd seen in her face and the sounds of her screams as the car made impact with . . . with what? There was no other vehicle involved in the accident; nothing had stood in the path of the car as she sped down the highway.

Unless . . .

My mind began to resurrect images from that night; frame by frame, the memories revealed themselves with perfect clarity. I watched the scene from a vantage point somewhere off stage, reliving the sequence as a spectator. My head began to throb as the reels turned. I flinched, clutching the sides of my head tightly as if to squeeze the memories from it.

"Beth!" Carl gasped. "What is it?"

I couldn't respond; I could only twist my head sideways, the pain lurching itself from side to side with each movement.

I watched myself unbuckle the seat belt and bend down to loosen the strap on my shoes. I watched my mom yell at me to sit back in the seat, and I saw her hand pull on the back of my shoulders, urging me backwards. I watched as I yanked my shoulder away from her and turned to yell at her.

"Knock it off!" I snapped.

"Beth, sit up, now," she ordered.

"Get off my back, Mom!"

"Beth!" she called anxiously.

"Leave me the hell alone!" I bellowed.

I turned to face her in time to see her eyes wild with panic as she stared directly ahead. She screamed, slamming her foot on the brake. The car swerved and spun, jolting me sharply against the side of the car. My head was slammed into something metal and became trapped between the side of the car and the front console. The center of gravity seemed to change repeatedly as the weight of my body shifted forward, sideways, forward again, and then hung awkwardly as if suspended in midair. The sensation reminded me of being on a full-revolution roller coaster. Then, in a final lurch, I was scrunched into a tight ball resting on my back, my legs pinned above my head. My mother sat, hanging from her seat, with her head dangling at a confused angle. I could see a spinning tire through the window and I smelled the odor of hot motor oil.

In a desperate movement, my mom struggled to free herself—but the seat belt restrained her. Horror stricken, she grabbed for me, clutching the air in front of her as if to pull herself closer to me. Her eyes darted forward and she began to scream, terrified by whatever it was she saw. The pressure in my head increased and my vision began to fade; but before darkness set in, I caught a glimpse of two yellow eyes peering through the window by my mom.

The car had stopped moving, I was sure of that, but the sound of twisting metal continued to screech in my head.

"Stay away from her!" my mom ordered. "It's me you want. It's me you need!"

Something hot, icy hot, burned against the palm of my hand.

"I can give you what you want!" she pleaded.

The deafening shriek of tearing metal ceased and my mother's focus shifted away from me. In an instant, an unseen force tore her from her harness and snatched her from the heap of wreckage that surrounded us. She kicked vehemently at the air, fighting for some kind of advantage against her assailant. And then, just as I had seen it a hundred times before, she disappeared.

Then something tight locked itself under my arms. The pressure in my head was causing excruciating pain that throbbed fiercely between my ears and behind my eyes. Then, there was nothing—nothing but darkness and silence—until someone's protective arms carried me to safety.

I looked up to find Carl kneeling next to me on the floor, his face anxious with worry as he listened to me recall in vivid detail the events surrounding my accident.

"She . . . saved me, Carl. She let them take her instead of me." Tears filled my eyes and I struggled to keep them from spilling down my cheeks.

"Yes," Carl whispered, "that's what I think."

"Why did they have to kill her?"

Carl shook his head. "Knowing your mom, she waited until she knew you were safe and then refused to give them what she'd promised."

"What did she have that they wanted so badly?"

"That's what we all want to know. I've been hoping your dad could shed some light on it. He was closer to her than anyone."

"My Dad . . ." I whispered.

"What about your dad? Did he contact you?" Carl was suddenly urgent.

"Yes. He sent me an e-mail telling me that a package would soon arrive, and that . . ." I looked earnestly into Carl's face, "and that *someone* needed to look at it."

Carl grabbed my shoulders intently. "What exactly did the e-mail say?"

I closed my eyes, concentrating. "Have someone look it over. No . . . that's not it exactly."

"Think Beth!" Carl urged, "It might be important."

"Wait, I printed the e-mail for my scrapbook. You can read it yourself."

We ran upstairs to my bedroom. I quickly retrieved the scrapbook from my desk and flipped through the pages. There it was:

Beth,

We finally received clearance to write. I hope all is going well for you at school. I miss you every day and wish I could see you. New orders arrived yesterday, but there is no word about how long they will need me here. I'm sure your uncle is taking good care of you.

I have to keep this brief as time is limited. If things have gone as planned, you can expect a couple of deliveries soon. One of them is quite peculiar; you'll likely need someone's help with it. The other is a Christmas present. I'm sorry I can't be with you for the holidays. I'll miss you shaking all the gifts.

This is important. We are fairly confident that the mail we send is secure; however, we can't be sure that the mail we receive won't be intercepted. Write when you can, but be aware that others may read the mail you send me.

I love you always,

Dad

P.S. Tell Carl thanks for me.

"Not a package," I muttered quietly. "What?" Carl asked. "All this time I've been expecting a package to arrive from him, but it's not a *package* that's supposed to arrive, it's a *delivery.*"

"The piano?" Carl thought aloud, but he shook his head. "It's been in storage for months. That can't be it. Did your father send you any other messages?"

"No, this is the only e-mail I've received since he left."

"Are you sure?" It was a rhetorical question. He covered his mouth with his thumb and finger, resting his hand on his chin as he thought to himself. His mannerisms were so much like his father's. I thought back to the image of Uncle Connor sitting across from me in his chair alongside the fireplace, the way he had when my computer had turned itself on!

"Of course!" I hissed.

"What?"

"There *was* another message."

Carl's eyes flashed to mine as he waited for me to continue.

"Something strange happened with my computer." I hesitated briefly, and Carl raised his eyebrows, silently bidding me to complete my thought.

I explained everything to him in as much detail as I could recall, including Uncle Connor's suggestion that my dad could have accessed my computer remotely.

"Could that be the delivery he was talking about?" I asked.

"Possibly . . . that would explain why he said you might need help." Carl exhaled sharply, deep in thought. "There has to be something we're missing."

The rumbling of my cell phone vibrating on the desk startled us both. I snorted a breath of relief as I reached for it and flipped it open.

"Hey."

"Er, hey yourself," Jonathan answered. "Did I interrupt something?"

"No, why?"

"You're out of breath."

"Are you coming over?"

"Uh, yeah."

"Okay, I'll explain when I see you."

"Beth?"

"Yes?"

"What's going on?"

"I'll tell you when you get here. Hurry, okay?"

"Oka—"

I flipped the phone closed before he finished speaking and tossed it onto my bed. When I looked back at Carl, he was laughing and shaking his head.

"What?" I asked innocently.

"That was Jonathan?"

"Yes . . . so?"

His annoying smirk made me realize I'd just done something stupid.

"What?" I demanded.

He shook his head and continued to laugh. "Clueless," he sighed. "Jonathan must have the patience of Job."

"What did I do?"

"Nothing," he chuckled. "Now stay focused." He began to repeat the words 'biological immortality' over and over as if saying the phrase out loud would spark some new meaning.

"It must have something to do with my mom's research, right? I mean, that would explain why they took her."

Carl raised his eyebrows.

"I suppose," he replied. "Your dad would've known what she was working on before the accident.

"Jonathan has been studying her binders. Mostly they're just her views on religion and science. I don't see how they could have anything to do with my dad's e-mail."

"When will my dad be home?"

"I don't know," I shrugged my shoulders. "He's with Marci."

"Okay. I'll be back." Carl rose abruptly and started for the door.

"But Jonathan's on his way—don't you want to see him?"

"I'm sure you can keep him . . . occupied until I return." He threw me a sly wink and headed out the door.

Jonathan arrived wearing the baseball cap I loved and a black T-shirt that made his eyes more brilliant than ever. I never tired of looking into them. And I never failed to blush when his eyes lingered on my mouth, which is what they did the minute I opened the door. He kissed me softly on the lips, then kissed me again more seriously before holding me tightly against him.

"Hi," he whispered in my ear. "Brought you something."

I backed away slightly as he held a perfectly shaped white rose to my nose. I took a deep breath and sighed. The rose had a powerfully potent fragrance that took me by surprise.

"Wow! That smells amazing. Where in the world did you find such a beautiful rose in the middle of December?"

"You'll never believe it. I was pruning the roses at the ranch and—"

"You were pruning roses?" I laughed.

Jonathan ignored my teasing insult and continued, "—when I spotted it. The rose bushes are nothing more than bare sticks right now, and yet there in the middle of them all stood this one lone rose looking regal as a pearl. When I got close enough to inspect it, I couldn't find any flaws—it's perfect—and its fragrance is even stronger than the roses that bloom mid spring. It reminded me of you," he said softly.

I reached for him and nestled against his chest.

"Wow," he chuckled, "I'm going to bring you flowers more often."

"It's not the flower," I blushed, "but thanks for the rose."

Jonathan followed me into the house and I filled him in on Carl's impromptu visit while I put the rose in a bud vase.

"Is Carl still here?" he asked.

"He left for a few minutes, but he'll be back."

"Good," Jonathan nodded.

"I can't wait to show you why he came," I said eagerly.

Jonathan raised his eyebrows in curiosity.

"Follow me," I said, dragging him through the kitchen and downstairs to the basement. He stopped abruptly when he spotted the piano.

"Whoa!" he said, stunned.

"He brought it all the way from California."

"I'm impressed."

"I guess my dad arranged for him to deliver it to me, so it's actually a gift from my dad, not Carl—but Carl brought me this." I skipped to the piano and picked up the book of compositions for the right hand and handed it to Jonathan. He handled the book carefully, gently turning through the pages and inspecting its contents.

"This is an amazing gift, Beth."

"I know. It's just like Carl to do this."

Jonathan smiled and tilted his head toward the bud vase that I still held in my hand. "I'd better upgrade my gift if I want to compete with your cousin."

"No. I love it . . . it's perfect."

Jonathan reached for the vase and set it on top of the piano. He took my hands in his and stared deeply into my eyes, then dropped my hands and pulled me into a warm, tender embrace. He held me close for several minutes. Nothing made me feel safer or more loved—and nothing made my blood rise to a rolling boil more rapidly.

After a few minutes, he pulled away and directed his focus at the piano.

"May I?" he asked, gesturing toward the piano keys. His eyes glistened in the soft light of the room.

"Of course," I replied.

As usual, Jonathan patted the spot on the bench next to him, expecting me to sit beside him as he played. The gesture had become so customary that my response was automatic.

I expected him to begin playing one of the many pieces from his memorized repertoire, but instead he hesitated, placing only his left hand on the keys. He eyed my right hand and with one eyebrow raised, shifted his eyes from my hand to the piano keys a couple of times. He adjusted his fingers on the keys so he could play octaves, and I instantly understood what he wanted—Moonlight Sonata.

We had played this piece together several times. It was an easy piece to play, requiring very little effort, but it showcased the right hand; I'm sure that was the reason Jonathan enjoyed playing it with me.

As we began playing, Jonathan folded his free hand around my injured one and lightly caressed my palm with his fingers, moving in perfect rhythm with the song. After a few moments, he raised my hand to his lips, gently straightened my fingers a little, and began to kiss the tips of my fingers, making it extremely difficult for me to concentrate. His part was easy; he didn't have to think about anything, so multi-tasking was effortless. But my part required more focus, and he was doing his best to distract me. I tried to ignore the warmth of his lips as they pressed on each of my fingers. When he dragged the tip of his tongue lightly over the soft pads of my fingers, I doubled my effort to remain focused on the music. I knew if I were to glance at him, he'd be grinning—that wickedly playful grin of his. My concentration crumbled, however, when he began to nibble and gently suck on the tips of each finger. My right hand hesitated, causing a pause in the music.

"Uh uh," he protested softly, and gestured with his eyes for me to continue. He enjoyed making me squirm. I forced myself to focus and finish the song in spite of his attempts to derail me.

By the time we finished the song, I could feel my cheeks burning and knew that a deep hue of pink flushed my face.

"That wasn't very nice," I scolded him.

"I disagree. I enjoyed it."

"Enjoyed what?" Carl's voice bellowed down the stairs and startled me. Jonathan chuckled as I jumped guiltily in my seat, but he still held my fingers to his mouth, refusing stubbornly to let them go as I tugged against his grip.

"So, Beth," Carl razzed. "Looks like I caught you with your hand in the cookie jar."

I jerked my hand away from Jonathan's mouth abruptly and growled, my face glowing red with embarrassment. I suddenly realized I was in the presence of two guys who could make me blush shamelessly with a single look or word.

Seeing Jonathan and Carl together made me pause and consider their respective ages. In my mind, Carl was older than Jonathan. Yet, technically, Jonathan had been alive longer. The age thing still baffled me—as did the issue of time.

"You see that blush in her cheeks?" Carl asked Jonathan.

"Mm hmm."

"It used to be me that put that color there."

"I see," Jonathan said, turning to look at me. "You never told me you had a crush on your cousin, Beth."

The familiar fire raged stronger in my cheeks. There was no way to conceal the truth.

"Seems her taste has changed in the past couple of years," Carl bantered.

"Improved, hopefully," Jonathan surmised.

"I dare say," Carl drawled in mock enthusiasm. "Even the mere mention of your name brings it on. You should see what happens when—"

"All right!" I snapped. "Knock it off." I tried to infuse as much warning in my tone as possible.

"Okay," Carl chuckled mercifully.

I had to admit they were glorious—both beautiful in their unique way. But where Carl's eyes danced with mischief, Jonathan's literally took my breath away.

"How's it going," Carl asked Jonathan.

"Good. You still traveling?"

My eyebrows shot up. "Traveling? Carl's a traveler?"

"Have you found out anything new?" Jonathan said, ignoring me.

"Possibly," Carl replied, also ignoring me.

"Hey!" I blurted scornfully. They both turned to me feigning annoyance. "Carl travels?"

It became instantly obvious to me that these two knew each other far better than I'd realized. I suddenly had the feeling that I'd been asleep for a very long time.

"Nice going, Jonathan," Carl moaned. "Now I'll be up all night answering Beth's questions."

Uncle Connor and Marci arrived shortly after six with two extra large pizzas, a bag of hot bread sticks, and a two-liter bottle of root beer. Their spirits were high as they came in, their heads and coats dusted with newly-fallen snow. Their faces brightened even more when they discovered Carl had arrived.

"How long will you be here?" Marci asked, hugging Carl tightly around the waist.

"Depends," he replied. "There's a lot happening right now. It could be hit and miss for the holidays, but hopefully I'll be here for a few days at Christmas."

"Really?" Marci exclaimed. She threw Uncle Connor a quizzical glance as she spoke. "We might need to modify our plans."

"No, don't change anything for me, I'm not that reliable."

"What plans?" I asked. It had never occurred to me that there would be plans for Christmas other than being at home.

"Well, nothing is decided yet," Marci responded reassuringly. Uncle Connor laid his hand on her shoulder before she could finish.

"Marci has invited us—"

"All of you—" she emphasized.

"All of us," Uncle Connor continued, "to spend Christmas Eve and Christmas day in Jackson Hole. Her daughter has a large place and she apparently goes all out for an old-fashioned Christmas."

I did my best to keep my expression neutral, but the idea of being away from Jonathan on Christmas day had never entered my thoughts. I felt a surprising wave of panic spread through me as the concept settled in my mind.

"What about Nick's family?" Carl asked Uncle Connor. "Aren't they coming home for Christmas?"

Uncle Connor shook his head. "No, they'll be with the in-laws—seems they're demanding equal time this year."

"Actually," Jonathan interjected, "I was planning to bring this up later, but Grace wanted me to invite you all to the ranch for Christmas. We're hoping to take in a couple of days of skiing as well."

Jonathan eyed Carl as he spoke, perhaps hoping Carl would prefer his offer to Marci's. I certainly would, but I didn't want to hurt Marci's feelings by voicing an opinion. I followed Jonathan's eyes to Carl and hoped that Carl would somehow read my thoughts, not that Carl had any final say on the matter, but he definitely could be persuasive when he set his mind to it.

"Well," Uncle Connor laughed, "looks like we have plenty of options don't we? We can decide all this later—right now, let's eat before everything gets cold."

Night had fallen, but the atmosphere inside was warm and festive as we enjoyed our pizza and bread sticks. Instead of eating in the kitchen as usual, we sat on the floor in front of the fireplace and listened to Uncle Connor and Carl tell stories. The two of them played off each other like a well-rehearsed comedy routine. It was impossible not to laugh at their anecdotes.

It was nearly two hours later when Uncle Connor's mood switched from jovial to serious.

"I hate to put a damper on the fun . . ." his eyes narrowed as he spoke directly to Carl, "but I suspect you have news for me. Shall we?" He stood and motioned for Carl to follow him.

"Actually," Carl's expression mirrored Uncle Connor's as he cast his eyes around the room, "*this* news affects everyone."

History Lesson
CHAPTER 15

*I*t was as if I were listening to stories straight out of a horror novel: crime sprees of robbery and rape, deadly attacks on individuals killed by human hands of unparalleled strength, and bodies that decomposed at an extraordinary rate. The list was astounding. It wasn't as if I'd never heard of violent crime sprees—California was riddled with them—but according to Carl, there was a rampant escalation of heinous crimes occurring in certain pockets of the world. They all followed a common pattern and were layered with overt evidence that led to the same implausible conclusion.

"And they suspect these crime pockets are somehow related to what's been going on in Jackson Hole?" Marci asked.

"Precisely," Carl replied. "The best we can tell, this is an organized operation, and not the work of mortals—not directly anyway."

"They think a possessor is behind it?" Jonathan asked. The mention of possessors sent an involuntary shudder through me.

"An organized *army* of possessors," Carl confirmed.

"Possessors working together?" Uncle Connor questioned. "That's highly unusual."

"Why?" I whispered to Jonathan, not wanting to interrupt, but unable to control my curiosity.

"That's what has the Lebas so baffled," Carl answered. He directed his next words to me specifically. "Possessors are generally self-centered and self-serving. They seek their own gratification above all else."

I tried to appear as though I understood, but Jonathan sensed my confusion.

"Possessors don't have a body, so they're unable to experience physical sensations or satisfy their insatiable cravings. Once they possess a mortal body, they work vehemently to satisfy those cravings. It's like a drug for them."

"But it's not always about violence and committing crimes," Carl added. "Sometimes, it's simply about jealousy."

"Jealousy? Why?" I asked.

"Because they're unable to enjoy common human experiences— no pleasure or passion associated with positive emotions such as love, joy, or even something as simple as the bonds of friendship," Jonathan explained.

"But Eric was angry when he threw me to the ground," I exclaimed. "There was no pleasure. . . ."

"Not for you, but pleasure and pain are closely related. Prior to being taken over by the possessor, Eric was in the heat of heightened emotions—torn between his desire for you and the fear of losing your friendship. The timing was perfect for a possessor—especially one wanting to satisfy . . . urges . . . similar to Eric's."

The lines in Jonathan's face tightened; he turned away and glowered at the flames in the fireplace. I could tell he was remembering the scene he'd encountered that night at the bonfire.

I adjusted my body so that my head rested against his arm. He reached across and stroked my hair, but continued glaring into the fire.

"Your situation is rather interesting," Carl interjected. "Based on your description, it appears you've been confronted repeatedly by the same possessor, but we can't seem to identify his motive. We don't know if he came to disable you, to control you, or . . ." he cleared his throat, "to . . . experience you, through Eric's body."

My stomach twisted as I thought of the wicked eyes that had bored into mine that night. It was one thing to feel the internal presence of a possessor, to feel his *influence* as I had in the room with the spiral staircase, but it was far more frightening to experience him externally, incarnate and tangible, knowing that in *that* form he was much stronger than I was. Jonathan had told me that this entity would come back, but he didn't clarify what *form* he would come back in. He'd prepared me to fight mentally, but we both knew I didn't have the strength to battle a possessor physically.

Jonathan pulled me closer to him, shielding me as if he knew what I was thinking. He tightened his arms around me, providing a sweetly protective barrier. It made me believe that as long as he was next to me, I had nothing to fear.

Marci had remained silent for most of the evening. She'd listened carefully to the conversation, content to be a spectator rather than an active participant, and it surprised everyone when she suddenly spoke.

"Carl, tell us what the police know about the crime sprees. Are they certain they're related to the rapes in Jackson?"

"They definitely share a connection. Even though the attacks in Jackson have been limited to rape so far, the modus operandi is identical to the more serious crimes being committed in other areas. Everyone is stumped," Carl huffed. "The evidence always suggests the impossible."

"It's the perfect plan if you think about it," Uncle Connor said pensively.

Carl raised his eyebrows. "How do you mean?"

"Think about it. Possessors take over the bodies of criminals: murderers, child molesters, and rapists. Then they go on a rampage, committing the vilest crimes of passion and lust—violating innocent women and children. Then they simply discard the criminal's body like trash. The body decomposes at an accelerated rate so that even when the evidence clearly identifies the perpetrator, the police find the perpetrator's corpse and determine the time of death to be months earlier than the dates the crimes were actually committed. The police never find a shred of evidence leading to a different suspect, so eventually the case goes cold."

Uncle Connor almost sounded impressed. "It's a brilliant plan, actually. It *must* be the possessors, but this is the most wide-spread, organized invasion I've ever heard of."

"Possessors aren't that sophisticated," Jonathan noted, "and they always work alone. Even if they did organize themselves, the Niaces would never allow this type of overt operation—it would call too much attention to them."

Carl shook his head. "Lebas Intelligence believes a rogue group of immortals are behind the organized movement."

"But possessors are subject to Niace control," Uncle Connor argued. "What could possibly motivate them to go against Niace law and risk banishment?"

"Whoever is behind it must have offered them something— something that the possessors want badly," Carl replied.

Uncle Connor nodded as he placed another log on the fire. The flames leapt to a roar as he stoked the logs into a new position, sending a blanket of heat into the room.

Jonathan continued to stroke my hair and stare into the fire, his mind seemingly miles away. I closed my eyes and allowed the heat to warm my face as I rested against him. Everyone seemed lost in their own thoughts, so it startled me when Jonathan's body suddenly stiffened. I glanced up at his face; his eyebrows were tightly drawn together in a deep frown.

"Biological immortality," he muttered, so low that only I heard him clearly.

"What's that?" Carl asked.

"Carl—remember Beth's computer? It was mysteriously logged on one afternoon."

"Yeah, Beth told me."

"The words *biological immortality* were typed in the browser window."

"Yes, she told me that too. We were talking about that before you arrived."

"What's the one thing a possessor wants more than anything? The one thing they can never have permanently?" Jonathan's eyes shifted rapidly between Carl, Uncle Connor, and Marci.

"Of course!" Carl hissed. "A body—they've been promised a body!"

"Not just any body," Jonathan corrected, "an immortal body." He paused, letting the idea sink in. "Don't you see? That's what Beth's dad is trying to tell us. He's warning us. He sent the message hoping that Beth would catch on."

A deadening silence followed. There was only the sound of logs splitting from intense heat as they burned with a blue flame in the fireplace.

"But how? Who?" Carl finally asked. "Only a handful of immortals have access to the codes for biological immortality, and the mortal world is twenty years away from any major breakthroughs in that field of research. No one else could possibly have—"

"Unless . . ." Jonathan interrupted as he glanced at me, "unless they've figured out where to find the knowledge . . . and the codes."

"Oh!" Marci flashed her eyes at me and gasped, cupping her hand over her mouth.

"What?" I mumbled. "What does this have to do with me? And how is my dad involved?"

"Beth," Carl replied, "I think you hit on it earlier. Your mother had the codes."

"But the message came from my dad. He doesn't know anything about immortals."

"Beth, what do you think your father is doing in Europe?"

"Carl, stop!" Uncle Connor snapped.

"He's on military assignment, isn't he?" I implored, staring at Carl.

"Do you really think he would've left you so soon after your mother's death for some voluntary military appointment?"

"Carl!" Uncle Connor said, cutting him off.

"Don't you think she has a right to know?" Carl argued.

"It's not up to us," Uncle Connor said coldly.

"Ah, bull!" Carl snorted.

"Carl," Jonathan cut in, "Don't."

"*You're* going to tell me to follow the rules? Are you serious?" Carl accused as he threw Jonathan a harsh glance.

"Yes," Jonathan replied, "But not for the reason you think."

"Why?" Carl insisted.

"Because *your* standing with the Lebas is critical right now."

"She has a right to know."

"I agree," Jonathan said calmly. "I'll tell her."

"Jonathan," Uncle Connor and Marci both spoke at the same time. There was more than just caution in their tone, there was pleading. "You can't afford to violate Lebas regulations," Uncle Connor continued.

"Good grief!" I bellowed, frustrated that they were all behaving as though I were not in the room. "Somebody tell me what's going on with my father!"

"Her father involved her when he sent that coded message—so technically, I'm not the one breaking the rules," Jonathan argued.

Uncle Connor glared; his eyes shifted back and forth between Carl and Jonathan. He wasn't going to win this one.

"She's even more involved than we are," Jonathan said earnestly. "The possessors have attacked her—twice—she's entitled to the truth."

"If you ask me," Marci interrupted, "I think you're all making this far more complicated than it needs to be. Beth, your father is investigating your mother's death; it's as simple as that."

"But . . . there's nothing to investigate," I insisted. "They already determined that when they went over the scene of the accident."

"Your father didn't want you to suffer more than you already had. He made your Uncle promise not to tell you anything, not until he had some answers. That was the one condition he had for sending you here instead of to your grandmother's."

"But the police found no evidence of foul play. They insisted that my account of what happened was a fabrication—then they locked me away." I was on the verge of an emotional outburst that was not going to be pretty. Jonathan tried to calm me by rubbing his hand against my arm, but I snatched it away from him.

"No! I don't want to be protected. I want the truth! What does my dad know about my mom's death?"

"We don't have the answers yet," Carl replied.

"But why would he do this to me?" I complained. Tears were building in my eyes and I knew I wouldn't be able to keep them from spilling over, but I didn't care. My father had lied to me. He had tried to convince me for months that my mother's death was a tragic accident, and when I continued to insist there was more to it, he had admitted me to the trauma center.

"He did it to keep you safe. Don't judge him too harshly, Beth," Uncle Connor cautioned. "Everything your father has done—and continues to do—is for you. When you came out of that coma and told him about the accident, he notified the police immediately. He convinced them to investigate the scene, but as you know, they found nothing. For the police, the case was closed. But for your father, the lack of physical evidence was not convincing; in fact, that was what made him suspect you were telling the truth. It was too convenient, too clean. That's when he decided to look into it himself . . . but he needed help."

"Help how?" I asked.

"His military clearance affords him many privileges, but he's not an immortal. He needed help from the inside."

"You mean he's known about immortals all this time?" I couldn't believe that first my mother and then my father had kept something this huge from me.

"Not necessarily," Uncle Connor replied. "I'm not exactly sure when your father found out about Hattie, but he didn't learn about the rest of us until your mom started her research on biological immortality."

Jonathan gently pulled me next to him again. I wasn't sure if it made me calmer or if I'd simply gone numb, but I welcomed the security of his arm. Questions were swimming in my head in cluttered disarray.

"If Jonathan is right and your father is on to something, then he's trying to warn us—without the Niaces or the possessors finding out."

"Warn us about what?" I asked.

"He wanted to let us know that the Niaces have already acquired the genetic codes," Carl revealed.

"I don't understand. What good are the codes to an intruder?" I asked.

Marci responded before Carl could answer. "Perhaps it would help if you understood the origins of the Lebas and the Niaces," she suggested. She stood and reached for Uncle Connor's hand. "We've heard this before. Why don't we give Jonathan a chance to tell Beth our story," she said as she pulled Uncle Connor out of his chair and headed for the kitchen.

Jonathan stood and held out his hand to help me off the floor. "You might want to sit on the couch for this. It's a long story. I know you're going to have a lot of questions."

Carl chuckled at that, but Jonathan ignored him.

"The legend begins with Adam and Eve."

I couldn't help it; eye wrinkles or not, I rolled my eyes. Here we were again—back to Adam and Eve.

"All right," Jonathan conceded, "for the sake of science, forget Adam and Eve. Let's start at the time when immortals first realized they were confined to a mortal world."

"No . . . I'm sorry," I apologized. "Don't change the story for me."

"Okay. When Adam and Eve chose to eat the forbidden fruit, it impacted the entire world. Every living creature on Earth became temporal—subject to death—except for a small band of immortals."

"Yes, that's what Uncle Connor told me when I found out about you. You're not a descendent of Adam or Eve."

"Right," Jonathan confirmed. "During the first millenniums, the differences between mortals and immortals were essentially unde-tectable because humans lived so long. According to legend, it was several centuries before the immortals became aware that they were not aging in the same manner as the Adamic people, nor did they experience prolonged illnesses or suffer mortal wounds in battle.

"One of the most significant signs that they were 'different' surfaced through mortality rates. It was common for mortal women to die during childbirth. Likewise, it was common for mortal children to perish at a young age due to exposure or disease. Although immortal births were rare, there were never reports of infant deaths—or even illnesses."

"Why were immortal births rare?" I asked.

"We aren't sure, exactly. It had something to do with insufficient hormone levels among both males and females. Anyway, by the second millennium, the life expectancy of humans had decreased to under a hundred years. Humans grew, married, had children, grew old, and died. Immortals never followed that pattern: they 'aged' at a far slower rate. To the world, the immortals were outsiders—witches, magicians, mystics—entities to be avoided or even eliminated. When mortals discovered they didn't have the power to destroy us, they began to fear us; and ironic as it may seem, some even worshipped us. That's when the great division among the immortals really began."

"What made them split?" I asked.

"The immortals couldn't figure out why they were still here, trapped in a world clearly meant for mortals. There was a lot of contention on the matter and eventually, two basic schools of thought emerged. First, that immortals were here to rule over mortals and make them subject to whatever purposes the immortals declared. Second, and the more accepted theory, that immortals were here to fulfill some noble duty to protect the agency or free will of mortals and support the cause of humanity.

The first group referred to themselves as supporters of Cain. They maintained that there was no afterlife for immortals, so they should grab all the power and glory possible as long as they existed in this world. They despised and capitalized on mortal weaknesses and interfered constantly with their agency. They were particularly powerful in early Rome and Greece as well as several parts of Africa and South America. Ironically, humans often considered the immortals to be gods or mythical beings, and they would go to great lengths to please them—even to the point of offering sacrifices to them."

"How you doing over there, Beth?" Carl cut in. He was watching my reactions carefully.

"I'm okay." I felt no sense of surprise or shock as I listened to Jonathan tell the legend of the immortals, yet it was obvious to him that something was troubling me.

"What?" Jonathan asked.

"Well . . . I was wondering why this history is considered a *legend* and not accepted as fact. If immortals never die, wouldn't there be firsthand accounts of these events?"

"Only *pure* immortals never die," Carl corrected me.

Jonathan nodded in agreement. "There are a lot of theories about what happens to immortals after they've lived beyond the length of time known as the *age of primes.*"

"Age of what?"

"Primes. You've heard of prime numbers?"

I nodded yes.

"Remember, I told you that immortals don't age, they progress. Well, they progress in a pattern known as the progression of the primes. It takes about a thousand human years for the progression of primes to complete its pattern, although the period can vary a little with each immortal. Where the natural lifespan of a mortal is one hundred years, an immortal's lifespan is closer to a thousand years. They refer to the full lifespan as the *age of primes.* When the progression is complete, an immortal becomes an elder. The controversy—and mystery—is that there are very few elders in existence."

"How's that possible?" I asked.

Jonathan shrugged his shoulders. "Don't know. No one seems to know for sure. Some claim that elders pass on to another realm of existence—a fourth dimension—but there's no proof to substantiate that theory. They just cease to exist *here.* Some say their bodies evaporate and become part of our atmosphere, others claim they're reincarnated. There are no concrete answers. Those who believe we pass to another physical realm are considered *believers,* a little like mortals who believe in life after death. Anyhow, it's the elders who have passed down the legends through the generations."

"Fascinating, huh?" Carl asked. "I still don't get the progression of the primes, though," he added. "It's too much math for me."

It occurred to me that Carl had only learned about all this a few years ago.

Jonathan chuckled and turned back to face me. "Does that answer your question or do I need to explain it better?"

"That's what I get for asking questions," I grunted. "It's pretty much way over my head." My brain was spinning so fast my head throbbed, but I was anxious for Jonathan to continue his story. "Tell me more about the legends," I urged. "You said the immortals divided and one group considered themselves to be supporters of Cain. What about the other group?"

"The other group comprised the majority of the immortals," Jonathan continued. "They wanted a way to distinguish themselves from the followers of Cain, so they took the name of Abel and spelled it backwards—becoming known as the Lebas."

"Really!" Carl interrupted. "I never knew that's where they got the name."

"Then, in an attempt to mock the Lebas, the sympathizers of the opposition took the name of Cain and spelled it backwards too. The names have been symbolic of good and evil since the beginning—literally and figuratively."

"Cool," Carl nodded.

Jonathan shrugged. "The Niaces soon became aware of their powerful ability to influence mortals, so they devised a plan that would make them lords over the world. Soon after, they discovered a large group of . . . spirits . . . for lack of a better term, entities that have no physical bodies and are known as *intruders*. They're neither mortal nor immortal; they simply exist with no other purpose than to torment mankind because they can never be like them. They can't reproduce in their current state, so you can imagine how anxious they are to have a body.

Anyway, the intruders united with the Niaces in a common cause to seek power and control over the entire world. Though the immortal members of the Niaces maintained leadership of the group, they promised free reign to the intruders if they could influence mortals to follow them and subject themselves to Niaces control. They also gave them a new name, a name that would appeal to their sense of pride and ego." Jonathan hesitated, giving me a chance to put the pieces together myself.

"Possessors?" I guessed. Carl and Jonathan both nodded.

"Possessors!" Jonathan repeated. "The name not only pleased them, it was prophetic. They began their attempts to possess mortal bodies immediately."

"Wow," I muttered.

"Their plan was so successful that the Lebas intervened. They formed a council known as the COR, to monitor and set limits on interactions between mortals and immortals. They wrote strict laws forbidding immortals to interfere with mortal development. Their aims were quite noble, actually. Their mission was to protect the agency of all humans. I think the wording was something like, *protect humans' right to life, and their right to choose for themselves how they will pursue their personal growth and happiness*—something like that, anyway. They began to oppose the Niaces actively. Eventually, there was a great battle between the two organizations—but even with the added numbers of the possessors, the Niaces were no match for the Lebas. The Lebas fought and defeated the Niaces, but the loss of numbers on both sides was astronomical, almost wiping us out completely."

"Wait a minute—if they were immortal, how could they be wiped out?"

"It's not simple to destroy an immortal, but it is possible; it requires special skills and training. The immortal has to be disabled first, its body drained of all life-sustaining fluids, and then its remains destroyed. The Niaces believe that drinking the fluids of another immortal provides added powers and strength. As a result, they've become a very hideous and bloodthirsty organization. That isn't all—the possessors discovered that if they inhabited a mortal body after drinking the fluids of an immortal, it temporarily gave them enhanced physical abilities and heightened pleasures. It became a ritual for them after winning a battle—sort of like a reward from their leaders. The whole process is gruesome and wicked."

I was completely engrossed in Jonathan's account of these two groups of immortals, to the point that I couldn't even question whether any of it was possible. He recounted the story with such firmness and confidence that I hung on his every word. I didn't doubt what he was telling me. Even though my mind questioned everything he said, in my heart I knew it was all true.

"Can't possessors be destroyed?" I asked.

Jonathan shook his head. "It's difficult to destroy something that isn't tangible, especially in a physical world. Technically, only something made of spirit matter can destroy another spirit. Very few have the necessary training—but even then, it's not an exact science."

"Doesn't that make them more powerful than immortals?" I asked.

"On the surface it may seem so, but possessors can't destroy immortals. They can try to possess them and they can influence them, but they have no power over an immortal unless the immortal allows it. Immortals, on the other hand, have the power to destroy other immortals. Furthermore, they have the one thing a possessor wants more than anything else in the world—"

"A body." I finished his thought for him.

"Exactly. That will always be the Achilles' Heel for a possessor."

"Are possessors ever successful at taking over an immortal body?"

"Occasionally, but the immortal has to either be willing or incredibly weak—it's very uncommon. Immortals are most susceptible when they're going through puberty or 'immortal adolescence.'"

"What's immortal adolescence?"

"The same thing as human adolescence, except that the emotions, insecurities, and passions immortals experience are much stronger and more difficult to control than those of a mortal adolescent. It is particularly challenging for males because of their raised levels of testosterone—they're quite proud of their increased abilities and heightened senses. The possessors are experts at exploiting this; but then, they've had thousands of years to practice."

"What about female adolescents?"

"It's similar, except that female hormone levels don't peak until much later."

Jonathan shifted impatiently and began to pace.

"So what happened after the battle between the Niaces and the Lebas?" I asked.

Jonathan gestured for Carl to take over, and Carl willingly obliged.

"Like he said," Carl gestured toward Jonathan, "there was a lot of destruction on both sides, but the Lebas had the upper hand. Eventually, they called a truce and negotiated a treaty. Each side had to make concessions, but they finally reached an agreement known as the MIC—Memorandum of Immortal Compromise. After that the war ended."

"So the things that are happening now are a violation of that treaty?" I asked.

"Well, it's not that simple. As with all things legal, there are gray areas, loopholes that the Niaces take advantage of every chance they get. But up until now, they've been careful not to cross the line to the point of a full breach of contract. That's why the Lebas council doesn't believe the Niaces are behind the recent crime waves. It would be unlikely for them to overtly violate the treaty unless they were prepared to battle the Lebas again—and confident that they could win."

I shook my head like a dog shaking water out of his fur.

Just then, Uncle Connor and Marci returned. "How's she doing?" Uncle Connor asked.

"Uh . . . I'm right here, Uncle Connor," I chided. Carl chuckled. My tone of voice was sharper than I intended. I glanced at Jonathan and noticed that he was holding back a grin.

"That good, huh?" Uncle Connor laughed, and I couldn't help but smile. Then he turned to Carl. "So what do the Lebas plan to do about the current situation?"

"That's one reason they sent me home. They want to see *you*."

"I was afraid of that. When?"

Carl scrunched his mouth apologetically. "As soon as possible, they said."

"Before Christmas?" Marci complained.

"That's how it sounded," Carl nodded.

"I'm sorry, Marci," Uncle Connor said regretfully. "If I leave right away, I could make it back before Christmas day." He was trying to sound hopeful, but something in both his and Marci's expressions told me they both knew that was unlikely.

"Where will you have to go?" I asked.

"Austria," the men answered in unison.

"Don't worry," Marci said reassuringly. She sat down next to me on the couch and gently patted my knee with her hand. "I'll stay with you through the holidays—you won't be alone."

"I'll stay," Carl said, looking at Uncle Connor. "Then Marci can spend Christmas with her daughter's family. I just need to make some calls."

"Connor," Jonathan interjected eagerly, "I mentioned earlier that Grace has invited you all to spend the holiday at the ranch. Why not send Beth to stay with Grace for a few days? That way nobody has to change their plans."

"Er . . . I don't think that would be a very good idea," Uncle Connor replied, "not given the nature of Beth's relationship with you."

My cheeks burned instantly and I covered them with my hands. I was too embarrassed to make eye contact with anyone.

"I think it's a great idea," Carl interjected. "It'd be good for Beth to get away from here for a few days."

"It wouldn't be proper—" Uncle Connor protested, but Carl quickly interrupted.

"I'll go too. And I'll keep my eye on her—heck, on both of them." Carl grinned smugly as my cheeks flamed beneath my fingers.

I peeked at Carl. He was his usual smug, cocky self. He noticed my glance and winked at me, and even though part of me wanted to smack the smirk off his face, another part of me was sincerely hoping Uncle Connor would give in. It would be worth it, even if I did have to put up with Carl's razzing. I glanced at Jonathan and was surprised to see that his expression was the same as Carl's. It looked as if the two of them were in cahoots.

"Connor," Jonathan finally spoke. "Grace will take good care of Beth. She's very protective and . . . proper. Besides, she's starved for female companionship now that Janine is gone." My head snapped up immediately when Jonathan mentioned Janine.

"Janine's gone?"

"Yes. She left a few days ago. It was all quite sudden and Grace took it kind of hard."

"Why? Where did she go?" I asked.

"She didn't explain. She just left a vague note saying there were things she needed to take care of, and she begged us not to try to find her. Of course, we've tried to locate her—she's like a sister to both of us—but she hid her tracks well. It came as quite a blow to Grace."

"I'm so sorry," I said. "Poor Grace."

"You see?" Carl looked at Uncle Connor. "It's settled. Beth and I will barge in and annoy Jonathan's sister until she begs us to leave. Meanwhile, we'll take in snowboarding for a few days. Sounds like a fun holiday to me." Carl stood up and clapped his hands as if the decision was already made, but Uncle Connor had yet to respond.

"Beth?" Uncle Connor eyed me carefully. "Would you enjoy that?" My smile gave me away.

"Well, Jonathan," Uncle Connor sighed, "call your sister. It looks like she's going to have visitors."

"She'll be very pleased. When shall I tell her to expect company?"

"I'll stay here with Carl and Beth for a few more days," Marci offered. "How about Christmas Eve?" She glanced at Uncle Connor who nodded in approval.

"I'll let Grace know," Jonathan smiled, exultant.

A sudden thought hit me. "Carl, how long have you known Grace?"

"Never met her," he replied matter-of-factly. "Why?"

I couldn't help but laugh. Jonathan looked at me suspiciously and raised one eyebrow as if to accuse me of some devious plan involving his sister and Carl. I returned the look with wide, innocent eyes.

"This is going to be fun," I declared, and everyone in the room snickered except for poor, clueless Carl.

Darla

CHAPTER 16

The days leading up to Christmas Eve went by quickly, in spite of the fact that I didn't see Jonathan for most of the week. He'd left Uncle Connor's house in high spirits the night of Carl's news, eager to get to the ranch and help Grace prepare for our arrival.

Darla called on Monday morning, our first official day of Winter Break, and invited me to hang out with her while her parents were gone for the night. It had been a long time since we'd done anything together, so I welcomed the offer. Besides, I knew it would help the time pass faster.

We spent the afternoon doing what teenage girls do best: shopping, talking about boys, laughing, and eating—but not necessarily in that order. Somehow, between the stories and the giggles, we managed to get most of our Christmas shopping done. My list was short—Uncle Connor, Carl, Marci, Grace, Darla, and Eric. There was no way I could send my dad a gift, and Jonathan and I had agreed to do something I'd never done before—to make each other something. Actually, it was my idea, one I insisted on after hearing him tell me about his family's gift-giving tradition. While Darla and I shopped, I remembered what Jonathan had said.

"Once upon a time we celebrated Christmas the traditional way. But after many years passed it became so routine that it seemed meaningless; we just didn't enjoy it as much anymore. It doesn't take long to accumulate everything you want or need, then you start looking for ways to get rid of stuff instead of wanting more." He'd laughed at the irony of it all. "Besides, with three of us always traveling, it became difficult to keep track of how often we should celebrate."

"Three of you?" I'd asked.

"Grace doesn't travel anymore."

"Why not?" I'd questioned.

He'd said it was a long story and chose not to elaborate.

Jonathan's family had decided years ago that instead of purchasing each other gifts, they would each think of something they could do to make the world better for someone else. It began small and then escalated into larger projects, involving groups of people instead of individuals.

"That's the main reason my parents gave up ranching between travels," Jonathan had explained. "They enjoyed the humanitarian projects so much they decided to make it a full time profession. For the past few years, they've been working to build and furnish schools in Nigeria. They fell in the love with the people there, and haven't wanted to leave since."

"So they gave up traveling too?" I'd asked.

"Um, not exactly," he'd explained. "The Nigeria operation gives them a great cover to travel whenever necessary."

I knew what Jonathan's parents were doing was noble, but I had a difficult time understanding how they could stay away from Jonathan and Grace for so long.

"A few years seems like a long time when you're living on a linear time-line, but when time is irrelevant. . . ." He'd shrugged his shoulders.

"Beth?" Darla tugged on my arm. "You haven't heard a word I've said."

"I'm sorry," I apologized. "I . . . was thinking about Grace, Jonathan's sister. I don't know what to get her for Christmas." It was only half a lie; I really was stumped about what to get her. What could I give someone who wanted and needed nothing?

"What does she like to do?" Darla asked.

"She's . . . different, only in a cool kind of *Gone With the Wind* sort of way." I wrinkled my nose and pulled a face that made Darla giggle. "I don't suppose you know where I can find Rhett Butler, do you?" I snickered and she giggled harder. My banter made me think of Carl; he had the same ornery, devil-may-care attitude as Captain Butler.

Our afternoon passed swiftly into evening. Jonathan called me around nine o'clock, but Darla and I had been cackling so much that I could barely formulate a coherent sentence without bursting into laughter.

"Glad to hear you're having so much fun," he teased. "I've been feeling guilty all day thinking you'd be lonely without me around. Clearly I was mistaken."

It was not as though we hadn't been texting each other throughout the afternoon. He knew exactly what I'd been doing all day, and he seemed sincerely pleased to hear me laugh.

"Did you finish working on your, uh, project?" I asked, fishing for a hint of what it was he was making for me.

"Nope, and it's none of your business, snoopy."

He knew I was notorious for guessing what my presents were. "I'm usually right, too," I'd bragged.

"I'll keep that in mind when I wrap your gift," he'd warned.

"How about you? Should I let you off the hook and allow you to buy me something?"

"Hah!" I snorted. "I know exactly what I'm going to make for you."

"Hmm. Intriguing," he mused. I wished I could see his face at that moment; I knew exactly what his expression would be. I smiled warmly at the thought of him, and Darla rolled her eyes, crossing her hands over her heart in a mock, lovesick gesture. I tried to refrain from giggling, but the look on her face was too much for me.

"Okay, I give up," Jonathan finally said. "Try not to have too much fun. I'd hate to be replaced."

"Never," I assured him, followed by more stifled laughter.

Darla brought out two air mattresses, a stack of blankets, and several oversized pillows which she scattered across the floor of her bedroom. We nibbled on freshly popped popcorn, chocolate covered raisins, and cinnamon gummy bears. Come the early hours of the morning, we were still awake talking about everything from our early childhood to our first kiss.

"Tell me more about you and Evan," I asked, reaching for another handful of popcorn. I tossed the kernels in the air and tried to catch them in my mouth as I lay on my back. It was harder than I thought.

"There's nothing to tell," she insisted.

I didn't believe her. I'd seen the two of them together at school and at the basketball games. Even though Evan was quiet and shy, it was obvious he was totally into her.

"He likes you a lot," I said, pressing for more information. I threw another kernel in the air, this time aimed in her direction.

"I think he does," she sighed, batting the kernel across the room. "But it can't go anywhere."

"Why? Don't you like him?"

"Of course. But we can't be together like *that,*" she explained.

"Like what?" I asked, confused by the inflection in her voice.

"Like . . . boyfriend and girlfriend, *officially.*"

"Why not?"

She shrugged her shoulders and stared at the ceiling, then let out a big sigh. I knew the sound of that sigh.

"Because of Eric?" I accused.

She twisted onto her side and rolled a chocolate covered raisin between her fingers. "Evan is Eric's best friend. It doesn't matter how much we like each other, it's just never going to happen."

"That's ridiculous. You and Eric are ancient history. Has Evan told Eric how he feels?"

"It wouldn't matter, Beth. You don't know how it was with Eric."

I did know how it was, but I could never tell her that Eric had confided in me; she'd be too hurt. "Eric would be happy for you," I suggested. "After all, he doesn't seem to live by the same code you do. If he did, he never would have gone after me."

"That doesn't make it right," she insisted, making me sigh in exasperation.

"Have you talked to Eric about it?" I flicked the raisin away from her fingers and it spiraled into her leg. "Oops, sorry 'bout that."

She retrieved the raisin and tossed it at my head. "No, I can't talk to him." The sadness in her voice surprised me. "He sort of hinted something though. . . ."

"And?" I ducked, but the raisin managed to graze my ear.

"He said he wants me to be happy."

"Well, isn't that enough?" I asked.

She shrugged her shoulders. "It might've been easier if you and Eric had worked out."

"What's that supposed to mean?" I protested.

"Eric thinks he loves you, and I have to admit, I've never seen him like this before. Not even when . . ." she hesitated and threw a raisin forcefully against the wall. "Not even when he and I were together."

"Eric only thinks he loves me because I turned him down. You told me yourself he was that way."

"I know, but he's been different ever since Halloween night. He's sad. It's like he's lost his confidence. I always thought I'd feel vindicated if Eric ever got a taste of his own medicine, but I have to admit, I feel sorry for him."

I rolled over onto my back again. Halloween. Darla was more right than she knew; Eric hadn't been the same since then. I understood that more than anyone did.

"Watching you leave with Jonathan must have been the ultimate rejection for him, especially since it happened in front of so many of his friends." I cringed as Darla speculated about what happened.

"So, what you're saying is, all we need to do is find someone new for Eric, and then you can officially be with Evan." I was attempting to shift the focus and mood of our conversation, and it worked. Darla snickered and threw her pillow at me.

"Tell me honestly," Darla pursed her lips. "If it hadn't been for me or for Jonathan, would you have dated Eric—even though you knew he was my ex?"

"Eric asked me a similar question not too long ago. I never would've dated him as long as I knew how you felt about him, so it's a moot point."

"That's not what I asked," Darla pressed.

I released a heavy sigh. "In a different time . . ." the image of Jonathan's time-line rope flashed through my mind, "if I didn't know you or Jonathan, there might have been something between Eric and me . . . maybe. But you *are* my friend and I *did* fall for Jonathan, and there's nothing I would do to change either."

"You know," Darla shook her head, "Eric totally believes that if you'd give him a chance, even now—after knowing Jonathan—he could still win you over."

"Well, that's just never going to happen. So he'll never know, will he?"

"He *is* a really good kisser," Darla teased, but there was an odd hint of cynicism in her tone. "Maybe you should let him try."

I threw her pillow back at her, then grabbed my own and slammed it into her amused face. Popcorn, chocolate raisins, and gummy bears scattered in all directions. We started laughing hysterically, not because what she said was funny, but because it was nearly two in the morning and we were both punchy.

"What about Evan? Is he a good kisser too? Maybe I should just kiss both of 'em?" I could barely get the words out between roars of laughter, but Darla's response sobered me.

"I wouldn't know. I haven't kissed him," she revealed, heaving her pillow in my face.

Stunned, I let the pillow fall to the side. "After all this time, he's never kissed you?"

"There're times when I think he wants to," she said, "but we just don't go there."

"Argh!" I growled. I swear I could hear her eyes roll.

"Don't you *want* to kiss him?" I asked. "I mean, seriously, I *know* you like him. You must think about it sometimes, don't you?"

"Every single day!" she admitted. "It drives me crazy. Some days, all I can do is stare at his mouth. I don't hear a word he says because I'm too busy watching his lips and wondering how they'd feel and what it would be like. I swear he thinks I'm a complete freak."

"Whoa." I couldn't think of another response.

"I know, I'm an idiot, huh?"

"Uh, yeah! The two of you might be surprised."

"I think that's what we're both afraid of."

"Darla, everyone has a past. It's okay to move on. Heck, Tom is Eric's friend, and *he* asked you out." Ugh! The words flew out of my mouth before I could think about what I was saying.

The room turned silent, the kind of deafening silence you could hear—the kind that made your ears throb. I waited for what seemed like several minutes until I could no longer bear the silence.

"Darla?"

She didn't respond, but I felt the rustle of the blankets and knew she'd turned away from me. And then, although the sound was faint, I could tell that she was crying.

Great. Some friend I was.

I started to give up and drop the conversation. I'd obviously done enough damage by opening my big mouth. But something stirred inside me. I rolled over and reached for her shoulder. The minute my hand made contact, she started to sob.

"I'm sorry," I whispered repeatedly. "I'm really sorry."

I rubbed my hand along her shoulder and arm and waited for her to finish crying. I lay beside her, leaning my head against her shoulder, and held her until there were no more tears left for her to shed. I'd never shown affection of this kind toward a friend before—it was definitely uncharted territory—yet my desire to comfort her surpassed all feelings of personal awkwardness.

When she quit sobbing enough to gain control of her voice, she opened up and told me everything about her and Eric, even some things that Eric had left out—things that would only matter to another girl. She talked and I listened until exhaustion finally overcame her.

When I was certain she was asleep, I turned away and stared into the darkness outside her bedroom window.

Though it startled me at first, it didn't frighten me when I felt an unseen presence near me. A familiar breath sighed behind me as the sweet scent of lavender filled the room. This was not the dark, dreadful presence of a possessor, but rather a peaceful, familial presence that brought with it a calming sense of serenity. Eleanor had returned, and she remained with me until I woke in the morning.

"Good morning," Darla yawned. The light coming through her bedroom window told me we'd slept longer than expected.

"What time is it?" I replied sleepily.

"Almost time for lunch," she laughed. The melodic sound of her laughter made the brightness of the sun even brighter.

"Are you kidding?" I moaned. I raised my head and tried to focus my eyes on her clock. "Eleven-thirty?" I bellowed. "Ah, geez!" I threw my head back on my pillow and sighed. I was never one for getting up early, but this was ridiculous.

I didn't have a chance to think about it for long because in a surprise launch, Darla attacked me with her pillow, hitting me repeatedly until she ran out of breath. I was happy she was laughing because for a moment, I was afraid she was angry with me—especially by the way she was walloping me with her feathery weapon of mass destruction.

"Okay, okay, okay!" I hollered. "You win. Uncle! Uncle!"

She sat up in a huff and held her stomach until she finally caught her breath. I hid my face beneath my arms until the attack was over and I was sure it was safe to lift my head.

"What the heck was that for?" I asked.

"That's my way of saying thank you for last night," she giggled.

"Geez, you're welcome," I groaned.

"Are you hungry?" she asked, changing the subject.

I gazed around the floor at the mess of scattered popcorn kernels and candy. "Famished!" I chuckled.

We stumbled downstairs to the kitchen and Darla began rummaging through the refrigerator for something to eat. She decided on Canadian bacon and egg muffins, and then went to work frying the eggs while I toasted the muffins and heated the bacon in the microwave. She pulled a pitcher of orange juice out of the fridge as we sat down at a small dinette table in the corner of her kitchen to enjoy our brunch.

"What is Jonathan like?" she asked as she cut through her muffin.

"Amazing," I answered without hesitation.

"And is *he* a good kisser?" Darla probed.

I wasn't one to share personal details, but after last night, I figured it was a fair question.

"Amazing," I blushed.

"Is he . . . nice? I mean, he's older. Does he ever try to, you know?"

I knew what she was trying to ask.

"There was this one day when I was sure he wanted more, but it only happened once." It had been several weeks since Jonathan kissed me that way. Ever since that afternoon on the hill overlooking the valley, he'd been careful not to cross any boundaries that would make me uncomfortable.

I felt a sudden surge of panic. What if Jonathan no longer wanted me that way?

"Beth?" Darla stopped, her fork midway to her mouth. "What's wrong?"

I laughed nervously and took another bite of food, stalling for time to gain control over my overactive imagination.

"Nothing," I answered, shaking my head. I smiled and she returned the smile, but I could tell by her raised eyebrow that she knew I was hiding something. "It's just that since that one time, he's been different."

"Different how? Does he pressure you?"

"No," I said quickly, "not at all. It's just the opposite."

"Huh?" Darla's confused expression mirrored mine, but for different reasons. "That's a good thing, right?"

"Yeah, I guess."

"You guess?" Darla questioned.

"What if he thinks I don't want him in that way?"

"But you don't. Isn't that why you stopped him? You *did* stop him, didn't you?"

"Yeah, but not because I didn't want him. I stopped him because I was scared."

"Oh," she nodded slowly. "Does he know that?"

"We never talked about it, and it hasn't come up again."

Any outsider listening to this conversation would probably think I was too young to have a serious boyfriend like Jonathan. I was beginning to understand that Marci was right; eventually, Jonathan and I would have to talk about our relationship.

I felt like a walking contradiction. I wasn't ready for more—not yet—even though I thought about it and wanted it sometimes. On the other hand, I was afraid to push him away, afraid he might leave the way Adam did. Would he wait for me until I was ready, or would he eventually lose interest?

"Well," Darla said reassuringly, "if yesterday is any indication of how he feels about you, then I'm sure the topic is going to come up again."

The morning of Christmas Eve finally arrived and I couldn't wait to leave for the ranch. I'd packed my bags three days earlier: packed them and repacked them several times. In the spirit of keeping our gifts homemade, I wrapped Jonathan's present in butcher paper that I snatched from the workroom adjacent to Uncle Connor's office. I stenciled a horse-driven sleigh on the front of the package and tied a simple bow around the box with some twine that I found in the garage. I had to admit, it looked cool and very old-fashioned.

Grace expected us sometime around noon but I was ready and chomping at the bit by nine, which was unusual for me, the queen of sleeping late. Carl, in his characteristically annoying fashion, took his sweet time with the household chores, insisting that Uncle Connor would chew him out if he forgot even the minutest detail.

"You know how he gets," he chimed in feigned consternation. "The last thing we need when he gets home is a lecture on responsibility. Remember how he reacted when you got that speeding ticket?"

"I remember it was entirely your fault," I reminded him, "and that *you* weren't the one who ended up paying for it."

"Ah, but it was worth it, wasn't it?" he teased.

"Sure," I huffed, remembering how awkward I felt when Uncle Connor had to appear before the town judge with me. *That* was embarrassing!

Marci had left the day before so she could spend the holiday with her family, but before she left, she managed to bake a couple of blackberry pies. Although Grace had given Jonathan specific orders that we were not to bring anything, Marci insisted we not show up empty-handed.

"Fruits of the forest are a must for Christmas," she had claimed. I'd never heard of that tradition, but once I tasted the leftover pie filling, I decided the tradition was a good one.

Carl and I didn't leave for the ranch until nearly eleven. It would have been even later, but I pitched a fit when he said he wanted to balance his checkbook before we could leave.

"Fine," I snarled, "you stay here and be obnoxious. I'm leaving!" I grabbed the car keys and stomped out to the garage. I fully planned to leave him behind as my patience had reached its limit, but Carl stopped me before I could get the keys in the ignition.

"I'm just messing with you, Beth," he grinned. "I'm ready to go."

"It's about time!" I sputtered through clenched teeth. I wasn't truly angry with Carl, that was pretty much impossible, but I was unbearably anxious to see Jonathan and the wait was driving me crazy.

"Patience isn't one of your strong points, is it?" Carl joked.

"Hah! With you around?"

He laughed and held out his hand for the keys. "You know they aren't expecting us until noon, don't you? If we'd left when you wanted to, we'd have dragged them out of bed."

I pursed my lips and glared. He had a point.

"You need to pace yourself or you'll be a nervous wreck before we get there," Carl cautioned with a laugh. He jabbed the back of his fist gently against my chin so I'd look at him. "And that wouldn't be very sexy now, would it?" he teased.

"Ewww!" I hissed. My cheeks burned a bright shade of red and Carl nodded with satisfaction.

"I've still got it," he declared triumphantly.

"You. are. a. brat," I informed him, but it only made his smile widen.

"Unfortunately for you, I'm okay with that," he chuckled.

Traditions

C H A P T E R   1 7

*S*pending the holiday at the ranch proved to be quite enlightening on several levels, one of which was Carl's unexpected, supportive attitude toward my relationship with Jonathan. I'd expected him to keep a watchful eye on us—not because he'd promised Uncle Connor that he would, but just to torment me. However, I didn't expect him to become my *coach*.

"Don't be too eager to jump out of the car," Carl warned when we pulled up to the house. "Let Prince Charming wait a few seconds longer." Jonathan was standing on the front porch when we arrived.

"You're suddenly an expert at relationships?" I asked, dubious of his unsolicited advice.

"Suck at them," he admitted.

Not once in all the years I'd known Carl had I ever met one of his girlfriends; and from what I'd heard, there were plenty of them.

"Sure . . ." I replied sarcastically, "I doubt you've ever had trouble finding a girlfriend."

"Finding a girl isn't the problem, it's *keeping* one that's the hard part."

Although I was curious, I had more pressing things on my mind—like getting out of the car. I unfastened my seat belt and reached for the handle, but Carl discreetly pulled my hand away.

"I may not be an expert on girls—heaven knows, I'll never figure out what goes on in the female psyche—but I *am* an expert at being a guy." He spoke softly, no hint of teasing in his tone. "Relax and savor the moment. Let *him* come to *you.*"

He held on to my hand as I slowly lowered it away from the door handle and rested it in my lap. He squeezed the top of it gently and glanced toward Jonathan, gesturing with a nod for me to look. Jonathan was already walking toward the car.

"Remember," he said in a low voice, *"savor* the moment."

When Jonathan reached for my door, he was smiling. It wasn't a smile of amusement, nor was it the mischievous, lopsided grin that I was so used to seeing; it was a joyful smile that nearly took my breath away. My pulse raced with anticipation as he opened the door.

"See what I mean," Carl whispered, so low I barely heard. He nudged my arm before opening his own door and climbing out of the car. He moved with such finesse that no one would suspect he'd coached me to wait. He was smooth—no doubt about that.

Jonathan reached for my hand and helped me out of the car, then pulled me close to him. Without letting go of my hand, he bent down and kissed me on the cheek. Carl winked at me from the trunk of the car where he'd gone to retrieve our things.

"Here, let me help you," Jonathan offered.

Carl handed him the bag with the pies. "Be careful with those—Beth will slice your throat if you let anything happen to them."

I rolled my eyes to object, but then I thought twice.

"He's right," I admitted. "Guard those with your life."

Jonathan peeked in the bag and spotted the pies. "Did you make these?"

"No, Marci did, and she'll kill me if they don't make it to Grace in one piece."

Characteristically, Carl pretended to pull a muscle as he hefted my suitcase out of the trunk and handed it to Jonathan. Jonathan grinned. I fully expected him to give me a hard time about packing so much, but he made no comment about the size or weight of my bag as we climbed the stairs to the front porch.

The inside of the house was exactly as I remembered it except for the elegantly laced holiday sprays and thick, white candles that adorned the entryway tables. The living room walls were trimmed with spruce and pine clippings woven together in a delicate garland. Antique, hand-made stockings hung around the sleeves of the fireplace mantle which was topped with clusters of white candles in varying sizes. Grace had spaced them artistically throughout the weave of the garland. It reminded me of a scene from *House Beautiful* magazine. I noticed the crisp scent of pine the moment I stepped into the room and I instinctively drew in a long, deep breath, allowing the holiday aroma to penetrate my senses.

"Mmm," I sighed as I exhaled. "The house smells amazing."

"Yeah, Grace goes a little overboard with the pine cuttings. She's very particular about the mixture of pine, cedar, and spruce. She insists on fresh garlands so the house will smell like the holidays."

"She must have had the bows special ordered," I sighed as I admired the simple weave of the garland.

"I guess you could say that," Jonathan chuckled. "She's good at giving me special orders."

"You made these?" I asked, shocked.

"No, I only brought in the cuttings. Grace wove the garland."

"Wow, it's amazing," I marveled. Even the stair rails were laced with the fresh garlands. It must have taken Grace hours to weave all the cuttings together.

Just then I heard the sound of delicate steps at the top of the staircase. Carl stepped into the living room from the entryway just as Grace appeared at the top of the stairs.

"Beth," she called to me, "I thought you would never arrive."

Always the perfect hostess. I'd forgotten how incredibly charming she was. In angelic fashion, she descended the stairs—perfectly poised, completely confident, and overwhelmingly beautiful. Her eyes twinkled brightly as she held her hands out for mine and bent down to kiss me on both sides of my face.

Carl, now standing somewhere behind me, was noticeably silent.

"It's so good to see you again, Beth," she said warmly. Then she smiled approvingly at Jonathan. "She looks radiant as ever!"

"Yep," he agreed as he reached for Grace's arm and led her to where Carl stood.

I turned to follow them, but stopped dead in my tracks when I saw Carl's face. It was not so much his stunned expression that caught me by surprise as it was the deep crimson color burning in his cheeks. *Hmm. Must run in the family.*

He was blushing profusely. It was all I could do not to giggle at his expense. After all the times he'd teased me, he deserved it. I bit my lips together and controlled myself. I hoped for Carl's sake that he was able to pull it together before he made a complete fool of himself.

"Grace," Jonathan began the introduction. It sounded so formal, so old-fashioned, yet it suited Grace perfectly. "May I present Beth's cousin, Carl Lee. Carl, this is my sister, Grace."

Grace extended her hand to Carl and for a minute I was afraid he was too stunned to move. But as if by a will of its own, his hand raised to accept hers. His eyes never left hers as he held her hand gently in his. I suppose in the old days he would have bent down and kissed the top of his thumb as he held her hand in his; but Carl wouldn't know anything about that. And if he did, I doubted he could remember much of anything right now.

"You must be the adventurous son of Connor Lee, Beth's dashing uncle," Grace drawled in polite charm. I didn't think it was possible, but I'm certain the color in Carl's cheeks turned an even deeper shade of red as she spoke. Carl glanced over Grace's shoulder at me when he heard my name. We made eye contact only briefly, but it was long enough for me to silently mouth the words, "Savor the moment." It took a minute for the words to register, and then he grinned.

"I don't know about adventurous," Carl replied with an impressive half bow, "but you're right about my father—he is quite dashing."

Grace responded with a slight curtsy as Carl flashed a breathtaking smile. My jaw nearly hit the floor at his seamless recovery. Jonathan, who'd been watching the exchange, stepped over and nudged me gently with his elbow. I looked up at him, but he was still watching them. Carl had made no effort to release Grace's hand, and I wondered just how long she would allow him to hold it before pulling away from him. I didn't have to wonder for long because as if on cue, Jonathan cleared his throat.

"Grace, why don't you show Beth to her room and I'll help Carl with the bags."

She allowed her hand to linger in his for a moment and then slowly slid her fingers free. He didn't move until she'd turned around to face me.

"Beth," she took my arm and started toward the stairs, "I wonder if you would prefer to sleep in Janine's room rather than the guest bedroom. Hers has the best view of the mountains, and a private bathroom."

"Are you sure she wouldn't mind? I'm perfectly happy to stay in the guest room again."

"I'm quite sure Janine would be pleased to share her room with you."

"Thank you," I accepted.

"Jonathan," Grace called behind her, "have Carl put his things in the guest bedroom."

It only took me about fifteen minutes to situate myself in Janine's room. Her room was decorated in soft tones of creamy beige and white, the shade of three of the walls being slightly different from the other. French doors in the outer wall of the bedroom opened onto a narrow balcony that ran the entire length of the room. There were no curtains along the doors, only tan-colored, vertical blinds that pulled from the side for privacy. Grace had been right about the view; the twin peaks of the Teton Mountains painted a breathtaking scene from every angle of the room.

The room was devoid of ornamentation with the exception of two paintings that hung above the bed, both of which were colorful northwestern mountain scenes. The wall opposite the bed was paneled with floor-to-ceiling beveled mirrors. A large dresser sat in front of the mirrors giving the illusion of a barrier in the room. The opening to the bathroom was just to the side of the entryway, before the mirrored wall began. I got the feeling that this room had once been the master bedroom considering its size, the view, and the balcony. The thing that surprised me was that there was no trace of Janine in the room—no pictures, no mementos, nothing feminine except for a large vase of silk tulips that sat on the dresser in front of the mirror.

I put my things away and grabbed my wrapped Christmas presents to take them downstairs. Jonathan grinned when he noticed the packages in my hand and saw the confused look on my face.

"Where should I put these?" I asked, looking around the room. Had I missed spotting their Christmas tree when we arrived earlier? Nope. No tree.

"You can put them on the hearth for now, or . . . you could give them to me," he grinned jokingly.

"Um, no," I replied, "that won't be necessary."

"Which one's mine?" he asked, spying the gifts from around my body.

"None of your business."

"I'll show you yours if you show me mine."

His offer was too tempting to pass up. I was dying to know what he'd made for me, and I was certain if I were able to handle the package, I'd be able to guess what was inside.

When Jonathan showed me my present, it was all I could do not to laugh. I nearly chewed off my lips as I struggled not to make fun of his wrapping.

"Well," he stammered, "I couldn't find the right box, so it's not perfect."

The package in his hand appeared to be a wrapped shoe box—but the contents were too big, so it bulged out on one side. The wrapping was simple; there was no ribbon, only a single large bow on top, and a tag that said, "No peeking! Do not open until Christmas!" As I reached out my hand to take it from him he hesitated and pulled it away.

"Be careful," he cautioned, "it's fragile . . . whatever you do, don't shake it."

I rolled my eyes at him and reached for the package—which he handed to me with exaggerated reluctance. I knew what he was up to; he wanted to keep me from shaking or squeezing the gift so I couldn't guess what it was. He wasn't fooling anyone. As I held the package in my hand, I couldn't help but gently squeeze the side of the box. But as I did, I felt something give, and I heard a faint rattling that sounded like broken glass. I wondered if Jonathan had heard it too, but I could see by the shocked look on his face that he had.

"Did that just break?" He looked mortified for a moment. I thought I was going to be sick.

"No, it just moved," I lied.

"Oh, good, 'cuz it sounded like it might have broken." He scrutinized the package with a worried expression on his face.

"It's fine. I barely touched it," I stammered nervously. I held the present close to my body, afraid that he might reach for it and inspect it.

"I really hope it didn't break," he fretted quietly. "It's very fragile, and I don't think I could make another one."

I desperately wanted to change the subject. I felt like a complete idiot.

Jonathan held up the present I brought for him and inspected it carefully. "Cool wrapping, did you make this?" he asked, pointing to the stenciled scene on the paper.

I shrugged. I couldn't get excited about any of it now—I was too worried about the contents of the box I held in my hands. I wondered if I could glue the pieces back together without him knowing.

"So, when do we get to open our gifts?" I asked, trying to sound optimistic.

"Read the tag," he told me. He had an amused smirk on his face; he enjoyed watching me squirm.

"Fine . . . tomorrow." I made it sound as if I was disappointed, but actually, this was just what I was hoping for—a chance to see if I could fix whatever it was I'd broken. "So where's your Christmas tree?" I asked, looking around the room.

Jonathan tilted his head slightly to the side and shrugged. "We don't really do the whole tree thing, at least not in the traditional way that you're used to."

I looked at him quizzically, waiting for him to explain.

"Follow me," he smiled. We set our gifts on the hearth and he took my hand. He led me through the house to the backyard. It wasn't really a *yard;* it was more like a large park that sat adjacent to a vast wooded area. Off to the side stood a large, noble fir tree that must have been at least twenty feet tall. It was covered with thousands of clear lights; large, glittering snowflake ornaments; and icicles that dangled from the tips of every branch. It looked magnificent in the light of day, casting rainbows of light into the surrounding air. I imagined it would look heavenly when lit against the black sky at night.

"*This* is our tree," he said proudly. I stared at the tree—Jonathan stared at me.

"Wow," I gasped, "It's amazing."

Jonathan let go of my hand and I walked slowly around the base of the tree, admiring its beauty. It was so simple, and yet so graceful and elegant, and so obviously Grace.

"Grace did this." I said, awestruck.

"Not exactly," Jonathan corrected me. "She designed it, but—"

"*You* did this?"

"Don't sound so surprised. I've had a few years of practice," he reminded me.

"So, what made you decide to have an outdoor Christmas tree?"

He shrugged his shoulders and grinned. "It's sort of a symbol, I guess. We used to cut down a tree every year, but after so many years, we began to think of the number of trees we'd killed. It hardly seemed fair—here we are, immortal, never having to die ourselves, yet we were taking away the life of a living tree year after year."

"You could have gotten an artificial tree," I suggested.

"Yeah, but it's not the same. Besides, we'd already gotten to the point that the whole Christmas thing seemed artificial anyway. One year, we decided to plant a tree, instead—and we've had it ever since. It sort of symbolizes our life."

"That's really cool. It's like you've immortalized Christmas."

"Well, the tree anyway."

Jonathan stood behind me and wrapped his arms around my waist, pulling me snugly against him. He rested his chin on top of my head for a moment, then slid the side of his face along mine and rested his lips against my ear.

"I'm glad you're here," he whispered, sending a chill down both of my arms. It caused me to shudder slightly, so he wrapped his arms even tighter around me. He pressed his lips against the base of my ear and drew in a deep breath, nuzzling his nose against my cheek. "Your skin smells so good," he moaned as he exhaled slowly.

He twisted his arms and before I could catch my breath, he'd turned me around and pressed his lips to mine. He kissed me eagerly for several minutes before he broke away, leaving us both panting for air. He rested his forehead against mine and breathed deeply.

"We better go back in before you get too cold."

"Actually," I smiled, "I'm pretty warm right now."

He chuckled and squeezed my hands. "Okay, then, before Carl comes looking for us."

"That reminds me," I said, pulling on Jonathan's arm. "Did you see the look on his face when Grace walked into the room? I've never seen him like that before—ever."

"Yeah, for a minute I didn't think he was going to recover. Grace has a way about her. She can be quite disarming."

"No kidding!"

"But I'm afraid Carl will have his work cut out for him. Grace is . . . unusual when it comes to men. She's been alone for most of her life."

"How can that be?" I asked. Grace was beautiful, smart, charming, and she oozed elegance.

"She's fiercely loyal, Beth. She gave her heart once, and that was it."

"What happened?"

"He went to war and never came back."

"War?"

Jonathan nodded.

My mind was calculating backwards through the wars we'd been involved in. I wondered if maybe he was one of the soldiers killed in Iraq or perhaps the Persian Gulf. How tragic to think of Grace sending her love off to war, only to never see him again.

"She still waits for him, convinced that he'll return someday," Jonathan added.

"You mean he's missing in action? There's a chance he's still alive?"

Jonathan looked down at me somberly and shook his head. "It's been a very long time, Beth. If he *could* have come back to her, he would have."

"Which war was he in?"

Jonathan cleared his throat and studied my face for a moment before answering. "The Civil War," he finally said.

It took a minute for his words to sink in. My eyes narrowed as I began doing the math in my head.

"But that's over a hundred and fifty years ago!" I exclaimed.

"In linear time, yes. Like I said, she's fiercely loyal. That's why she quit traveling."

"So she could be here if he returned?"

"No, nothing like that. You see, traveling is what keeps us 'young,' relatively speaking, and she desperately wants to grow old. Even though she knows it's never going to happen, she hopes that she will figure out a way to make herself mortal."

"Why in the world would she want to be mortal?"

"As I said, she's fiercely loyal—and she was deeply in love with her soldier."

I thought carefully about what he was saying. The only outcome of mortality was eventual death. "Are you saying she wants to die?"

"She thinks it's the only way to be reunited with her love."

"Oh! Poor Grace!" I whispered.

"No," Jonathan corrected me, "poor Carl."

I thought about the expression on Carl's face when he saw Grace, and then I thought about his words to me in the car earlier: *Finding a girl isn't the problem, it's keeping one that's the hard part.* I closed my eyes and shook my head.

"Yeah, poor Carl," I sighed.

We walked back into the house and found Grace and Carl together in the kitchen. She was busily preparing what appeared to be an elaborate meal. Carl was following her around, hopelessly trying to be of some help. I couldn't recall ever seeing Carl do anything in a kitchen—except eat a meal or grab something out of the refrigerator. His awkwardness was comical, yet genuinely sweet. He looked relieved when he saw Jonathan and me enter the room.

"Where have you guys been?" he asked.

"I was showing Beth our Christmas tree," Jonathan replied.

Grace turned around to face him and smiled. Then she looked at me. "We sort of tamper a bit with tradition here," she said sheepishly. "I hope you don't mind."

I let the irony of her words simmer for a moment in my brain. With the exception of last year, which was the first Christmas without my mom, I'd spent Christmas with my parents and grandparents at our home in sunny California. We always cooked a traditional ham, decorated the outside of our home with traditional lights, sang traditional carols, and participated in the age-old tradition of opening presents that surrounded a traditional Christmas tree on Christmas morning.

Tradition. I laughed silently to myself as I wrapped a spare apron around my waist and began peeling potatoes. There I stood, in a room with three people who would never experience what it was like to grow old and die, something that at this time last year I would have sworn was impossible. Three people whom I had grown to love, and who were not part of the traditions of my Christmases past—yet whom I hoped would be part of all my Christmases yet to come.

"No," I smiled at Grace as I reached for another potato, "I don't mind."

As I began peeling the potato I glanced briefly around the room. Jonathan and Carl had wormed their way over to the snack trays that were spread across the buffet server. Jonathan met my glance and winked at me, then he started talking with Carl.

In fact, I thought, *I think the absence of normal tradition is a wonderful tradition.*

The Christmas Eve party lasted well into the evening. We ate until we could barely move; then we cleared away the dirty dishes and ate some more. We were miserable, but it didn't seem to stop us. Afterwards, we played games and gathered around the grand piano and sang Christmas songs. Grace accompanied us with flawless elegance—naturally.

When the chimes announced it was eleven, Jonathan called a halt to the singing. Grace glanced at the clock and then laid her hand on Jonathan's arm and smiled.

"I suppose I do get a little carried away," she admitted. She excused herself, and with Carl's help, began putting away the music and the games.

"Would you mind going someplace with me?" Jonathan whispered. I raised my eyebrows questioningly. "Please?" he added.

"Sure." I was happy to go anywhere with him. He smiled, and then looked over at Carl and Grace.

"Hey guys, care to join Beth and me for a midnight drive?"

"Not me," Grace replied. "I'm going to make some hot chocolate and enjoy the fire. You guys go ahead."

Carl opted to stay behind as well—no surprise there—but he didn't let us leave without performing his proper function as my "chaperone."

"You guys be careful. There's supposed to be another storm tonight." Then he winked at me. "I wouldn't want you to get stranded somewhere . . . all alone."

I promptly slugged Carl in the arm.

Many things passed through my mind as I climbed into Jonathan's car. I anticipated his motives for wanting to go for a drive at such a late hour, but I couldn't have been more off the mark. We drove for about half an hour and ended up parked in front of a small church at the edge of a neighboring town. The church building was closed, but the grounds were beautifully lit and decorated. Every tree and shrub surrounding the church was loaded with clear miniature lights. They wrapped around a simple scene that took center stage on the church courtyard—the Nativity.

We crunched our way slowly through the remains of last week's snow toward the manger scene. Jonathan sat down on a large boulder that rested alongside the wooden stable.

"This is one of the things I envy about mortals," he said, gesturing toward the glowing figures of a mother holding her child and her husband standing beside her. A lovely guardian angel was suspended above them, watching over the little family of three.

"I don't understand," I said, sitting down next to him. Tiny flakes of snow drifted sporadically across the sky, hinting that the new storm was not far behind.

"A mortal's life can be all wrong—full of mistakes, anger, hurt, regrets—and then, because of the birth of a single child over two thousand years ago, it can all be made right . . ." he snapped his fingers, "just like that."

"I'm not so sure it works that way," I suggested. "Besides, there are many who don't believe in any of this." I waved my hand at the simple scene before us.

"Yeah, but the ones that do . . . they get it. It's one of the few things they have that I covet."

This was a side of Jonathan that I'd never seen before. "Aren't you the one who told me you were angry with God?" I asked, recalling the night in Uncle Connor's study when we pounded each other with paper snowballs.

"I am."

"Why is that?" I asked.

"Why?" He glanced over at me for a moment and searched my eyes, then he turned back to stare at the nativity scene. "Because he left us here."

"Left who where?"

"The immortals. This world was meant for *mortals,*" he gestured toward the manger scene. "He gave them everything—directions, books, commandments, even his own child. He gave them a purpose for being here, and then he promised them everlasting life in a better world after they die. But us . . . ?" he shook his head, "there's nothing—no divine purpose, no salvation, no promise of anything more, and no redemption when we make a mess of things."

I listened, but I couldn't respond; I knew nothing of redemption or salvation.

"It's not supposed to be this way, Beth," he said, turning to look into my eyes. "Immortals aren't supposed to be here. Why did he leave us behind, trapped in a world that according to him," he pointed into the night air, "will soon come to an end? Then what? Mortals move on to their 'better world.' But for us, there's nothing. Just . . . nothing." The intensity of his words seemed to embarrass him and he laughed nervously. "So, yeah—that's why I'm angry at God."

I nodded to indicate that I understood, but I definitely didn't agree with him. "I don't think it was a mistake," I suggested. "I don't know much about God, but from what I do know, He doesn't make mistakes. There's always a reason for things even if we don't understand it."

A vision of my mother flashed through my mind and I wondered if I could apply those words to my own situation. I saw no reason for losing her—or for losing the use of my hand. Was I willing to trust in some supreme being and believe that it was all for some greater purpose? My eyes flickered to Jonathan and a wave of powerful emotion swept through me, causing a lump to rise in my throat. I realized that I wouldn't be sitting next to him tonight if things hadn't changed so drastically in my life. Yes, I believed there was a purpose. I had to believe.

"I'm sorry," he sighed, touching my cheek. "I didn't bring you here to depress you. I just wanted you with me this time."

"This time?"

He nodded. "I come here every year."

"Why?"

"I don't know . . . just to touch base I guess." He chuckled and reached into my jacket pocket so he could hold my hand. "He brought me you this year. I wanted to tell Him thanks."

A sudden throb pounded in my throat, making it impossible to swallow. A tear trickled down the side of my face; I tried to wipe it away discreetly with my coat jacket, but Jonathan stopped me. He traced the tear with his finger and then gently kissed my cheek where the tear had left its trail. He reached down to move a strand of hair that the wind had blown onto my face and rested his hand against the hollow of my neck. I closed my eyes and relaxed into the warmth of his hand. I wasn't surprised when I felt his lips press gently against mine. When I opened my eyes, he was looking at me.

"I am so in love with you, Beth," he whispered, and he kissed me again. His lips were soft and gentle, and his hand trembled slightly against my neck.

I recalled the question I'd had the night I stayed with Darla, worrying about whether or not Jonathan still desired me physically. I reached up and rested my hand over his, allowing his trembling to become my trembling as his lips moved gently against mine, and I realized that nothing could make me feel more loved or more desired than I did at that moment.

It was a long time before he broke the kiss. I wasn't sure if we were trembling because we were cold (my toes were tingling—I should have worn thicker socks) or if something else was happening.

"Beth, I'm going to have to go away for awhile," he finally said, clearing his throat.

"Why? Where?" I asked, suddenly nervous.

He looked at me thoughtfully, "There's something I need to do."

"What?" I didn't care how nosy I sounded.

"There's something I screwed up a long time ago—I need to make it right."

My heart began to beat anxiously, sensing something ominous coming.

"Where do you have to go?"

"I won't know for sure until I have more information. This thing with the possessors is going to get worse. I have . . . abilities that can help."

The nervous beating in my chest accelerated. "I don't understand. What do you have to do?"

"It's not what I *have* to do, it's what I *can* do that's important."

"Does that mean you're going to travel?"

"Probably."

"When?"

"I don't know, but soon."

I dropped my head and tried to mask my disappointment.

"It'll be okay, Beth, I promise."

"I don't want you to leave," I whispered.

He wrapped his arms around me and pulled me close. "There's more," he said, burying his face in my hair.

"More?" My heart sank as I felt him nod.

"I need to know that you trust me."

"I trust you," I assured him.

"I know you do *now,*" he said, "but that could change."

"No . . ." I pulled away so I could look him in the face, "that won't happen."

He let out a dark chuckle.

"What's all this about?" I pleaded.

"I'll tell you everything I can as soon as I know more." He laid his hand on the side of my face and rubbed his thumb against my cheek. "I promise."

I nodded, but I caught the exclusion in his promise.

He scrutinized my expression carefully and then smiled. "There's one more thing—a confession actually."

"Confession?" I questioned reluctantly.

He nodded slowly. "There are things in my past, things I'm not proud of—things that might cause you to doubt how you feel about me." I started to protest, but he shook his head, cutting me off. "I just want you to know that no matter what happens, I love you. Don't ever forget that."

His behavior seemed a bit overdramatic. Nothing could change my feelings for him.

"Will you tell me about your past someday?"

"Yes," he replied without hesitation. And then, as if anticipating my next question, he added, "soon."

By the time we arrived back at the ranch it was nearly two in the morning and snow was falling steadily, laying a thick blanket of white across the already frozen ground. Grace and Carl were still awake, sitting on the floor in front of the fireplace. Carl eyed me suspiciously as Jonathan and I joined him and Grace on the floor.

"Where'd you guys go?" he asked, glancing at Jonathan. I almost laughed at the accusation in his tone, but I decided to ignore it.

"Actually," I replied before Jonathan had a chance to respond, "he took me to church."

If it were possible for a jaw to literally hit the floor, Carl's did. His eyes flickered back and forth between Jonathan and me until he was satisfied that I wasn't pulling his leg.

"Well," he said, glancing at Grace, "there's one I haven't heard before."

Grace stood and suggested we call it a night if we wanted to hit the slopes early in the morning. According to Jonathan, Grace rarely left the ranch. There were only a few times during the year that she felt comfortable going out in public and Christmas was one of those times. Jonathan had explained that it was because there were usually no crowds at the ski resort on Christmas day.

"Beth, can I get you anything before I retire?" Grace stifled a yawn.

"No, thank you. You've thought of everything."

"Carl?" She reached for his empty coffee mug. I don't know if she meant to, but her fingers slid subtly against Carl's when he handed her his cup. Carl noticed.

"Well then, I'll say good night." She smiled and took the cups to the kitchen before we all retired to our rooms.

I waited until I was certain everyone was asleep before I crept back downstairs to snatch the gift Jonathan had made for me and take it to my room for inspection. I tiptoed over to the hearth, grabbed the package, and then scampered back upstairs to my room. I quickly went to work removing the wrapping paper, being very careful not to tear it so I could rewrap the box when I was finished. With every movement, I prayed a silent prayer that the contents of the box would not be shattered to the point that I couldn't repair them.

Understanding

CHAPTER 18

I finished removing the wrapping paper from Jonathan's present and confirmed that he had packaged it in a shoebox, just as I'd suspected. The bulge that had been so obvious earlier had disappeared—no doubt the result of my careless handling. Clearly, whatever was inside the box had been seriously altered.

I stared at the package for what seemed like an eternity, sickened by the inevitable. Reluctantly, I loosened the lid and peered nervously inside. It took a few minutes for my brain to register what my eyes were seeing. But then, in a fit of exasperation, I released a series of colorful invectives that embarrassed me, even though nobody was around to hear them. Part of me was so angry I could spit nails. Another part of me was so relieved I could cry. And then there was the third part of me—the part that was secretly impressed by Jonathan's creativity and clever ingenuity.

Nestled inside the box were two halves of a used brick, and wedged between the bricks was what used to be a light bulb. All that remained of the fragile bulb, however, were a thousand tiny shards of glass.

I realized I was in a precarious position. If I rewrapped the present and snuck it back downstairs, I'd have to act surprised when I opened it in the morning. I didn't think I could pull that off effectively. On the other hand, if I let on that the gig was up, I'd have to admit that I'd broken my promise and snooped. I was in the middle of weighing my two options when I heard my phone rumble against the nightstand.

He knows! I thought to myself, my guilty conscience taking root. *Nonsense Beth—get ahold of yourself. Just stay cool.*

I took a deep breath and flipped open the phone.

"Hey," I faked a yawn.

"Hey, yourself," he replied. "So . . . what'cha doing?"

"Um, getting ready for bed," I lied.

"Oh?" The raised inflection in his voice let me know that he didn't believe me. "Okay, then. I just wanted to say good night and . . . pleasant dreams."

"Uh, all right . . . thanks. You too."

"See you in the morning, Beth. By the way, Merry Christmas."

I glanced at the clock automatically, but I already knew it was well past two in the morning.

"Yes, you too," I replied. Could he hear the guilt in my voice?

"G'nite," he whispered.

"G'nite," I echoed.

Whew! Narrow escape. Carefully, I rewrapped the present and replaced the tag and bow in their original place—no harm done. I turned off the light, grabbed the gift, and headed out the door. I wasn't three steps down the dimly lit hallway before Jonathan whispered, "Going somewhere?"

"Yaaaaaaa!" I jumped, hurling the box several feet into the air as I screamed.

Jonathan's reflexes were impressively quick, yet he made no effort to catch the flying box as it plummeted to the ground. It hit the floor with an angry thud and tinkled with the sound of shattered glass as the package flipped over onto its side. I whirled around and there he was, leaning casually against the wall just beyond my bedroom door—his cell phone still clutched in his hand.

"Hmm. That's too bad," he said, shaking his head, his lips pursed together tightly. "I'm pretty sure it's broken this time." His eyes focused sternly on the damaged box, but the corners of his mouth twitched in a smug, satisfied grin.

"You!" I bellowed, slugging him in the arm. "I can't believe you did that to me!"

"Did what?" he laughed, his eyes wide with feigned innocence. "I just came by to say good night."

"Argh!" I slammed both of my fists into his chest, not even caring about the shooting pain in my left hand as I made contact—but it was a futile attack. Effortlessly, he grabbed my wrists and pulled me up next to him, laughing the entire time. His laughter was infectious, and soon I was laughing too.

"I can't believe you!" I struggled to keep my voice down, suddenly afraid that I might wake Carl or Grace. I tried to free myself from his grip, but he pulled me closer to him.

"Do you have any idea how worried I've been all day about breaking that stupid present?" I whined, pressing my face into his chest.

"I think I do," he grinned knowingly.

"As mad as I am at you, you have no idea how relieved I was when I saw what was in that box. I could just kill you for putting me through that!"

"Got you pretty good, didn't I?" He raised his eyebrows and his twinkling eyes bore shamelessly into mine.

"Yes!" I admitted weakly. "Very impressive I might add, and creative."

He smiled victoriously and wrapped his arms around my waist. "Would you like to see your *real* present?" he whispered into my ear.

"Now?" I asked, looking around as if I were about to do something wrong.

"Why not? Technically, it *is* Christmas," he reminded me.

"Then . . . yes! I'm dying to see my present. Where is it?" I asked impatiently.

"Follow me."

He led me downstairs to his bedroom and switched on the light. Propped up against the wall in the far corner of the room was a large rectangular shape with a sheet over it.

"There it is," he said. "Go ahead, take a look."

I glanced up at him anxiously, pausing briefly, then walked quickly to the corner and removed the sheet. I was utterly speechless when I saw what lay hidden underneath. Painted in rich, classic baroque hues was an exquisite portrait of a boy and girl sitting side-by-side at a grand piano.

"It's beautiful!" I gasped, awestruck.

"Look closely," he insisted, redirecting my gaze.

I stared dumbfounded at the painting, and then one by one the details began to leap from the canvas. The girl in the painting was leaning her head against the boy's shoulder. She was playing the piano with her right hand, and when I looked more closely, I noticed that her left hand was lying on top of his, exactly the way Jonathan and I had been the day he taught me to play Eleanor's theme. Jonathan had captured every detail of my disfigured hand perfectly, but instead of appearing grotesque and misshapen, it was delicate and beautiful. The position of our hands on the keys was not that of Eleanor's theme, but of Chopin's Étude in E. I don't suppose anyone else would have noticed that. Sitting on top of the grand piano were three items: a metronome, the instrument used to help a pianist keep perfect time; a clock; and a piano book with the word "Étuden" printed on the cover. Etched across the bottom of the artwork was a title which simply read, "Timeless."

I'd always heard it said that a painting captures far more than a photograph ever could, and judging by this piece of art, that was definitely true. Jonathan had managed to portray beautifully the very essence of our relationship. I was stunned. I'd never seen anything so exquisite, and I'd certainly never received a more meaningful gift.

"I-I don't know what to say," I stammered.

"You like it?"

"Are you kidding? It's the most beautiful thing I've ever seen. I can't believe you did this! I had no idea you were . . . are an artist."

"I'm glad you like it." He seemed honestly relieved, as if there were ever a chance that I *wouldn't* be pleased.

"I love it!" I shook my head in disbelief, still amazed by his offering.

"So, can I open *my* gift now?" he said, reminding me that we weren't finished yet.

My gift to him was going to seem very anticlimactic after this.

"I'll be right back," I replied as I started for the living room.

"Not necessary," he said sheepishly. "I already brought it in here."

I eyed him scornfully but he raised one eyebrow, daring me to say anything about it. After my shenanigans with his gift, I had no choice but to back down graciously.

He untied the string on my package and tore through the hand-made wrapping paper without hesitation. He pulled up a DVD case from the wads of tissue paper I'd used to disguise the box. The sleeve of the case read, "For Jonathan," in bold print across the top, and scripted beneath were the words, "From your little étude." He appeared a bit perplexed, not certain what was actually burned onto the DVD, so I explained.

"It's a collection of videos from some of my piano performances, beginning with my debut at age seven and ending with my audition for the scholarship last year."

"Wow," he said, flipping the case over in his hand to read the list of piano pieces I'd performed.

"I know it's silly, but playing the piano is the only real talent I've ever had, and I'll never get to share it with you now—not fully. I wanted you to have a glimpse of me when I was whole."

Jonathan stared at the DVD and then at me. I didn't understand the expression on his face.

"I'm sorry," I mumbled, "it's sort of a selfish gift now that I think about it."

Jonathan pressed his fingertips against my lips. "Stop," he sighed,

"I love it. The gift is perfect. But please, don't ever refer to yourself as not 'whole.'"

"But—"

"Not ever," he ordered gently. "Understand?"

I nodded my head and he released my lips.

"This is very thoughtful of you," he said, holding the DVD in his hand. "I can't wait to watch it. Thank you." He bent down and kissed me.

I started to kiss him back, but I yawned instead. I couldn't help it. The day had finally caught up with me. He chuckled as we both glanced at the clock on his chest of drawers. It was half past three in the morning.

That's when I noticed that the picture of Eleanor was gone. I didn't say anything, but I'm sure he was aware that I noticed.

"Come on," he said, "let's get you to bed."

The hauntingly simple melody of Eleanor's theme floated softly through the air as I was drifting to sleep, but there was something strange about the way it sounded. It was like a music box, distant and detached, devoid of the dynamics that enhanced its natural emotion.

The melody grew louder and more determined as I lay listening, too tired to clear the fog from my brain. It wasn't that the volume of the music was increasing but that its proximity to my room was changing. It grew closer with each new phrase.

The melody began to pound loudly just outside my bedroom, no longer melodic and sweet but determined and angry as it hammered at my door, bidding me to rise. I couldn't get out of bed. My legs were too heavy to obey the command.

Ignoring the boundary of my closed door, the music entered my room. It was accompanied by a rush of swirling air that ripped the covers from my bed. I sat up, not out of fear—which was uncharacteristic for me—but out of annoyance.

The melody softened as I sat up, urging me to get out of bed. I suddenly realized that I was in my room at Uncle Connor's, but for some reason that seemed normal. I swung my legs off the mattress and forced my feet onto the floor. At once the music quieted to its beautifully soft and morose tune. It continued to slow and soften as if the music box had wound down, expending all of its energy. In distinct bell-like tones, the music came to a standstill and the room was silent.

I sat on the edge of my bed listening, waiting for the music to begin again—but the room remained quiet and still. I waited for several seconds before deciding that whatever the music wanted from me had passed. I reached down to grab my comforter from the floor, but the instant my hand made contact with it, the music began again. The melody was below me now, and this time, it wasn't the bell-like tone of a music box; it was coming from my piano. I would have recognized that sound anywhere.

I stiffened and bent my ear in the direction of the music, trying to discern who might be playing. Every pianist has a uniquely personal style—the trained ear can differentiate among those styles rather effortlessly—but as I listened more carefully, the only style I recognized was my own.

Compelled by some unseen force, I climbed off the bed and moved quietly across the room. I opened the door and crept down the hall toward the source of the music. At the top of the basement stairs, I stood surrounded by darkness; the only light source was the bright green numbers that glowed from the microwave clock in the adjacent kitchen. I stared from the open doorway down the stairwell into pitch blackness, looking for any sign of movement or light from below. I could hear the faint sound of a clock ticking in the background, but it was discordant with the timing in Eleanor's theme.

I clutched the stair rails tightly and hesitantly stepped down into the darkness. Each step brought me closer to the source of the melody, but once I reached the bottom of the staircase, the direction from which the sound originated had changed. Once more, I felt the melody coming from below me. I turned away from the piano and noticed that the door to the closet beneath the stairs was ajar; a faint light illuminated its frame.

Fear seized my chest, gripping my lungs until I couldn't breathe normally. Every instinct warned me to hasten back up the stairs; but as I started to turn toward the stairway, a gentle wind blew across the room and directly past me—only instead of frightening me, it warmed and calmed me. The sweet scent of lavender saturated the air and beckoned me to follow. I had no choice. My legs moved of their own accord, independent of any conscience command from my brain. I stood at the closet and reached for the doorknob, but the door opened on its own.

When I bent down to climb through the door, I noticed that the light was coming from the edges of the trap door in the floor of the closet. The throw rug had been removed and was folded neatly next to the wall. I reached down and pulled the trap door open; as I did so, the music shifted into an unfamiliar bridge.

I paused and listened to the change in the melody. That was it—the missing element of Eleanor's theme—the interlude that bridged the gap between the beginning of the melody and the end of the composition! I closed my eyes and visualized Eleanor in my mind, sitting at the pianoforte as she composed her song for Jonathan. The interlude seemed to bind her to me, beyond our mutual love for the same man. I breathed in deeply and exhaled slowly as the conclusion of the melody connected the present to the past.

When the music stopped, I knew what I had to do. Although it went against every grain of my common sense, I climbed into the hole in the floor and descended the ladder that led to the vortex cellar.

The soft plink of dripping moisture echoed along the walls of the room and the rich smell of earth and minerals confirmed the fact that I was underground. My mother's binders sat unmoved, spread across the table in the center of the room. The room was exactly as I remembered it.

I panned the perimeter of the room carefully, examining every inch of the walls and floor. There was nothing unusual. Uncle Connor had said that my mother loved this room because she felt spiritually connected here, enlightened by some higher power that enhanced her abilities to reason. I recalled his exact words: "She believed that in the heart of a vortex, science and faith united harmoniously; and she was convinced that when she was here, her mind opened to an influx of inspiration, melding the conflicting worlds of science and religion. She described it once as receiving pure light and knowledge from heaven leading to new perspectives on old ideas."

Confused, I sat down at the table and began flipping through the pages of my mother's research binders. They were all here, with the exception of the two I'd taken upstairs to read. I carefully moved the other binders to the side and opened the one bearing the title *Biological Immortality*—the one Uncle Connor had insisted I leave under the protection of the vortex.

I perused the pages of the binder, but nothing unusual caught my eye. Mostly it contained information related to cybernetics, genetic codes, DNA, and cloning experiments. The language specific to DNA and genetic encoding was way over my head, and once more I found myself marveling at the depth of my mother's intellect.

I closed the binder and slid away from the table. But when I began walking toward the ladder, a wall of air stopped me in my tracks. I pushed against the invisible force but it was too powerful to penetrate. I persisted—but a blow to my chest by invisible hands knocked me backward onto the floor.

"What?" I screamed. "What do you want?"

My cries echoed into the empty space around me.

"You brought me here!" I bellowed. My eyes circled the room for some hint, some clue that I was obviously missing. "Tell me why I'm here!" I demanded.

I paused . . . there was no response. Of course there wasn't. This was obviously part of some morbidly cruel trick to frighten me. It was working.

The peaceful sense of confidence I'd felt when I first entered the room faded, giving way to frustration and fear. Tears welled up in my eyes and spilled down my cheeks in steady streams.

"Please," I called, my voice now barely more than a whisper, "show me why I'm here."

I doubled over onto my knees and buried my face in my hands. There was nothing more I could do; I'd reached the edge of reason. I clenched my hands into tight fists, too upset to notice the piercing pain in my left hand and too upset to care.

I stood and focused my attention on the ladder across the room. With renewed determination, I stomped angrily toward it. In an instant, I was flying backward again. This time, the force struck me with so much strength that it knocked the air out of my lungs. As soon as I regained my breath I stood up, even angrier than before. I stared at the invisible wall of energy that held me prisoner in my Uncle's cellar. Frustration overcame me, and in one violent swoop I shoved the research binders off the table, sending them flying across the room. I leaned over the table and slammed my fists on it repeatedly.

"What do you want from me?" I screamed. "What?"

Nothing. No response. Nothing but the sound of my breathing.

I lowered my head in despair and stared at the top of the table. Then I saw something move from the corner of my eye. My eyes flashed instinctively in the direction of the perceived motion, but there was nothing there. I started to turn away when I noticed something unusual, something out of place. I stooped to pick up the binder on biological immortality and when I did, a cluster of papers fell to the floor.

The pages were pinned together with a small binder clip and appeared to be a collection of children's drawings. I recognized the familiar scenes; they were pictures I'd drawn when I was a child—pictures of the toys that I used to play with.

I flipped expectantly through the drawings and there it was—the reason I was brought to the cellar. It was the picture of a man, a man I knew only as "Bailey": an imaginary friend who had once lived inside my bedroom mirror. The drawing was unimpressive, a simple child's rendition displaying no real artistic ability, yet containing an unusual amount of detail. But that didn't matter. What mattered was the cold chill that coursed through my veins because there, staring back at me from the face in the drawing, were two brightly colored yellow eyes.

A loud rumble of thunder blasted repeatedly through the room, causing the light bulb on the ceiling to flicker on and off several times. The light buzzed noisily, then sizzled and smoked in a furious rage until it finally exploded, sending slivers of glass rippling through the room in a single blast. Instinctively, I buried my face in my hands to avoid the shooting splinters.

I'd experienced this type of violence before, every time a good-sized earthquake struck Southern California, which had happened rather frequently when I was a child. But to my knowledge, earthquakes were not common in Wyoming.

I was acutely aware that underground was the worst place to be during a quake. I braced myself, not yet certain if it was safe to move. I rose slowly to my feet, reluctant to take my hands from my face and leave it unprotected.

By all logic, the cellar should have been black once its only light source had been destroyed. Nevertheless, as I surveyed the room, a glimmering sheen along the limestone walls brightened the room enough that I could discern objects and shapes. It was as though the walls were magically generating their own power.

When I reached down to pick up the drawings I'd dropped, I had the eerie sensation of being watched. It felt like someone was standing directly behind me. The feeling was foreboding yet familiar. It was accompanied by the pungent stench of rotting flesh.

The room grew so cold I could see my breath. My labored breathing seemed to echo loudly through the chamber; but as I listened more carefully, I realized it was someone else who was breathing.

I wasn't alone!

I clung tightly to the picture in my hand as I stood frozen in place in the center of the room. The breathing behind me deepened and within seconds, the presence was so close that I could feel its cold breath against the bare skin of my neck. I wanted to run or turn around and confront whatever it was that stood behind me or do something—anything—besides stand there like a statue. But my legs wouldn't budge.

And then, as quickly as it had come, the disgusting odor and the cold air dissipated. The breathing behind me ceased and a warm, calming wind flitted past me. The room brightened softly and the sweet fragrance of lavender permeated the air.

"Beth," a voice whispered behind me.

I was afraid to turn around.

"Beth," the voice called again—or were there two voices?

"Beth, honey?"

I shook my head in confusion. The voice didn't fit with the feminine smell of lavender, yet it was familiar. I was powerfully drawn to it.

"Wake up, Beth."

Awareness struck and my eyes snapped open. For a moment, I felt disoriented, confused by my surroundings, then I saw Jonathan's face.

"I've heard of the sleeping dead before, but you put them to shame," he chuckled.

His adoring smile was the most welcome sight I could imagine.

Still groggy, I sat up and threw my arms around his neck, holding him as tightly as I could. He let out a grunt of forced air and then started to laugh as he reached up and tried to pry my arms loose.

"Oh, sorry," I apologized, releasing my death grip.

"No problem," he sputtered, pretending to cough. He twitched his face and shook his head as if trying to shake his features back into their proper place. "My nose will grow back."

I blushed, embarrassed, but finally fully awake. "Good morning," I yawned.

"Good morning," he replied, grinning. "I hate to wake you, but Carl and Grace are already downstairs anxious to hit the slopes."

"Oh," I said, shaking my head. "Right."

"Everything all right in there?" he asked, tapping the top of my forehead with the tip of his finger.

I nodded in response. "I'm fine."

"You sure?"

"Just give me a minute to get my bearings."

"Are you always like this when you first wake up?" he teased.

"Afraid so," I shrugged. "I don't do mornings, remember?"

"Do you want me to tell them to go ahead and leave without us? We can always meet them later," he suggested.

I considered his offer for a moment because I suddenly realized there was something else I needed to do—something that couldn't wait.

"Jonathan, would you take me home?" The words sounded like an urgent plea.

He raised one eyebrow but said nothing, obviously taken by surprise.

"Please?" I begged.

"What's wrong? Are you okay?" His countenance fell; I could tell that he'd misunderstood.

"I need your help with something."

"Beth, you're not making any sense. I thought you wanted to go skiing."

"I do," I replied. I shook my head, trying to stay focused.

"You're talking in circles . . . back up a minute."

I bit my lips together and sighed heavily. He was right; I wasn't making any sense.

"I need to do something," I explained.

"Something that can't wait?"

"Yes . . . no . . . that is, Jonathan, it *is* something that can't wait."

"Will you please tell me what's going on?" He was trying hard not to sound impatient.

"It's Eleanor," I whispered.

"What?"

"I had this dream. I think she's trying to tell me something, something that has to do with the possessors."

Jonathan froze.

"I need to go back to Uncle Connor's cellar."

Jonathan raised both eyebrows, bewildered. His eyes dissected mine for several moments. He knew I was deathly afraid of being underground—that I'd rather walk alone through a haunted cemetery in the middle of a moonless night than go back into that cellar. The very thought caused me to panic. I was sure that was the reason he stopped questioning me and agreed to the detour from our plans.

Jonathan left me alone to shower and change while he filled Grace and Carl in on our sudden change of plans.

"Are you sure you don't want me to go with you?" Carl asked when I finally made it downstairs.

"No, it's okay. You go ahead. We'll meet you there later," I promised. I could tell that Carl was torn between wanting to know what it was that I might find in the cellar and his desire to hit the slopes. The fact that he was smitten by Grace's charms made it difficult for him to decide.

"It's okay, Carl," Grace assured him. "I'll wait here if you want, and we can all go later—"

"Really," I interrupted, "you go ahead. You'll miss the best snow if you wait for us."

Carl hesitated a moment, but finally decided in favor of the slopes and some time with Grace. He pulled his car keys out of his pocket and gestured toward the front door. "Grace, shall we?"

The shimmer of Carl's keys (actually, *my* keys since he'd given the car to me) reminded me of something.

"Wait," I called after them, "the key—where does your dad keep the key to the cellar?"

Jonathan and I made it to Uncle Connor's house in record time. I wasn't sure if he drove so fast because he was anxious to get to the slopes or if he wanted to find out what was waiting for us in the vortex cellar. Either way, I didn't care. I had an agenda. I filled him in on the details of my dream and he listened patiently, nodding on cue at each pause.

The key was exactly where Carl said it would be, tucked away in a box in the top drawer of Uncle Connor's dresser. We didn't waste any time getting into the closet and pulling the rug away from the trap door, but when it was time to step into the dark hole and climb down the ladder, I hesitated.

"I'll go first," Jonathan offered. I gladly stepped aside and watched him climb to the bottom of the ladder and disappear. He switched on the ceiling light and quickly returned. He must have read my mind because he climbed the steps to where I stood, paralyzed on the first rung. I was dead set on seeing my plan all the way through, but all my determination couldn't force my legs to climb down another step.

"Hold on, Beth."

I experienced a feeling of déjà vu as he climbed up behind me—something about his words echoed in my mind. When he reached the rung just below where I stood, it placed his head level with mine. He wrapped one arm around my waist and pulled me closely against him.

His lips pressed gently against my ear. "Hold on, honey," he whispered.

I couldn't put my finger on it. It wasn't only the words or the way he said them, it was the feeling of him so close behind me speaking into my ear that was strangely familiar.

Once we reached the bottom of the ladder and I could stand on firm ground, he released his hold on me.

"Okay," he urged. "What are we looking for?"

"*Biological Immortality*," I responded.

His eyebrows raised in a quizzical expression.

"It's one of the binders," I added, pointing to the stack of research on the table that sat in the center of the room.

He quickly located the binder and slid it across the table to where I stood. I stared for a moment at the book, afraid to consider the possibility that my dream was just that—a dream. What if I'd forced Jonathan to drive here for nothing? What if I had simply been over-tired last night and my mind had gone into overdrive? What if . . . ?

I looked up at Jonathan, silently pleading for some sign of reassurance, some sign that he wouldn't be angry with me if this was all for nothing—but his face was expressionless. I swallowed hard and began flipping through the pages, slowly at first, then faster as each page revealed nothing unusual or extraordinary. Finally, I picked up the binder, held it upside down by the binding, and shook it—but nothing happened. There was no stack of pictures clipped together as there had been in my dream. I shook the binder again and then a third time, but the result was the same. Dejected, I slid the book away and looked apologetically into Jonathan's eyes.

"I'm sorry. They're not here," I murmured. "I was sure they would be here."

"What exactly are you looking for?" he asked patiently.

"It doesn't matter," I mumbled.

"Beth, if you tell me what you're looking for, I can help."

"Pictures," I muttered. Jonathan looked at me curiously. "Drawings, actually. They were clipped together, and they fell out of that binder in my dream."

"Dreams can be a little disjointed, Beth. Perhaps they're in one of the other binders."

"But it was so vivid."

"Okay, think," he insisted. "What were you doing in the dream just before you saw the pictures?"

"I . . ." I furrowed my eyebrows in deep concentration. It was difficult to remember in the correct order. Some of the details had become fuzzy.

"I was angry because she . . . it . . . whatever it was wouldn't let me leave the room. Something kept striking me in the chest and knocking me backward every time I tried to get near the stairs. I got so angry that I shoved all the binders onto the floor—like this." I pretended to scoot my arms across the table as if I were heaving its contents onto the ground.

"So it's possible the pictures came from one of these other stacks." He glanced at the pile of research and then shifted his gaze back to me. Then, as if the idea struck us both at exactly the same time, we began hurriedly rummaging through the binders.

We were two-thirds of the way through when Jonathan held up a green file folder, twisting it in his hand. The grin on his face told me he'd found what we were looking for. The folder was labeled, "Beth," and contained several examples of early work from my pre-school and kindergarten years. I wasn't interested in a trip down memory lane, but Jonathan was enjoying himself as he chuckled through each sample of my early artwork.

And there they were—just like in my dream—four drawings clipped together. I removed the clip and found what we'd come for—the drawing of the man with the bright yellow eyes.

I gasped when I saw it in spite of the fact that I'd known what to expect. Somehow, holding it in my hand and knowing it was real was significant to me. It was tangible evidence that there was a power greater than logic and reason at work here. Even if I had fabricated the whole paranormal thing—the music, the breathing, the tremors, and the cold—I could not have fabricated the pictures. I had no way of knowing beforehand that my mother had saved them or that she kept them locked away in a cellar beneath Uncle Connor's basement.

Whether it was Eleanor that led me here or some other mystical power from the earth's vortex, I couldn't say. Nevertheless, even the scientist in me could not dispute the hard, cold evidence that now stared up at me with glowing yellow eyes.

"Here he is," I whispered to Jonathan. "My possessor!" Once Jonathan had examined the drawing, his mouth fell open and his eyes glazed over. He stared past me as if he were seeing something that his mind refused to accept. After several seconds he closed his eyes and sighed, breathing heavily.

"Jonathan?"

His eyes opened, but he still didn't look at me. I moved my hand slowly in front of his face to get his attention. He tilted his head to the side and gazed sullenly into my confused eyes. "I'm so sorry, Beth," he uttered remorsefully.

"Sorry? Sorry for what?"

Jonathan shook his head slowly from side to side, but said nothing.

"You know something," I said in a half-accusatory tone.

He nodded once, slowly. "Beth, I need to talk to Carl—as soon as possible."

Fear was cold inside me. "Jonathan, what is it? What does Carl have to do with this?" But he was already stacking the binders back on the table and preparing to leave. "What are you keeping from me?" I demanded.

"Beth, would you please just trust me on this? I can't tell you everything—not yet."

"Why not?" I sputtered. But he didn't reply; instead, he just looked at me with pleading eyes.

"Please, Beth, I can't."

His tortured expression made me believe that he wanted to tell me more, but for some inexplicable reason he couldn't.

"Why do you need to see Carl?"

He paused, battling something inside of him.

"It's complicated," he sighed.

There it was again, that *feeling*—no, stronger than a feeling, that *knowledge* that I'd heard those words before—those exact words in the same voice with the same pleading agony behind them.

My mind darted back in time, searching through the past few months for any memory that would explain this feeling of déjà vu. Then, as if resurrected from the dead, the memory surrounding the night of my accident unfolded before me and the search ended.

A heavy weight pressed against my shoulders and my legs started to tremble. My stomach contracted and I collapsed forward, losing my balance. I reached for the edge of the table in time to steady my footing, but the words continued to beat in my mind like a loud echo against a canyon wall. "It's complicated, it's complicated, complicated, compli. . . ."

And then, as if joining the chorus of echoes, someone saying, "Hold on, honey, hold on. It's complicated, compli . . . Hold on, honey."

Then another echo. "God, no, not her. Hold on Beth, hold on. God no, not her. Hold on, honey. It's complicated, it's compli. . . ."

They weren't just words, they were *his* words, the same words he spoke in my ear the night of the accident as he cradled me in his arms and comforted me.

My trembling legs gave way and I crumpled to the ground.

"Beth!" Jonathan was at my side immediately.

My head spun violently and I struggled to catch my breath. I tried to regain my equilibrium—then seconds before the spinning stopped I thought I heard Jonathan's voice. "God, no!" His words hung in the distance. And then, like the night of the accident, my world faded to black.

Guardian

CHAPTER 19

$\mathcal{I}$ pressed forcefully against thick blackness, inching my way along the metal staircase as it twisted upward in a familiar, circular pattern. I'd been here before, but not like this. Ice cold metal singed the palms of my hands as I clasped the stair railing. It felt as if I were clutching red-hot coals in each of my hands. Every natural instinct screamed at me to release the rail and free myself from the fiery pain, yet letting go meant wandering in the dark and risking the loss of my footing.

Determined, I pushed upward, reaching hand over hand, clinging to the frozen rod that kept me firmly mounted to the narrow staircase. A frigid wind gusted fiercely against my chest and face halting my progression—daring me to take another step forward. I ducked, snapping my head from side to side in angry protest; but each twist of my body exposed another part of me that recoiled against the slicing cold. My chest tightened as my muscles contracted; it was an instinctual act of self-preservation.

If only I could let go. I wanted to give in to the urge—to buckle my knees and pull myself into a huddle—maybe then I could shield myself from the icy darts and sub-zero temperatures that needled me. I eased my grip on the handrail and a gust of glacial frost exploded against my chest. The wind could perceive my weakening resolve and it howled furiously, throwing me off balance. I reacted without thinking. I wrapped my arms around the handrail and clutched it as tightly as possible. The burning cold of the railing sent unbearable tremors darting through my arms and shoulders, across my neck, and into the pit of my stomach. I opened my mouth to scream, but my frozen breath was no more than a labored grunt.

Push! Keep pushing!

I battled unsuccessfully against the wall of cold air that repeatedly stifled me.

Push! I ordered myself again. *Don't give up!*

The air became solid, like a sheet of ice. I searched laboriously for a weakness, a vulnerable spot that would give way under pressure.

And then I heard it, the shrill snap of ice splitting into a thousand tiny fissures. A pattern formed in my mind: *push* with your feet—*pull* with your hands—*embrace* the ice. Push-pull-embrace. Push-pull-embrace. Like an icebreaker in the Arctic, I forced myself forward with new resolve. Crack-split-separate. Crack-split-separate.

Finally, a glimmer of sunlight penetrated the blackness. The sun's warmth traveled through my veins, thawing my icy body as the room filled with light.

"Welcome back, Beth," a kind voice greeted me.

I turned toward the sound, shielding my eyes from the brightness of the light, and found myself staring into the eyes of the man in the white suit who had greeted me once before at the top of the staircase. He had a pleasant smile and an alarmingly bright countenance. His eyes twinkled just as they had the first time I saw him—just as Jonathan's did—and his smile widened the moment he realized that I recognized him.

"Are you ready for that tour now?" he asked cheerfully. His deportment was calm and comforting.

He gestured for me to join him, offering me his arm in gentle-manly propriety, and waited patiently for my response. "Shall we?"

I took his arm and walked with him across a spacious court-yard. We passed several rows of buildings and went through a wide archway that led to a lush, green garden. Before us was a path that was ornamented with fountains every ten or fifteen yards. Water flowed freely from the fountains and overflowed through narrow channels into a long, narrow pool that ran the entire length of the garden. Thick, flowering shrubs, accented by tall purple lupines, lined both sides of the pool. Spaced symmetrically throughout the garden were white, wrought iron benches whose backs curved up into intricate floral designs. Water lilies grew randomly in the shal-low pool and as I watched, they swayed in gentle unison to a calm breeze. I felt like I never wanted to leave this beautiful place.

"There's someone who is very anxious to see you, Beth," the man in the white suit said. He smiled warmly and backed away from me, freeing his arm.

I was so awestruck by the beauty of the garden that I'd almost forgotten about the man in the white suit. I turned toward him, but his eyes were focused on something beyond me. My eyes followed his gaze. In the distance I beheld the figure of a woman sitting peacefully on one of the white benches. She was turned sideways so I couldn't see her face, but she appeared to be intrigued by some-thing moving in the water. She wore a green silk dress that flowed loosely around her calves, revealing her ankles and bare feet. There was something familiar about her profile—something that tugged at my memory and caused a pounding ache in my throat. My heart throbbed relentlessly as I walked toward the angelic figure.

Could it really be her?

I was too afraid to embrace the hope, afraid she might disappear. I approached slowly, inching my way on tiptoes to keep from startling her; but she sensed my presence and turned toward me.

She was a vision of heaven—too perfect to be real.

"Mom!" I cried. Tears burst from my eyes without warning as I ran to embrace her. A low voice of reason cautioned me that I was only dreaming, but I didn't care. It was a dream I welcomed, and one from which I did not wish to awaken.

Sobbing, I dropped to my knees at her feet and wrapped my arms securely around her waist. I wept openly as I pressed my face into her lap, just as I had as a child. She lifted her perfect, delicate hand to my head and weaved her fingers through my hair.

"Elizabeth," she whispered, stroking my scalp tenderly with her fingertips. "My sweet Elizabeth."

Never had the sound of my real name sounded more beautiful.

I sobbed in her lap, clutching her waist, drinking in her touch, her voice, and her smell—the heavenly fragrance of sweet spices and subtle florals. I pulled her arm to my face and drew in a long, deep breath, nuzzling my nose against her skin.

"Mom," I whimpered.

"Shh . . ." She hushed my cries as she caressed my forehead, comforting me as only she could. She was so real! So tangible. So beautiful.

There was something I wanted to tell her . . . something I needed her to know.

"Mom," I muttered through my tears. "I'm so sorry!"

"Shhh . . . sweetie, you have nothing to be sorry about."

"I was so awful to you that night . . . I yelled at you," I choked through broken sobs. "I didn't mean it."

"I know honey. I know. It's okay. Everything is okay." She cupped her hands gently around my cheeks and lifted my face to look into my eyes. There was nothing but pure, unconditional love in her gaze as she smiled warmly down at me.

"I love you, Mom."

"I could never doubt that," she replied.

As I began to gain control over my emotions, I thought of all the things I wanted to tell her. So much had happened I wasn't sure where to start. Then, as if she perceived my thoughts, she cut me off before I could begin.

"I haven't much time, Beth," she informed me.

"No, Mom . . . don't say that. Stay with me."

"I can't stay here honey. This is no longer my world."

"Then take me with you," I pleaded. "I want to stay with you. I need you."

"No, sweetheart, you don't. Not really. Your beautiful life is just beginning."

"But I miss you so much."

"I miss you too, honey, but I'll always be a part of you—no matter what."

I sensed that my time with her was coming to an end; I felt powerless to change it. I needed more time, I longed for it desperately. Just a few days or even a few hours—I didn't care—I'd take whatever I could get.

"Sweetheart, I need you to listen to me."

How many times had she said those words to me before? Would I ever hear her say them again?

"Okay," I said obediently.

"Trust what your heart tells you. Your heart knows what your brain isn't ready to comprehend." She focused her eyes intently, as if mentally transferring knowledge from her mind to mine.

"I don't know what that means."

"You will. Right now your mind cannot accept what your heart embraces as truth, but the time will come when the two will merge."

She put her palms together and weaved her fingers into a tight braid.

"Until then, trust your heart and wait for the rest to catch up. Don't fight it with logic."

"I'm sorry, Beth," the man in the white suit interrupted. When had he returned? Or had he been standing there the whole time? It didn't matter; it was too soon.

"No," I pleaded. "Please, just a little longer."

He glanced at my mother apologetically and then shifted his gaze to me. "It's time," he replied softly.

"Beth, it's all true. Everything I told you."

I gazed up at my mother's face questioningly. She was the vision of an angel; I wanted to remember every minute detail. One solitary tear slid from the corner of her eye, and I quickly reached up to capture it on the tip of my finger. She pressed her face against my hand and kissed my palm. She held my hand against her lips for several moments and then sighed.

"I love you, Bethy," she whispered against my hand, and her eyes spilled over with tears.

"I love you too, Mom." I reached around and hugged her waist tightly with my free arm, burying my face in her lap again. I closed my eyes and clung to her with all the strength I could muster, and wept as her fingers gently smoothed my hair.

I knew the exact moment my surroundings changed, but I fought against the impulse to open my eyes.

A hand held mine, but it was not my mother's hand. My palm was pressed against familiar lips, but they were not my mother's lips. The lips moved in quiet whispers against my skin.

"Beth, honey?"

I recognized his familiar voice at once, and on so many different levels. It was so obvious now. How could I have not made the connection sooner?

"Beth," he whispered, "open your eyes."

I couldn't find it within me to resist; I was compelled to obey—just as I had been the night he forced me to face the man with the yellow eyes. I opened my eyes slowly, disoriented at first. I was no longer in the vortex cellar; I would have recognized the smell of wet limestone. I wasn't lying on a bed or a couch, but I was in a safe place. I tried to sit up, but Jonathan's arm held me so snugly I couldn't move.

My eyes searched the room and the cloud covering my brain dissipated. Jonathan sat on the floor of Uncle Connor's basement with his back against the wall and held me cradled securely in his arms. My eyes found his and he smiled. This reaction confused me. I'd expected to gaze into tortured eyes filled with worry; instead, I stared into the twinkling blue eyes I'd grown so accustomed to. Yet something more was reflected in them as he smiled at me.

I raised my fingers and touched his face.

"You were there!" The words escaped in a muddled murmur, but he understood.

"Yes," he nodded, breathing a subtle sigh of relief.

My heart ached with doubt and confusion. The night of my accident had haunted me for months; he knew how important it was for me to find out the truth about what really happened, and to discover who else was there. How could he have kept the truth from me all these months?

Every sensible cell in my brain told me I should be angry with Jonathan, that he owed me an explanation. No matter what his reasons were, they couldn't begin to erase the fact that he'd betrayed my trust by keeping this secret from me.

Fighting with the angry emotions that swirled in my head was the yearning to reach out to him. I wanted to hold the guardian who had protected me both on the night of the crash and on the night of Halloween when I'd been attacked in the woods.

Comprehension dawned. I must have always known on some level that he'd been there that night. Of course it was him—it had always been him.

I studied the peaceful expression in his eyes and the relaxed lines on his face, and I realized that he'd known this moment would come some day. He'd been waiting for it—waiting for some pivotal event to occur that would turn the key and unlock my memory. He must have dreaded it, yet at the same time longed for the secret to be out in the open. And he knew me well enough to know that I would not be satisfied until I had all the answers.

All these thoughts flitted through my mind in a matter of seconds, and though a part of me questioned what other secrets he might be hiding, I realized it didn't matter. None of it mattered. Everything he had done, every emotion he had experienced, every thought he'd ever had made him who he was today—made up the whole of his being—and I realized at that moment that I loved him completely.

I brushed my hand against his face and his eyes closed.

"You're getting better at this," he said, breaking my train of thought.

"At what?" I whispered hoarsely.

He traced circular patterns along my forehead and then tapped on my temples lightly.

"What?" I asked again.

He grinned as he caressed my face.

"The first time you fainted in my arms, you went into a coma for a long time." The side of his mouth lifted into a wry grin and he shrugged his shoulders. "The second time you stayed unconscious for several hours. This time you were only out for a few minutes."

"Hmm, impressive," I huffed sarcastically.

"It's how your mind handles an overload. It shuts everything out until it can process things."

"So I'm weak-minded? That'll look good on my college application."

"Your mind isn't weak at all," he grinned. "Quite the contrary. It reverts to inward energy . . . and it's becoming surprisingly efficient at it."

"What are you saying?"

"That I believe your destiny—your fate—lies among the immortal realm."

I could tell by the look on his face that he wanted this to be true.

"That's just wishful thinking on your part," I muttered.

He started to argue, but I lifted my deformed hand and held it in front of him. One-by-one, I pulled my bent fingers away from the palm of my hand and held them straight. When I released my fingers, they moved involuntarily back to the spot that had become their permanent home—evidence that I was every bit a mortal.

"No, Jonathan," I sighed, "these," my eyes flickered to my fingers, "are proof that I am not of your world. I'm not special like you or Uncle Connor or Carl."

He folded his loose hand around my bent fingers and pulled my hand to his face. "I don't know why this happened," he said, kissing my wrist, "but it doesn't matter. It won't always be this way. Trust me. You carry royal blood in your veins. I *know* it."

"You see what you want to see," I argued. His feelings for me had obviously clouded his judgment. "Mine is the blood of a mortal."

"Perhaps for now, but I already see it in here." He tapped my forehead again.

"What if you're wrong, Jonathan? What then?"

"So what?" he asked.

"You know what I mean. What if I *am* just a mortal? What then?"

"Then, nothing. It doesn't change anything," he reassured me. "Look at your mom and dad . . . your dad is mortal. It didn't matter to them and it won't matter to us."

He pulled me closer and kissed my forehead. "Truly, it won't matter," he whispered, his lips soft against my skin. What Jonathan had neglected to mention, however, was that there would be a steep price to pay if he married a mortal.

I was satisfied to drop the subject for now—his hungry lips were way too close to mine—and for a few minutes, we were lost in each other.

But there were matters to consider that were urgent and too many questions that remained unanswered. He must have been thinking the same thing because although he continued to hold me close, he suddenly switched gears.

"Beth, tell me about the drawings."

"Can we get out of here?" I asked, unfolding myself from his arms.

"Are you all right?"

"Yes, but I need to get out of this basement."

"And then will you tell me about the pictures?"

"Yes, but then it's your turn. I want to know everything—beginning with why you were there the night my mom died."

The drive back to the ranch took much longer than usual. It had started to snow shortly after we arrived at Uncle Connor's house and had been coming down heavily ever since. It wasn't easy to discern exactly where the road was because of the thick blanket of white that covered the ground. Fortunately, Jonathan was an experienced driver and maneuvered his way through town with little difficulty.

It felt good to be outside. The scenery, though not great for driving, was like something from an old-fashioned postcard. I'd forgotten that today was Christmas until we drove through the main part of town. Main Street was a ghost town; even the gas station on the corner was closed. We made small talk until we were headed down the main highway toward the ranch, then we talked about the pictures.

"I'd forgotten about them, Jonathan. Geez, I was only four or five when I drew them."

"That long ago?" Jonathan asked, grinning smugly.

"Yeah," I shrugged. "Bailey—that's what I always called him—was my imaginary friend when I was little."

Jonathan glanced at me quickly and then shifted his eyes back to the road.

"Go on," he urged.

"He lived in my bedroom mirror—at least, that's where I'd see him. He was invisible otherwise."

"You *saw* him in your mirror?"

"Yeah, all the time. He liked to watch me play."

Jonathan balled his fingers into fists around the steering wheel but said nothing.

"Anyhow, one day he showed up while my mom was brushing my hair. I thought it was funny that I could see him and she couldn't. That's why I drew the pictures."

"Your mom never saw him?"

"No, not that I know of."

"And you only saw him in your mirror?"

"Yes. I could feel him watching me when I played in other rooms, but I only saw him in my bedroom mirror."

"What else do you remember?"

"Nothing. It was too long ago. I didn't remember any of this until I saw those pictures."

Jonathan bit his lips together.

"Except . . ." I suddenly remembered something else. "I remember he got really mad when I showed him the pictures."

"You showed him the pictures?" Jonathan gaped at me for a moment before turning back to watch the road.

"He wanted me to burn them, but I refused. Then—wait a minute, there *was* a time I saw him when he wasn't in the mirror."

"When?"

"He came in the middle of the night. He wanted the pictures. I remember I grabbed them off my nightstand and hid them under my pillow. He was furious! He yelled at me and made things fly across my room. He knocked over all my toys and all my books." I reached up without thinking and touched the scar in my eyebrow. "That's how I split my eyebrow open," I said, rubbing the spot where the corner of a book had slammed into my head. "They always told me it happened during an earthquake," I chuckled.

"What happened after that?"

"Nothing. That's the last time I remember seeing him. We moved when I started kindergarten and I figured my imaginary friends stayed behind."

"Friends? There were others?"

"Yes. I had imaginary friends all over that house. I was never alone."

Jonathan pulled to the side of the road and put the car in park.

"Why are we stopping?"

He shifted his weight in the seat so he could face me. I met his troubled eyes with confusion. What had I said?

"They weren't imaginary, Beth," he said seriously. "They were watching you. They've probably been watching you ever since. I'm sure after you drew those pictures they were ordered to keep their distance from you."

"Why would they watch me?"

"Like I said, royal blood flows through your veins; they want you on their side—and they'll take you regardless of whether you're human or immortal."

He relaxed his fingers around the steering wheel and rested his forehead on his hands. After a few seconds, he reached into the pocket of his jacket and pulled out the drawings. He unfolded the pages and set them before me. It was disconcerting to see so many sets of yellow eyes peering back at me. They were the same yellow eyes that had glowered at me through Eric's body weeks before, the same eyes from my dream of the spiral staircase, and the same eyes that had glared through the window of my mother's car the night of my accident.

I shivered as a cold chill ran down my spine. Jonathan adjusted the heat, but it wasn't the air that made me tremble.

"That explains why he called me Beth Anne," I said pensively.

Jonathan raised one eyebrow. "When?"

"In the woods . . . with Eric. He couldn't have known me by that name unless he'd been around when I was younger. I just couldn't make the connection that night."

"Something isn't right." He paused for a minute, rubbing his chin between his thumb and forefinger. He shook his head. "No—it's not right," he repeated again.

• "What's not right?" I asked, as if anything about this nonsense was *right*.

"Possessors are entities that take over the bodies of others. They have no descriptive traits of their own that would distinguish one of them from another. Your depiction of the one you call Bailey is too specific, too detailed to be that of a possessor."

"It's him, Jonathan. I'm sure of it."

"I know you are, and I believe you. It just doesn't add up." He stacked the pictures on top of each other and refolded them. "Do you mind if I hang on to these?"

"No," I said, confused. "I don't mind."

He replaced the pictures in his jacket pocket and pulled back onto the highway.

The snow was still falling heavily, making it difficult to see clearly. Jonathan drove for several miles before I finally asked the question that had troubled me all afternoon.

"Why didn't you tell me you were there that night . . . the night of my accident?" I tried not to make it sound like an accusation, but my words had an edge to them.

"I wanted to," he said regretfully. "I wanted to tell you the minute you came out of the coma. I wanted to scoop you up from that hospital bed and take you as far away as I could."

"You were at the hospital?"

He nodded as if the answer should have been obvious.

"When?" I asked.

"Every day. I came as an intern doing research on coma patients."

"And nobody ever questioned you? Not even my dad?"

"Actually, nobody seemed to notice." He smiled at me and then he shrugged. "I usually visited in the middle of the night, and I always brought music."

I drew in a quick breath of air. "I remembered the music when I woke up," I recalled. "My dad thought it was just because there was so much music tucked away inside my memory."

"It's supposed to help coma patients," he explained.

"But why didn't you say anything afterwards, when I came out of it?"

"Say what? 'Hey Beth, I've been stalking you. By the way, I'm sort of immortal.' They'd have committed one of us for sure." He was smiling, but it was only a half smile. His eyes reflected no hint of humor. "I confess though, I've broken several rules since the night of your accident."

I coughed a chuckle and struggled to keep myself from laughing. He looked so serious—so guilty.

"Go ahead and laugh," he said sarcastically, "but a lot of people are unhappy with me because of how I handled things with you."

"Like who?" I asked suspiciously.

"Like your uncle for one. He had a fit when he found out I signed on as a tutor at the CRC. I figured he'd forbid you to see me—I was prepared for it. I was actually shocked when he let you go to the Palisades that day."

"If it makes you feel any better, he thinks you have a good aura." I reached over and nudged his arm with the side of my hand and he grinned. However, we'd gotten off my intended topic, and I wondered if it was merely by accident.

"So," I continued, "why were you watching me all those months?"

"It was an observation assignment—just like hundreds of others I'd been given."

"An assignment? Who assigned you?"

"The Lebas, indirectly. It's just standard procedure, nothing unusual. Do you remember what your uncle told you that day in the vortex room? As a hybrid gets closer to the age of adulthood, the Lebas observe them carefully for signs of reclamation—and for signs that a possessor might be trying to control them. As you know, immortal offspring are quite vulnerable during the early stages of reclamation."

"So when I first met you, that day at the practice rooms, that wasn't by chance?"

"Not completely. Obviously, I had no way of knowing you'd come to the music department that day, but if we hadn't met there, I would've figured out a way for you to run into me."

"Am I still your . . . assignment?" I asked, amused yet irked by the notion as well.

"My little étude," he said affectionately. He smiled and reached across the seat to brush the back of his hand down the side of my face. I scrunched my lips together and furrowed my brows, but he chuckled warmly.

"When were you first assigned to observe me?"

"Last year, when you auditioned for your scholarship."

The surprise must have shown on my face because he chuckled when he glanced at me.

"That's an evening I'll never forget," he said, ignoring my stunned reaction. "Never."

He allowed the car to roll to the side of the road again and shifted into park. When he turned to face me, the twinkle in his eyes seemed brighter than usual. He cupped my chin gingerly between his thumb and forefinger and fixed his gaze on mine.

"Seeing you walk onto the stage was like seeing an angel, like some heavenly being had been sent to wipe away years of frustration and guilt."

I started to roll my eyes, but he shook my chin gently in protest. I closed my eyes when I felt the flush in my cheeks burn.

"Then something strange happened. You raised your hands to the keyboard and I swear I saw something . . . something ethereal pass through you. I was convinced that I was witnessing the onset of reclamation, something nobody has ever witnessed in action."

The look of bewilderment on my face surprised Jonathan. It was instantly clear to him that I could not deny that something supernal had taken place that night. I quickly turned away. Was it possible? Had Jonathan actually seen what happened?

"Look at me, Beth," he said softly, turning my face toward his. "I can't explain everything that happened that night—what happened to you or to me—but I *knew* we'd be together eventually."

His eyes searched mine for a minute and then slowly their expression altered. My blood reacted to the change and my heart began to pound. The pattern of his breathing shifted as his eyes fully embraced mine. In a slight movement that was nearly undetectable, he moved his head from side to side.

"Beth," the sound of my name on his lips ignited an unexpected flame. "Do you feel what I'm feeling?"

If by that he meant could I burst into flames at any moment, then the answer was yes. The look in my eyes must have answered his question because before I could respond, he kissed me—slowly and gently at first—then more urgently, until we were both out of breath. Our lips parted spontaneously as we gasped for air and he laced his fingers through my hair, pulling me closer to him. His tongue caressed the top of mine, sending electric tremors pulsing through my veins. His body trembled.

We held onto each other for a long time, wrapped together in a kiss that I wished would never end. He finally pulled away slightly, his mouth a fraction of an inch from mine. But as our eyes met and held our breathing became even more staggered. The hunger in his eyes made me yearn to give myself to him completely; I had no doubt that I would—someday.

He closed his eyes and held me firmly against his chest for several minutes, his breath hot on my neck, his hands caressing my back. My willpower was turning to jelly. Then he released a deep sigh and started to laugh.

"I'll be right back," he said abruptly. With that, he climbed out of the car and disappeared into the blizzard. The windows in the car had fogged over so badly I couldn't see where he'd gone. I waited for several minutes, but when he didn't return I started to get anxious. I slid across the seat and climbed out his door. I could tell by the footprints in the snow that he'd walked around to the back of the car.

"Jonathan?" I waited. "Where did you go?"

I heard a faint groan that sounded like it was coming from the other side of the car, so I followed his path, stumbling awkwardly through the snow, until I reached the back of the car. That's when I saw him, lying face down—spread eagle—against a three foot bank of snow. I thought for a minute that he'd tripped or something.

"Jonathan?" I cried in alarm.

He rolled over onto his back and wiped the snow away from his amused face. He was grinning and groaning in mock agony.

"What are you doing . . . ?" I demanded, holding back a sudden urge to laugh.

He stood, covered head to toe in snow. He looked ridiculous, like a comical version of the abominable snow man.

"Ahhhhh!" he bellowed. He shook, throwing snow in all directions. "That's better."

"What's the matter with you?" I scolded jokingly.

"*You're* the matter with me!" he groaned. He walked straight up to me, gave me a quick peck on the cheek, and then strolled past me toward the front of the car. I stood, bewildered, as I watched him walk away. My eyes shifted back and forth between him and the place where he'd fallen in the snow.

"Are you ready?" His question hung in the distance.

I hesitated, considering my options.

"Beth?"

I took another look at the snow embankment, turned toward the car, and then back again to the pile of snow that still held the impression of his sprawled body.

Ah, what the heck! I decided, and with one leap, I threw myself face first into the snow.

So much for theatrics. The snow was much colder against my

face than I'd expected, and my cheeks instantly burned with the icy bite. I flipped over onto my back, quite gracelessly I might add, and let out a loud, uncontrolled shriek.

"Good grief . . . it's *cold!*"

Fortunately, it only took us another twenty minutes to reach the ranch. Once the snow thawed on our clothes, both Jonathan and I were soaking wet and uncomfortably cold—even with the heater blazing. Oh well, if I caught pneumonia, at least I had two more weeks before the new semester started.

We ran shivering from the car into the house where Jonathan immediately went to work building a roaring fire in the fireplace. All I wanted to do was get out of my wet clothes and soak in a tub of hot water.

When he took our coats and hung them in the entryway to dry, he noticed the light flashing on the answering machine. The first message was from his mom.

"Hi kids, guess you're already gone. We just wanted to wish you a Merry Christmas. I'll call you later tonight. Love you."

His mother's voice rang through the air oozing optimism, and Jonathan smiled pensively. He glanced over at me and shrugged.

"My mom."

The second message was from Carl, and it wasn't quite as optimistic.

"Hey, call me as soon as you get this. I tried the cell, but the call wouldn't go through. We need your help."

Uninvited Guest

CHAPTER 20

*J*onathan called Grace immediately. At first, I thought it was strange that he didn't call Carl, but I soon understood why.

"Grace, are you okay?" he asked as soon as she answered. He listened for a moment. "What happened?" He waited, listening intently, and then closed his eyes. "Are you sure you're all right?" He listened again, and then nodded his head quickly. "I'm coming to get you, don't worry. Let me talk to Carl."

He listened while Carl explained what had happened. I watched anxiously, only getting half of the conversation. Jonathan hung up the phone and I waited impatiently as he disappeared for a moment and then returned wearing dry clothes. He grabbed the keys from the entryway table before he finally explained.

"They're okay, but some idiot driving a truck tried to pass them around a blind curve. He ignored the double yellow lines and apparently didn't see an on-coming car in the opposite lane. Carl pulled as far to the right as possible to make room, but the driver of the truck either panicked or loss control and side-swiped Carl's car, knocking them into a ditch off the shoulder of the road."

"Oh my gosh!" I gasped. "Was anybody hurt?"

"No, but Grace is pretty freaked out. I knew she would be. It's hard enough for her to leave the ranch as it is." He pursed his lips and shook his head. "Carl says the kid stopped, walked over to the car and peered at them from the side of the road, and then took off. The other car never stopped, probably didn't even know there was an accident."

"Just like that? Hit and run?"

"I guess," Jonathan shrugged. "Carl wanted to call for help, but Grace made him wait until he heard from me."

"They must be freezing stuck out there all this time. Didn't anybody notice them in the ditch and stop?"

"I don't know . . . I didn't get all the details. Although knowing Grace, it wouldn't have mattered. She won't interact with strangers."

"Where are they?" I asked.

"From Carl's description, they're about forty-five minutes from here, maybe an hour. By the time I get there it'll be too icy and dark to do much about the car. I'll have to bring them back and deal with the car tomorrow."

"Should I go with you?" I asked.

"Of course. Unless . . . you'd rather stay here." He hesitated. It wasn't a pause that made me feel like he didn't want me to go, it was the kind that indicated there was something more important for me to do.

"And?" I waited for him to finish his sentence, but then he seemed to change his mind.

"Nah, I'd rather you came with me. I don't want to leave you alone."

"Wait a minute. Is there something else you need me to do?" I asked.

"No. Really, it's fine." The last thing he needed was an argument, but I could tell he was covering.

"Just tell me how I can help the most. What can I do?"

"I was thinking about Grace. It would be good if there was something to eat already prepared."

I looked at him as if he were crazy. Was he really thinking about food?

"I know it's preposterous, but she won't rest when she gets back—she'll step right into hostess mode."

Knowing Grace, that made sense. "No problem, I'll figure something out and have it ready." Jonathan seemed to appreciate the offer, but he still looked hesitant.

"Are you sure you won't mind?" he asked reluctantly.

"No. I'm happy to help. No problem. Just hurry back, okay?" A smile replaced the concern on Jonathan's face and he bent over and kissed me quickly on the mouth.

"Thank you," he sighed.

I followed him to the door and then rose onto my tiptoes to kiss his cheek.

"I love you, you know," he said, folding his arms around my neck. He gazed silently into my eyes for a brief moment and then smiled radiantly.

"I do know," I said as he brushed the side of my face with his fingers. He bent down and kissed me again—a lingering kiss that said he hated to leave.

Jonathan started out the door, but stopped short as a thought suddenly occurred to him. "Beth, if you need anything, *anything,* call Mason.

"Okay, get going," I ordered, "and hurry back."

It took me awhile to inventory the food in the kitchen, mostly because I didn't know where anything was. I was nowhere near the gourmet chef that Grace was, so I decided to keep it simple and make a stew using the leftover prime rib roast Grace had served the previous evening. I chopped some onions and potatoes, added carrots, celery, and tomatoes, and then topped it off with shredded cabbage.

Once I had all the ingredients simmering, I decided to look for a book to read. I meandered through the living room—watched the clock—added wood to the fire—watched the clock—flipped through a magazine—and watched the clock.

It felt like Jonathan had been gone forever, but in reality, it had been less than an hour. I finally wandered over to the piano and plucked a few melodies absentmindedly. I thought about the first time Jonathan and I met—at least, it was the first time for me—and I began playing Étude in E. Without the left hand, the piece was flat, lifeless, so I decided to try something different.

I opened the piano bench and sorted through a variety of books until I found what I was looking for—Eleanor's theme. I studied the music carefully and noticed that it was an old photocopy of the original with several notes marking different variations of the theme.

I recalled the bridge I'd heard in my dream. I could hear it playing clearly in my mind; it was just a matter of figuring out the notes. I trotted back into the kitchen, stirred the stew, and grabbed a pencil and some paper. I quickly drew several staff lines across the page and as I plucked through each measure of the bridge, I drew the respective notes on the staff. It didn't take long to frame the melody—it never did once a melody took hold in my mind—but composing the intricacies of a melody's counterparts was a different story. That required total concentration.

It wasn't uncommon for me to lose touch with my surroundings once I began composing, so it took awhile before I realized someone was knocking on the front door. I was so absorbed in the music that I was inclined to ignore the unexpected caller, but eventually the persistence of the knocking caused me to lose my train of thought.

"Ahrrgg!" I barked, throwing my pencil against the sheet music. "Who is it?!"

The knocking continued.

I stomped from the room wondering who on earth could be visiting on Christmas night. The ranch certainly wasn't "just in the neighborhood." I hesitated as I neared the double doors that led into the formal entryway. I considered turning around, but realized that whoever it was had probably heard the piano and knew somebody was home. Besides, what if it was important? Maybe there was an emergency at the stables, or perhaps it was Uncle Connor, back early from his trip.

The moment I stepped into the entryway hall, the knocking ceased. I waited for several seconds, listening, but there was nothing. I approached the door and peered through its diamond shaped window. All I could see through its beveled grooves were differing shades of white and gray.

A sudden gust of wind rattled the door and I jumped back. *Moron*, I thought. *Spooked by the wind. You're supposed to be the level-headed daughter of a scientist.* I let out a disgusted sigh and opened the door, determined to prove something to myself.

"Good grief!" I gasped as I stepped onto the porch. Snow flurries immediately enveloped me, snatching my breath away. The temperature had dropped drastically, probably into the single digits, and by the look of the roiling clouds darkening the sky, the storm had yet to unleash its full fury.

No one was there, so I clutched my shivering arms around my chest and stepped back into the house, shutting the door behind me. Then I turned the latch on the dead bolt until I felt it snap securely into place. Locking the door gave me a sense of comfort. It somehow made me feel safe from the impending storm.

"Drama queen," I murmured to myself.

"Oh, I wouldn't say that," a voice said calmly.

"Aghhhhhgh!" I whirled around so fast it made me dizzy.

"Geez, Beth! Relax. It's only me."

"Eric!" I took a deep breath, but my heart continued pounding. "What are you . . . how did you. . . ?"

"Merry Christmas, Beth." The overconfident, cocky grin on his face would normally have made me roll my eyes, but this time it raised the hair on the back of my neck.

It was obvious by Eric's attire that he'd been snowboarding. He still had on his beanie, and there was an almost yellow-looking ring around his eyes and the bridge of his nose where his goggles had been. His cheeks glowed with the type of dull rose color that resulted from spending an entire day unprotected from the sun's ultraviolet rays. They can burn even through thick cloud cover. I was sure Eric didn't care. He'd think it just made him look more macho.

"How did you get in here?" I demanded.

"I came through the back," he said, pointing to the back of the house.

"You what? Eric!"

"Hey, I tried knocking but nobody answered. I heard the piano, so I—"

"So you what? You decided to just let yourself into somebody else's house? Eric, you need to leave—right now," I insisted.

"What's the matter with you, Beth, calm down. I was out this way snowboarding and just decided to stop by and wish you a Merry Christmas. I tried to call you on my cell, but there's no signal out here. How do these people survive without their cell phones?"

"Eric . . . I mean it. You can't be here."

He ignored my protest and looked around the room. "Where's your boyfriend?"

"He'll be here . . . in a minute."

"You're alone." It was not a question.

An uneasy feeling formed in the pit of my stomach, like all of my internal organs were twisting into a tight knot. Eric and I were alone!

Jonathan's warning echoed in the back of my mind: "You have to be very careful around him, Beth."

"Jonathan's coming right back," I said casually. I knew I had to act as if everything was normal, but I wasn't sure I could pull it off.

Eric shrugged, indifferent.

"So, how was snowboarding today?" I asked, making small talk.

"Funny you should ask. I had a major wipeout and totally annihilated my board."

"You're kidding! That had to suck." My words sounded forced—or was it just my imagination?

"Yup." Eric's eyes continued to survey the room.

"Were you hurt?" I asked, trying to sound concerned.

"Yup," he said flatly.

"What happened?" I asked, afraid of the lack of emotion in his voice.

"Took a pretty hard hit to the back of my head. And here, look at this." He pulled his T-shirt away from his shoulder and revealed a nasty scrape along his shoulder and back.

"Oh my gosh!" I gasped. Blood was still oozing from the deeper parts of the gash. "Eric, you need to go have that looked at. You need stitches."

"I'll take care of it when I get home. It's not the first time I've been scraped up. Here, feel this." He grabbed my hand and rubbed it across a large lump on the back of his head. It had to be at least two inches in diameter.

I pulled my hand away quickly—too quickly. Eric raised his eyebrows and smirked.

"Not a great day on the slopes for you, was it?" I chuckled nervously.

"Well, yes and no."

"How so . . . ?" My words stuck in my throat. Eric smiled smugly as if this somehow pleased him.

"Getting hit in the head can do strange things to your memory. Sometimes it makes you forget things, but other times it can have the opposite effect. It's funny actually, one minute I was surveying a great jump, and the next thing I knew, I was flying into a grove of trees." He laughed. "Must've taken the jump with too much speed."

He paused for a moment as if he were reflecting on something. The knot in my stomach tightened.

"Yeah, that must have been it. Too much speed." He glanced at me briefly and then turned his focus to the flames in the fireplace. "You know, the instant the back of my head slammed into that tree, I had one of those *déjà vu* moments. I seemed to remember another time when I flew backwards into a tree. And then—*bam!*" He snapped his fingers and opened them into the air as if he'd just had an epiphany. "I remembered everything about that night at the bonfire."

He turned to face me, smirking. "It seems I have some unfinished business with your boyfriend," he declared. He stepped closer to me and touched my stunned face. "And with you!"

I jumped back immediately, putting as much distance between us as possible.

"Eric, you don't know what you're saying. You weren't yourself that night. You were drinking. . . ."

"So I've heard," he said, dismissing the fact. "You know what's funny?" He looked at me, waiting for me to respond. When I didn't, he shrugged his shoulders and went on. "I was so pissed off when my memory came back that all I could think of was getting home so I could call your boyfriend out. Imagine my shock when I saw *your* car on the drive home. Fortune was certainly smiling down on me. I was quite miffed when I discovered you weren't in the car—but then I saw your cocky cousin and your boyfriend's frigid sister, and a plan began to formulate. I think of it as a Christmas present from fate. So I decided to drop by and pay the two of you a visit."

Eric paused in mock disappointment. "Pity your boyfriend isn't here but look on the bright side, it gives me more time with you."

Terror gripped me and my chest tightened in a primordial response to his threat.

"Eric, please . . ."

"Eric, please," he mimicked, disgusted. His mouth twisted into a mocking smirk. "Although I have to admit, I kinda like the sound of you begging." He closed his eyes for a brief minute as if savoring a memory, then sighed heavily. "It *so* turns me on."

"Eric, listen . . . this isn't you. You aren't yourself right now." I circled around behind the sofa and eyed the staircase. I was too far away to make a run for it. Could I make it out the front door? Where would I go? Could I make it to the guest house? Eric was a star athlete; he'd overtake me effortlessly. Maybe I could make it to the kitchen. If I had a knife I could buy some time and figure out how to get away from him.

I backed away slowly toward the kitchen, but Eric mirrored each of my steps in perfect synchronization. I surveyed my surroundings, shooting quick glances around the room and making a note of each door and obstacle. If I could just keep away from him until Jonathan returned, then maybe. . . .

"You know Beth, I'm really disappointed in you. All this time you knew the truth about that night and you didn't care enough about me to tell me. I thought we were friends. I thought we had something special. You even had me convinced that you truly cared about me."

He followed my every move. With each step, he inched a little closer to me.

"We *are* friends, Eric. You know I care about you." I tried to sound brave and confident, but my voice cracked.

"I'm glad you said that, because in a few minutes you're finally going to *show* me just how much you care about me. And maybe if you're convincing enough, I won't hurt your boyfriend."

"Eric—*please!*" I begged.

"Eric, please . . . Eric, please. Hell, you're starting to sound like a broken record. You almost remind me of Jonathan's sappy little sister. She begged a lot, too."

"What are you talking about?"

"Don't be too upset, Beth. After all, Janine is the one who told us where you were. It's amazing what jealousy can do to a person."

"Told who? You're lying!" I screamed. "Janine would never hurt Jonathan that way!"

"She really didn't have a choice, but she did require a lot of persuading. In the end, we were merciful. She didn't suffer *too* much."

His words struck like heavy boulders plummeting from the sky. Janine destroyed? The thought was too unbearable. She was so meek and fragile. Why her?

"She was just a child!" I sputtered. "She was no threat to you."

"She tried to desert—AWOL—we couldn't allow that."

"Why do you keep saying *we*? Who is *we*?" I demanded.

"No one you need to worry about. Oh, and by the way, Janine was much, much more than a mere child. My time with her was very . . . satisfying. Although she wasn't very convincing—if you know what I mean—so I had to go back on my agreement not to harm Jonathan. I actually felt sorry for her. I would have enjoyed spending more time with her." He closed his eyes and smiled as if savoring a sweet memory. "I would hate to run out of time with you—"

"Stop it, Eric!" I demanded.

"Beth . . ." he shook his head pitifully, "I'll make this very simple. We're alone. Your boyfriend won't be back for at least another
half hour, and while I would prefer to have more time, that's plenty
of time for us to finish what we started in the woods . . . and for you
to *convince* me not to hurt him. I have to warn you though—you'll
have to be *very* convincing."

My stomach wrenched with nausea. Despair was crushing me,
just as the darkness had a few hours earlier in the vortex cellar. I was
shutting down. Jonathan had told me that this was how my brain
handled an overload of trauma, but I had to fight against that defense
right now. I couldn't allow myself to black out—not here—not like
this. I had to remain aware, to keep my brain alert. I pushed against
the despair with every ounce of strength I could muster. I just needed
to hold on until Jonathan returned. *Hold on, Beth. Hold on.*

"Eric, he'll kill you," I warned with renewed confidence. "You
have no idea what you're up against."

"Not if I kill him first," he chuckled darkly.

"You won't kill him! You can't."

"Oh, but I can," he murmured, "and I will."

"Eric, you don't understand. He's not human. You can't fight
him and win!"

"Now . . . you see," he said condescendingly, "that's where you're
wrong."

"He's too strong for you."

Eric laughed loudly and glared at me. "So confident, aren't
you!" He reached into his pocket and pulled out a knife. He flipped
it open, revealing a shiny silver blade. He held the blade up as if to
threaten me, and then pulled his eyebrows together in a tight line. I
thought he would lunge forward, but instead, he held the knife against
his own skin. With a lustful smirk on his face, he cut through his
skin and sliced his forearm open. The flesh beneath his skin turned
white instantly and then, as if a floodgate had opened, a rich pool
of bloody fluids covered his arm. Mixed among the red streams of
blood was a thick, clear liquid—exactly like the fluid that oozed
from Jonathan's wound the day we were at the lake.

"Impossible!" I hissed. I gaped at the bloody fluid as it dripped into small puddles on the floor. "Only an immortal has blood like that."

"Yes," he agreed wickedly, "that's why I needed Janine's fluids."

Eric's head began to twitch and his body jerked in awkward, unnatural spasms.

"Oops," he chuckled, "I don't think Eric liked cutting himself like that."

His words hung in the air, hovering.

He lifted the knife to his face and made another cut, this time slicing the skin along his jawbone. More blood formed and dripped in a stream to the floor. A growl rose in Eric's throat and his head twitched violently from side to side.

"Hmm," he said heartlessly, "he didn't care for that one, either."

Satisfied that he'd made his point, Eric tossed the bloody knife onto the floor. He stood with his eyes closed and his arms extended; it looked as though he were concentrating on something. Then, as if some invisible force were stitching his wounds together, the flesh along the edges of his cuts began to move back into their original place, reuniting the flesh until there was not a trace of blood present. The skin scabbed over before my eyes, leaving deep red marks where the open wounds had been. I wondered how much worse the cut on his back had been before he showed it to me. It had probably healed by now too.

I watched, horrified, until I realized his eyes were still closed. I took advantage of the opportunity and ran for the kitchen. He was behind me in seconds—I had to think fast. I grabbed the pot of simmering stew from the stove and heaved it into his chest and face. He gave an ear-piercing shriek and began to shake convulsively. He spat and sputtered and his face twitched, jerking violently from side to side. He growled loudly, clutching at his face.

I ran as fast as I could up the stairs, hoping to reach my bedroom before he caught up with me; but as soon as I reached the door, a sharp blow in the center of my back knocked the air out of me and sent me reeling to the floor. I doubled over, gasping for breath as

I tried to crawl to safety. He flung his body over mine, then rose slightly and forced me onto my back.

Still gasping for air, I writhed beneath him and struggled to get free. He pinned my right arm beneath his knee, trapping me under his weight. Then he lifted my left arm above my head and held it down with his hand. His face was just inches from mine. I relived the horror of the night in the woods and resigned myself hopelessly to the fact that this time, Jonathan wouldn't arrive in time to save me.

"Leave!" I demanded, remembering my experience on the spiral staircase. But my attacker just chuckled. "Leave now!" I commanded more intensely. This time he roared with laughter.

"It won't work, Beth. You can't order me out of someone else's body, especially not one with immortal fluids running through its veins. Only Eric has the power to force me to leave, and he's busy right now. You see, deep inside, he dreams of experiencing you—he longs for it. He won't resist when he knows he's this close to having you—even if he has to share the experience with me."

I couldn't win. I couldn't order him away and my body was no match for his. Even if I were stronger, my human body was far too weak to withstand the strength of an immortal. My mind was the only weapon I had left. I searched frantically for ideas, for help, for the right words to reach Eric before it was too late. I struggled to recall the words Jonathan had spoken to me while I was under the possessor's influence. Perhaps I could bring Eric out of his darkness and back to the forefront of his mind, the way Jonathan had brought me to the top of the spiral staircase. I wasn't sure how, but I had to try.

I made a concerted effort to relax every muscle in my body, giving in to Eric's hold on me. I allowed his weight to press against me.

"Ahhh," he sighed, pleased. He rested his face on mine, panting heavily into my ear. "That's much better."

He brushed his lips several times against my ear and then began passionately kissing my neck, my jawbone, my shoulder. . . .

"You taste just the way Eric dreamed you would," he whispered, moving his lips back to my ear. "Yes . . . he likes this very much."

"Eric, listen to me . . . you can fight this," I said calmly. "You can make him leave."

Eric's body jerked slightly and I could sense that he was able to hear me, but he continued panting in my ear and letting the full weight and length of his body press against mine. It made it difficult for me to breathe, and impossible for me to move. He reached for my mouth with his lips, but I turned my head away from him.

"Try, Eric, please . . . please!"

A deep groan rose in Eric's throat and his head began to twitch from side to side like it had earlier.

"Eric, you can fight him. Try!"

He flung his head back and growled furiously. His muscles tightened around me and he dug his fingers into my shoulder with his free hand, tearing at my shirt angrily. I wanted to scream, to rant and rail and force him away from me, but I knew that would only excite him further. I had to remain calm if I was going to reach Eric.

"Eric, you're hurting me," I cried. Tears spilled down my face. "Please . . . don't hurt me," I pleaded desperately.

A loud moan echoed from his throat and for a split second, I thought I saw something flicker in his eyes. I peered into them; but before I could look too closely, he closed them.

I suppose I should have predicted what was coming next, but it caught me off guard and ripped away my confidence. Eric opened his eyes—and he was gone. Totally. There was no hint of Eric in the bright yellow eyes that stared back at me. I screamed as loudly as my strength would allow. I screamed repeatedly, trying futilely to twist my body out from under his.

"Ah, Beth, and you were doing so well. I guess it'll be up to Jonathan's other sister to save him. Perhaps she'll be better at convincing me to let him live."

"NO!" I shouted. "I'll do it. I'll convince you—I promise. Leave Grace alone!"

I began to sob uncontrollably. I was beaten. I knew it and the possessor knew it. My only hope was that it would be over before

Jonathan got home. I couldn't bear the thought of him walking in on this.

"Hmm. There must be something very special about Grace. Maybe I'm working on the wrong girl."

"No! I'll do whatever you want—anything. I won't fight you." My words reverberated through the air in broken sobs of desperation.

"That's not enough anymore," he said coldly, his yellow eyes burning into me like fiery darts.

"What more do you want from me?" I whimpered, distraught.

"I want you to convince me that you *want* it, that you want *me* the way you want Jonathan. I want you to make me believe you love me. And then I want you to beg me to love you back." He looked down at me smugly. "Can you do that for me, Honey? Can you do it for Jonathan? For Grace?"

"Why are you doing this to me?" I blubbered, closing my eyes.

Where was the blackness now when I needed it? Why wouldn't it overcome me and render me unconscious. It was the only way I could endure the inevitable horror that awaited me.

"Oh, Beth Anne, surely you already know the answer to that. You *belong* with me. You see, whether your cells reclaim their immortal state or stay mortal, you have the power of the bloodline running through your veins, making you a rightful heir to all the privileges and powers invested by the covenant of the Lebas. With you by my side, we can further our work among the possessors and the immortals and overturn the power of the Lebas.

Your body, my spirit, male and female united as one—the perfect union. We'll become as the gods, and nobody will ever strip us of our power and glory."

"You're insane!" I cried.

"Perhaps. But I've waited nineteen years to bring you under my control. I was so close the night of your . . . *accident.*" He said the word mockingly. "If your boyfriend hadn't interrupted me that night, we wouldn't be going through all this right now. You would already be mine. That's twice he's thwarted my plans."

He reached around, grabbing for my left hand, and pulled it in front of him. He inspected it carefully, rubbing his thumb over my scar. "I am sorry about this, however. I always loved hearing you play the piano. I really miss that."

I pulled my hand away defensively, but he pulled it under his knee, pinning it to my side.

"Twice your boyfriend has stopped me from having what belongs to me. It won't happen a third time," he said coldly. "Now, we've wasted enough time. Do we have a deal, or not?"

"Just get it over with," I begged. "Please."

"No, no, no," he hissed tauntingly. "The stakes have been raised, remember?"

The sobs rose again in my throat, only this time they were the sobs of a helpless child. I had nothing left. No options. I knew he would go for Grace before he went for Jonathan, and I couldn't bear to think of her broken, abused, and discarded the way Janine had been.

The possessor became annoyed. He grabbed my shoulders and shook me roughly.

"I'm growing impatient, Beth. Do we have a deal?"

I closed my eyes as tightly as I possibly could and nodded. Even with my eyes closed, I sensed the elation in him; I could feel his growing anticipation.

"Goooood," he sighed hungrily. "Now, let's do this right. Go wash your face and get rid of those tears. I want to see you smile at me the way you smile at him—but don't take too long. The deal's off if we're interrupted, and I plan to take my time and savor every part of you.

The possessor released his hold on me. Robotically, I walked to the bathroom and splashed cold water over my face. There were no tears left to cry—there was only emptiness. It was the loss of my mother, the loss of my hand, the loss of my friend Eric, and now the loss of my happiness all rolled into one empty black hole.

In total despair, I dropped to my knees and buried my face in my hands.

God . . . if you're there, please . . . please tell me, how do I do this? How do I survive it? They were the words of a silent prayer, but I had no idea to whom I was praying. If there was a God, why should he help me tonight? Who was I to him?

I waited. Silence was my only answer.

My mother had been wrong. She'd told me to listen to my heart, but my heart was dying with each second that passed, bringing me closer to a hideous doom. I resolved that even though I would die tonight—if not physically, then definitely emotionally and spiritually—at least I would know that Grace was safe. As for Jonathan? I knew he would try to kill my attacker, but how do you kill something that never lived? How do you kill something that feeds off the life of others? I had no answers, only questions—too many questions.

A sudden knock on the bathroom door startled me.

"It's time, Beth," Eric's voice chimed impatiently.

Sacrifice
CHAPTER 21

*R*eluctantly, I opened the bathroom door, resigned to my fate. Two yellow eyes glared lustfully at me from across the room as Eric's possessor stood beside the bed that would soon become my coffin—perhaps not literally, but definitely in every way that truly mattered. I stepped hesitantly through the doorway, dragging my feet as if they were dead weights.

I forced myself to move toward Eric, one unbearable step at a time. I would have to be convincing, to make him believe that I wanted to be there—or the deal was off. I had to try. No, not try—succeed. I had to keep the possessor from going after Grace. I knew deep down that I couldn't protect Jonathan. I prayed he would be strong enough to protect himself.

I took another labored step toward the monster who had over-powered Eric's mind and body. Each daunting step brought me closer to the thick cloud of darkness that would soon embrace me, body and soul. I inched forward until at last I stood face to face with my destiny. The evil inside Eric groaned, relishing the thrill of victory. He licked his lips as his eyes traced the shape of my body with obvious deliberation. Unable to conceal his morbid excitement, his eyes widened, wild with the anticipation of sealing our deal. My stomach lurched as his hideous gaze burned through every inch of me. But I forced myself to stand erect and not turn away.

Then, through the window, a stream of brilliant light cut briefly across the room. It was no more than a fleeting glimpse—appearing and then disappearing as quickly as it came. But somehow it gave me a glimmer of hope.

Then a thought coursed through my mind. *Eric's feelings—focus on Eric's feelings for you.*

At first I was confused, unable to determine how Eric's feelings could help me in this situation. After all, wasn't it his feelings for me that had made him vulnerable to the possessor? Then, just as clearly as if another person were present in the room, I heard a voice. It was a reassuring voice which I *felt* more than heard.

Look through his eyes. Find Eric.

I only had a split second to formulate a plan. I glared scornfully into the yellow eyes that calculated my every move. My resolve recoiled at the hideous sight; everything in me screamed to turn away. But I was compelled by the voice to remain firm. Those eyes were the key. I must force myself to look into them; rather, I must look *through* them. My gaze had to reach beyond the evil that stared at me greedily.

You must find Eric. He is still there.

I dug deep, clutching at whatever courage I could muster. I fixed my gaze on the yellow eyes that now glowered back at me with an ominous wickedness that was intended to intimidate me into total submission. But at that moment, it wasn't fear that coursed through my veins, it was courage—fierce, undaunted courage. I focused intently on the possessor, reminding myself repeatedly to focus on Eric in my mind.

I recalled something Eric had said to me—that I had never given him a chance to make me forget about Jonathan. They were silly words at the time, downright pathetic, but they burned in my memory now as though he'd said them only moments earlier. And then a plan unveiled itself.

"Eric," I spoke calmly, funneling all my mental energy toward him. "You were right about Jonathan. I never gave you a chance to prove that you love me more than he does."

The golden eyes blinked involuntarily.

"I'm offering you that opportunity now."

Eric's face twitched as I spoke, and his left shoulder jerked stiffly. *Don't look away,* I told myself.

"Do you remember the day you tried to kiss me?" I continued. "You insisted that if I'd let you kiss me, I'd know how you felt about me. You were positive that you could make me forget about Jonathan. Do you remember that?" I held his gaze firmly, refusing to free his eyes when the yellow orbs twitched.

"No, Eric, look at me," I demanded abruptly. "I *need* you to look at me. I *want* you to look at me." I reached up and unbuttoned my blouse, letting it hang open.

His eyes fixed on my body, but they were tortured eyes that shifted nervously from side to side.

"Kiss me now Eric," I ordered, "only let it be *your* lips that press against mine, *your* breath that I taste, and your body that takes me—not *his.*" Eric jerked and his eyebrows furrowed into a hard line.

"I want *you* to love me . . . not the monster that's inside you."

It was a sensual plea intended to mask my desperation. I shook my blouse free and let it fall to the floor.

"If you *want* me, I'm yours. *Yours alone.* Don't allow *him* to take this from us. This is *our* moment. It belongs to you and me—alone."

Still fixing my gaze on his eyes, I reached up and wrapped my arms around Eric's neck. His body trembled beneath my touch. Undeterred, I stepped onto my tiptoes and pulled his face to mine, pressing my lips hard against his. His reaction was instant. He moaned as my lips parted, and then he circled my waist with his arms and pulled me tightly against him. He groaned as he slid his hands hungrily up and down the full length of my back, connecting our bodies with every motion. He pulled me closer to him as his desire grew more and more urgent.

After several moments, he pushed me away abruptly with a painful, shrill cry that sounded like an animal about to take its last breath. The tremors in his body transformed into violent shudders and his cry became a terrifying growl that raised all the hair on my arms. His head snapped back and forth violently and his face twisted into hideous contortions. I heard a loud pop, a crack, and then he screamed. His agonizing roar ripped through the room with so much power that it shook the walls. He began clawing at his own skin, slashing and tearing until his fingers were soaked with his own blood.

I backed away—terrified that he would unleash his anger on me at any moment. I reached down and grabbed my blouse, but he ignored my movements. I hurriedly flung my arms through the sleeves before I heard another bone-splitting crack. Both of Eric's shoulders dislocated and twisted sideways, rendering his arms useless. The growling intensified, but the clawing and scraping had ceased. His eyes began to vibrate fiercely; then they rolled up and down in their sockets, each time revealing the whites of Eric's eyes. This horrifying sequence was repeated several times as his body continued to twist and bend grotesquely. Finally, as if all his strength had left him, Eric's body folded into a limp heap on the bedroom floor.

A paralyzing scream pulsated through the air as several dark shapes swirled around him, hovering above his motionless body. Suddenly, they whirled into a spinning funnel that turned every loose object in the room into a dangerous flying missile. I wanted to run to Eric and help him, but the primordial instinct to save myself dominated. I whipped around to flee, but there, staring balefully at me from the floor-to-ceiling mirror adjacent to the door, were eight shadowy figures—each with glowering golden eyes. One stood out from the rest. I recognized him immediately. His features were an exact match to the drawings I'd made as a child. His familiar and once friendly smile was now one of sarcasm and rage.

"Bailey!" My whisper was barely audible.

"We're not through here, Beth Anne," he hissed. "Do. not. think. you. have. won!"

His threatening voice sent cold chills down my spine. Instinct took over and I scurried as fast as I could through the door into the darkened hallway. The pictures that hung on the hall walls swung violently from side to side, then detached themselves and flew across the narrow space, slamming into the opposite wall so hard they shattered into hundreds of lethal crystals. The house quaked violently. I clamored down the long hallway, tripping over a thick, wooden frame. As I sprawled forward, awkwardly trying to break my fall, I sliced the palm of my right hand on a jagged fragment of glass. I staggered, half-crawling across the floor, until I reached the stairway. Grabbing for the railing, I held on tightly as I braced myself against the shaking of the house, then I stumbled my way down the stairs. Halfway down, a sudden force crashed against me, knocking my legs out from under me and flipping me over the railing. It left me dangling in the air, clutching frantically to the swaying handrail.

Then the shaking suddenly stopped and the house was still.

I heard the rattle of a door opening and closing and footsteps quickly crossed the entryway. I turned my head in time to see Grace, Carl, and Jonathan rushing in, panicked by the devastating scene in front of them. Grace gasped when she saw the bloody knife on the floor, and Jonathan's eyes flashed swiftly around the room until they focused on me. His eyes widened in horror. He sprang quickly across the room and up the stairs, two at a time.

"Dear God, no! Beth!" he yelled. "Hang on!"

"Jonathan!" I wailed. In a moment he was by my side. Relief washed over me, but my body began to shudder in violent convulsions. I wanted to reach for him, but my arms were locked around the railing—welded in place. Blood oozed from my hand in streams, running down my arm and over the railing.

In one fluid motion, Jonathan reached over the handrail, wrapped one arm around my waist, and pulled me back to the stairs. He set me down gently and held me to him, stroking my hair and rocking me back and forth.

"Beth," he choked, "what happened?"

I was too hysterical to respond. All I could do was cling to him while my breath heaved in sporadic waves. My mind whirled with images of Eric's body lying upstairs in a limp mass.

"Beth," he choked, "what happened?"

All I could do was cling to him while my body shook violently. My head whirled with the image of Eric's body lying upstairs in a limp mass. I knew he was dead; there was no way a human body could survive the torture that had been inflicted upon him. I also knew that I was wholly responsible for what had happened to him.

"E-Eric!" I managed to sputter between gulps of air.

Jonathan stiffened. "What about Eric?"

"Up . . . stairs," I choked. Jonathan jerked his head around to look up the stairway, then he spun around and looked wildly at Carl.

Carl flew up the stairs in a rage and disappeared around the corner. I could hear his footsteps crushing the shattered wood and glass as he made his way down the long hallway.

"No!" I screamed after him. "Carl. No!" He didn't respond.

"Jonathan, stop him! They'll kill him!" I bellowed in panic. He loosened his grip on me and handed me over to Grace.

"Get her downstairs," he ordered. Grace scooped me away from his arms and steadied me down the stairs.

Once again I heard the sound of feet clattering on broken glass and debris as Jonathan went to find Carl and Eric. Grace settled me on the couch and hurriedly grabbed a blanket to wrap around me. Working quickly, she tore a strip from her shirt and wrapped it around my hand to stop the bleeding.

"I'm so sorry." My shaking voice cracked through my tears. "I . . . didn't know. I. . . ."

"Shh, shh." Grace brushed a dampened lock of hair away from my tear-streaked face. "It's okay, Beth. Of course you didn't know. It's okay. Shh." Her calm voice was reassuring and I was so exhausted that I slowly began to relax into the cushions on the couch. I raised my hand to my forehead and squeezed, trying to relieve the pounding throb that hammered against my brain.

A few moments later, Jonathan appeared at the bottom of the stairs. Carl was only a few steps behind him. Jonathan looked anxiously at Grace and then glanced at me. Something unspoken passed between them as she studied the expression on his face. She shifted her glance to Carl who slowly shook his head and said nothing. She sighed despairingly, lowering her glance to the floor.

"I'm so sorry, Beth," she whispered.

The meaning behind her words didn't sink in at first. There was pain behind them, the kind of pain reserved only for news that is too devastating to bear. The same kind of pain behind the words I'd heard when I came out of my coma and asked to see my mom. I stared blindly in front of me for a moment. Then my gaze shifted to Jonathan. The bleak expression on his face confirmed what Grace was trying to tell me.

"Oh, no! No. No. No," I screamed. "No!"

Jonathan was by my side in an instant, pulling me into his arms.

"Oh, Eric . . . Eric."

"Shh," Jonathan hissed softly against my ear. "He wants to see you," he whispered.

"He's not . . . ? He's okay?" I sobbed, suddenly hopeful.

Jonathan shook his head. "No, Beth. I'm so sorry. There's too much internal damage for his body to bear."

"But he's still alive?"

Jonathan cupped my face between his hands and looked somberly into my eyes. "Barely."

"He doesn't have much time, Beth," Carl said in a low voice. "He's asking for you."

I struggled to pull the blanket away from my body. It no longer warmed and comforted me; it restrained me. Grace reached down and gently removed it, freeing my arms and legs. I swung my feet to the floor, but the minute I stood the room began to spin and I lost my balance. Jonathan quickly lifted me into his arms and carried me upstairs to Eric.

The grotesque sight of Eric's crumpled body made me instantly ill. His legs were sprawled beneath him, bent in unnatural folds under the weight of his torso. His shoulders appeared hunched behind his head which hung sideways, making one of his shoulders much higher than the other. His arms lay limply at his side. Deep, bloody gouges were etched in his hideously torn face, arms, and chest. It looked as if someone had taken a jagged scalpel and sliced into his body at random intervals. Dark red blood flowed from each laceration, collecting in a pool beside his body. There was no sign of the clear fluid that had been there earlier.

With enormous effort, I hid my shock at the mangled sight before me. Although Eric's eyes were open, they were devoid of light—their expression dull and filmy. I cried at the painful contrast to their usual bright, playful countenance. He didn't seem to notice when I entered the room.

"He can't see," Carl whispered quietly behind me.

"Oh, Eric. . . ." My whisper was barely audible.

Eric's mouth twitched into the hint of a smile. It was the only indication that he was aware of my presence. Jonathan led me closer to him and then whispered softly into my ear. "You need to get very close in order to hear him."

I tiptoed across the floor to where Eric lay and slowly dropped to my knees so I could get as close to his face as possible.

"Eric!" I whimpered. "I'm so sorry."

"It's not so bad," he muttered in a broken whisper, and to my utter amazement, he was trying to smile. "Not as bad as being sacked by eleven football players."

I couldn't believe it; he was trying to be funny. The absurdity of it was more than I could handle. I made no attempt to stop the tears that now flowed in a steady stream down my face.

"Thanks, Beth," he whispered, "for helping me fight him. I wasn't . . . strong enough . . . on my own." He coughed, choking on the words. He winced each time he coughed and I knew he was in far greater agony than he would admit.

"Eric, we're getting you some help. You'll be okay, you will!" I spoke the words fervently, but with false conviction. I needed to believe there was a chance that he would pull through this. Eric blinked his eyes and then held them shut for a lingering second. It was his way of disagreeing with me. He had already accepted the inevitable.

I spun around when I felt Jonathan's hand on my shoulder; I sensed by his touch that the end was near. I turned back to face Eric and noticed that his lips were moving again, but the sound was so low I couldn't make out his words. I bent my head so that my ear was next to his mouth.

"Do me a favor?" he whispered.

"Of course," I choked.

"Better hear . . . first," he stammered, trying to laugh.

"What is it?"

"Don't let anyone . . . find me here. Not like . . . this." I didn't understand. But Eric didn't have much strength left so I readily agreed.

"We won't, Eric. We won't."

He blinked his eyes slowly again and started to gag. His eyes widened in reaction to his obvious struggle to breathe. I rested my face against his and stroked his hair as his breathing regulated somewhat. He moaned faintly and I turned again to look into his eyes. They were closed, yet he was smiling.

"Tell Darla . . . she was right," he whispered.

"Right about what?" I asked, but he never had a chance to answer. His chest rose as he gasped his final breath and just like that, his body went limp. His eyes slowly opened but there was no light in them.

Eric was gone.

The remainder of the night passed in a dark fog. I heard Carl and Jonathan talking in low voices, but I couldn't understand what they were saying—nor did I care. I didn't want to focus. I couldn't bear the finality of both Eric and Janine being dead, their bodies abused and mutilated. The reality of losing them churned like a violent, twisting storm inside me and wrapped in the vortex of that storm was an all too familiar pain—the pain of grief, coupled with guilt.

At some point during the evening, Jonathan carried me downstairs and laid me in a makeshift bed on the floor in front of the fire. Faint snatches of the conversation between Carl and Grace registered in my mind while Jonathan worked to clear the upstairs hallway of the broken glass and debris.

Eric's lifeless body lay upstairs in Janine's bedroom. Fleeting thoughts of his parents, his friends, the football team, and Darla weaved in and out of my mind, but I kept shaking them away. I wanted my mind to be empty—void of all thoughts.

And then there was Janine, beautiful Janine. She'd suffered a fate worse than death. Jonathan and Grace hid their emotions from me when I told them what had happened to her, but I understood more than they knew.

"Shouldn't we call the coroner?" Grace asked Carl.

"Grace, he didn't want to be found like this."

"But we have to take care of him."

"Your brother has an idea," Carl explained. "It might work."

What? What was Jonathan's idea? I was so tired. I could only grab fragments of their conversation.

I fought the urge to close my eyes, afraid of what I might see in the darkness. I must have dozed off at some point, however, because I was suddenly aware that Jonathan was lying beside me on the floor, his arm locked securely around me, cradling my back against his chest. And that's where he stayed until dawn broke a few hours later.

When I awoke, I was surprised to find Grace curled up on the couch above us. But then reality hit, and I broke into a new round of tears. Jonathan jumped, startled by my abrupt outburst. He used his free arm to turn me toward him. I rested my head against his chest and cried. Without saying a word, he folded his arms tightly around me and held me close, stroking my back until my sobs finally subsided.

Death

CHAPTER 22

The unexpected news of Eric's death stunned the small town of Andersen. The story ran on the local news just moments after Eric's parents were notified of the tragic "accident" that had ended his life. It was by far the most devastating shock in the town's recent history.

Andersen High School's most promising athlete, Eric Daniels, died yesterday in a tragic snowboard accident at Grand Targhee Ski Resort. The body of eighteen-year-old Daniels was found early this morning by one of the resort's search and rescue crewmembers. Daniels was reported missing late last night when he failed to return home from a snowboarding trip. Local officials are calling the tragic death an accident. According to investigating officer Anthony McKay, Daniels was snowboarding in an area that was off-limits. Local searchers located his body at the bottom of a deep ravine where he had apparently lost control after attempting a dangerous jump. One resort official claims that as many as nine accidents in the past two years have been attributed to daredevil antics by overconfident teenagers snowboarding in areas that are out of resort boundaries. According to teammate Thomas Stewart, Daniels was well-known for his willingness to take risks, both on and off the football field.

The news channel followed the story with a series of recommended safety precautions for skiers and snowboarders, and even sponsored free snowboarding lessons in honor of Eric's memory.

Nearly every citizen of Andersen attended Eric's funeral. It was a closed casket service due to the severe nature of his wounds. Members of the high school football team signed a team ball and gave it to Eric's grieving mother while members of the school band played a melancholy version of "Amazing Grace." In a ceremony immediately following the graveside service, the team retired Eric's jersey number. The school held a special service honoring his achievements over the years that provided an opportunity for his friends to speak about their memories of him.

I participated dully in each honorary service, dutifully going through all the motions. I offered my condolences to his family, helped Darla and a small group of her friends serve at the luncheon that followed the funeral, and worked with the senior class officers to take up an offering to help the family with funeral and burial fees.

I felt like a hypocrite through every act of service. I knew the truth about Eric's death—but the truth could never be told. And although Eric would have appreciated Jonathan and Carl's efforts to make his death look like an heroic accident, it went against everything I believed to perpetuate the lie, no matter how noble the cause. I went along, however, because I owed Eric that—and so much more.

Jonathan and Carl tried their best to convince me that Eric's death was not my fault, but I couldn't escape the reality that if it were not for me, he'd still be alive.

"Beth, trust me on this," Jonathan sighed, exasperated. "The possessor would have killed Eric no matter what happened with you. It was his plan from the beginning to use Eric's body to get to you and then dispose of it. He would have taken you by force either way—if not through Eric, then through someone else. Eric saved you. In the end, he was a hero. He wouldn't want you to blame yourself."

I heard the words and I knew I was being irrational, but I needed someone to blame. If I'd never moved to Andersen, Eric would still be alive. Nobody could dispute that fact.

Darla was amazing throughout everything. She maintained a noble posture, always thinking of others' grief before her own. She visited Eric's family daily and took care of all the small details that Eric's mom couldn't handle. She drove Eric's younger brother and sister to school each morning and helped them with their homework at night. She made sure dinner was prepared so that Eric's mom could rest. I waited and watched, certain that eventually she'd have some sort of an emotional meltdown; but she managed to hold herself together long enough to help Eric's family through the worst of those first few days following the initial shock of his death.

When I first met Darla, I wondered if she were for real. I'd searched for flaws in her character; of course, I never found any. She was by far the most sincere person I'd ever met. In the days following Eric's funeral, I watched her focus so intently on putting other's needs before her own that I was convinced she was far more angel than human. If any mortal deserved to become immortal, she did.

It was nearly two weeks after the funeral when she finally broke down and allowed herself to mourn. It wasn't until then that I realized Darla still secretly loved Eric. I remembered Eric's last words to me, and I knew I had to find a way to tell her what he'd said. The trick was figuring out a way to relay the message since by all accounts, nobody was with Eric when he died. I could never tell her that they were his final words.

If I intended to honor both of Eric's last requests, I'd have to be party to another lie. The decision was not an easy one for me to make, but once I witnessed the depth of Darla's grief, I realized I had no choice.

The lie came as naturally as telling somebody about the events of my day.

"I used to think we were kindred spirits," Darla reminisced. "We could finish each other's sentences effortlessly, and we always knew when one of us was keeping something from the other." She paused, but her silence didn't feel like an invitation for me to talk, so I remained quiet and waited for her to continue.

"We used to play house when we were little, and we always teased each other that if we weren't married by the time we were twenty, then we'd marry each other. It was a funny joke until we turned sixteen."

Darla's countenance dropped when she said the word *sixteen*. "I guess twenty seemed a little too close for comfort by that time," she muttered sadly, "at least for him. It's no wonder he started putting distance between us."

"He loved you, you know," I offered, searching for some way to comfort her.

"I thought he did once," she lowered her eyes, "but it was never the same way I loved him. I realize that now."

She sighed and paused for a moment before continuing.

"You know, I was never so sure of anything in my life than I was that we'd be married someday. I know you probably think I'm nuts," she glanced at me and half rolled her eyes, "but I honestly believed that someday, when all the cards had been dealt and played, it would just be him and me. That's how it was when we were kids—and that's how it was supposed to be when we grew up." She choked through the words, unable to hold back her tears. "At least, that's how I felt. If I hadn't believed it, I never would have. . . ."

She broke down and sobbed in my arms like a small child.

"Darla," I said as I consoled her, "Eric told me something, something that he wanted me to tell you some day—when I thought the time was right."

She lifted her head and studied me quizzically, raising both her eyebrows. "What?" she sniffled.

"He said for me to tell you that you were right."

She pulled her eyebrows together and tilted her head to one side. "When did he say that?" she asked, confused.

This was the part where the truth became fuzzy, but I owed it to Eric. I owed it to both of them.

"Right after I asked him to kiss me," I admitted guiltily. It was only half a lie.

"What?" she gasped. "You did what?"

She gaped at me incredulously, waiting for an explanation. I didn't want to say any more because up until this point, everything I'd told her was technically true. But I could tell by the look on her face that she wasn't going to let it go.

"I . . . needed him to kiss me," I finally answered.

"But what about Jonathan?"

"Remember when you told me that Eric was sure if I'd give him a chance, if I would kiss him—really kiss him, just once—he could make me forget about Jonathan? I-I suppose I wanted to be certain . . . before I-I—"

"Before you could sleep with Jonathan?" she interrupted. Her icy words of accusation made me sound so shallow that I wanted to protest immediately, but this wasn't about me, this was about Eric.

"Yeah, I guess." Every muscle in my body cringed.

I expected her to hit me or scream at me or do something to let me know how upset she was, but I didn't expect her to laugh.

"I knew it!" she accused scornfully. "I knew you had something for Eric!"

"No, it wasn't like that—"

"Shut up, Beth! Admit it for once. You aren't so perfect!"

"I never claimed to be perfect," I retaliated.

"Always so noble, the faithful friend who would never break the code when all along she was going behind my back."

"No!" I shouted. "I never went behind your back!"

"Stop lying! How many times were you with Eric before you dumped him for your precious Jonathan?"

If she only knew the irony of her words. How could I make her understand without telling her what really happened? This was so much harder than I expected.

"Darla, I'm so sorry. I never meant to hurt you, please believe me. I only. . . ."

"It doesn't matter anymore, does it?" She slumped, her voice suddenly low and calm.

The lie wrenched my gut. "Darla, listen to me. Eric said you were right about him. I didn't know what he meant, but don't you see? He must have been fighting his true feelings for you all along." The deception was firmly entrenched. I would carry the guilt for lying for the rest of my life.

Darla looked up at me, cheeks tear-streaked. "I knew it," she whispered. "I knew something must have happened." Her tone had shifted from accusatory to resolved.

"You lost me," I said, confused.

"Right before Christmas Eric called and said he needed to see me. We went for a drive and ended up at the hot springs—you know the place I'm talking about."

I nodded. My stomach churned with renewed angst.

"It was the first time we'd talked openly about what happened between us. Anyway, he told me that it bothered him to see me with Evan. I told him that deep down he must still have feelings for me, that he really did love me after all. He didn't say anything, he just kissed me, I mean he *really* kissed me, in a way he'd never kissed me before. Suddenly, it was just like the other time at the hot springs. He wanted me, and I knew . . . I knew he loved me."

My heart fell. Surely she wasn't implying that they'd—

She looked at me and then grinned through her tears. After a quick minute, her grin broadened into a perfectly angelic smile.

Although the facts were heavily obscured, Eric had given me the very message Darla needed to hear—and it didn't matter if it made her think less of me to hear it this way. She had closure, and that was all that was important. I would probably never know the full truth behind Eric's final words, but in the end, he'd left this world with Darla's name on his lips.

Obligations

CHAPTER 23

*W*hile the town of Andersen was coming to terms with Eric's death, Jonathan and Carl were gathering intelligence about the recent activities of the possessors. Uncle Connor returned from his meeting with the Lebas council, having cut his trip short when Carl contacted him about Eric's tragic death. He was full of questions.

"Was this the same possessor that victimized Eric the first time?"

Jonathan and Carl nodded in unison.

"And the same one that tried to take over Beth's mind?"

"Yes," Carl said.

"Not only that, he was there the night of Beth's accident," Jonathan clarified.

Uncle Connor raised both his eyebrows in shock. "How can you be certain?"

"He told me," I answered, joining in the conversation.

"That isn't everything," Carl continued. "He's been watching Beth since she was a child."

This news made Connor noticeably uneasy.

Jonathan explained about the pictures I'd drawn of my imaginary childhood friend Bailey, and I recounted what Bailey had said to me the night of Eric's death—deliberately skipping over his vulgar intentions. I assumed Uncle Connor could figure that part out by himself.

The morning after Eric died, Jonathan had insisted that I tell him every wretched detail of that horrible evening, no matter how appalling it was to recall. And though he did his best to listen calmly, I could see the anger and hatred festering inside him. I watched the pain and torture he and Grace felt as I told them about Janine, and I knew that Jonathan would not rest until the possessor had been destroyed. According to Carl, Jonathan was one of the few who had the training to do just that.

"It requires a special skill," he'd said. "I don't have it, but Jonathan . . ." he paused, glancing briefly at Grace and then Jonathan before turning back to me, "Jonathan is one of only three who have mastered the skill as far as I know."

The memory of those prior conversations floated randomly through my mind as I explained everything to Uncle Connor. Jonathan observed me intently as I spoke, as if he were hearing it for the first time and was listening for some small piece of information that I'd forgotten to tell him previously. It was Carl, however, who ended up surprising us with new information.

"They'll come back," he announced.

That was no surprise; I'd already told them that.

"No," he clarified, "I don't mean just the intruders who possessed Eric."

"What *do* you mean?" Uncle Connor demanded.

"It's what Eric told me when I found him lying on the floor."

"What Eric told you?" I gasped.

"Yes. When the possessors had control of him, Eric saw their collective minds. This thing with Eric is only the tip of the iceberg. The one possessor's obsession with Beth is personal. He plans to take her before the others get to her, and he's vowed to destroy Jonathan in the process. But according to Eric, it's Beth's birthright the others are after. They plan to either turn her or destroy her, and they don't care which."

I sucked in too much air at once and lost my balance. Jonathan quickly grabbed my shoulders and pulled me close. Carl's words confirmed what the possessor had said to me; but until then, I hadn't realized *more* of them wanted me. I sat down on the couch and stared blankly at the faces before me.

"How many are there?" Jonathan asked.

"The word Eric used was *legion*," Carl replied.

Jonathan closed his eyes and sighed heavily. The silence that followed solidified the gravity of our situation. Jonathan sat down next to me and rested his chin on his fingers.

"I won't let them take her," he whispered resolutely.

Silence followed for several minutes. Carl stood and cleared his throat. He poked at the fire, pretending to adjust a log that had slipped sideways in the fireplace.

"Dad," his tone made it obvious he was about to change the subject. "Tell us what you found out when you met with the council."

Uncle Connor stood and began pacing back and forth absent-mindedly. His stride revealed no hint of nervous anxiety; rather, it was as if he were methodically collecting his thoughts and carefully choosing his words. Jonathan raised his head, waiting for him to talk. Uncle Connor abruptly paused mid-stride.

"They're convinced that the leaders of the possessors are immortals who have obtained inside access to specialized Lebas research. It also appears they may have been trained in Lebas Intelligence."

"The COR plans to form regiments specially trained in warfare against possessors," Uncle Connor informed us. "We have no way of knowing how many there are, who's organizing them, or where they plan to strike next—so obtaining covert intelligence is going to be a critical component of the training."

"That's the same thing I heard from leaders in the northeastern division," Carl commented. "I've already asked to be assigned to the western contingent."

Jonathan nodded his head slowly in approval of Carl's

announcement. Uncle Connor seemed to ignore the comment, waiting instead for Jonathan to turn and meet his gaze. When he finally did, Uncle Connor's eyes narrowed to a squint.

"They want you, Jonathan."

Jonathan immediately shook his head in response. "No. I'm not the one they want."

"You're the only one who has the . . . background necessary to fight them." Uncle Connor glanced at me and then quickly focused back on Jonathan. It was apparent that he was choosing his words cautiously. "It's highly probable that there's a connection between what has happened here and the unexplained crime sprees that have been occurring elsewhere."

"No!" Jonathan replied flatly. "I can't. I won't."

"This isn't going to be easy for any of us," Carl reminded him, "and they will come back for her."

"That's precisely why I can't go," Jonathan insisted. "I won't leave her."

"She wouldn't be alone," Uncle Connor argued. "Marci and I will be with her constantly until you return."

"Really? And you're both trained to fight possessors?" he replied sarcastically.

Uncle Connor opened his mouth to protest, but closed it and sighed.

"Exactly," Jonathan muttered.

Carl shook his head. "It would only be for a couple of w—"

"No, Carl," Jonathan insisted. "I will not leave her. Period."

The discussion ended there, but it was far from over. In the days that followed, Carl and Uncle Connor each took turns trying to convince Jonathan that it was his duty to lead one of the regiments as the Lebas had requested. They were adamant that his specialized skills were necessary in order to effectively prepare the Lebas regime for battle against the legion of immortals and possessors who would soon come.

It was not difficult for Uncle Connor to convince the COR that setting up one of the regiments in Andersen was necessary, especially after they were informed of the possessors' knowledge of my alleged royal bloodline. That was the part I had the most trouble comprehending. I wasn't a royal anything. I was just me, and I was mortal.

In spite of the Lebas's concession to gather immortals in Andersen, Jonathan stubbornly refused to be the one to lead them. Although part of me was relieved by that fact, it seemed oddly out of character for him. I was convinced there was something deeper going on—something Jonathan had not elected to share with me.

School became a challenge; I trusted no one. I was constantly distracted, unable to focus on the lessons in my classes. I waited and watched for signs that a possessor had gotten to somebody else. I grew suspicious if anyone said anything even remotely out of the ordinary. Uncle Connor and Carl did their best to try to convince me that possessors would not attack in the open. "They're far too cowardly for that," Uncle Connor had explained.

Even so, Uncle Connor drove me to school each morning and he was there the moment my classes ended, except on the days that Jonathan tutored. Even when Uncle Connor picked me up, Jonathan wasn't far behind. He would arrive as soon as his other obligations permitted. I knew he was sacrificing a great deal of his time to act as my personal bodyguard, and I couldn't help but wonder how long he could manage to keep his affairs balanced around my schedule. At night when I went to bed, the four of them—Uncle Connor, Carl, Marci, and Jonathan—took turns sleeping down the hall on the couch in the living room.

My life had taken an insane turn. I'd always been one to treasure my personal space and downtime. Before the accident, I spent countless hours alone at the piano; since the accident, I'd resorted to listening to music and reading novels. With the exception of a rare weekend morning or an occasional afternoon in the practice room at school, my "alone" time was now virtually nonexistent.

The only time I truly found myself alone was when I was at school—but not in the literal sense. The gloomy cloud that hovered over the campus ever since Eric's death brought the students, particularly the seniors, closer together. They became an even tighter-knit group, and I wasn't part of it. The pain of losing their lifelong friend and hero gave them a new sense of camaraderie that I didn't share. What made it worse was that I was seen as the girl who had "dissed" Eric. To some, that was unforgivable.

Even Darla had changed, although her change was far more subtle. She still posed as my closest friend, but there was something different about her, something that created a gentle distance between us. Maybe it was because she came down with a lingering flu at the end of January that frequently kept her out of school, sometimes for three or four days at a time. She didn't want visitors so I just waited, hoping that when she fully recovered things would get back to normal—as normal as they could be under the circumstances.

Fortunately, Justin was a bright spot in my life. Next to Jonathan, spending time with Justin was what I looked forward to the most. It gave me a welcome sense of normalcy and purpose. I rarely discussed Justin with Jonathan because I knew Jonathan wanted me to sign on as Justin's official piano instructor. By doing so, my name would appear on the program at the Bach festival. This seemed to be particularly important to Jonathan, though why, he wouldn't say. I knew he and Mr. Laden were secretly plotting behind my back, but I chose to ignore them both whenever they dropped their not-so-subtle hints.

Some afternoons, Jonathan would stand in the hall and listen to me as I worked with Justin. He wouldn't admit it, but I knew he was there. It was something I sensed, usually because I always kept my ear peeled in the direction of his practice room, even while working with Justin. When the music stopped, I knew Jonathan was nearby listening.

I sometimes returned the favor. I loved watching Jonathan at work. I particularly enjoyed watching the young girls swoon over him when he helped them with their drills. On a few occasions, three or four of them would gather around at once and beg him to play for them. He always pretended that they were twisting his arm, but Mr. Laden was definitely right about Jonathan—he thrived on a captive audience. I didn't mind. I loved listening to him play too.

On occasion, when I found myself alone at the piano (usually while waiting for Jonathan's tutoring sessions to conclude), I'd try my hand at the book of compositions Carl had given me the day he delivered my piano. I had no idea the pieces would prove so challenging. I put them on the same level as the Hungarian Rhapsodies or the more difficult Études—barring the exclusion of the left hand, of course. I often found myself frustrated, sometimes spewing colorful metaphors at the piano. I would've given anything for Mr. Stydle's guidance, a thought that often made me chuckle to myself. I'd hated him for so long because of his moodiness and bad temperament.

In spite of the distractions of piano and school, the cloud that hung over my family became heavier and darker with each passing day. The storm was on its way, of that we were all certain. The tension between Jonathan and Carl grew stronger each time Carl tried to convince Jonathan to head up the immortals' training. Uncle Connor seemed heavily conflicted when it came to Jonathan. He knew Jonathan's expertise was necessary to train the immortals, yet he understood that Jonathan was the only person who could keep me safe from another attack, be it internal or external.

We each struggled with our conflicts, and those conflicts were causing an inadvertent division among us. The unity that should have been our strongest asset was now weakening the seams of our tapestry. We soon found ourselves walking on eggshells. Even though we tried to remain positive, an unavoidable, ominous undertone filtered through every conversation. This pattern persisted until a surprise visit from Grace changed everything.

Jonathan and I were in the basement of Uncle Connor's house. He was playing selections from a book of Chopin nocturnes as I lay sprawled out on the floor doing my homework. I was forced to endure an analysis of *The Jungle* in the form of a persuasive essay.

"Perhaps I should switch to something a bit more sinister," Jonathan teased. "Judging by the frown in your forehead, the Nocturnes seem a bit too romantic."

"Blech! There is nothing romantic about Upton Sinclair!" I growled.

"Agreed." He tossed the piano book on the floor and traded it for another. "How's this?"

Jonathan immediately raged into Chopin's Étude in A Minor.

"That's much more appropriate . . . thank you very much," I moaned.

Neither of us heard the doorbell ring so we were both startled when Grace appeared at the bottom of the staircase. She stood nervously on the bottom step, her hand lightly touching the handrail.

"Hello, Beth," she said quietly, "Jonathan."

"Grace?" Jonathan and I both gasped—me from surprise and pleasure but Jonathan from utter disbelief. I stood immediately and greeted her with an embrace.

"Grace, what's wrong?" Jonathan hurried over from the piano. He affectionately offered her his arm in an age-old gesture that she responded to as though they'd rehearsed it a thousand times.

"Jonathan, I need to speak with Beth," she said, patting his arm with her free hand.

"How did you get here?" he asked, ignoring her request.

"Oh, I saddled up the old horse and buggy," she said winsomely. Then she laughed. "I drove, you idiot."

"You *drove?* Alone?" He was shocked. Jonathan had told me that Grace never left the ranch except on rare occasions; even then, she'd never do it alone. According to Jonathan, she was petrified of driving. I'd thought he was merely feeding me tall tales of his sister's peculiar ways; but judging by his reaction to her unexpected arrival, he wasn't teasing at all.

"I'm sorry to show up uninvited and unannounced—"

I interrupted her. "No, Grace, don't apologize. You're always welcome here."

She smiled graciously and nodded. "Thank you."

"What's so urgent that it brought you away from the ranch?" Jonathan urged.

"I'd like to speak with Beth."

A confused expression crossed Jonathan's face. He turned and looked at me and then raised his eyebrows, as if he suspected I knew something I wasn't telling him. I shrugged my shoulders and we both turned to look at Grace.

"Jonathan, if you don't mind, I'd prefer to speak to Beth alone . . . although if you insist, you may stay."

Grace's tone startled me, but I tried not to let it show. What could she possibly want to say to me that she didn't want Jonathan to hear? Then a thought suddenly struck, and I couldn't help but smile. She must have come to speak with me about Carl. Jonathan saw the smile on my face and stared at me quizzically, hoping I'd let him in on the secret.

"Jonathan, would you please excuse us for a minute," I asked, amused.

Jonathan scrutinized my expression for a moment. Suddenly, his eyes lit up and he broke into his adorable lop-sided grin. "Uh, could this be about Carl?" he drawled, elbowing Grace in the side. Although her cheeks glowed pink at the mention of Carl's name, she shook her head.

"No. This would be about you," she retorted flatly. Her face remained pleasant and smooth, but her tone indicated that she wasn't kidding.

Jonathan's demeanor changed instantly. "*What* about me?" he muttered.

"I came to tell Beth the truth."

Jonathan said nothing—he simply stared at his sister for a long, uncomfortable minute. He pursed his lips and then turned to study my expression. I was very confused. After another moment, Jonathan drew in a deep breath and sighed.

"Grace, I wish you wouldn't," he whispered quietly.

She stroked the side of his face with her hand and gazed lovingly into his pleading eyes. There was absolutely no hint of anything besides pure adoration in her expression. "Jonathan, it's time."

He winced and closed his eyes.

"The time has come for you to finally make everything right," she said.

Jonathan took his sister's hand in his and shook his head.

"I'll not stop you from saying your piece to Beth, but that's the end of it." He looked over at me, held my gaze for a moment, and then turned back to Grace. "She's all yours." He dropped her hand and disappeared up the stairs.

"Is there somewhere private where we can sit down for a minute?" Grace asked once Jonathan was gone.

I led her into Uncle Connor's study. Although she'd asked for a place to sit down, she remained standing. It was clear that I was the one who was expected to sit. I obeyed the unspoken request and waited for Grace to begin.

"How much has Jonathan told you about our family?"

Jonathan knew just about everything there was to know about my background, yet his remained a mystery. So much had happened during the past few months that on those rare occasions when Jonathan's past did come up in our conversation, I never pressed him for more information than he was ready to share. I knew he had secrets, he'd told me so himself, but I'd insisted that his past didn't matter. If I let my imagination run wild, I could conjure up all kinds of unpleasant scenarios—mainly involving former relationships. So whenever thoughts of Jonathan's past crept into my mind, I tossed them out.

Grace stood next to where I was sitting for a moment, then knelt down beside me and laid her delicate hand over mine. "Is it very hard for you, knowing there was someone else for Jonathan once?"

Her frankness caught me off guard, it was so unlike her.

"Yes, but . . . it doesn't change how I feel about him." I had to be honest with her.

"I'm glad." She squeezed my hand gently. "What else do you know about him?"

"I know that something happened, something that causes him to suffer a tremendous amount of guilt." I searched Grace's eyes questioningly. She knew his secret. "He told me on Christmas Eve that he was leaving—that he had to make something 'right.' He didn't give me any details, though."

"No, I suppose he didn't."

Grace took a deep breath and stood. She wandered around the study, running her fingers lightly over the backs of the books that lined Uncle Connor's shelves. Her back was to me when she continued.

"Our family, the Rollings, was one of the more prominent families in Pennsylvania prior to the Civil War. Mind you, we weren't among the elite, but we were accepted in society and that was very important in those days. My mother and father moved to Pennsylvania from England when Jonathan and I were very young." She stopped when she heard me gasp and then turned to face me, puzzled at my response.

"Jonathan never mentioned being a child," I explained. "I didn't know when—"

"Surely he has explained reclamation to you."

"Yes, of course, but I didn't know when he. . . . I'm sorry. I didn't mean to interrupt."

Grace smiled politely and then turned around and continued. "We were among a select few immortal families permitted to play an interactive role among mortals in preserving the unification of the states. Normally, we do not form allegiances in conflicts involving mortals. You can imagine it would be impossible to maintain the secrecy of our existence if we fought side-by-side with them."

Grace turned and smiled reluctantly. She had protected her family's privacy for so long that it was obviously difficult for her to share their history with me now. I listened attentively to every detail, nervous about what she might reveal but unable to temper my prickling curiosity.

"The Civil War was . . . different." She hesitated.

I waited for her to explain.

"The Lebas took sides—they aligned themselves with the northern states. Jonathan was young and handsome and all of fourteen years old when the war broke out." She grinned, realizing that from my perspective, this was difficult to imagine. "And he was the promising son of a respected businessman. Jonathan was too young to enlist, but by the time he was older, there was no holding him back. He was eager and determined and . . . foolish. Honor was everything back then. If a child, no matter what his or her age, did something disloyal to their community or country, the entire family suffered. Likewise, if an immortal child did something to defy the authority of the Lebas, the consequences stained the family name for generations to follow. A soiled name among immortals requires generations of recompense before the 'stain' can be blotted out."

"Jonathan did something dishonorable?"

Grace smiled sadly. "It's more complicated than that," she replied. "As I mentioned, ours was a prominent family. Marriages were arranged by mortal families back then, at least, among the old wealth. In many cases, it was more of a financial merger than the result of two people falling in love. What's worse is that even the Lebas arranged marriages among certain immortals, depending on their bloodlines. It was important to the Lebas that the bloodlines remained as pure as possible. However, with the advancements in science over the past century, they've learned that nearly all royal bloodlines have been diluted—or as they refer to it, 'polluted.' So their earlier efforts to protect the integrity of the bloodlines were fruitless."

"Were Jonathan and Eleanor one of those arrangements?" My jealousy demon made an unwanted appearance when I thought of the two of them together; I forced myself to ignore it.

"No, Grace replied. "By the time they discovered how they felt about each other, their families had already arranged other matches for them."

"I see," I lied. But I didn't see. It made my stomach wretch to think of him married to someone else.

"Jonathan openly refused the arrangement, and news of his rejection caused my parents a great deal of embarrassment. Naturally, they never would have forced him to marry someone he objected to, but the girl's family was greatly offended. It helped that Jonathan was away most of the time due to the war; in fact, my parents tried to use that as his excuse for not wanting to enter into an 'understanding,' as they called it. When Jonathan and Eleanor's 'friendship' blossomed unexpectedly, it was nothing less than scandalous. She was already promised to another."

"Wow, it sounds so unbelievable," I commented. "And so unfair."

"That's just the way it was. People accepted it. Well, most people. You may have noticed that Jonathan tends to be a bit, uh, what's the word . . . ?"

"Stubborn?" I chuckled.

"That works too. I was thinking more along the lines of free-spirited . . . or dare I say, rebellious?" She smiled at me and we both snickered. Her clear green eyes twinkled exactly the way Jonathan's did, a startling sight when you weren't expecting it. She was so like him in her own peculiar way.

"Well, I won't bore you with the minor details, but Eleanor was to marry another and there was no getting around that obstacle. However, it didn't stop Jonathan from trying, especially once he learned that she did not love her suitor. He could have handled knowing she was happy, but he couldn't handle the thought of her being forced into a loveless marriage.

"Eventually, her father intervened and arranged for Jonathan to be 'reassigned.' Jonathan was belligerent about the assignment, but he followed orders and did what was expected of him. But the fear of Eleanor acquiescing to her father's wishes drove Jonathan crazy."

"What did he do?" The story of these star-crossed lovers enthralled me. I'd disconnected myself from the story, viewing Eleanor's Jonathan as someone other than *my* Jonathan. That was the only way I could feel compassion or empathy toward my would-be rival.

"Not knowing what was happening became such a distraction that Jonathan requested temporary leave, but leave was denied. He appealed to the Lebas, but they refused to intervene on his behalf. Then, one afternoon Jonathan made a serious mistake that resulted in the loss of several of his men."

"Oh, no!" I whispered.

"He took off in the middle of the night. He wrote a note to his commanding officer telling him that he would return, and then he left—absent without leave."

"Wow," I hissed.

"You can't imagine what it did to our family when news of his 'desertion' became public." Grace ducked her head. "It affected all of us . . . me in particular."

"Why?"

"I was engaged to a soldier of my own. With our name tainted, his family called off the arrangement. I received a letter from my would-be husband telling me that he would come for me anyway, that he didn't care about their approval." Grace's eyes flickered to mine. "I've been waiting for him ever since."

"Oh, Grace," I gasped. "How angry you must have been at your brother."

"Angry?" she chuckled softly. "How could I be angry with him? I understood how he felt. I could never blame him for what he did."

"You love Jonathan very much." It was meant as a rhetorical statement, but she responded anyway.

"More than my life. More than my very soul. The anguish he experienced following his separation from Eleanor would have killed any mortal. There were many times when he damned himself for being immortal. I understood his pain completely."

"What finally happened with him and Eleanor?"

"He returned for her, but their reunion was short-lived. They planned to go away, but then she disappeared. Jonathan went crazy."

"Disappeared? You mean . . . she died?"

"We don't know. She simply disappeared. Jonathan refused to accept that she was gone. He was convinced that the Lebas had somehow intervened."

"Would they do something like that?"

"I suspect they would do almost anything to preserve a pure bloodline. Regardless, nothing else made sense—after all, people do not just disappear. Jonathan went to them and asked for help, but again, they denied him. They begged him to let it go and to trust them, but that just made him more suspicious. Eventually, he abandoned everything he knew, vowing to find out the truth about what had happened to her. It became an obsession with him. He was no longer driven by love. He had exhausted all his resources going through the proper channels, but had gotten nowhere. Finally, he did the unspeakable."

Grace hesitated. This was what she'd come to tell me—what Jonathan didn't want me know—the secret that he feared would cause me to stop trusting him, to stop loving him.

"He made a deal with the Niaces," she said sadly. She hesitated briefly when I gasped and then continued. "Beth, Jonathan swore an allegiance to the Niaces, and in return, the Niaces promised him unlimited freedom to travel and to intervene at will in mortal affairs."

My mouth dropped. "No," I whispered.

Grace scrutinized my expression for several moments, waiting for me to absorb this information before continuing. She moved closer to me and took my hands in hers. She paused slightly, distracted by my bent fingers, and then looked pleadingly into my eyes.

"Obviously, Jonathan's reputation as a Union deserter had a major impact on our family's social standing. My Father's business failed. He lost his contacts when other reputable companies refused to do business with him. My mother became an outcast in society and her friends shunned her. But these were *mortal* repercussions, and they would have been relatively short-lived in the grand scheme of things. On the other hand, Jonathan's open rebellion against the Lebas was another story; it completely devastated our family and tainted the Rollings name in the immortal community. Jonathan was gone—absorbed in his obsession to find Eleanor—so he had no idea of the price the rest of us paid for his actions until much later."

I didn't know what to say. "Your . . . family," I stammered, "you're all so close. How did you get through all this?"

"Love, actually. In the end, there was love. After what must have been decades, Jonathan finally gave up his search for Eleanor and came looking for us. By then, of course, our family had traveled several times. We severed our ties with Pennsylvania and set up a new base for traveling—somewhere remote."

"The ranch?"

"Yes. After that, Jonathan immersed himself in traveling. He's been a soldier in nearly every war this country has been involved in since that time, hoping to make restitution and redeem our family name."

"And now?" I asked.

"According to the Lebas, Jonathan now has a chance to restore all honor to our family."

"I see. He can restore your honor . . . if he agrees to lead the fight against the possessors." I choked on the words and lowered my head. I was numb. Grace hadn't come to tell me Jonathan's secret—she wanted me to encourage him to train the Lebas.

Grace nodded slowly. "Beth, Jonathan is the one best equipped to train the immortals. Because of his former ties to the Niace, he has inside knowledge of their operations. His experience is unparalleled."

I nodded blankly.

"He will never agree to it unless you ask him. Even then . . . I'm not sure you can convince him to leave you. The thought of losing you is unbearable to him. He can't survive that kind of torture again. It would destroy him—permanently."

"What are you asking me to do?"

"I'm asking you to speak to him, that's all." She paused for a moment. "But before you do," she added, "you need to understand something. The dishonor Jonathan brought on our family's name haunts him to this day. He has never forgiven himself. This is his chance to put the mistakes of his past behind him and finally find peace."

She squeezed my arm gently and smiled a soft, doubtful smile. "I will support whatever you decide to do. If you cannot bear to let him go, I will understand. Truly."

A timely knock along the stairway wall ended our conversation. My head whirled from the information Grace had shared.

"I need to think," I muttered. "I can't make any promises."

"That's all I'm asking," she said reassuringly.

I knew by the sincerity in her voice that she wouldn't hold it against me if I couldn't bear to let Jonathan go. The thought of being separated from him frightened me. If the possessors came back for me, they'd do so when I was vulnerable, when Jonathan wasn't around to protect me. He would never agree to it, not as long as he knew I was in danger.

"Are you ladies planning to stay down here all night?" Carl's voice rang from the top of the staircase. No doubt he was anxious to spend time with Grace, and her eyes began to twinkle the moment she saw him.

Decisions

CHAPTER 24

*W*hen I drifted off to sleep that night, I wasn't surprised to find myself standing on top of the familiar hill overlooking the same vast green valley I'd dreamed of so many times since my arrival in Andersen. I recognized the place at once. And once again, I watched as forces gathered on each side of the rolling hills that were spread out before my view. The soldiers valiantly took their places, forming two lines—each facing the other—just as they had in previous dreams. Approximately a thousand yards separated them. The ones to my right were young men, bold and strong and eager for the battle to begin. The ones to my left were shapeless figures clustered together in a dark cloud. Centered in the cloud was the figure of a man with glowing yellow eyes. This time, however, there were no swords, no rifles, and no canons. This was not a battle between flesh and blood—it was a battle between the forces of life and the forces of death.

I saw the details of each soldier's face as they waited anxiously for the call to advance. Jonathan stood among the soldiers to my right, scrutinizing the opposing force. He was searching the front lines for someone in particular. I understood immediately who he was looking for; he was searching for Bailey among the crowd of shadowy figures. After a few moments, he cast his eyes in my direction, seeming to search the hillside where I stood. His eyes focused on me and he bowed slightly as though he were in the presence of royalty, just as he had in previous dreams. He appeared to be waiting for my command. Again, I held the fate of the soldiers within my power; one signal from me would launch both sides into a massive scene of destruction.

While Jonathan waited patiently for my signal, I hesitated, not sure what I should do. I sighed remorsefully. The familiar golden scepter was heavy in my left hand. I clutched it tightly and marveled at the strength in my fingers. Every muscle in my hand was strong and powerful. There was no sign of deformity.

Intuitively, I knew that in the next second I would straighten my hand out and hold the scepter horizontally in front of me to study its magnificence. I also knew that the moment I did, Jonathan would interpret my action as the signal for him and his men to advance. He would nod in obeisance, and the battle would begin.

Although I knew what was going to happen, I couldn't resist the compelling force that told me to stretch forth my hand. I met Jonathan's eyes and silently mouthed, "I love you," and then raised the golden scepter high into the air for him to see. This time, there would be no inadvertent command. No mistake. This time, I *wanted* him to fight—and I wanted him to *win!*

"Beth," someone called from the distance. I didn't respond.

"Beth," the voice repeated, closer this time. As it had so many times before, the scene of advancing soldiers disappeared to be replaced by the soft, rolling silhouette of foothills in the distance.

"Beth, honey. Are you awake?" Marci's voice pulled me from the battlefield to my bedroom. "Your uncle and I are going to breakfast. Do you and Jonathan want to join us?"

I shook my head in immediate protest. "I need to talk to Jonathan."

"What is it? What's wrong?" Marci asked, alarmed by my abruptness. "Did you have another encounter?"

"No. But I need to talk to Jonathan right now. Actually, I need to talk to all of you."

I probably should have spoken to Jonathan alone before springing this on him in front of the entire family, but I wasn't exactly thinking that far ahead and I was afraid I'd change my mind if I didn't act swiftly. My dream had given me the answer. Jonathan was *my* soldier, and he would fight—he would fight for me. He would fight for Grace and her lost love; he would fight for his family's name; he would fight for Janine; and he would fight for Eric. He would fight because it was his obligation. And most importantly, he would prevail—I knew in my heart that he would prevail!

I quickly showered and dressed, then I joined the family in the living room. Uncle Connor had the usual fire sputtering away in the fireplace and the morning edition of the Andersen Daily lay scattered across the coffee table where they had been reading it. Jonathan was pacing the floor, waiting impatiently for an explanation.

"Where's Carl?" I asked brusquely. It was difficult to mask the sense of urgency I felt.

"Right here." I turned around quickly at the sound of Carl's rough voice. To my shock, Grace stood beside him, her hand in his arm. I stared at the image of them together and for a split second, I envisioned their hands clasped together, fingers intimately entwined. I realized I was staring, but I couldn't tear my eyes away.

"Beth?" Carl finally said.

"I'm sorry," I sputtered, shaking my head as I abruptly turned back to the others. "I really need to talk to all of you."

"We're all here, dear," Marci replied as if that fact were obvious to everyone but me.

I stared into their faces one by one, allowing my heart to swell with emotion as I considered how much I loved them: Marci, my surrogate mother who was helping me sort through my mixed-up emotions and insecurities; Uncle Connor, who had taken on the role of father and protector; Carl, my brother and comrade in arms; Grace, the older sister I never had; and Jonathan, my music partner, my friend, my love, and my reason for trusting that there was something beyond this life.

"Beth?" Jonathan said softly, reading the emotion in my face. He moved to my side and wrapped his arm around me in a gesture that had become so automatic nobody else noticed, but I did. Having him close to me felt as natural as breathing. His gentle hug let me know he felt the same way.

"You might want to sit down for this." I shot Grace a quick look and bit my lip. She understood immediately and encouraged Carl to take a seat on the couch.

"You, too," I said to Jonathan, who was becoming more suspicious by the moment.

"What are you up to?" he whispered.

"Trust me," I whispered back.

Once everyone was seated and I had their complete attention, I told them the details of my dream. I explained that the dream had recurred several times since I'd moved to Andersen, but its meaning hadn't been clear to me until this morning.

"Jonathan," I began, "you *have* to train the immortals and lead the fight against the possessors."

Everyone looked at Jonathan with apprehension. He ignored them and stared at me. His jaw tightened and his eyes narrowed as he slowly moved his head back and forth in a negative motion.

"No," he said flatly.

"Jonathan, listen to me." I knelt in front of him and rested my hand on his knee. "You have to do this for me . . . for us."

He drew in a long, deep breath and closed his eyes for a second.

"Are you satisfied?" he said coldly, turning to glare at Grace. She met his gaze for a moment and then slowly lowered her eyes.

"Jonathan, please," I begged, "don't blame Grace. I'm glad I know what happened. I won't let you forfeit your chance to make things right."

"It's not your decision to make, Beth."

"I know it's not. But I'm *asking* you to do this."

He closed his eyes again and dropped his head, rubbing his forehead with the palms of his hands.

"I can't do it, Beth," he muttered. "I can't leave you unprotected."

"I won't be unprotected," I insisted. "You can train Marci, Uncle Connor, and Grace—"

"You have no idea what you're saying," he snapped. "Do you think this is some kind of game?"

"Of course not, but I'm only *one* person in the whole equation."

"You're the *only* person in the equation," he said sharply, "the only one I care about."

"That's not true, Jonathan."

His eyes searched mine pleadingly. "Beth, please. Don't ask this of me. If something happens to you, I won't survive it."

I stared into his eyes for a long, tense moment. I knew he was right. There was honest pain behind his tortured expression. He was not going to back down—he couldn't. It wasn't in him to leave me vulnerable to another encounter with the possessors.

Jonathan finally stood and took my face in his hands. "I can't leave you, Beth," he said in a tortured whisper. "There'd be no way to protect you."

Tears collected in my eyes and I conceded the argument, nodding in quiet defeat.

"There is a way." Grace spoke so softly it was almost a whisper, but her voice pierced through the awkward moment with clear resonance.

"How?" Marci asked.

Grace took a deep breath before answering. "I could travel," she said to Jonathan, resigned.

Jonathan and Grace stared at each other for several moments.

"I can hide her Jonathan . . . they won't find her."

Jonathan continued to stare at his sister in disbelief.

"What does she mean?" I asked. Nobody responded. Every bit of energy in the room seemed to be suspended in midair.

"Grace, it's too risky," Jonathan whispered.

"Not necessarily," Marci interjected. We all turned in unison to face Marci.

"Possessors can't travel . . . they're limited to linear timelines," Marci explained.

"What are you talking about?" I was getting exasperated, but again my question fell on deaf ears. It was as if I were no longer in the room.

"Where would you take her?" Uncle Connor asked. He sounded uneasy, yet at the same time there was a glimmer of hope in his voice.

Grace thought for a moment and then smiled. "Wherever she wants, but it would have to be at least a century back to be clear of any connection to the present."

"Even if you could do it," Jonathan said doubtfully, "it's too risky for mortals."

Grace must have sensed that Jonathan was beginning to wear down, because she suddenly exhibited renewed enthusiasm. She walked over to him and put her small hand on his arm.

"It will work," she said confidently, nodding her head.

"What do you think?" Marci asked, looking quizzically at Uncle Connor.

"Grace, how long has it been since you traveled?" Uncle Connor asked.

"It's been a very long time," she began, "but I know the procedures as well as I know how to breathe."

Uncle Connor raised one eyebrow and then looked at Jonathan.

"She does," Jonathan confirmed.

"Would you please tell me what you're talking about?" I screamed. Every head snapped around. I was embarrassed. "Somebody please tell me," I echoed softly.

Jonathan pulled me down onto the couch next to him and slid me close to his side. He looked into my eyes. "You remember what I said about us being travelers?"

I nodded slowly. I remembered.

"Grace has the ability to take you across time—anywhere you want to go."

"Are you serious?" As incredulous as it sounded, the scientist in me instantly stood at attention.

Jonathan's amused smile was a welcome contrast to his tortured expression of moments before.

"The question is," Grace said, "if you could choose a time and place in history that you'd like to visit, when and where would it be?"

Now she was tempting me.

"Wait!" Marci said abruptly, "don't say anything Beth. Nobody in this room should know."

A chorus of "whys" hung in the air.

"It's too risky. If the possessors should perceive our thoughts, they might enlist the help of an immortal to get to Beth. Only Beth and Grace should know her whereabouts."

"Not even Jonathan?" I asked.

"*Especially* not Jonathan," Carl declared.

"And the possessors wouldn't be able to find me?" I asked Carl. I turned to Grace. "You're certain of that?"

Grace nodded slowly. "Yes, I'm certain. The only possible way they could find you is if your possessor had access to an immortal body—someone who knew where you were. As long as nobody knows where you are, you'll be safe."

"How long would I be gone?" I asked.

"That's up to Jonathan," Grace replied. She turned to her brother. "How long would it take you to adequately train a regiment?"

"It depends on the individual members," he replied. "Normally it would require at least a month, but there's no way I'll agree to a month-long separation."

"If the possessors are on their way, we don't have that much time anyway," Carl stated. "Can we learn enough to make a difference in two weeks?"

Jonathan considered for a moment. "Possibly, but the training would be intense. It would require long hours of preparation."

"When do we start?" Carl said enthusiastically.

"I haven't agreed to this yet," Jonathan reminded him.

"This would put you in a positive position with the Lebas," Carl encouraged.

"I could really care less about—"

"Uh, Jonathan . . ." Uncle Connor interrupted, clearing his throat. He stole a sidelong glance at me and then focused on Jonathan again. "May I speak to you privately for a minute?"

Jonathan looked confused as he studied Uncle Connor's expression. He hesitated for several seconds but then followed Uncle Connor into the kitchen. I watched them disappear without explanation. I looked at Carl questioningly but he just shrugged and said, "That's odd."

Marci stared after Uncle Connor and Jonathan for a moment. Then she grinned. "Not really," she replied, a sly expression on her face. She was responding to Carl but she never took her eyes off me.

Grace quietly caught my attention and mouthed the words, "Thank you." I half smiled in reply. I had no idea what I'd just agreed to do.

Although nothing had been decided yet, I had to admit I was intrigued. The idea of actually traveling through time fascinated me. What scientist's daughter in her right mind would pass up such an opportunity? The fact that I'd be safe from my enemy and that Jonathan could fulfill his obligation to restore dignity and honor to his family name made the idea triple tempting.

"And we'd only need to be gone for two weeks?" I asked Grace when the others had started buzzing among themselves.

"*You* will. I won't be able to stay with you. I'll need to come back here and stay until we know it's safe to bring you back."

"Oh," I sighed. It was a good thing Jonathan was out of the room. He'd sense my hesitation and that would be enough to make him reject the idea. I'd have to hide my emotions well.

"How soon would we go?" I did my best to sound brave, but apprehension stabbed relentlessly at my insides.

"The sooner the better," she replied. She sounded so nonchalant about it—like she was just planning a trip to Hawaii. "There are arrangements I need to make first, but those shouldn't take long. If all goes well, we should be able to leave at first light day after tomorrow."

"That soon?" I gasped.

Grace nodded.

"I can't leave that soon. I made a promise to someone."

"Who?"

"It doesn't matter. I have to keep that promise."

"How much time do you need?"

I knew exactly how much time I needed. "One week."

Grace drew in a sharp breath. "Well, I suppose that would give Jonathan time to work out his strategy and me time to make all the arrangements. Still . . ." she eyed me skeptically. "Beth, are you sure you can't leave any sooner?"

"I can't leave until the Bach Festival is over."

Grace looked puzzled.

"Please understand, I have an obligation. I can't back out now."

"All right, then. One week it is." Grace smiled, resigned. She started to get up, then stopped and rested her hand on my knee. "This will work, Beth. I promise," she assured me.

She stood and caught the attention of Marci and Carl who were involved in a lively discussion of their own. "Would you excuse us for a moment? I need to speak to Beth in private."

She looked in the direction of my bedroom. I understood and led the way. She followed me in and shut the door.

"Thank you for doing this, Beth."

"It's the right thing for Jonathan," I replied.

She took both of my hands in hers and smiled graciously. "Now then, where and to what time period would you like to go—as if I didn't already know!"

I raised one eyebrow as I surveyed the confidence in her eyes. Of course she would know.

To be sure no one could hear me I leaned forward and whispered, "I want to go where Jonathan lived, before he was immortal."

"I assumed you would want that, but it might be a little tricky. The Lebas won't allow any travel that changes the past. It could disturb the linear continuum, resulting in a parallel time-line. The consequences of that could prove catastrophic." She watched the confusion wash over me and grinned. "Let's put it this way. If Jonathan meets you in the past, it could change the present."

"I just want to watch him. He doesn't even have to know I'm there."

"It's not always that simple, especially with someone who's mortal. We won't know how traveling will affect your memory until after you're there."

She watched as my countenance fell. She probably feared I might change my mind about going because she bit her lip and sighed.

"I'll tell you what. I'll discuss your request with the Lebas, but I can't make any promises. I'll do everything in my power to get you as close to Jonathan as possible. Will you trust me on that?"

I grinned and hugged her.

"Don't get too excited," she cautioned. "He may only be a two-year-old when you see him and trust me, he was a holy terror at that age."

I had to laugh. I'd hoped to be able to watch Jonathan when he was close to my age, but suddenly the idea of being able to watch him as a little boy made me almost giddy. The very thought made me anxious to go.

"I would love that, Grace," I giggled.

"I'll do my best." She extended her graceful hand and I accepted it readily. "Thank you," she said quietly, suddenly more serious. "Jonathan has carried the weight of his mistakes for well over a century. Nothing will bring me more happiness than to know he's finally free of the weight of those burdens."

"That would make me very happy too," I added.

"You obviously love him very much," she stated rhetorically. She smiled when she saw the surprise on my face. "Well, it's no secret. I knew that the first time I saw you."

"Really?"

"Beth," she chuckled, "your eyes are a dead giveaway. You couldn't hide your feelings for him if you tried." She smiled and hugged me the way I'd always imagined an older sister would.

"Now then, there's one more thing you need to know," she added. "None of this is happening by chance—it's part of a much bigger plan."

"I don't follow."

Grace smiled. "Just trust me when I say this was meant to be."

I nodded because I trusted her, not because I understood.

"Let's get back before Carl accuses me of kidnapping you."

"That reminds me." I muttered the words before my brain could tell my mouth that it was none of my business. "You and Carl seem to get along very well."

A shimmer of color rose in her smooth cheeks, but she brushed aside my observation.

"We better get back," she grinned.

I couldn't help but notice how her emerald eyes started to twinkle, however, reflecting the shimmering light of the morning sun.

The Competition
CHAPTER 25

*W*hen Jonathan returned with Uncle Connor, there was a peculiar change in his expression. I couldn't put my finger on it exactly, but whatever Uncle Connor said to him had convinced him to move forward with Grace's plan. Grace said she would leave immediately to begin her "preparations"—whatever that meant. Carl offered to assist her and she readily accepted. Within the hour, the two of them were gone.

My preparations were simple. First, I was to send an e-mail to my father with a coded message explaining that Eric's death reminded me too much of my mom, so I wanted to get away from Andersen for a few weeks. I was to tell him I was planning to visit my mother's cousin in Canada. That would be enough to signal my father that something unusual was happening. Apparently, 'Canada' was a code word for 'traveling.' Second, I was to speak to my counselor and teachers and request home study assignments to be completed while I "visited my relatives up north." Third, I needed to talk to the friends who normally called my cell phone or sent me e-mails and explain to them that I'd be unreachable by phone or e-mail while I was gone, and not to worry—that I'd contact them as soon as I could. My sudden trip needed to sound planned and normal, just in case I was being watched. Finally, I was to return home immediately following the Bach Festival (which would take place the following Saturday afternoon) and say my good-byes that night. I was to be ready to leave before first light Sunday morning.

Everything was happening so fast I didn't have time to think about how difficult it was going to be to leave. The idea was exciting in theory only. The reality of it was overwhelmingly frightening. I did my best to suppress my emotions, especially around Jonathan, but I knew he sensed my anxiety. In light of whatever Uncle Connor had said to him, however, he made no effort to convince me to change my mind.

Ultimately, it was thinking about my mother that gave me the courage to forge ahead. She would have jumped at this opportunity, if only for the sake of science. She'd told me to follow my heart, and that's exactly what I was doing.

During the afternoons leading up to Saturday, I worked with Justin to help him prepare for his debut into the arena of classical music. He was amazing, far surpassing my expectations. Mr. Laden was extremely pleased as well which, I had to admit, gave me more satisfaction than I thought it would. I knew it would give Mr. Laden a great deal of pride to introduce Justin at the Festival.

Whenever possible, I worked furiously at mastering the first right-handed composition in the book Carl had given me. It was something I needed to do for myself—in secret—and something I wasn't ready to share with Jonathan yet.

By the time Saturday arrived, I was a nervous wreck. I convinced Jonathan that it was because I was anxious about Justin's performance; I wanted him to do well. Though that was true, it wasn't the only cause of my anxiety.

Jonathan and I spent the morning together. We walked in the snow and recalled our first date when we went horseback riding. He confessed that he'd wanted to tell me he loved me that day, but he figured he'd scare me away if he dropped a bomb like that so soon after meeting me. I made a confession of my own; I was so enamored with him by then that nothing he said or did would have scared me away—not too far away, anyhow. We laughed about how angry I'd been just moments before our first kiss and the shocked expression on my face afterwards. We talked about everything. But mostly, we just enjoyed being together.

The morning hours ticked away too quickly. It was soon time to get ready for Justin's performance at the Bach Festival. This was an important day for me on many levels, so I wanted to look especially nice. I had enlisted Marci's service and she'd helped me purchase a semi-formal dress for the occasion, something I didn't mention to Jonathan. It wasn't that I was trying to keep it a secret—it was standard dress for an afternoon recital of this type—but Jonathan's reaction took me by surprise. He looked at me as if he were seeing me for the first time. It occurred to me that I looked similar to the way I did at *my* piano competition—a lifetime ago.

We took our seats in the twelfth row, dead center. I took a deep breath and smiled. Jonathan noticed and chuckled.

"Ever notice that performance halls all smell the same? It's like . . ."

"Musty old wood and stale floor wax," I finished, sighing affectionately.

Jonathan raised his eyebrows. "Yeah . . . that's it exactly."

The first row was reserved for the panel of six judges, each from a different area of the state. Behind them sat visiting dignitaries: school principals and assistant principals; heads of music departments; talent scouts from various colleges; and, of course, the mayor of Andersen. The Master of Ceremonies was the distinguished, silver-haired Dean Randall Josephson, chairperson of the SCAA— the State Committee for Advancement of the Arts—and head of the music department at the University of Wyoming. He stood an intimidating 6 feet 4 inches tall and looked even taller in his tuxedo tails. His very presence in the room commanded respect and seemed to raise the prestige of the program to a higher plane.

In this leg of the festival, there were fifteen performers, each representing a school or a legally organized group of piano teachers in the western half of the state. Some had traveled as far as a hundred and fifty miles through winter road conditions to participate, making our thirty minute jaunt to Jackson Hole seem like a small effort in comparison.

Justin's name was ninth on the program. I fidgeted nervously in my seat through what felt like hours of other performances. I had a difficult time concentrating on most of them, with the exception of a young Asian girl named Sung Yim. Her performance was stellar—technically flawless—but it lacked emotion. Granted, it's difficult to perform a prelude and fugue with much emotion, but it's not impossible.

By the time Mr. Laden introduced Justin, I thought I was going to be sick to my stomach. It made me appreciate how my parents must have felt the numerous times they sat through my recitals. I was too nervous to hold Jonathan's hand. I twisted my wrists, tapped my fingers against my knee, and shook my foot uncontrollably. I was a wreck.

"Beth," Jonathan whispered. "Relax!" He put his arm around my shoulders and squeezed gently. "He's going to be fine."

"He's never done this before. What if he chokes?"

"He'll make it, you'll see," Jonathan reassured me.

"What if he goes blank? That was always my fear—walking onto the stage, sitting at the piano, and then, bam! The notes are gone." I looked around, aware that I was talking louder than I should. "It could happen, you know," I whispered.

I felt Jonathan's shoulders shake.

"It's not funny . . . Justin would be mortified."

"Beth," he covered my tapping fingers with his calm hand, "have some faith in the kid, okay? Laden wouldn't put him on the program if he had any doubts."

I nodded. He was right. Mr. Laden was particularly protective of Justin. But deep down, I knew it wasn't just Justin's performance I was nervous about.

When Justin took the stage, I stopped breathing. For the next six minutes my body would have to survive without air. I relaxed minutely when I recognized his confidence and determination, but I could only grab enough breath to keep me from fainting. By the time he was halfway through, I was sitting on the edge of my seat, focused intently on his hands. He was perfect. Beyond perfect. Not only was his technique superb, he was able to effectively draw on the emotion of the piece—something I knew the judges would notice.

When Justin finished, I waited patiently for him to stand and take a bow. Then I flew out of my seat and clapped and hollered in an embarrassing show of pride that probably embarrassed Jonathan and the rest of the audience, but I didn't care. I was high as a kite. I soon noticed that I wasn't the only one standing; two of the six judges and several members of the audience also stood. A rush of emotion overwhelmed me. I didn't even attempt to stifle the tears of joy running down my face. Justin's triumph was my triumph, and I relished every minute of it.

But the afternoon wasn't over yet. There was more for me to be nervous about—including, but not limited to, the announcement of which performer would advance to the state finals.

"You can relax now," Jonathan said, trying to calm me. "He was great, just like I knew he'd be."

"He was perfect," I agreed, still agitated. Jonathan was still unaware of why I was so nervous, and that's how I intended to keep it.

I wasn't surprised when Dean Josephson announced Sung Yim as the first runner-up. She'd earned it. I was elated (but again not surprised) when I heard Justin announced as the candidate who would advance to the state finals. In reality, the competition hadn't even been close.

Next came the moment I'd anticipated with excitement and dread all afternoon; it was time for Justin to introduce his instructor—and for his instructor to perform for the audience.

Justin spoke with ease into the microphone as he introduced Mr. Laden. Then Mr. Laden stepped proudly to the stage.

"I wonder what piece Laden has in mind," Jonathan whispered in my ear.

My palms were sweating.

"Good afternoon ladies and gentlemen," Mr. Laden said. The crowd quieted, awaiting his announcement of the selection he would perform.

"I am very honored to serve as the supervisor over Justin's instruction. He has certainly put Andersen, Wyoming, on the map." The crowd applauded politely, then Mr. Laden continued. "But I would not be honest if I took credit for Justin's performance here this afternoon. Beth? Would you please stand for a moment?"

Mr. Laden gestured in my general direction and immediately a parade of heads turned to look at me. Obediently, I stood and offered a shy wave before sitting down again.

"Ladies and gentlemen, judges, distinguished guests—this is Miss Elizabeth Arrington, winner of the National Piano Player's Guild Scholarship Competition two years ago." There were a few audible gasps and then an obligatory round of applause.

"As some of you who follow the National Guild may know, Miss Arrington lost the use of her left hand in a tragic car accident shortly after that competition." A few heads nodded knowingly. "Miss Arrington has been kind enough to work with Justin—unofficially of course—in preparation for today's performance."

Jonathan nodded approvingly. "That's pretty cool of him."

The audience offered another show of appreciation. Perhaps it was a bit more enthusiastic this time because now they all knew about my accident.

"Miss Arrington, would you please stand again?" The crowd quieted.

"What's he doing?" Jonathan whispered, placing his hand protectively on my arm.

"Miss Arrington, I believe you and Justin had a little bet going, is that correct?"

Again, nearly every head in the audience turned in my direction. I smiled and nodded.

"Would you please join me here on stage?"

An usher appeared at our row and offered me his arm.

"Beth," Jonathan said apprehensively, "what's he doing?"

I turned around and flashed Jonathan a knowing smile. Then I bent down and kissed him on the cheek. "Happy early Valentine's Day," I whispered against his ear.

"What?"

To say that Jonathan was stunned would be a gross understatement. His face froze in utter bewilderment.

I reached down and put my hand against his cheek. "I love you," I said softly. It was the first time I'd ever said that to him. It wasn't planned—the words simply flowed from my throat as though I were saying hello. The shock on his face turned to emotion. He opened his mouth as if to say something, but he was speechless. Another first.

I turned and took the arm of the usher who led me to where Mr. Laden stood at the microphone. Mr. Laden greeted me with a quick hug before continuing.

"If I understand the nature of this bet, you promised Justin that if he won today, you would take my place as his instructor for the final performance. Is that correct?" He squeezed my back gently.

"Ladies and gentlemen, I would like to invite Justin back on stage." A round of applause followed as Justin pretty much jogged to the stage, taking his place by my side after throwing me a big high-five. I'd never realized how tall he was before; he was almost taller than I was—and I was wearing three-inch heels.

"Beth, uh . . . Miss Arrington . . . was recently made aware of a body of compositions by an obscure composer named Frydric Khuammerle. During the past few weeks, she has managed to write a simple base accompaniment to complement his first composition. While it is customary for the instructor to conclude with a Bach selection, I have secured the approval of the Festival committee for a deviation from protocol. This afternoon, Beth will perform one of Khuammerle's works, accompanied by Justin."

Mr. Laden paused, allowing time for the audience to clap their approval. I searched for Jonathan in the audience. If I wasn't mistaken, he hadn't moved since I'd left his side. He was still staring at me in awed disbelief.

"You two ready?" Mr. Laden asked as he gestured toward the piano. Justin offered me his arm, and together we walked to the grand piano that stood proudly in the center of the stage. "Ladies and Gentlemen, I present, Miss Elizabeth Anne Arrington and her accompanist, Justin Miles Bradshaw.

I didn't hear the applause as we took our seats. I didn't even feel the presence of the audience. Nor was I aware that this should be a life-altering moment for me. There was just Justin and me, sitting together at the piano, about to have the time of our lives.

And that's exactly what we did.

Yearning
CHAPTER 26

*J*onathan and I returned to Andersen around six that evening. We'd stayed in Jackson long enough to join Justin and his family and Mr. Laden for dinner at a local steak house. Jonathan was glowing—I'd never seen him so excited. His eyes twinkled so brilliantly that I thought for sure our companions would notice. If they did, however, they never said anything.

Shortly after we arrived at Uncle Connor's house, we found ourselves sitting at the piano. We didn't speak much. Instead, we let our hands speak for us, through music. We began with the song that had started it all—Chopin's Étude in E. Our separate hands played as if controlled by one mind, in perfect synchronization. We continued with *Moonlight Sonata*, the emotion of which made my heart tremble. No one played with as much feeling as Jonathan did. My own emotions became so staggered that it was difficult for me to make it all the way through the piece. It would soon be time for us to say goodbye to each other.

We went through as many of our favorite songs as we could remember without using the music. Later, after we'd run through our entire repertoire, Jonathan began to tap out the tune to "Three Blind Mice." He began simply, then turned the melody over to me and picked up the accompaniment. We attempted to outdo each other in what rapidly became an all-out piano war—his left hand and my right hand, battling each other on a field of ivory. And yet, the battle produced a glorious, free-spirited composition that eventually became so ridiculously embellished that it bordered on the absurd.

Eventually, we were laughing so hard that we could no longer focus on playing. Jonathan wrapped his right arm around my neck in a mock head-hold until I admitted defeat.

"Okay, okay, you win!" I giggled.

Then, as if he had been holding back and could no longer resist, he pulled my face to his and crushed his lips against mine. We were both on fire. When he finally broke the kiss, we were breathless. I laid my hand on his chest and felt the pounding of his heart against my palm. He covered my hand with his and raised my palm to his lips.

"Sorry about that," he muttered into my hand, "sort of."

"You should be," I chuckled weakly. "You . . . interrupted my creative flow."

Everything in me wanted him to kiss me again and never stop, but I was distracted by a gnawing desire to hear him play Eleanor's theme. Hers was the last melody I wanted in my memory when Grace came for me in the morning.

A rapid tapping along the stairway wall startled both of us and we swung around to find Marci and Uncle Connor watching us. *How long have they been there?* I thought, embarrassed.

"Your uncle and I have decided to drive to Jackson for a late dinner and a movie," Marci announced, elbowing Uncle Connor gently. "We'd ask you to go with us, but Beth shouldn't be up too late tonight."

The announcement surprised me; it was noticeably a contrived plan. I stared at each of them for a moment. Why would they leave when I only had a few hours remaining? Before I could protest, I caught a very subtle movement in Marci's face. Did she wink at me? I hesitated—then I understood. She'd convinced Uncle Connor to give Jonathan and me time alone, time to say our good-byes in private. I met her gaze and nodded.

"You'll be back before Grace comes for me?" I asked.

"Of course," they both assured me.

"We'll be back before two," Uncle Connor replied. His eyes flickered to Jonathan briefly and then back to me. There was a slight hint of warning in his glance.

"Grace and Carl won't come for you until at least four," Marci added.

I glanced up at Jonathan and he nodded once in agreement.

"Don't worry Beth," Uncle Connor said quietly. "We'll all be together when it's time for you to go."

"Thank you," I whispered fervently, hoping he understood just how much I appreciated what he was doing for me.

"Okay then, we're off," Marci exclaimed enthusiastically. She looked at Jonathan and pointed a stern finger at him. "Don't keep her up too late. She has a long day ahead of her tomorrow." Then she winked at Jonathan and to my surprise, he blushed.

Uncle Connor and Marci disappeared up the stairs and Jonathan and I listened until we heard the faint sound of the garage door opening and the car engine roaring to life. A short minute later the garage door closed and everything was silent. We were alone.

Without speaking, Jonathan turned back to the safety of the piano.

"Chopsticks?" he grinned, challenging me to another piano war, "or have you had enough?"

I hesitated. "Jonathan . . . would you play Eleanor's theme for me—as many variations as you know."

"That could take awhile. Wouldn't you rath—"

"It would mean a lot to me," I interrupted. "I want her theme to be the last piece of music in my memory."

He swallowed hard and tenderly brushed his fingers along my cheek. Then he pulled me tightly to him and bent his face slowly to mine. His kiss was long and gentle.

"You don't have to do this, you know," he whispered in my ear. "There's still time to change your mind."

I wanted to cry. "No, Jonathan . . . I have to do this. We *both* do. But only for two weeks, right?" My voice broke and I clung to him. The way I felt, two weeks might as well be two years.

Jonathan's eyes searched mine for any hint of hesitation, but he found none. There was no doubt in my mind that we were doing the right thing. Still, I was apprehensive and a little frightened. Okay, I was a lot frightened, but I'd keep that buried for Jonathan's sake.

"Two weeks," he whispered. "I promise."

I turned my head and cradled it on his shoulder. His arms were still around me—a safe haven. "Jonathan," I asked softly. "What's it like to travel?"

"It's different for everyone, Beth. It takes some getting used to. . . ." He paused to read my reaction. "Grace is an expert traveler. I'd never have agreed to this if I didn't trust her implicitly."

"I'm just curious, that's all. I'm nervous about being away from you." I hoped he didn't sense the reluctance I was feeling.

His comforting smile was conflicted. The separation would be difficult for him as well. "Just two weeks," he repeated reassuringly.

I stayed in the warmth of his embrace for a few minutes. We were both silent, lost in thought. I loved him so much.

Finally I drew away—time was getting short. "Will you play for me now? Please?"

For the better part of the next hour, I lay on the floor next to the piano and listened to variation after variation of Eleanor's theme. I allowed the melody to resonate in my mind until I'd memorized every detail and experienced every emotion behind the phrases. I must have drifted off to sleep at some point because the next thing I knew, I opened my eyes and found Jonathan lying next to me on the floor. He was propped up on one elbow watching me pensively.

"How long have I been asleep?"

"Not long," he smiled, stroking my arm with his fingertips.

"I'm sorry," I apologized. Then I chuckled. "I think your playing hypnotized me."

His eyes radiated love as he silently looked at me. He caressed my face with his free hand. The tenderness of his touch caused familiar prickles of electricity wherever he touched me. Tonight it was almost painful—how could I leave him?

His eyes followed his fingers as they traced circles along my forehead and then slid slowly down the side of my face and into the hollow of my neck. He studied every contour of my face and neck as his fingers continued to caress their way lightly across my collarbone. I trembled involuntarily under his touch and my breathing became heavy and uneven.

I watched his eyes when he paused, his fingertips lingering on the skin exposed by my blouse. His expression slowly transformed from adoration to something I'd never seen before. It wasn't passion or hunger or even desire, but something much deeper.

He raised his head slowly until his eyes embraced mine. I started to close my eyes so I could focus on controlling the tightness in my chest, but then his thumb gently tapped on my throat. Before I could respond, he pressed his lips to mine and rolled forward so that the weight of his body rested firmly against me.

I can't describe the emotion his kiss aroused other than to say that I knew he needed to be as close to me as possible—and my need mirrored his. He'd never kissed me that way before. There was no urgency in his lips, no eagerness in the tempting caress of his tongue, and no pent up passion in his embrace, there was only raw need—his need for me and mine for him. We became one heart, one body, one spirit separated only by the physical barrier of our clothing.

The fact that he could reveal his need for me so openly and so willingly made me love him even more. I slid my hand beneath his shirt and the moment I felt the bare skin at the small of his back, an electric current raced through my blood. A low moan formed deep in his throat and he pressed his lips more feverishly against mine.

He rolled to the side, pulling me with him until I was directly above him. Wrapping his arms tightly around me, he held me even more closely to him. His hands slid easily beneath my blouse and moved feverishly across my back, pulling the small of my back against his body. A fire ignited between us making it impossible to breathe evenly—but his lips never left mine.

"Beth," he whispered against my lips, "do you know how badly I want to make love to you?"

I wasn't sure if his question was rhetorical or if he was waiting for me to respond, but hearing him utter those words made my blood boil. My body yearned for his in a way that I didn't know was physically possible—a yearning so powerful that it was painful.

"I love you," I whispered back. Instantly, his tongue found mine and he kissed me passionately, holding nothing back.

In one flawless movement, and without breaking the kiss, he rolled over and I was beneath him again. He pulled away only so we could catch our breath, but his mouth never stopped kissing me— my face, my throat, my neck. He sighed heavily and then groaned softly in my ear.

"Beth," he whispered, "I'm on fire." His staggered breathing caused the blood in my veins to explode and I pulled his mouth back to mine. He moaned, pressing his body as tightly to mine as he could. Several minutes passed before he pulled away again, panting. He paused, staring anxiously into my eyes, worry lines etched on his forehead.

"Beth . . . I love you . . . I don't want to stop."

I wasn't sure if he was asking for permission to keep going or if he was warning me to stop him. Either way, I had a decision to make.

Everything in me and every part of my body wanted him to keep going—to give ourselves to each other completely. All it would take was two simple words—*don't stop*. One whisper from me, and the throbbing desire in both of us would be satisfied.

I ached to say those words—anything else would be a betrayal of our yearning need for each other. How could we deny the burning passion that consumed us? *Just say the words—give yourself to him.*

I examined the anxiety in his face for a split second. His eyes pleaded with mine for a response. And then it struck me. Jonathan *truly* loved me. He would not cross the physical boundary I had set months earlier without receiving my permission first. How unlike Adam he was . . . how unlike Eric . . . how unlike anyone I'd ever known. Could any other man love a woman so unselfishly?

Involuntarily, my mind flitted to the future, something I rarely permitted myself to think about. I envisioned the two of us standing together, promising to love each other forever and uniting our lives through the bonds of an everlasting commitment. And then I saw the two of us as lovers preparing to consummate that promise in a physical union that would bind our bodies and our hearts as one. It was an image my mother had painted for me several times while trying to convince me that waiting until marriage was the right thing to do. For the first time, the image seemed real—it struck at the very core of my soul—because this time the image included Jonathan.

That vision, that split-second snapshot, brought to my mind two equally small, yet vitally important words—two words that would preserve the virtue of the moment I had just glimpsed. They were the two words I needed to utter right now. I struggled to find my voice, to find the strength to say the words before I gave in to the heat of the moment.

As badly as I wanted Jonathan, as deeply as we ached for each other, and as desperately as we needed to be together at this moment, it was neither the right place nor the right time. Not here. Not a stolen night on the floor of Uncle Connor's basement. And not as a way to say goodbye to each other! Finally, I managed to choke out the words I needed to say.

"Not yet."

That was all it took.

Jonathan stopped.

"Give me a minute," he smiled. Whether it was a smile of understanding or one of frustration, I couldn't tell, but he kissed me softly and then sighed heavily—several times.

He rolled over, releasing me from his hold for a second. Then he repositioned us so that I lay on my side with my back against him. He folded his arm around my shoulders and held me close. It was several minutes before our breathing calmed.

"I love you, Elizabeth Anne Arrington," he whispered gently against my ear.

A new wave of emotion engulfed me and I fought back the urge to cry, but the effort was unsuccessful. I was full of mixed emotions—complete, utter joy that he wanted me so badly, and deep gratitude that he loved me enough to wait. I didn't want him to know I was crying; I thought I'd hidden it from him until I felt his thumb stroke my cheek, wiping the tears from my face.

"Shhh," he soothed. "It's okay . . . really. We'll wait."

He stroked my hair tenderly for several minutes. Slowly, our bodies began to sink into a peaceful pattern of relaxed breathing. Our emotions had exhausted us.

Although my eyelids were heavy, a question flashed through my mind.

"Jonathan?" I murmured.

"Hmm," he responded lazily.

"What did Uncle Connor say to you last week?"

"When?" he yawned.

"When he took you into the kitchen after I told you about my dream."

He chuckled softly. "I wondered when you were going to ask about that."

"Well?" I prodded.

"Part of it was a mini-lesson in Lebas politics," he said evasively.

"Meaning?"

"Well, apparently because of your bloodline, and mine for that matter, the Lebas have a vested interest in your future. They prefer that your marriage *not* be to someone with a stain on his family name." He paused, watching my face closely as his words slowly sunk in.

"Marriage?" I whispered incredulously.

"Yep."

"Marriage," I repeated as if to double-check my hearing.

"Mm hmm," he chuckled. He didn't expound, and though it took every ounce of mental constraint I possessed, I didn't press him any further.

"What was the other part?" I asked.

"A personal request," he said, amused. He seemed to enjoy giving me vague answers.

"A personal request for . . . ?"

"I asked for some time alone with you before we were separated for two weeks. Connor agreed . . . on one condition."

He hesitated, waiting for me to pry it out of him.

"That being . . . ?" I sighed impatiently.

"That I promise to be good—or else."

We both laughed at that one.

"Or else what?"

"I think he said something about draining my immortal fluids and selling my body parts to science . . . one at a time."

"And you agreed to that?" I snickered teasingly.

"It sounded like a reasonable request at the time." He gave my shoulder a squeeze.

I felt safe and protected as I nestled against him and he wrapped his arms more tightly around me. It was only a matter of moments before both of us drifted to sleep, and that's exactly how Uncle Connor and Marci found us when they arrived home sometime early in the morning. I slipped in and out of awareness as I heard them whispering. Uncle Connor wanted to wake us, but Marci stopped him.

"Leave them be, Connor," she whispered quietly. "I told you they'd be fine. You had nothing to worry about. That boy loves her."

"That's exactly what I'm worried about," Uncle Connor grumbled under his breath; it was so low I wasn't sure I heard him correctly.

A minute later I felt the weight of a heavy quilt covering us and soon after, I drifted back into a peaceful sleep. Jonathan and I were two spoons perfectly nestled together, and that's how we remained for the rest of the night.

Journey

CHAPTER 27

Carl and Grace awakened us about an hour before dawn. Within half an hour, the family had gathered in the kitchen for coffee and a light breakfast. I was too nervous to eat, and although nobody said anything, the rest of the family appeared to be nervous as well.

The morning was surreal. There was no way for me to grasp the reality of what was about to take place. A lump hardened in my throat and I fought against the emotions that swelled inside me. Grace and Carl were animated—both excited about the idea of me traveling. Grace, in particular, seemed uncharacteristically pleased about something. Marci, however, seemed apprehensive. She spent the morning scrutinizing Uncle Connor's every expression. He was unusually quiet, adding little to the conversation.

Jonathan was also quiet, but unlike Uncle Connor, I could see the wheels spinning in his head. He had accepted the fact that I was leaving for two weeks and he had already begun to move into soldier mode. He wanted to get the next two weeks over with as quickly as possible. The sooner he could begin gathering forces and training them to fight possessors, the sooner Grace could bring me home.

I'd come to Andersen seven months earlier hoping to find answers about the night my mother died. As her twin, I had believed Uncle Connor's connection to her would allow me to feel her spirit near while I searched for those answers. I had also hoped Andersen's close proximity to the earth's vortex would assist me in my attempts to solve the mystery surrounding the night of my accident. It was a night that had changed my life forever—and it was the night that Jonathan had held me for the first time.

My answers had come, but not at all in the way I had expected. My mother had often quoted a familiar phrase: "A door never closes without a window opening somewhere else." I understood now what that meant. I'd lost my mother, my piano scholarship, and the use of my left hand; but I'd gained a new family, discovered I was part of a world I never knew existed, and found a love more powerful than any I ever could have imagined.

I'd also discovered that my dream to make my mark in the world of piano performance had not died in the crash with my mom. It had changed, yes—significantly so—but the dream was very much alive. I felt a subtle twitch in my left hand. Perhaps I'd never master the Hungarian Rhapsodies; but in the end, mine could be a different kind of rhapsody.

Although my emotions were on the verge of spilling over, my mind was working overtime trying to sort through the myriad of new questions now facing me. Would I survive traveling to another time? Would Jonathan clear his family name and finish training the immortals before the possessors returned? Would the Niaces find out where I was hiding and come for me while I was away from Jonathan?

Finally, there was the one question that I refused to allow myself to ask, the question that caused every cell in my body to constrict in agonizing concern. How long could Jonathan love me, as he did now, if I remained mortal? I couldn't bear to think of the answer.

A solitary tear trickled down my cheek and before I could reach up to wipe it away, Jonathan caught it on the tip of his finger.

"Beth?"

"I'm okay . . . I'm okay," I assured him.

He put his arms around me. "Two weeks," he whispered. I held his face between my hands and smiled weakly—I was too nervous to manage more than that.

Grace stood and my heart skipped a beat. Then it began hammering fiercely against my chest. Although her face was bright and eager, I couldn't help but feel like an inmate on death row whose executioner had just arrived.

"It's time," she said enthusiastically. The six of us stood and waited for her to continue. She addressed her next words to Uncle Connor. "I understand you have a cellar that borders along the vortex, is that correct?"

Ah, geez! Not the vortex cellar again.

My knees began to shake, but Jonathan steadied me.

"You'd think by now I'd be used to it," I moaned. I tried to laugh but it sounded more like I was choking.

"I'll be right next to you," Jonathan assured me. "Don't worry."

Uncle Connor opened the door under the stairs and we descended the familiar ladder that led to the vortex chamber. I expected to find the room in disarray—still in chaos from when Jonathan and I had found my drawings of Bailey—but everything was in perfect order.

Grace took a long, deep breath, drinking in the rich fragrance of the surrounding minerals. She exhaled very slowly and her eyes brightened as her smile widened.

"This will do," she announced, glancing at Jonathan and Carl.

"Why do you travel so early in the morning?" I yawned.

"It's best to travel in complete darkness," she explained, "and this is the darkest hour—the hour just before dawn."

I didn't understand, but I accepted her reasoning. Jonathan had tried to explain the physical process of traveling during our conversations the day before, but it went over my head. My mother, the physics major, would have understood. It had something to do with separating molecules and organizing matter—or was it disorganizing matter? I couldn't remember.

The urgency in Grace's face told me she was anxious to get going.

"What do I do now," I asked nervously, "tap my heels together, and chant?"

The others in the room paused until they caught on: that's what Dorothy did in *The Wizard of Oz*. We laughed to relieve some tension, although I wasn't enjoying the joke as much as they were.

"I'm serious," I murmured, interrupting their fun. "I don't know what to do."

"Say your good-byes, Beth," Grace gestured, nodding toward the others.

One at a time, I hugged my family: Marci, Carl, Uncle Connor, and finally—Jonathan.

"Promise me," I whispered into Jonathan's ear, suppressing the urge to cry. "Two weeks!"

"I'll come for you myself if I have to," he promised. He kissed me hard on the mouth and folded his arms around me in a lingering embrace. He didn't care that everyone was watching, and neither did I. I clung to him until Grace reached for me.

"Now, Beth," she ordered quietly.

She faced me and clasped her hands firmly around my forearms.

"I know you can't hold on to me with your left hand, but try to keep it as close to my forearm as possible. Hold on extra tight with your right hand, okay?"

I nodded.

"In a minute, I'll ask you to close your eyes. When I do, I want you to concentrate on your breathing. Breathe in slowly until your lungs completely expand, then hold the air in and count to twenty in your mind. Follow the rhythm of one-one thousand, two-one thousand, three-one thousand, and so on. Do you understand?"

I nodded yes.

"Good. When you exhale, I want you to pretend you're in an elevator that's on its way down. When it arrives at the first floor, your lungs will feel empty. But I want you to continue to exhale as if the elevator were going further down to the basement. That's all you need to do."

I glanced one more time at Jonathan. When my eyes met his gaze, he mouthed the words, "I love you," and winked. I studied his eyes one last time, suddenly desperate to memorize them and to remember their pattern as they twinkled. There just wasn't enough time. Grace squeezed my arm with her hand and I reluctantly turned away from Jonathan to face her.

"Remember what I said, okay?" She studied my eyes, making sure I was focused. "You will feel a little strange, perhaps even nauseated for a few moments, but I want you to ignore it. It will pass quickly. I'll be right next to you, and I'll talk you through it."

This time, the excitement in Grace's expression made me smile.

"Okay," she said. "Close your eyes, and breathe."

I began the slow ascent to the top of the elevator, counted to twenty, and then followed the elevator as it slowly descended to the first floor. I ignored the burning in my lungs as I neared the bottom and then I forced the elevator into the basement.

Somewhere in the distance I heard the opening measures of Eleanor's theme. It was the last thing I remembered before the world went black.

Epilogue

eth. The word swam in my head, floating endlessly along a path that seemed to lead nowhere. I knew the word should fit inside the small circumference of my brain; instead, it meandered aimlessly through a vast space that had no bounds.

"Beth, listen."

The familiar voice echoed indeterminately from one corner of my conscious mind to another. I tried to clutch the words and hold them still, but they bounced around in motions that made no sense. There was no pattern to the words or their meaning.

"Your body cannot travel."

But I *was* traveling. I couldn't see anything because my eyes were clamped shut, yet I felt my weightless body—void of shape or structure—dissimilate into a blur of unorganized matter.

Like a distant dream whose details were fuzzy, the faint sound of Grace's voice cried anxiously through the darkness. Something was wrong, of that I was certain. Her words bounced recklessly around me.

Your body cannot travel.

My body? I struggled to open my eyes but there was no movement. My hands. I had been holding Grace's arm with my right hand. Did something happen? Had I accidentally let go? I had no memory of it if I did. I commanded my hands to tighten, but there was nothing there: no movement, no feeling. I ordered my deformed hand to stretch; I knew the familiar pain associated with the movement would confirm what I desperately needed to know. But there was nothing. No movement. No pain. Nothing.

"Trust me, Beth," Grace called through the darkness. "I'll explain everything when you return."

When I return? Explain what? What had gone wrong?

"It's all according to plan," a man commented.

His was also a familiar voice, but not one I readily recognized. I ran through all the male voices I could clearly remember—Jonathan, Uncle Connor, Carl—but theirs was not the voice I heard now. My father? Eric? No. Who was it? Where had I heard the voice before?

"The breach must be timed exactly. She must enter the exact moment that the girl's spirit leaves."

He spoke urgently, yet his voice was calm and gentle. I was certain I knew him—only I couldn't pinpoint from where.

"Hang on, baby." A sweet, angelic voice pierced the darkness. I recognized her voice immediately.

Mom? Mom, are you there?

The words only formed in my mind. I tried to speak, but there was no voice box to create the sounds, no air to compel the voice forward, no tongue to formulate the syllables, and no mouth to utter the sentence.

Was I dead? Was that what had gone wrong?

Your body cannot travel! I heard the words again in my mind. Oh, crap! That's it! I died. My body couldn't make the journey. That was the problem. My body was dead.

"Ready?" The man's gentle voice was more urgent now.

"I'm going with her," Grace's voice announced.

"It's forbidden—you know that," he insisted.

"Please, I must explain what happened," she begged. "Please!"

Silence followed. What did she want to explain? That she'd killed me? That I was doomed to float around in darkness, having no shape or substance to call my own? That she'd forgotten to tell me about this one itty-bitty little risk?

"Please." She spoke the words so desperately that I felt guilty for being angry with her.

"It's very likely she won't remember anything you tell her," the man replied.

"I have to try."

A long pause followed.

"Two minutes. That's all I can give you."

"Thank you . . . thank you," Grace replied.

"It's time!" my mother's voice rang clearly.

She didn't seem saddened by the fact that I'd died; she seemed intrigued. Perhaps she was pleased that I would join her soon. Shouldn't there be a light? I thought I was supposed to walk into a light and be greeted by my loved ones. This was too dark; not how I had envisioned death at all.

"Beth . . ." Grace spoke as if her voice came from somewhere inside of me instead of next to me as it had done earlier. "You're going to feel a great deal of pressure for the next few moments. Don't panic. You may feel a tingling, perhaps even a slight burning sensation, but it will only last for a minute. No matter how badly you want to, try not to move until I tell you to open your eyes. You'll have to force your brain to issue the command. It's going to seem difficult at first, but keep trying."

So many instructions. Pressure? Tingling? Open my eyes? What eyes? I tried to push my eyelids closer together, but there was nothing there. What was she talking about?

"Now!" the man's voice thundered.

As he spoke the words, a pounding throb pulsated through my head. Ahgr! The pressure squeezed my brain, my eyes, my nose, and my mouth as if a vice were cranked around the entire parameter of my head. Fiery darts penetrated every pore, and then disappeared in a trail of needling jabs that left behind a tightened cast that formed into the shape of a human head.

The pressure moved throughout my body beginning with my neck and shoulders. It burned a smoldering path as it worked its way downward along my arms and hands. It continued on through my chest, my pelvis, my thighs and calves, and finally, my feet.

I was immediately aware of cool, crisp cotton sheets pressing against my skin. I no longer felt the freedom to float, but rather was confined to a definite form. Although I felt constrained, the sudden awareness of my sense of touch comforted me. The tingling darts crawled to the edges of my extremities, and exited in one final fiery wisp through the tips of my fingers and toes. Then, as quickly as it had come, the pressure was gone.

"Beth, open your eyes," Grace ordered.

The command was simple. I had been opening and closing my eyes for nineteen years. All I needed to do was lift my eyelids—so why wasn't it happening?

"Concentrate, Beth," she demanded in a low, restrained whisper.

I couldn't remember how to make them open. I squeezed both eyes shut as tightly as possible—that was easy. Then I relaxed. But my eyelids still didn't open. *Think!* I fretted. I pressed my eyes tightly shut again, only this time I sucked in a deep breath and held the air in my lungs. The air felt cool and satisfying. It was like I'd been under water for several minutes and had finally broken the surface. When I could no longer hold my breath, I forced it out in a loud puff—and my eyes flew open.

Disoriented, I stared at unfamiliar surroundings. The room was large and dimly lit, but the light didn't come from an electric lamp, it came from some sort of lantern. Off to one side of the room was a fireplace; burning embers glowed in brilliant shades of orange. The rest of the room was obscured in shadow. I could barely make out a large wooden rocking chair next to the fire and a vanity table directly across from the bed. There appeared to be a small oval mirror on top of it. As my eyes adjusted to the darkness, I discovered another mirror in the corner of the room. This one was tall and oblong in shape. Its wooden frame was intricately carved, but it was too dark for me to distinguish the design.

A gentle hand pressed my shoulder and my eyes flashed at once to find Grace quietly seated in a small chair next to the bed.

"Grace?" I whispered hoarsely. She reached for a pitcher sitting on the nightstand beside me and poured some water into a small cup. She handed it to me.

"Here," she said softly, "drink this." She watched me carefully as I sipped the cool water. It trickled down my throat, a wave of cool relief.

"Mmm," I moaned, and then drank some more.

"Beth, I only have a minute. Please listen carefully."

I nodded in response, remembering that her time was limited.

"Your mortal body couldn't travel, so we had to place your soul in another body temporarily. It's very complicated, but trust me when I tell you that it's part of an intricately designed plan."

"Grace—" I started to speak, but she stopped me.

"No. Please let me finish. You're mortal. No one knows for sure how traveling might affect your mind. It's possible your memories could fade, until you think they're nothing more than a dream. You might not recognize me when I come for you. You might be disoriented, like one feels when waking from a deep sleep. On the other hand, your memory might remain clear. We just don't know."

Something caught Grace's attention and she snapped her head around quickly. Then she reached into her pocket and retrieved several sheets of parchment paper rolled into a narrow tube. It was tied with a delicate crimson ribbon that shimmered in the glow of the lantern. She pulled back the sheets and placed the tube into my left hand. Then she quickly tucked the sheets around my shoulders.

"Find Jonathan, Beth, and be sure to give this to him. Do you understand?"

I nodded. "Find Jonathan. Yes. Wait . . . no! You said it was forbidden for me to make contact with him." She had told me that herself before we left. It would interfere with the course of linear time.

"I don't have time to explain. Just trust me Beth, please. Find Jonathan . . . and give him the parchment as soon as you can."

"Grace, get out!" a low voice ordered, the same voice I'd heard earlier. I gazed around once again at my surroundings, but I couldn't see anyone else in the room. Grace bent down and kissed my forehead.

"As your memories fade, keep hold of the music in your mind. Don't ever let Eleanor's theme leave your mind."

With that, her eyes flickered across the room toward the faintly glowing fireplace. My eyes followed hers but when I turned back, she was gone.

I slowly pulled the covers away from my body and slipped my legs over the side of the bed. The bed was much higher from the floor than I was used to, but somehow I knew there was a stool placed strategically on the floor near my feet. I located the stool with familiar ease and pulled myself off the bed and onto the floor. My nightgown shifted and draped gracefully to my ankles. My legs were unsteady so I clutched the top of a chair to balance myself.

A large, oval-shaped woven rug covered the dark wood floor. As I walked on the loosely looped carpet, my toes curled automatically around the material. I felt as if I had done this a hundred times before. The thick weave was soothing to the bottoms of my suddenly sensitive feet.

I stepped toward the vanity and then stopped short—I was holding the rolled sheets of parchment paper in my left hand, the hand that had held nothing for almost a year. I peered down at my fingers folded around the tube and slowly opened my hand, palm up. My fingers stretched into four elegant, straight lines. I marveled at the beautiful symmetry of the perfectly shaped hand. Amazed, I folded and unfolded my fingers around the rolled papers repeatedly, enjoying the restored use of my hand.

I continued to step forward until a sudden movement in the corner caught my eye. I glanced up quickly and beheld a beautiful woman dressed in a white flowing gown staring at me. She looked surprised at first, but then she must have recognized me because she smiled. I'd seen her beautiful form so many times in my dreams, but this was different—this wasn't a dream. She was real, and she was here in my room.

I took another step forward and her movement mirrored my own. She also held several rolled sheets of parchment paper in her hand and she extended them to me, just as she had done so often in my dreams. We approached each other silently. She mirrored my movements exactly as we drew closer. Her movements were too perfect, too symmetrical. We both looked down at our hands at the same moment and then raised our heads to face each other with the same bewildered expression on our faces. I reached forward with my free hand. She did too. We both stepped back quickly. Then I gasped as I realized there was nobody else in the room—I was looking at my own reflection in the mirror.

But it wasn't *my* face that stared back at me—it was Eleanor's face.

I dropped the roll of parchment paper on the floor and listened as it thudded against the wood and rolled to one side. Instinctively, my hands flew to my face, examining every feature of it in detail. My fingers cupped two perfectly round cheeks and then slid slowly downward to the edge of my lips—her lips—which turned up slightly at each corner. Everything about her face was stunning, far more beautiful than I recalled from my dreams.

I reached behind my head and found the ribbon that held my hair bound. I loosened the knot, allowing the ribbon to fall to the floor. Long, thick waves of curls cascaded down my shoulders and caressed the tops of my breasts. Curiously, I wove my fingers into the silky curls and brushed them lightly through to the ends, pulling the curls straight. Then I released them and watched in awe as they bounced effortlessly back into shiny ringlets.

I bent forward and stared into Eleanor's deep green eyes— emerald eyes—similar to Grace's but deeper in tone. They didn't twinkle the way Grace's did, but they were mesmerizing in their own peculiar way.

I took several graceful steps backwards until I could once again see the full length of Eleanor's body—my body—captured in the frame of the mirror. She was breathtakingly beautiful, far more so than any girl I'd ever seen, even in fashion magazines. The open slit in the front of her nightgown subtly revealed the promise of two very full, delicate breasts, and her tiny waist curved outward slightly into round yet slender hips. It was the perfect hourglass figure that girls hope for and men desire. Hers was a captivating, natural beauty, and though I'd seen Eleanor many times in my dreams, I'd never viewed her in such striking detail before.

But now I wasn't dreaming. Tonight, and apparently for the next two weeks, I *was* Eleanor.

Watch for Melinda's next exciting book in *The Birthright Legacy*

Intermezzo

The darkened sky that hovered overhead added its seal of regret to the small gathering at the Hastings' family cemetery. Only members of the immediate family and a few close friends attended the intimate ceremony led by Patrick McKay, or as the members of his parish fondly referred to him, "Reverend Pat." The Hastings didn't particularly care for Reverend Pat; his sermons were too rigid and unforgiving. But, despite their dissatisfaction, a Christian burial was of utmost importance to the prominent family—so they made do.

The modest gathering formed a somber circle around a small mound of mud and a grave that would soon give rest to the tiny pine box that now held the body of Eleanor Hastings' baby brother. Christopher, once a bundle of endless excitement and unconditional love, now lay cold and still. His death came unexpectedly, and Eleanor's father, Charles Frederick Hastings II, did not take it well. His two eldest sons, Charles Frederick Hastings III and Miles Harrison Hastings, had both died at Gettysburg, leaving Christopher as the only surviving male of the Hastings family. Christopher's premature death meant the end of the family line.

Eleanor stood between her mother and her younger sister and watched as the two men who served as Reverend Pat's assistants struggled to lower the casket gently into its final resting place. Dressed in black, the three Hastings women, each with veiled faces, stepped forward to gather a handful of dirt—now thick as mud—and cast it into the young child's grave. This they did without any outward show of emotion, for such a display would not be proper, and propriety was a way of life among the Hastings women. But Eleanor was not like the other women of the Hastings family, at least not since she had recovered from a fever that by all the laws of nature should have claimed her life. She knew she didn't belong here, and try as she might she could not mask her emotions with the same poise and grace as one would expect from a lady of proper upbringing.

Tears streamed down Eleanor's face and a painful lump lodged itself at the back of her throat. *How could this be fair?* she wondered in silent anguish.

She looked toward the sky, pleading, as if she might somehow find the answer revealed there; but the only thing she saw through her black lace veil was the ominous motion of the clouds that threatened to turn what was presently a light, scattered rain into a steady downpour.

"It figures," she mouthed silently. A bitter taste of sarcasm coated Eleanor's tongue as she lowered her gaze back to her brother's grave.

"Father, we give Thee but Thine own. Take this child into Thy bosom and give him eternal rest . . ." Reverend Pat said as he began the final portion of the service, which led flawlessly into a recitation of the twenty-third Psalm. In a few moments, those gathered around the grave would join in chorus to recite the Lord's Prayer, signaling the conclusion of the service. Then the Hastings family would make its way along the wooded path that led back to the main house.

Death was no stranger to the folks of Marensburg, Pennsylvania, a modest township located west of Gettysburg between Chambersburg and Greencastle. In Marensburg, news arrived with unsettling frequency announcing the latest casualties of the war. The postings always arrived on a Wednesday. Families of soldiers would gather in the town center and search frantically through the list, relieved when the name they hunted for wasn't there. Too often, however, more than one family would learn that a father, son, or brother would never come home, and once again, Marensburg would mourn.

Eleanor longed to give her family and the people of Marensburg hope, to let them know that the war was over and their fallen fathers and sons had not died in vain; but of course, she could not tell them this. That was against the rules. She couldn't tell them that history books would report that more Americans died in the Civil War than would die in two subsequent World Wars. Nor could she tell them that President Abraham Lincoln would be assassinated in Ford's theater.

Eleanor couldn't tell them these things, *because they hadn't happened yet.*

Just as promised, the sky soon crackled with the sound of thunder and began to dump a heavy, sustained rain on the small party of mourners. Umbrellas did little to protect the Hastings women from the sideways sweep of rain which seemed to shift directions randomly. Christine, now the youngest member of the Hastings family, folded her arm through Eleanor's and leaned close to her.

"Do you think he's happy?" she whispered.

"Who?" Eleanor whispered back.

"Christopher."

Eleanor was quiet for a moment as she fought the urge to shrug her shoulders, something she had learned—and learned the hard way—was never appropriate for a lady.

"I don't believe I'm the best person to ask," she finally said.

"Why not?" Christine asked.

Eleanor's mother turned slowly, but she didn't say anything. Eleanor knew she was listening.

"I'm sorry, Christine, I'm not myself today," Eleanor replied.

Christine nodded. "I know . . . neither am I." She squeezed Eleanor's arm. "But he's in heaven, right? So he must be happy."

Eleanor breathed deeply and sighed. "Yes, I'm sure Christopher would be happy there." It was the best she could do.

A bright flash lit up the atmosphere as several bolts of lightning danced across the sky in rapid succession. A fierce rumbling of thunder followed, shaking the ground around Eleanor and her family. Christine tightened her hold on Eleanor's arm.

"Let's go, Eleanor, please . . ." she begged. "I don't like storms."

Eleanor lowered her umbrella and wrapped her arm around Christine. Rain swept across both their faces as they started back to the house. Lightning zigzagged in front of them as if it were searching for something it had lost on the ground. It frightened Eleanor and made her stop short. She tightened her hold on Christine, who started to cry.

"Let's hide in the trees," Christine pleaded, referring to the woods that surrounded the small cemetery on three sides.

"We're not safe near the trees," Eleanor yelled above the now pounding rain.

"The lightning is too close!" Christine screamed. "We need to hide!"

"Trust me!" Eleanor said, jerking Christine along the path to the house.

Another series of lightning bolts lit up the forest beside them and an ear-piercing crack let them know that the lightning had found a victim. A few seconds later, a large section of a mature pine tree tumbled to the ground. Christine screamed and tore free of Eleanor's grasp. She started running back across the cemetery to where the family had sought cover under a canopy of trees. Eleanor ran after her sister, but before she could catch up she lost her footing and fell into a sinkhole hidden by the dense undergrowth. Christine continued to scream as she ran—unaware that Eleanor had fallen. Eleanor clutched at the ground, struggling repeatedly to get out of the hole, but her heavy wet skirts and the saturated soil prevented her from gaining purchase.

The next series of lightning bolts lit up alternating sections of the cemetery. Headstones hidden in the darkness now jumped into view just long enough to announce their presence and disappear again into the backdrop of the storm. Each flash of light made it more difficult for Eleanor to see clearly.

She clawed frantically at the slushy mud beneath her, trying to release her feet, but each struggling movement forced her deeper into the ground. After several fruitless attempts to straighten herself, she lost what little footing she had and fell face first into a pool of saturated soil. The lace veil that shielded her face was plastered against her skin, making it difficult to breathe.

"Help! Somebody help me!" Eleanor screamed into the wet blackness, but her cries were no match for the angry sky that bellowed continuously with pounding thunder and blinding flashes of blue light. "Please help me!" she sobbed.

"Eleanor!" a man's voice called from the distance, but the violent vibrations of the ground distorted the sound making it impossible for Eleanor to discern who was calling her or how far away he was.

"Beth!" another man's voice called, only this voice came from somewhere beneath the ground. Eleanor struggled to grab hold of anything that might give her enough leverage to pull herself out of the sinkhole.

"Beth . . . !" The voice echoed in the thunder as something wrapped itself around one of Eleanor's legs and started to pull her down.

Eleanor screamed and began to kick frantically against the unseen force pulling her deeper into the earth. "NO!" she screamed, louder this time.

"Eleanor!" the first voice called again; it was closer now.

Eleanor fought, clutching desperately at the ground. Finally, she found something to wrap her hands around; it felt like a large root. She tried to pull herself up, but the harder she pulled the tighter the pressure grew around her leg, pulling her back down.

"Beth! Let go! I've got you."

"Eleanor, hang on!"

Eleanor was being pulled by two forces at once, but which command should she obey? One offered to pull her to certain safety, out of the miry mud that seemed determined to claim her. The other meant letting go of that safety and allowing herself to be swallowed up in the depths of the ground.

The thunder rumbled impatiently as sheets of rain swept across Eleanor's face and arms. She lay outstretched, clinging to life on the one end and fearing death on the other.

"Beth, there's no time. Let go—now!"

For a brief second, Beth—now housed in Eleanor's body—thought she recognized the voice.

But that's impossible, she thought to herself. *Grace is the only one who knows where I am. This can't be right.*

Before she could make sense of what was happening, a man's strong arms wrapped around her and pulled her from the ground. She felt the hold on her leg slip away—she was finally free.

"Hang on Eleanor, I've got you." Eleanor recognized her father's voice as he folded her in his arms and carried her through the storm toward the house.

Eleanor's mother and sister were waiting at the door when her father arrived. As soon as he was in earshot, he began barking orders to the staff.

"Get her bed ready," he said, pointing to Mrs. Weddington, the head servant. "And get the fire going in her room."

"Bring hot water and rags," he ordered another servant.

"Get her out of these wet clothes," he said, motioning to Eleanor's maidservant.

Before she knew it, Eleanor was tucked snugly into bed—dry and safe—and completely unaware of two yellow eyes that watched her from the mirror in the corner of the room.

Acknowledgements

Of the many people who helped me to write *Étude*, I especially wish to thank Raechel and Ellen who spent numerous hours reading and rereading each chapter and providing critical feedback that helped me create a believable story line and characters with whom my audience might identify. I also want to thank my husband, Ron, for convincing me to take Beth and Jonathan's story from mind to paper, and for his patience and understanding during the many nights he spent alone while I played the absentee wife, locked away in my own world.

About the Author

California native Melinda Morgan's first novel, *Étude*, reflects her love of the mountains of eastern Idaho and Wyoming. She lived in Idaho in 1980–81 and enjoyed the grandeur of the Tetons, an area that is significant in her book. As a displaced homemaker and single mother of four, she went back to school and in 1998, received her BA in Liberal Studies from California Baptist University. She then went on to earn a Master's Degree in Education and Administration from Azusa Pacific University—all while teaching full time and raising her children. In 2002, she married Ron Morgan, who is also an educator and musician.

Melinda has served as a staff developer and district liaison for the California Math and Science (CaMS) K–12 Alliance. In 2006, she received the Region 10 California League of Middle Schools Teacher of the Year award. She is currently serving as an assistant principal for Temecula Valley USD Alternative Education Center and spends the bulk of her time helping students complete their high school education.

In writing *Étude*, Melinda has drawn upon more than thirteen years of experience as a language arts and science teacher. Her story has a scientifically intriguing plot, endearing characters, and elements such as foreshadowing, symbolism, and imagery that enhance the book's literary value. Melinda is also a classically trained pianist. Her performances landed her on the Piano Players Guild's National Role with a superior rating for five years in a row.